July 2002

Malignant Decisions

to Ed and Carole

Enjoy the intrigue
and always check up
on your Doc

Wad
M Connell MD

Malignant Decisions

Walt McConnell, M.D.
and D.A. Campbell

CADUCEUS
PUBLISHING

To all the competent, compassionate, and
ethical physicians who continue to provide the
highest level of care to their patients.

One . . .

At the time of Janet Mitchell's accident, her husband was forty-five miles away saving another woman's life. Ironic? Yes. To be expected? Certainly. And Janet would have approved. It could be said with accuracy, however, that her husband was involved in, or even caused, the accident. For on this gray December day of wet shoes and windshield wipers, it was he whose words had, since breakfast, preoccupied Janet to the point of distraction. Even before she got into her aging Volvo, she had spent her day rummaging through his remarks as one might sort through dirty laundry when the closet is empty, looking for something still wearable. She didn't like any of what her dear Loring had to say, but grudgingly she had to admit that he knew the ills of the modern medical profession as well as she did. She just couldn't stomach selling her pediatrics practice to a creep like James Perkins Harvey III. And that, as Loring had pointed out, was chief among her limited options. So during the day, as she had examined one child and the next, her thoughts returned to their talk that morning. Of course Dr. Loring English was right. If she wanted to spend less time on paperwork and more time practicing medicine, Jim Harvey offered an answer. Her dislike for the man was only a gut thing.

His medical credentials were stainless. As the morning turned into afternoon and Janet found herself immobile in front of a computer screen, immersed in health plan documents, Loring's arguments took on added weight. She was caught by her partner, Natasha Wilson, venting a prolonged sigh.

"What's eating you, girl?" Natasha chided, using the feminine familiar from her childhood in the projects to gently tease her friend and partner. "You've been preoccupied all day. Go on down to the hospital and start your rounds. You better clear your head, girl, or you're going to need some doctoring yourself." She steered Janet toward the coat closet and helped her into her jacket.

The temperature had dropped several degrees and the rain was now a fine mist. Janet shivered and turned up the old Volvo's heater before she had her shoulder belt buckled. Pulling away from the faded Victorian that served as her and Natasha's office, she slipped a Bach tape into the dash. The tape was one of Loring's. She thought of his promise to be home for dinner and worried whether she'd finish her rounds at Port Hancock General in time. She thought of Carmella Parente, Loring's patient, whose aging heart he was repairing this afternoon in Riverton, an hour's drive to the south. There were parallels between the lives of Carmella and Janet Mitchell. Carmella was a workhorse who had operated a wholesale produce business while raising a family. Janet also pursued her career at the same time she raised a family. Gabriella was born the summer after Janet finished medical school. Rather than open a practice, she stayed at the clinic where she had interned and traded shifts with Loring, so one of them could always be with the baby.

It was during those years that Loring's practice began to flourish. At first, he was the only cardiologist in Port Hancock. The emergency rooms of the city's two hospitals, Port Hancock General and Valleyview Medical center, referred patients to him exclusively. He became known to the community's bankers and swindlers, its drunks and deacons and dowagers, as the man who kept their hearts beating, and he was quickly transformed into one of the valley's most prosperous men. But with prosperity he shouldered a burden, like the sole lifeguard on a beach, responsible for hundreds of men and women, those who could pay and those who had no means. He belonged to the community, whose claim on him came even, and always, before the claims of Janet and Gabriella.

Janet admired and was first attracted to Loring's dedication. When they met in medical school, she two years behind him, she was unmoved by his appearance. Were he a dog, he would have been a terrier, nothing regal. His ears were big and tilted out elflike at the top. His chin was a sturdy anchor at the bottom of a triangular face that narrowed sharply from his wide brow and prominent cheeks. His nose was straight and thin, his hair dark and brushed, not combed, to the side, like dead grass bent by a sleeping animal. His eyes, pale blue, cavorted under thin, velvety eyebrows in permanent merriment and the corners of his mouth were habitually upturned, as if humor were about to erupt uncontrolled from his lips. He had the build of a middleweight wrestler, which he had been in high school, and fingers long enough to play clarinet. He charmed Janet with his wit and warmth, and she was moved by his compassion, although the power of his intellect was what dazzled her. Years later, when she realized that the glitter of early love had faded, Janet found she still had a good and thoroughly enjoyable companion capable of caring. The sex continued to amaze them both.

And yet, although she found the feeling uncomfortable, she was jealous of Loring's devotion to his patients. The unfairness was clear. She dealt with the same burdens of a private practice. She was as devoted to her patients as Loring was to his. And she managed to do it with time left for home. He could, too, if he cared. The thought slipped before her, unwelcome, and, Janet thought immediately, dead wrong. He does care, she thought. He cares so deeply, that's his problem.

"So why doesn't he sell *his* practice to Jim Harvey?" she said aloud and laughed as she motored along the familiar streets skirting Port Hancock, toward the hospital only a few blocks away. Before she could give the obvious answer—that Loring English had a problem with authority that compelled him to work alone—she was startled by a silent splattering on her windshield and then a second. Almost instantly, the mist had been replaced by snow, falling in fat, wet clumps. The sudden, unseasonable conditions reminded Janet that she had not fastened her belt, and she reached for the shoulder harness and drew it across her jacket toward the buckle. Somehow she could not find the slot in the buckle. No one was coming, so she glanced down at her side, then back up to the road. Another glance and she saw that her jacket was covering the slot. She drew the tab end of the harness toward the slot. As the two metal parts clinked against each other, she felt a sudden, jarring pressure across her chest—and intense pain.

All was quiet. She held her breath, or, more accurately, her breath withheld itself. There was no motion. She could see the windshield was shattered. She could not see whether it was still snowing beyond the glass. Her breath returned and, with it, the sound of her own voice, groaning. Then the sound of another voice, husky but feminine.

"Lady, you okay?"

Inevitably, someone would come between Loring English and his wife Janet. Today it was Carmella Parente. Carmella was the perfect temptress, the irresistible test of his ethic, his whole philosophy. Even at age seventy-two, with her body fading, Carmella's voice strutted, sharp-tongued. Her words were still strong as oak rafters, emblem of the spirit that, through almost half a century, kept her proud back straight raising five children and managing the family business. For years a cigarette, glued by dried saliva to her lower lip, wagged up and down as she talked—until she gave them up at last. But she still talked. Talk was the currency of her trade. With it she had made buyers out of melon-squeezers and honor students out of her three hell-raising sons. She talked right up until her heart attack. Talked

4

and, against the advice of her doctor, consumed a hearty, fat-soaked diet. The rich food was what invited disease. And disease did what it always does, undermining all the strength that was within Carmella, secretly laying layers of paste, like mortar for a brick wall, inside her heart arteries until the blood stopped flowing and the pain came in her chest, a dreadful pain that stopped Carmella's talking in mid-sentence.

In the next week, after the ride in the eerie quiet of the ambulance—she knew vaguely its siren would be wailing, but she could not hear it—and after the injections of clot-dissolving drugs through an intravenous line, Carmella's pain vanished and her voice returned, sassy, gravelly. But the swagger was gone, and when Loring entered the catheterization laboratory at Riverton University Medical Center, he wondered if he would ever see Carmella looking other than she now appeared, the sparkle sedated out of her dark eyes, her hair a white halo, matted against the thin pillow, her once robust body now but a small deposit of bones and gristle under the blue paper drapes. His concerns would soon be relieved.

Mike Bernstein, a cardiology fellow who was assisting in the angioplasty, had already shoved a hollow-tipped needle into the femoral artery in Carmella's right groin. He had adjusted the two x-ray cameras, large as trash baskets and mounted on tracks that encircled the table and Carmella. On four video monitors suspended from the ceiling over the table were live, black-and-white images of her beating heart. On a fifth monitor, in color, were digital calibrations of her pulse, blood pressure, and other functions, and there was a digital clock, ticking off the seconds of Carmella's day, a sort of open-ended countdown toward either her restored health or her demise. From some hidden speaker came beeps each time Carmella's heart pumped; the beeps came faster than the seconds on the clock, which now read 3:16 p.m.

"You read all those pamphlets I gave you, Carmella, right?" English asked, looking over his shoulder at her as he selected a long wire, thin as vermicelli and encased in plastic, from atop a stainless steel cart behind him.

"Every one, Dr. English." The old woman's voice was soft, but more than a whisper.

"Good! At least someone in here knows what we're supposed to be doing," English said, winking at Carmella as he removed the yard-long wire from its wrapper and expertly shoved its tip through the hollow end of the needle in her groin. In matters medical, Loring English was as sharp as a surgical blade. In matters personal, he liked to fuzz the edges, keep his patients comfortable and interested.

"You want some advice, a lady likes a softer bed than this rock," she said. He could see, through the leaded glass partition that shielded him from the x-rays, that her lips, creased by years of smoking, were twisted in a smirk. Loring liked Carmella. He looked up. On the overhead screens he saw the guide wire following the curve of Carmella's aorta and entering her flinching heart. His ability to focus, remarkable even among doctors, was fully engaged on that video image. Yet even as he fed the guide wire into Carmella's heart, English was thinking of how, as he walked around the property with Janet earlier in the day, the cold drizzle had dripped from the back of his hat brim, trickled under his collar and down his spine, and disappeared, he had thought at the time, like a half-formed thought. This notion—of the incomplete thought—first came to him, unsummoned, while he and his wife were preoccupied with a small crisis. The storm had arrived during the night, the leading edge of winter thrown across darkened Port Hancock with gusting winds. The temperature had fallen, as had several branches. Some shrubs were flattened. Now, hours later, Loring knew that the notion of an incomplete thought held some meaning, that some unresolved issue was attempting to break into his consciousness. But what issue? The question hovered briefly before him now as he turned to the cart to select a balloon catheter, the device that, when inflated, would open Carmella's heart artery, allowing blood to flow unimpeded.

"I'm inserting the balloon, like we discussed, Carmella," he said, looking not at her but at the monitor above. "You'll be able to see a little dot on the screen. That's where the balloon is. When we get it to where your blockage is, we'll inflate, and the balloon will squish the plaque against the artery walls. Chances are two to one that'll fix you. There, see the dot?"

He glanced at Carmella's face, checking on her alertness. For the angioplasty to proceed, he needed her to be aware of how she felt, whether there was pain. A nurse standing beside the table at Carmella's head kept her talking. Loring asked Bernstein for Carmella's vital signs. They were normal. With a stainless steel wire in her heart, though, that meant little. A bettor must see a horse at post time. He can't just rely on the tables from the *Daily Racing Form*. And Loring needed to look into Carmella's eyes. The greatest gem Loring English took from medical school was his appreciation of the art of diagnosis. "Technology is great for confirming a diagnosis," he would tell his students at Riverton University. "But your hands, your ears, your eyes and even, at times, your nose and tongue, these are your first and most reliable instruments. Keep them engaged at all times."

Loring drew out the guide wire, over which the balloon catheter had ridden into Carmella's heart, and he replaced it with a wire thin as a human hair. He maneuvered this wire into the fine stem of the heart artery that was blocked, preparing a track for the balloon to ride. Then he pushed the catheter further into Carmella's groin, until, on the screen, the dot was in place.

"In a minute, I'm going to inflate the balloon, Carmella," Loring said. "When I do, there's going to be some pain, like when you had the heart attack. I want you to rate the pain for me, from one to ten. Okay?"

"Loring, you're a frustrated plumber, Hon," she said, attempting a wink. "You just can't wait to get out the old Roto-Rooter."

"I'm easier to get on short notice than a plumber, Carmella. Now don't let the music put you to sleep." Softly, from a portable tape player, came the music of Bach, played on guitar. Loring's thoughts drifted once again to the morning, to Janet.

They were in the kitchen, and Loring, who was ready to leave for his hospital rounds, stirred his coffee, the spoon clink-ing against the mug. He lifted the mug to sniff the aroma.

"Will you be home for dinner?" Janet asked.

"I hope so. I have Carmella Parente's angioplasty this afternoon. I don't see any complications. What's your day like?"

"A bunch of kids with winter colds, bronchitis, croup, ear infections, and Natasha and me chasing after them when we're not filling out some HMO's paperwork. Not as exciting as angioplasty. Then I have to make afternoon hospital rounds. With luck, I'll get home in time to put together some chicken Marsala," she said, dumping the remains of her coffee into the sink.

"Oooo. I love it when you speak French, bay-bee," Loring said, reaching for her hand and drawing her to him so that he could smell the damp wool of her sweater and feel her warm against his paunch. She was small. With her head tipped back to look up at him, her chin reached only to his second shirt button. Her eyes had the translucence of polished walnut. Her dark hair was short, above the ears. At the corners of her mouth were the creases left by forty-five years of constant smiling. She reached up and wiggled his ears.

"What I'd love is a thirty-hour day." She pouted. "I swear, I became a pediatrician to care for children. At times, I feel like a clerk for all those medical plans."

"Jim Harvey would be happy to relieve you of your troubles, Jan. I really think you should consider his offer." He felt her stiffen in his arms. Digging in her heels, he thought.

"You want me to sell my practice to that bozo? Loring, for someone who's an incredible diagnostician, you're sometimes blind."

"Look, you complain about the paperwork? Jim's group takes care of that for their docs, so they've got the extra time for patients. I've always said that you will do well if you practice good medicine, and the proof that the man's doing great work is in his group's expansion."

"Jim Harvey is spreading all right. Like a *virus!*" Janet said, stepping back and holding his hands.

"I'll tell you where the virus is, Janet Mitchell. It's the

damned accountants at the HMOs and insurance companies. The only pulse they can feel is in their cash flow. Take Darlene Phipps. She switched to an HMO and, because of her colitis, she picked a GI guy as her primary physician."

"Ouch, that must hurt! A GI over a cardiologist!"

"No, seriously. She starts getting chest pains, he treats her for gas and won't ship her back to me because the HMO will charge him. In the end, Darlene pays for this efficiency with an ambulance ride! It's criminal!"

Janet pulled Loring back to her and, with a smirk, whispered up to his ear.

"I'd suggest that you sell out to Jim Harvey, but he's probably already heard about your trouble with authority figures."

"Damned proud of that little reputation, too!" Loring said with a grin and a rough hug that lifted Janet off her feet. "Public enemy number one for three years running on the Port Hancock General board of trustees but, I need not remind you, those were also the years the medical staff voted me their chief."

"You're hopeless, Loring. Idealistic, but hopeless."

"We're two of a kind, Jan. But I think you should reconsider Jim's offer."

"Brilliant as he is, Jim Harvey's not my hero, Lor. So, we'll have dinner tonight for a change? It's been more than a week. And you'll call our daughter?"

Call my daughter! he thought now as he began twisting a device the size of a small flashlight, inflating the balloon, big as a seed, inside Carmella's heart. I've never got enough time for Gabriella. Hell, I never even have time for Janet. He broke from his reverie to ask Carmella if she felt pain.

"On a scale of one to ten?" he asked.

"Is ten childbirth or slamming a car door on your thumb?"

"I don't have any experience with childbirth, Carmella. You pick."

"It's about a six," she said, her voice dreamy with drugs. "But go ahead. I trust you."

Most people in the Hancock River Valley trusted Loring. They would describe him as sensitive, caring. If they measured him by the time he spent with his family, there would be a different verdict. Or if they could look into his mind and know what moved him. The reality didn't quite meet the ideal, a fact that Loring accepted the way one is compelled to acknowledge any other permanent feature of one's being: their height, the curl of their toes. Loring's fallibility—his recognition of it—slipped now through his consciousness and he sensed its appearance had something to do with his earlier, troublingly incomplete thought, when the rain dripped down his neck.

He deflated the balloon and, looking up at the video screen, gauged the size of the opening in Carmella's artery.

"We'll do this a couple of times, Carmella," he said. "That's normal."

"I do this every day," she said, closing her eyes as the nurse dabbed perspiration from her brow.

"Inflating," Loring announced, and a second clock on the video screen began counting. When the balloon was inflated, he injected an iodine dye. On the screen, the opaque dye filled Carmella's heart vessels, tangled like a root-bound plant, and outlined the sausage-shaped inflated balloon. After two minutes, he deflated again. The artery was still pinched.

"We're shooting for a seventy percent opening," he told Carmella. "We're going to inflate again in a minute, a little longer this time."

"If you want to know, the pain is up to about an eight."

"I haven't inflated yet, Carmella," Loring said, deep furrows appearing across his broad brow.

"She's sweating profusely," said the nurse at Carmella's side.

"She's Brady, Loring!" said Bernstein, his eyes fixed on the screen as Carmella's pulse slipped from eighty to fifty and then to thirty.

"Give her point five milligrams of atropine," Loring said, calmly, as if he were ordering a side of peppers.

"Atropine on board," another nurse echoed.

"Okay, I'm proceeding to finish up," Loring said.

Carmella gave a weak moan as Loring began to reinflate the balloon.

"I'm finished inflating. Perfusion appears adequate," Loring told Bernstein. "How are you doing, Carmella?"

She did not answer. Her blood pressure had slipped sharply. Without warning, her body stiffened.

"Loring! She's starting with a seizure!" Bernstein looked to Loring, waiting for instructions.

"Dammit!" Loring whispered. "She's in v-fib!" On the color monitor, the jagged green line representing Carmella's heartbeat had become erratic and, on the black-and-white screens, her heart had stopped moving. Carmella was silent. The nurse at her head held Carmella's brow and looked back to Loring, a "Do something" expression in her eyes. Carmella's heart was contracting—like a bag of worms, Loring might say. Its rhythm was chaotic. Her blood stopped flowing.

Anticipating Loring's command, the second nurse was moving toward the defibrillator. The nurse at Carmella's head tore away Carmella's coverings and stood back while the other applied the paddles firmly to Carmella's chest. The jolt of two hundred watts bounced her body.

The green line remained irregular.

"Damn! Reshock at three-sixty and give one milligram of adrenaline!" Loring ordered.

"Given!" Carmella's body jolted and bounced once again.

"We've got a rhythm," Bernstein reported. "Brady with multiple VPCs."

"Mary, give her a hundred milligrams of Lidocaine and start a drip at two milligrams a minute." Loring's brow was beaded with sweat. "Come on baby, can't lose you now," he said, his voice still just above a whisper.

Hearing his own voice, he was moved, in one of those bursts of awareness that takes an instant and yet encompasses enormous ideas, to reflect that he was not unlike a gambler who has put his money on red and is urging the roulette wheel to work for him. Carmella's a wonderful woman, and yet I'm indifferent, truly, to her immediate pain. She could be anyone and I would react the same. Again, the sense of a half-completed thought returned, the notion of reality failing to meet the ideal,

But what ideal gnawed at him this day? And what question was his subconscious anxiously throwing up for him to answer?

"She's waking," Bernstein said. "Pressure one hundred. Sinus tach at one-twenty with good pulse."

"Great, we're out of the woods. Let's finish up," Loring said. He reinflated the balloon and injected more dye.

"Dr. English, phone call," a control room nurse said over the intercom.

"Take a message."

"It's Port Hancock General's emergency room, Doctor. They have your wife."

Loring set the inflate-deflate device gently on Carmella's thigh and turned toward the control room. His heart beat hard against the inside of his chest. Without knowing Janet's condition, he wanted to escape from the cath lab to her side. And yet his duty was here.

Instantly, Loring English understood the answer to the vague question the dripping rain had posed.

At 6:05 p.m., Loring English took the unusual step of asking his assistant, Dr. Bernstein, to finish the paperwork on the angioplasty.

"Carmella, you were lucky today," he said, smiling at his patient and holding her hand. "We opened that artery like the drain of your kitchen sink."

"That's what I hired you to do, Loring," Carmella said, her voice thin, sleepy. "I knew you're the best!" She squeezed his hand, as Janet might have. Again with clarity came the answer he had been seeking all day. It had to do with caring. At times, he had let his enthusiasm for medicine override the chance to nourish a relationship. This had been true with Gabriella. It had been true with Janet. Even, and perhaps particularly, it had been true with his God. He would, he decided, address the more terrestrial of these relationships first, and see how he fared.

"Look, Carmella, I've got to run. My wife's in the emergency room at Port Hancock General."

"Nothing serious, I hope."

"Not my Janet," Loring said. "She's healthy as a horse, thanks."

The voice was somewhere beside her, to her left. She tried to turn, but the steering wheel was against her chest.

"Don't move, lady," the voice said, and she heard the complaint of bent metal as her rescuer yanked open the door and she felt a breath on her cheek. It was a woman—she could smell the perfume—a woman wearing a United Parcel Service cap, leaning into the Volvo. Again the woman's voice, this time farther away. "Dial 911! She needs help!"

"What . . ." her own voice sounded distant, nowhere near as close as the pain in her chest or the warmth that flowed down her forehead.

"You ran off the road, lady. Hit a tree, hard. I can hear the ambulance coming," the delivery woman said, reaching across Janet to turn off the ignition. "Good thing we're so close to the hospital. That's a nasty gash. Must have hit the windshield."

Each moment moved with strange and exaggerated slowness, like a cinematic dream sequence. Medics worked over her, and a red tint pulsed through the falling snowflakes. Soon, however, Janet found herself passing back into the familiar, strapped to a backboard and wheeled feet first through Port Hancock General's emergency room door, into the warm bright lights and comforting antiseptic smells of medicine. Even on her back, she knew the place by its details—the striped wallpaper, the glass of the trauma nurses' booth. She had treated many of her young patients here. But she also felt embarrassed at finding herself the center of the activity.

"I'm sorry," she said when Karen Larsen, the nursing supervisor, a redhead with the demeanor of a first sergeant, appeared alongside the rumbling ambulance gurney. She would have apologized for the carelessness that had brought her here, but a searing pain shot through her chest and her entire body stiffened in response.

"Take her in trauma, Bill," Larsen barked to the paramedic at Janet's head. "Don't worry, Dr. Mitchell. Dr. Callahan's waiting for you." She squeezed Janet's arm. "Sue," she called. The gurney came to a halt inside a room filled with the tubes and gauges of life-saving apparatus, and Janet saw a petite nurse wearing a crisp blue button-down blouse and snug jeans take her wrist in one hand and, with the other, pump up the blood pressure cuff wrapped around her biceps.

Bill Callahan's voice came from the other side.

"Dr. Mitchell?"

She turned slowly. Callahan, tall with sandy curls, was bending over her, a practiced but sincere smile in his blue eyes.

"Bill, sorry to bother you like this," she whispered, forcing her own smile and using as little breath to speak as possible in hopes of sparing herself more pain. She was certain some ribs were broken, her only diagnosis so far. A second nurse had unfastened the backboard straps and was cutting her clothing away.

"Chest pains, Janet?" Callahan asked. She nodded. "Let me peek at your forehead." He leaned closer and drew stainless steel sheers from the pocket of his white smock. She felt the cool metal against her brow and felt cool air as he lifted the dressing that, until now, she had forgotten was there.

"BP one-twenty over sixty, pulse one-twenty, Doctor," Sue Czernicki reported. Callahan glanced toward the nurse, then back at Janet. His smile had faded.

"Guess I got scratched," Janet said, again whispering. "How serious is it?"

"The medics tell me your car was badly damaged. You uprooted a tree. There's a deep laceration on your forehead, but the medics did a good job. Let's see how the rest of you fared." He began bombarding Janet with questions: How she felt, what she remembered, how Loring was, where Gabbie was going to college, where it hurt; and his hands and stethoscope moved about her naked torso, systematically as a dowser with a forked stick, a prospector with a Geiger counter. All the while, Callahan was getting data from the trauma nurses.

"Vitals stable," Sue reported.

"Keep that IV at KVO," Callahan replied. "What's her pulse-ox reading?"

"One hundred percent on four liters, Doctor," the second nurse said.

"Good. Have Lab draw the usual trauma blood profile. Get X-ray in here to do a cross table of her cervical spine and a chest."

As Callahan drew a blue paper drape up over her chest, Janet glanced at a wall clock. 3:16. She had pestered Loring to be home by seven. She knew from the questions Callahan asked that he worried she might lose consciousness.

She was hooked to an IV, perhaps with painkillers, certainly with tranquilizers, flowing into her veins. She hurt, but nothing she could not stand.

"Bill, I'll be okay to leave? I feel a little foolish."

"You've got a severe laceration on your noggin, Janet," he said, taking her wrist in his hand. "I'll get Dr. Jankowski, our best plastic man, to take care of it. You also have a bad chest bruise with a steering wheel tattoo, so we need to check that out. I don't want to rule out something more serious than a cardiac contusion."

Janet tried to add it up, but the bottom line escaped her. "Am I here for the night?"

"Definitely," Callahan said. "Sue," he called to the nurse. "Sue, get me a stat cardiogram." He looked back to Janet and was about to say something when, behind him, Karen Larsen leaned through the door.

"Dr. Callahan, you're needed in the cardiac room! Arrhythmia!"

"Shit!" Callahan said. "Sorry, Janet. Sue, give Dr. Mitchell seventy-five milligrams Demerol IV. Jan, I'll get right back as soon as I've got cardiac under control." As he stepped out the door, he spoke quietly to Larsen: "I'm really concerned about that chest injury. We've got to consider everything, even a lacerated aorta."

Janet, watching Callahan go, heard the word "aorta" but nothing more. She looked for a nurse. "Sue, could you find out who's covering for Barry Siedel?" she whispered. Sue came closer. "I know he's out of town. I can trust whoever's covering for him." She closed her eyes. The pain in her chest was growing more distressing. She inhaled deeply and let her breath seep out slowly as Sue inserted the IV needle and the Demerol began working. It was, she thought, like falling asleep knowing you would return to a bad dream. The Demerol made her drowsy, made even her toes and her cheeks relax. Her skin seemed to sag loosely from her bones. But, as if sensing her slack defenses, the pain marched forward, occupying not only her back but also her chest. After Sue left, she felt a surge of nausea and told a passing nurse, who put a small, curved pan by her head. Then she was alone, but only briefly. She was trying to doze when she heard Jim Harvey's voice outside her door. She opened her eyes a slit and thought of feigning sleep when Harvey stepped into the room. He was looking back over his shoulder, probably at one of the younger nurses, Janet thought. The topic of Jim Harvey's moves was, among the female employees at the hospital, normal grist for conversation. Everyone knew that he used nurses for a tune-up. The big game, notwithstanding his wife, was women with money or power. But he flashed that smile and wore his tanned, blond beach boy good looks like a diner wears neon. Always open! Everyone welcome! You could talk to any woman who knew him and her eyes would roll in disgust. Yet Harvey's revolving door kept spinning.

When Janet's eyes met his, Harvey's face grew serious.

"I'm covering for Siedel, Dr. Mitchell. I'll be handling your case." He had picked up her chart and was reading it while he spoke. "Is the pain any better, Doctor?"

"Yes, better," she said.

"You're the last person I expected to find in here, Janet. With your huge patient base? I'm surprised you took time off for this nonsense." He winked.

"Loring says I should take your offer, Jim." Her own words surprised her. They leaped from her lips, as if the IV were dripping Pentothal.

16

"Your husband is a wise man, but I'm certain that's a decision you can make based on the merits and without help," he said, and he fashioned an expression that even Janet found appealing and, perhaps, sincere.

"I like doing my own thing," Janet said. "No offense. Ohh!" She moaned reflexively. It felt like a giant jumper cable clamp had been applied to her back and chest. At the same time, her head spun dizzily.

"Let me take a look," Harvey said. Warming the disk first in his palm, Harvey placed his stethoscope against her chest and listened. His brow knit like he was on a phone with a bad connection. "Your heart sounds are good, your lungs are clear," he said, looking up and smiling. Then he returned to his examination, palpating her abdomen.

"Any ideas, Jim? Why the pain in my back?" she asked, and as she did she felt her concentration slip, so that his words seemed to come to her delayed.

"Probably muscular pain in the back," he said, looking again at her chart. "Cardiac contusion in the chest. We'll check it with some thoracic spine x-rays, and I'll talk to you after I see your labs and ECG. They should be taking you up to radiology any minute, Janet. Meanwhile, I'll give you more pain medicine to get you comfortable. I have to go up to intensive care to check a patient. I'll be back."

A gathering discomfort filled Janet. Alone in the trauma room, visited by waves of pain, she heard herself moan. One nurse or another would appear to take her pulse, pat her shoulder. After several of these visits, Bill Callahan stuck his head in the door.

"Feeling any better, Dr. Mitchell?" he asked. "Not so good," she said.

"What does Dr. Harvey say?"

"I haven't seen him for a while."

"What?" Callahan stepped full into the room. "For how long?"

Janet looked up at the wall clock, but she could not make sense of it. She closed her eyes. "A long time," she said.

"Sue!" Callahan called. The nurse arrived and Callahan asked her to take Janet's vitals. Janet felt the cuff inflating around her arm.

"It's dropped," Sue told Callahan.

"Damn! Where's Harvey?"

Sue shrugged. Callahan leaned out the door. "Karen, page Dr. Harvey. Stat!"

Janet heard the call go out, then saw Harvey step into the room behind Callahan, who was listening to Janet's chest. Janet noticed that Sue smiled, a bit too sweetly, at Harvey.

"Doctor, your patient's blood pressure has dropped while you were out." Callahan was scolding, even as he made room for Harvey at Janet's side.

"The Demerol," Harvey said casually.

"Her pulse is up, too, and she's pale, Doctor. I'm concerned."

"Look, we're dealing with cardiac contusion. Serious, but no big problem," Harvey said, stepping to the doorway and calling.

"What's the holdup with X-ray? Dr. Mitchell's getting hypotensive from the Demerol. Let's get moving!"

At that moment, another nurse called Callahan back to the cardiac room. Janet closed her eyes, attempting to collect her scattered thoughts. The voices beyond her eyelids continued to invade her scrambled mind.

"Sue, bolus five-hundred cc's of saline into the IV to see if that raises Dr. Mitchell's blood pressure," Harvey said. "If not, we'll have to give Narcan to reverse the Demerol and try a different analgesic. I want her moved to the observation room."

"Sue, they need your help in cardiac."

Janet knew this as the voice of Karen Larsen. She opened her eyes and saw Larsen take the hypodermic from Sue. Larsen was tough, protective of her nurses and willing to put doctors in their place when necessary.

"Dr. Mitchell? How are you doing?" Karen asked, her smile genuine. Janet saw in the arrangement of Larsen's features a hint of tension. Larsen and Harvey had exchanged neither

18

words nor glances, like a feuding old couple, Janet thought. When an orderly, a tall, bony woman with acne and stringy hair, appeared in the doorway, Harvey ignored her, Janet noticed. Larsen spoke to the woman, who bent and unlocked the gurney's wheels. Now the examination room ceiling began spinning, and Janet thought about clutching the sides of the gurney. She vomited instead. Karen was looking down, holding the pan at Janet's cheek as the gurney rolled across the emergency room and down a corridor. Janet felt lightheaded. Time was losing significance, shoved ruthlessly into the background by her pain. At some point, she discovered, she had been hooked to an electronic monitor. She was in the observation unit, and Karen was bent over her. The ceiling light, blocked by Karen's head, shimmered behind her like an aurora, leaving Karen's face in shadows. Her features, barely visible to Janet, were drawn with concern.

Janet's pulse was unchanged, but her blood pressure had dropped again. She heard Karen's voice, distant, urgent.

"Doctor, this looks serious!"

"Nurse, I don't have time," Harvey snapped, stepping into the hallway to look at Janet's chest film on a wall-mounted view box.

A panic swept up through Janet. She wanted answers. But now even Karen was leaving her side, following Harvey into the hall, where Callahan had joined him. They were out of sight, but Janet could hear their voices, their muffled, hostile words.

Callahan, at first. "The chest x-ray's suspicious, Doctor."

Then Harvey, irritated. "That film was done supine. That'll distort the findings."

Now Karen. "It's definitely more than cardiac contusion, Dr. Harvey."

"Jesus, now a word from the Girl Scouts! If we do anything, it'll be an arteriogram."

"Then let's do it!" Callahan nearly shouted. "She's been here an hour, Doctor, and in my opinion it should have been done a long time ago and the OR put on notice."

Janet's head was spinning, the pain in her chest searing.

Harvey's next comment gave her little reassurance.

"I'm in charge here and you're the junior physician, Callahan. Get X-ray ready and we'll take her over!"

Janet's gurney was rolling now, Harvey trotting at her side, his hand on her arm. "It's going to be fine, Janet." And then the gurney had stopped and a nurse was preparing her groin for the insertion of a catheter and Stanley Raphire, the radiologist, was at her other side, unhappy, it seemed, with the x-ray.

"Shouldn't she be on her way to the OR?" asked Raphire, a man of constant uncertainty. Janet felt like she was on a heavy locomotive that was gathering speed. "I mean, geez, Jim, don't you think she looks bad? That is, she's quite pale and really diaphoretic and, uh, are you sure we should be wasting time with the arteriogram?"

"Dammit, Dr. Raphire!" Harvey said. He was injecting Lidocaine in Janet's groin. "Just shoot the dye so we know what's going on here!"

"Okay, okay! I'm going to put the dye in. But, Jim, I mean, look, her pressure's going down!" He mopped his brow as he looked up at a monitor to see the path of the dye.

"Okay, Stanley, shoot the first film," Harvey ordered.

"Geez, it looks like a tear in the thoracic aorta!" Raphire's words were a cry. His fear penetrated Janet's grogginess. "She needs to be in the OR!"

Just then, Janet writhed on the gurney.

"Oh, God! I'm feeling terrible!" she cried, a panic rising in her voice. "I feel like I'm going to pass out!" She gasped for breath, panting now, a flood of perspiration rising on her brow and around her lips and trickling down into her ears. "The pain is getting worse! Ooooh! I'm dying!"

"Dammit, Jim," Raphire screamed, a voice too distant from Janet for her to identify. "It's a tear and a large hematoma! Call the OR! We're going up!" Her right arm and leg were suddenly numb. She tried to move but could not. Her own petrified scream was lost on it way to her lips. Her pulse raced. Her blood pressure dropped again, sharply. Stanley Raphire's anxiety boiled over in a smear of words.

"Bolus her with a thousand cc's of saline," Harvey shouted. "We're going up!"

As the saline raced through the clear plastic IV tubes and into her blood stream, Janet Mitchell lost consciousness.

"Call a code! Call a code!"

On the hospital paging system, Dr. Heartwell was summoned and, in seconds, the gurney banged through the OR doors. It was 6:05 p.m.

Two . . .

Loring and Gabriella remained in the limousine, parked in front of the church, while two men with white carnations in their lapels rolled the polished mahogany casket bearing Janet Mitchell's body from the hearse. Loring recognized one of the men, a stout fellow with a few oily strands combed along his crown, as William Podgell Durant, the funeral director and a member of the board of trustees at Port Hancock General. Durant's substance was further swelled this morning by his immediate authority, directing six men in suits, all physicians, uncomfortable in their doubly unfamiliar duties as pallbearers and as subordinates. Waving his stubby arms, Durant assembled the doctors around the casket at the base of St. Anthony's steps, two dozen granite slabs rising to dark, wooden front doors massive as vault lids. He ran a hand back over his scalp, then turned toward the limousine and opened the door on Loring's side, as he buttoned his jacket across his stretched white shirt. Durant's cologne hung like a fog into which Loring rose, thinking: I never wore cologne for Janet, and then: That's a trivial concern to engage me now, and then: How disconnected everything feels, like I've been anesthetized. Durant motioned for Loring to follow the casket. Loring turned and took Gabriella's hand and squeezed. He saw her chin quiver and the tears flooding her eyes and he felt her return his squeeze. A now familiar tension seized his throat as he saw Janet's casket, lifted by the hands of six other men, rising away from him toward the church doors. Eager to stay close to Janet, he led his daughter up the steps.

They had spent the last two days together, seldom leaving the big, old house. They had searched there for memories to share. There were too few photographs, too few of any of the normal trinkets that collect around a happy family. Loring assumed the blame. With Gabriella, he had gathered as many albums and envelopes of photographs as they could find boxed in the dusty attic. They were still sneezing when they brought a shopping sack full of snapshots to the parlor and heaped them on a table near the piano. Sitting together on the sagging, mauve sofa, its upholstery itchy as the stubble of a day-old beard, they slowly analyzed each picture, as if piecing together fragments of a magic urn with the power to restore Janet to them.

Loring put his arm around Gabriella. She fit there under his wing as comfortably as she did in grade school, which was, he thought, about the last time they had sat like this. Where was I, he wondered, that I wasn't holding my daughter. In his hand was a picture of a nearly-teenage Gabriella, standing knee deep in water, practicing a coy smile. On the back of the snapshot was written "Gabriella's seventh grade class canoe trip."

"I don't remember taking this picture," he said, tilting the photograph toward a lamp.

"You didn't, Dad. Mom was the chaperone on that trip. Remember? You said you were coming but had an emergency at the hospital?"

He did not remember. Yet he saw that even now, ten years later, the memory of his absence was as sharp for Gabriella as broken glass.

"I'm sorry," he said. There was something in the shape or substance of his words, some trigger that released a force from inside his chest, a force until then trapped in some bodily chamber undiscovered by medical science, and that force came as suddenly as unexpected death, overwhelming him

22

with roaring, unwashed grief. A shower of tears streamed down his cheeks. "Oh, God, I'm sorry!" he sobbed, hugging his daughter's shoulders and tasting his own tears, then whispering: "I'm so sorry!" A confession to his child; an apology to Janet.

It would only be later that he realized Gabriella had understood him completely when she moved closer to him and assured him: "She loved you so much, Dad. She really did."

Now, climbing the stone steps behind the casket, Loring again put his arm around his daughter and she reached around his waist, there to steady him if he needed her, just, he thought, as her mother would have done. Gabriella, while in her own right a woman—an adult with her own apartment near the college and her own PIN number at the bank—was in every way his wife's daughter, short with dark wavy hair, dark eyes that smiled easily and a ready laugh.

A laugh now silent in Janet, Loring thought, watching as the pallbearers rolled her casket through the tall doors. Inside the sanctuary, Gothic arches soared toward Heaven and down from them echoed a soprano's voice, accompanied by an organ, singing "Precious Lord, lead me home." Whole families, scores of them, were crowded the length of both walls and across the rear of the church, and every seat was filled. It felt, as the procession moved slowly along the aisle, as if Loring and Gabriella and Janet's casket were passing between two massed, silent armies.

Ahead, ranks of candles flickered on the altar, and one tall white candle stood in the center. There, the pallbearers left the casket, draped in a white cloth. An usher led Gabriella and Loring away from the casket, toward seats in the front pew. Loring went slowly, wanting to linger with Janet, to wrap his arms around that awful box and embrace her one last time, as if, despite two decades of treating men and women who often died in his care, he believed that if he remained at her side, she would not be gone and the dreadful ache in his heart would be healed.

Gabriella tugged gently at his hand and Loring, blind with tears, allowed her to lead him away.

The soprano finished her hymn and the priest stood above the casket, repeating a prayer. Behind him were dozens of potted flowers, purple, white, and yellow, with tags roughly cut from bright construction paper and tied to each pot with ribbon. Loring and Gabriella had asked for charitable contributions instead of flowers and Loring wondered, without anger, who had ignored them. Janet loves flowers, he thought, then corrected himself: Loved flowers. The tears rose again, and he glanced at the casket.

"Let us not dwell on Janet Mitchell's death," the priest was saying, his amplified voice a resonant bass that penetrated Loring's chest. "For within her, as within the rest of us, God had his hand, prepared to take her home when the time was right. No, let us look at her life, which God gave her as He has given each of us every breath we take. And let us look at how she used that life, whether it was spent as God wishes us to live."

The priest paused and leaned his elbows on the pulpit, resting his chin on his hands. Looking down, he continued, "Please look behind you, Gabriella and Dr. English." They turned in their seats. Directly behind them were two pews filled with children, and beyond the children were the faces of Port Hancock: smooth, pimply, wrinkled, whiskered.

"There is the answer. Like a farmer who has labored honestly and planted well, Janet is rewarded for her life with an abundant crop of love. And a special love it is. For in a world that seems at times overrun with those who would use their skills solely for their own enrichment, we were given Janet. One child at a time, she spread the kind of love our Lord taught us."

The priest stood and gripped the sides of the pulpit. "I knew Janet, but in the last two days I've heard the stories of others, as well. To her, giving was its own reward."

Even in death, Loring thought. Her heart was now beating in another woman, and her kidneys, corneas, lungs and liver had been harvested. The only good to come from Jim Harvey's bad doctoring, Loring thought. Janet had died from a thoracic artery rupture. She had bled to death internally while Harvey called for more tests and ignored not only the obvious but,

24

Loring had been told by someone who had been a witness, the protests of other doctors and nurses. If Harvey had been competent, Janet would be recovering now and soon would be back with her patients. Back with her family. Damn Jim Harvey! Loring thought, and his fists balled in a rage he had never before felt. Harvey's image rose now and Loring's clenched fingers squeezed and he felt as if he were shaking the doctor. Damn him! he thought, his whole body wracked with silent sobs, Damn him for taking her! And just that quickly, Loring's intellect stepped in front of these strange emotions and he remembered the patients he himself had lost. He saw some of the faces, warning him against this anger that had seized him. Loring looked up to the shadows between the arches, perhaps searching for some symbol of the surviving soul of his wife. Instead, he saw the image of her corpse, lying a few feet away, disemboweled like a cleaned fish. To avoid another flood of grief, he returned his attention to the priest.

"While those of us who could have bought flowers have instead contributed to Janet's favorite charities, there were some who felt she deserved nature's own perfume on her journey from this life. The children of Raleigh Gardens Elementary, where Janet volunteered as school doctor, brought in these lovely plants, which they have been nurturing since September." He smiled at the children seated behind Loring and Gabriella, and a small girl with black braids reached up and tapped Gabbie's shoulder. "We loved her," the child whispered.

Loring returned the little girl's smile and, despite a new flood of tears, his pain began to lift, buoyed by the love left by Janet on earth, love with the purity of spring water that rose from the children and the adults who had poured into the church.

Outside, the sun hung like a silver coin in the hazy sky. The air, still damp from the storm three days earlier, had already warmed by the time they left the church to follow the hearse to the cemetery. They rode along West Avenue, past rows of run-down mansions, monuments erected by industrial barons to themselves. Many remained boarded up. Others had been divided up into apartments and seedy looking professional

25

offices. In front of one old Victorian, its paint dull and peeling, a small white sign with black letters still announced "Janet L. Mitchell, M.D." Natasha hadn't yet the heart to remove it. The limousine turned north on Mill Street, passing the Raleigh Gardens housing project and then the old frame houses that, a hundred years before, were built by the sawmill for its employees. The houses got smaller, closer together, and more run-down with each passing block, until the land started to rise from the river to the bluffs north of the city. Here the decrepit houses of the poor yielded, after a buffer of parkland, to the suburbs.

Outside the city, the hearse turned off the street through a stone arch that, like a bank facade of the same vintage, was meant to convey a comforting sense of eternity. The motorcade climbed a knoll and stopped near a green and white canvas canopy, under which were more potted flowers. The knoll was shaded in season by several sheltering oaks, and when Loring noticed the now naked limbs, he remembered the tree branches that fell on the shrubs that morning and how, in the kitchen, they had held each other and how her hair smelled like shampoo and how her back felt to his fingers through her soggy sweater and how her breasts felt against his paunch. He did not want to put her into a hole in this hill. He wished for some kind of magic that would return her to him. For the first time in his life, he acknowledged the futility of his profession.

They did lower Janet into that damp earth. Holding Gabriella's hand, Loring reached down and snapped a single blossom from a spray, setting it on the casket lid, a final gift for his lover.

Unsettled, he turned away. Nothing was left to be done except to receive, in Janet's honor, the sympathy of the several hundred mourners who had traveled to the cemetery.

Among the first was Natasha Wilson. Janet had been Natasha's doctor as a child, and was instrumental in encouraging the younger woman to pursue a career in medicine. They kept in touch while Natasha earned a pre-med at Villanova, and finally an M.D. from Temple University. As

26

soon as she finished her residency, in pediatrics, Janet invited Natasha to join her practice in Port Hancock. At thirty-three, Natasha still had the physique of a hurdler, and the unblinking eyes of the seasoned competitor that took Villanova to two division championships. Those eyes now glazed with tears as she reached for Loring's hand.

"You know how much I loved her," she said. She cupped her free hand over the back of Loring's, then extended it to Gabriella. "Your mom was the best big sister I ever had, and I've had a couple," she said.

After Reginald Wilson, Natasha's husband, took Loring's hand and offered his condolences, Loring turned to Natasha.

"What will you do, Natasha? With the practice?"

"It's too much, Loring. I know how strongly Janet felt about independence, but with only four years under my belt, I'll have to find someone else. You can't go it on your own in this new world."

"We were talking about Jim Harvey's overture that morning. I told her I thought she should look into it."

"She told me about that, and she was stewing about it all day," Natasha said. "She said maybe you were right."

"She always had better instincts than me," Loring said. He restrained the words more critical of Harvey that his tongue pleaded to throw.

"She will always be my inspiration," Natasha said, and noticing that a line had formed behind them, gave Loring and Gabriella each a kiss on the cheek and she and her husband stepped away.

The impromptu reception line wound back around the grave. There were mothers and fathers, some of whom had been Janet's patients before they brought her their own children. There were nurses from both Port Hancock General and Valleyview Medical Center, and there were physicians of every stripe, each with her or his own tale to tell Gabriella and Loring, each story another reason to grieve her loss.

When James Perkins Harvey III reached them, he did not extend his hand or offer a kiss, but rather, clasping his hands low before him, tears welling in his reddened eyes, he bowed his head and softly, pleadingly said simply: "I'm sorry."

The anger Loring had felt toward Harvey in the church and several other times in the last three days returned now. It tightened the muscles in Loring's jaw and set his eyes in a critical cast. He overpowered this emotion and rearranged his expression.

"I'm sure," Loring said.

"These hands failed when it counted most. I should have . . . I keep looking for an excuse, Dr. English, and there just is none. I have the training, the experience. I was certain I knew what I was doing, and I missed it. And the worst part is that I know I can't make it up to Janet or to you or to your daughter."

"We feel her loss enormously," Loring said, burning with anger, unwilling to betray Janet's memory with a kind word for Harvey, despite the look in the younger doctor's eyes, as if the weight of her death pulled them toward the ground in search for answers.

"Will you ever forgive me?" Harvey looked into Loring's eyes for the first time, then to Gabriella.

"Of course we will," she said, and she tightened her hug around her father. "God requires it."

Three . . .

Jim Harvey spoke with a few of the mourners and then, ignoring the path, cut across the grounds to his Range Rover, parked just beyond the cemetery's rear wall. It was consistent with Harvey's approach in all things that he would avoid the bottleneck at the front gate. The cunning that propelled him to the top of his class at Johns Hopkins Medical College continued to serve him in each detail of his life. Knowing his absence wouldn't be felt in the crush at the funeral, he had glanced at a street map the day before and located the cemetery's rear entrance.

He arrived just as the priest turned from the grave. He moved swiftly but subtly through the crowd of mourners toward Loring English, avoiding eye contact until a few others had already consoled the father and daughter. It was important, Harvey felt, that the focus not be on Loring's grief but on his own sincere remorse.

Arriving back at the Range Rover, Harvey took a cellular phone from inside his silk suit jacket and dialed.

"Tiffany, sweetheart, I'll be there in ten minutes," he said, slipping off his jacket and tossing it across to the passenger side.

"Good, then ask them to assemble in the conference room. Have you set out the iced tea for Neil?" He turned the key in the ignition. "And Jerry's cigars?" He spun the wheel and stepped vigorously on the accelerator. "Don't forget the napkins for Dr. Urizar," he laughed. Driving swiftly, Harvey took inventory of his morning. A phone call to Tommy Bettenfield, his broker, at 7:00, after a half hour of exercise. An hour on the phone with Jerry Wiegenstein, laying out the goals for the noon directors' meeting. At 8:30, breakfast with his wife Sonia, who by then had driven the kids to school. Then a trip across the river to a small ranch house in an older development. That took from 9:00 until 11:10. Then the drive to the cemetery. Now it was nearly noon. He dialed the car phone again.

"Tiffany, honey, could you put Neil on?" He bent to the side to look at himself in the mirror, brushing back his short, trimmed sideburns with a fingertip. "Neil, what's the mood?" A pause. "I guess that's to be expected. See you soon."

A solid teak table, thirty-two feet long, ran nearly the length of the conference room, a half-scale reproduction of the deck of Harvey's yacht, *Carassius Auratus*. When he opened the conference door, there were six men gathered at the squared end of the table. Without speaking, Harvey walked toward them, his steps muffled by an antique Oriental rug, layered over a deep carpet. The other directors of Osler Medical Group fell silent and parted, taking their seats on the table's curved sides.

29

Harvey's seat, at the end, clearly controlled the helm. Still silent, he surveyed his crew.

In the first chair to his left was Dr. Dennis Ross, a classmate of Harvey's at Johns Hopkins where Ross tried to poke everything that walked and not without success. It wasn't his good looks. Even then he was dumpy, with pale skin, small eyes, and a brow that spread back, like a rising flood, through his thin, curly hair. In the place of witticisms or manly deportment—his handshake may have suggested his lovemaking: eagerly offered, yet limp as a bag of giblets—Ross carried an impressive roll of cash. He never wanted for companionable flesh, and he graduated and became an allergist.

Beside Ross at the table was another of Harvey's classmates, Dr. Steven Nightingale, an orthopedic surgeon, skillful in his art. Steve wore the only beard in the room, if not the only Rolex. He was scrawny, with a non-existent chest, a characteristic accentuated by his posture—hunched, as if he were always cold—and he habitually tugged on his nose when he was impatient for a chance to speak, as he now apparently was.

Next to Nightingale sat Neil Dunmore, at sixty-eight the elder on Osler Medical's board and the only director who was not a physician. Dunmore, his dark hair combed straight back from his deeply furrowed brow, had the thick hands of a bricklayer, which he had been in his youth. Now, he owned and developed real estate. His bushy eyebrows and kindly smile were deceptively grandfatherly.

Across the table from Dunmore sat Dr. Bradley Barnett. Barnett—Brad to all—had struggled through Johns Hopkins. He needed to work to pay for his education, and his work ethic pulled him through where he lacked genius. Despite inferior intellect and finances, Barnett was able to develop friendships above his station, particularly with Jim Harvey, whom everyone at Johns Hopkins jokingly called J.H., in part to distinguish him from his legendary father and grandfather.

Wedged between Brad Barnett and Jerry Wiegenstein, who, as lawyer for the Osler Group, sat at Harvey's right hand, was the other doctor on the board, Ari Urizar, the only physician member who lacked the Johns Hopkins diploma. Urizar, a gastroenterologist, gave corporeal ballast to the table's right side in the manner that Dennis Ross held down the left. A thin salt-and-pepper mustache crossed under his nose from one jowly cheek to the other, small crumbs of breakfast impaled on its bristles. Urizar had earned a masters in finance at Harvard and then, seeing the financial potential in the medical field, got his M.D. at U. Mass Medical.

Wiegenstein, who kept his slender physique and chestnut tan by playing tennis with clients, slid a blue plastic folder across the table toward Harvey. Wiegenstein, a polished lawyer, could be either ruthless or fawning, depending on the demands of the moment. He was very efficient in achieving his personal goals. Now, covering his mouth and looking down at the table before him, he cleared his throat. The signal that the meeting was to start, which normally came amidst noisy conversation, sounded odd in the quiet that surrounded the table this morning.

"Could we have a moment of silent contemplation over the loss this week of an outstanding physician, Dr. Janet Mitchell," Harvey said, bowing his head and resting his clasped hands on the table edge. Urizar took a peanut bar from his shirt pocket and peeled the wrapper.

Harvey stood as the rest bowed their heads. He walked to a sideboard and, bending, brought out a silver tray with seven crystal glasses and an iced bottle of champagne.

"When one door is closed, another is opened," he said quietly. "Could we now share a toast!"

The startled board members looked up, unable to interpret Harvey's priestly smile. He circled the table, filling their glasses and then his, which he raised high, proclaiming:

"To the newest member of our group! Natasha Wilson!"

Slowly, the bewildered faces broke into smiles of their own, and the glasses were all raised.

"It seems that young Dr. Wilson, left on her own by the loss of her partner, believes we may have something to offer that she needs. I spoke briefly with her at the cemetery, casually, you understand, and she asked if we could meet. If she comes, she brings the whole patient base, by my estimate thirty-five hundred children from fourteen hundred families!"

"I think it's great we're getting some of Janet Mitchell's business, J.H." Brad Barnett said, leaning forward on his elbows to look down the table. "But I'm not all that excited about Wilson's welfare mothers and their snotty little brats."

"Quite right," said Nightingale, tugging on his nose. "But we can cull what we don't want. We can re-engineer Wilson's practice, just like all the others—"

"Gentlemen? If you will," Harvey interrupted, settling into his seat. "You have raised some important issues, but there are opportunities for us here that perhaps you have not yet imagined. We must be visionaries, not reactionaries, if we are to survive in the changing medical environment."

"Well put, J.H.," said Dunmore, throwing a glance across the table at Barnett. "There's money to be made in every game. You just have to learn what the rules are." He paused, smiling, the understanding grandfather. "And how to avoid them."

"Today, we need to examine the health of our body, the corpus Osler Medical Group," Harvey began, rising to stand behind his high-backed oxblood leather swivel chair. He inhaled slowly through his nostrils, his mouth closed, his eyes gazing at a point somewhere distant, above the heads of the others, giving them a moment to focus on his words and his every choreographed gesture. Then, arching his brow, he looked at each of them as he continued. "We've done well, and I'd like to take a moment to examine what has brought us this far in our development."

Osler's seed was planted on a Saturday night fifteen years earlier when Harvey, an intern, was working a weekend shift at Riverton University Hospital's emergency room. Dunmore's wife, habitually "tipsy," had burned herself on the backyard grill. As she was being treated, Dunmore and Harvey fell into a conversation, and the elder saw a spark he admired in the younger. He mentioned that he needed a physician's office to anchor a new strip shopping mall and outlined the benefits a young doctor might realize by joining such a venture.

Harvey was interested, but not at Dunmore's price. Why not a partnership, Harvey suggested. He mentioned an investment he might make "after my accountant has examined your prospectus." Harvey even suggested some creative tax benefits.

Dunmore was charmed. Harvey finished his residency and opened his practice, bringing Nightingale with him. Referring patients to each other, Harvey and Nightingale saw their practices grow, and so within a year they brought in Ross and Barnett and, later, Urizar.

"Each on our own," Harvey continued, "might have struggled to get half the business. Instead, you will recall, our schedules were always filled to bursting."

Osler, the partners decided, was not so much a practice as a deliverer of medical services. Now the group expanded by taking in tenant physicians, creating a critical mass of specialties like no other group in Port Hancock, sixty-seven physicians in all. And doctors were happy to join. They got access to Osler's huge patient base and the advantage of a consolidated administration. No worries about billing, scheduling, laboratory testing or patient records. These tenant doctors could devote their time to medicine alone. In return, they paid Osler a monthly overhead fee and, as a sort of membership dues above that fee, a portion of their monthly billings.

"And, in simplest terms, our achievement can be measured this way," said Harvey, walking behind Ross and Nightingale to stand beside Dunmore's chair. "Every one of those doctors, through their overhead payment alone, is contributing, in current dollars, as much to Osler Medical's vitality as any one of us would have paid fifteen years ago in rent at Neil's shopping mall."

Harvey paused. "That's a healthy organization, gentlemen. If I'm not mistaken—and Ari, you can correct me here from your books—this overhead fee alone represents three quarters of a legitimate million a year that we're splitting seven ways, simply because we had foresight." He nodded toward Wiegenstein, who rose, tugged at the hem of his double-breasted jacket and checked his foulard tie with long, slender fingers.

"Thanks, J.H.," the lawyer said. "Indeed, through our main lines of business, we have done and continue to do well. But there is change," he said, drawing a pair of half-glasses from his breast pocket and using them like a pencil to punctuate his words. "And, as with a disease in the body, if we do not continue to anticipate and to, if you will, medicate in advance, the disease of change could enter the body of Osler Group and destroy it."

Under the old medical game, physicians were paid fees for each service they performed. Doctors who saw more patients made more money. Consequently, at Osler, there was an unwritten rule for tenant doctors. Refer your patients to other doctors in the group, and refer them often. Tenants who were lax could, at the end of the year when memberships were reviewed, find themselves expelled from Osler. In Port Hancock, where Osler's owners sat on the boards of both hospitals, the threat was implicit: refer within the group or you will lose your privilege to practice in those hospitals. So the tenant doctors rang up the charges and, through the fees they paid, contributed a growing stream of cash into the Osler vault.

Tenants were also expected to order tests whenever possible, a form of malpractice insurance, Osler's administrator told them. In fact, the tests were all funneled to labs in which Harvey and his friends had hidden investments.

Finally, Ross, Nightingale, and Barnett individually and independently managed, within their separate medical specialties, to create a variety of special deals. While regulators might have found them suspect, these schemes contributed as much to the expansion of their personal wealth as did their profits from the group.

"This worked well, gentlemen," Wiegenstein said, slipping his fingers into his jacket pockets to the knuckles. "But change is on us like a bull on a cow, and the old way is fucked, like it or not. My advice, learn to like it."

Under "managed care," insurance companies gave doctors a flat fee every month for each of their clients. In return for collecting this guaranteed money, the doctors were to provide whatever medical attention each patient needed. But work as hard as they could, the doctors could not increase their income from any one patient from managed care, Wiegenstein explained.

"We've reached the point where twenty percent of our patient base is covered by managed care," the lawyer said, opening another folder and passing some charts to his right. "The proportion will rise constantly. Expect fifty percent in three years. Then the old way will start costing you boys money. Perform as many tests as you like. You pay for them out of your capitation fee from the insurer. Call patients in every day—as you are so fond of doing, Steve—you won't get a dollar more. Which means," he said, unbuttoning his jacket and settling into his chair, "that while you weren't looking, the gravy train has switched tracks." He tilted his seat back and turned toward Harvey, who had returned to his place.

"We were visionaries once. Now is the time to embrace managed care for all the good it can do," Harvey said.

"I'm not all that eager, J.H.," said Brad Barnett. "I think I speak for most of us when I say that we can prosper without getting tangled up with HMOs and these Kaiser Permanente-type scams. In fact, I insist that we spend our resources looking for ways to keep our edge right where we are!"

The swiftness with which Harvey's fist rose and the ferocity with which it pounded the table created a silence in which his whispered words sounded like cannon shots.

"This ship has one captain," he said, barely audible but heard by all. "If you must insist, Bradley, do so on your own vessel. Do you wish to sign off, or are you with us?"

Barnett's voice had to hurdle a knot in his throat before he could respond, in a crackling gasp: "I'll reserve my comments, J.H."

"Good," Harvey said. "Here is our path."

The path Harvey outlined was nothing less than conquest. In three phases, the group would take control of literally every aspect of medical care provide in the Hancock River Valley. First the group would acquire as many practices from existing physicians as it could. The Janet Mitchell and Natasha Wilson practice would be the first. Natasha would become an Osler employee. Then Port Hancock General would be driven out of business. The hospital, the city's oldest, was already suffering. Employers were cutting back on insurance coverage and the insurers had imposed other limits in the name of efficiency.

"We hit them hard, it'll be nothing but brick dust as they crumble," Harvey said, unbuttoning his jacket for the first time, slipping it off his broad shoulders and draping it over the back of his chair. "And we'll pick up some new lines of business in the same process. Steve, your surgicenter will be our model," he continued, circling behind Wiegenstein. "I want to see us opening our own mammography center, our own imaging center, birthing center. We'll siphon this work away from General, and they won't have the resources to continue with acute care, so they'll collapse." He unbuttoned his cuffs and rolled his sleeves up over the downy blond hair on his forearms. Patting Ari Urizar on the back with one hand, Brad Barnett on the shoulder with the other, he continued.

"Finally, I want control of Valleyview, which we will need for our acute in-patient facility. Neil has some ideas on how to do it. We'll hold a special meeting on that."

He walked to the far end of the conference table, and with the bow of his ship aimed squarely at his crotch, Harvey spread his feet, raised his right hand over his head, and once more brought his fist crashing down on the oiled teak:

"And we'll do this all in two years, dammit!"

Tiffany had been chosen not for her name but for those of her qualities that justified her name. She was, in every aspect, exquisitely assembled. Tall enough to look most men shorter than Jim Harvey in the eye. Slender in the manner of a fast horse, which is to say full-boned in those areas where it is appropriate for a woman, and in those places carrying enough flesh to not only cover the bones but to call out the juices in even the most lethargic of men. And smart. He met her at a

36

symposium at Cornell, where she was a student majoring, it could be said, in the acquisition of power. Their affair was, by mutual desire, short. Her subsequent employment at Osler was nominally as Harvey's receptionist, although her duties—none of them sexual—were more intriguing.

Harvey had left the conference room intercom on, and when his fist hit the table the second time, Tiffany waited a moment then quietly opened the door. Two Hispanic men in white uniforms pushed cherrywood carts to the near end of the table and began serving lunch to the directors. The meals, presented on bone china trimmed in gold, were prepared by the valley's finest restaurant. Caesar salads for Nightingale, Barnett, and Wiegenstein. Two cheeseburgers for Ross. Penne rigate with a sauce of herbs, egg whites, and olive oil, and a fresh pitcher of iced tea for Dunmore. A hefty plate of lasagna for Urizar, served with extra linen napkins. With two hands, Urizar stuffed one of the napkins into his collar and began scooping forkfuls of pasta, trailing long strings of cheese, directly into his mouth. The cheese stretched from the plate to his lips like high voltage wires climbing a hill, and they broke and fell to the teak only when the next mouthful was on its way.

Tiffany stood by the door until the waiters had withdrawn with their carts, and then she brought a wrapped Dominican cigar to Wiegenstein and set it, along with a lit candle, at his place.

"Will there be anything else?" she asked Harvey, who took only decaffeinated coffee for his lunch. He shook his head, and she, too, retreated from the board room. It was time for Harvey to work this small crowd, to whip it into a team. He pulled out the seat on the far side of Brad Barnett, set his cup on the table, settled into the chair and, speaking with enough volume that Barnett knew everyone else could hear, began his pitch.

"The linchpin for us is going to be capitation, Brad. I want you to handle it."

"Don't the insurance companies pretty much tell us what they're going to pay? I don't remember that we've had any voice in the past."

37

"You're absolutely correct, Brad. But here's where our vision comes in." He tilted back, crossing his ankles and stretching.

Insurers want predictability, Harvey began. A promise to reduce uncertainty is a bargaining chip. Osler's dominance in Port Hancock puts that chip in its pocket. The group dealt regularly with dozens of smaller insurers, as well as Coastal Insurance, the largest. Many of them were pressuring their customers, both individuals and the employers who financed group insurance policies, to turn toward managed care. This meant capitation—flat fees paid to the group or to individual doctors for each man, woman, and child covered by that insurance policy.

Brad Barnett had handled negotiations for all of the services commissioned by Osler, from trash removal to archiving records. He was a skillful wrangler. The same ability, focused on the insurance companies, would result in more favorable capitation fees for the group's doctors and, in turn, for the directors. The little insurers would have to compromise, give up something, if their policy holders were not going to be shut out of care from Osler, Harvey said.

"Of course, what we show our tenant docs will, as with the rest of our finances, be from the front set of books and will suggest the standard capitation fee offered to our peers in the community," Harvey said. "The back books will reflect the true fees. Our group does what, Ari, forty-four million in billings annually?"

Urizar mumbled through the lasagna and nodded, the strings of cheese whipping between the plate and his lips.

"If we can shave five percent, that's another two-point-two million if everything's under managed care. I'd say it's worth the effort."

Barnett grinned and reached out to shake Harvey's hand. "You're a genius, tops in your class," he said. "Always were, always will be!"

The other directors had finished their lunches and, shoving aside their plates, leaned toward Harvey, an expectant audience, prepared to be surprised by the maestro's next move. Wiegenstein, who knew what was coming, twirled the tip of the cigar in his mouth and brought its clipped end to the candle flame. A cloud of smoke billowed, like the puff from a gun barrel, above the table.

"As with the Asian martial arts," Harvey said, "those who will prosper under managed care are those who yield to its power. Don't be mistaken. Managed care isn't about cost effectiveness. It's about acquiring money. We find a way to make more money for the insurance companies, we'll make more money."

The door opened, and Tiffany smiled at the directors and then at Harvey. "Are you ready for the charts?"

Over the next few minutes, Harvey, flipping pages on an easel, outlined the duties for each of the directors. Brad Barnett negotiating capitation rates. Nightingale overseeing the development of satellite facilities to compete with Port Hancock General's operating room, maternity ward, and mammography lab. Dunmore aligning Coastal Insurance, by persuading its chief executive to favor Osler Group. Urizar keeping the books. Ross's name was beside the headings "Medical Supplies" and "New Lines of Business."

"We're netting from the group about eleven million annually, gentlemen," Harvey concluded. "We are poised at the threshold of seventy million."

When she heard these words, Tiffany went to the outer office. She smiled at the gentleman who sat on the sofa working through papers in a briefcase. "Dr. Harvey and the board are ready to meet with you, Dr. Chen."

In his undergraduate years at University of North Carolina, Harvey had shared dorm rooms, books, and lunches with Robert Chen. He was the skinny kid from Guangzhou who had fled the poverty and tyranny of China through relatives in Hong Kong and the United States. The man who now entered the board room was almost unrecognizable, carrying half again the weight of his youth on a frame still five-feet, seven inches tall. But, as at UNC, his grooming was impeccable, as was his English.

"Gentlemen, I am so pleased to be welcomed into your midst," Chen said, taking a seat drawn to the head of the table beside Harvey.

"Robert, this is our pleasure. We never could have dreamed that our good fortune would blossom from your hardships, but we are thrilled that you might consider joining Osler Medical Group as an employee physician. While I can't speak for everyone at this point, from my perspective, your acceptance is a foregone conclusion. But why don't I let you tell the board why you're here."

The reason was managed care. The reality of the system's arrival in California, where Robert Chen, a cardiologist, established his practice after medical school, was that there was work for fewer doctors. Chen had joined the staff of a group serving the Chinese community. He had felt an obligation to aid those less fortunate than he. He did as much charity work as he did paid work. But as managed care expanded, the amount of money available to the group dwindled, and the staff was cut to leave enough income for those who remained.

"I am longing to return to medicine, to be with patients. I can assure you that I will be an asset to your group."

"Beyond our greatest expectations, I am certain, Robert," Harvey said. "Gentlemen, there will be a special board meeting at which we will vote on Dr. Chen's membership. Robert and I are going to have a nice chat by ourselves now, to catch up on recent history." He smiled at Chen, who bowed from his seat. Harvey nodded, and then, as abruptly as a cloud can hide the sun, his face reassembled its features darkly. "I almost forgot. I want to note that Dr. Grimes has raised some concerns that we must address. That, too, at the special meeting."

To become a man, each son must escape his father's shadow. Some are driven to great achievement as a means of distinguishing themselves. Some are driven to drink or other anes-

40

thetics. Some fathers stand like tall oaks at sunrise and cast shadows that seem to their sons to wrap around the entire globe. Others are less imposing, the shadows of a smaller tree, or of a cloudy day. But each son, if he is to escape his childhood, must find his way out of the shade.

James Perkins Harvey III was the seed of two generations of towering oaks. James Sr., at his death, was the world renowned chief of medicine at Johns Hopkins Medical College in Baltimore. Harvey remembered summers at his grandfather's plantation on the eastern shore of the Chesapeake Bay. He remembered the cool breezes of the verandah, remembered smelling honeysuckle and watching the ospreys glide over the water as he and his sister played Clue, but he could remember little of his grandfather, who by then was in his late seventies and who had little interest in children. James Sr.'s life was the stuff of legend. After lying about his age to join the Army, he became a corpsman at age sixteen and distinguished himself on the front lines of the Battle of San Juan Hill. He was decorated for bravery and offered a scholarship to the United States Military Academy. He graduated from West Point, then from Johns Hopkins. During World War I he served as the commander of the Medical Corps. In 1918, the year his first son was born, he returned to Johns Hopkins where his work on battlefield trauma earned him international acclaim and the college's top job.

James Jr. pursued an accelerated academic path that found him entering Harvard Medical School at nineteen and, four years later, accepting a residency in general surgery at Peter Bent Brigham. He was called from his residency into the military as a battlefield surgeon. He was awarded a Bronze Star for bravery under fire during the Battle of the Bulge and was credited with developing innovative surgical techniques that saved the lives of thousands of soldiers during World War II. He returned to Harvard as chief of surgery and wrote several texts that remained on the shelves at Johns Hopkins' medical library when his son entered medical school.

Two matters were predestined for James Perkins Harvey III.

41

His understanding of the first of these predated his awareness of independent thought. He would become a medical doctor. The second he recognized while he was still a towhead boy: It would be futile to try to set himself apart from his father and grandfather through medicine alone. Indeed, given that the world viewed its doctors as the authority second only to God, he must redefine for himself the nature of success, for it was success against which he found himself competing. And what he discovered, upon observing his father, was that the only men to whom he or James Sr. need bow—though without acknowledging any inferiority—were those who controlled the money.

The shadow cast by Robert Chen's father competed with a forest of shadows that darkened the twisting alleys of Guangzhou, where his father ran opium dens for the Yellow Gang Triad, an ancient criminal organization that controlled commerce and the government. The options for Chen and his brother, Ching Huo, were minimal. Become his father's mule or his customer. Or take the lifeboat offered by his uncles in Hong Kong and San Francisco: the United States and its promise of opportunity.

For a time, the opportunity was great. Then Chen's dreamy American success began to dissolve as the control of wealth shifted in the land. Now he was forced to seek a new opportunity.

Harvey ushered Chen into his office and led him to two Queen Anne chairs set beside a lamp table in a reading alcove.

"I'd like to be able to offer you more," Harvey began, "but with managed care eliminating the need for specialists, your field of cardiology has become incredibly crowded. I know the figure I've suggested may seem low, but it's my experience that the rest of the board will go no higher."

"The salary is not a problem, J.H.," Chen said, folding his smooth, manicured hands in his lap. "It is a wise step, given that your income will be increasingly fixed under capitation. We experienced this same trend many years ago in California. I assume you will need to renegotiate with the other physicians in the group to place them on salary."

"That's an issue we have not yet faced, Robert. But, yes, something must be done to allow us to survive in this new environment. There's an immediate concern I must address with you, though, and it need not go beyond this room. I remember something from our time at UNC. About a brother of yours?"

"Yes, Ching Huo. He lives now in Manhattan."

"My recollection, and please excuse me if I'm confused, Robert. But if memory serves me, he had some involvement in organized crime. This is something that concerns me, should there be any reason for this to come to the attention of the other directors. I want everything to be above board."

"I understand, J.H. I have had no dealings with Ching Huo in several years. That business when we were in college is the last time he has bothered me. I am the family disappointment, all but forgotten," Chen said, smiling to himself.

"That's reassuring, Robert. But I must insist that you give me as much detailed information about your brother as possible, including his last known address. To be comfortable that I can return you to the board for a membership vote, I'll need to initiate a background check."

Six days later, after Neil Dunmore's friends finished their work, Harvey boarded a flight that landed in Newark, New Jersey. He drove a rental car to East Orange where, on a bitter, sunny morning, he found the nondescript restaurant. The man at the cash register picked up a menu which Harvey waived off. "I'm to meet a gentleman, 'The Dragon'?" The man said something in Chinese to a young, short waiter, who gestured for Harvey to follow across the vacant dining room. The waiter pushed open a swinging door on the rear wall and Harvey stepped through. Beyond the door was darkness, except for a red glow in which two large men seemed to float like fish in a still pool. Each seized one of Harvey's arms firmly, frisking him. Then with one ahead of Harvey and one behind, they led him along a narrow corridor with doors on each side, stopping at the door at the end. The first man knocked on the door and, when it opened, stepped in. The second man nudged Harvey from behind, and the doctor stepped into a room where a thin man sat at a table, lit by a low hanging lamp with a turquoise glass shade.

"My brother is a doctor like you. He did not choose to stay with our family. I have no respect for him," Chen Ching Huo said, his words hissing through his teeth, exposed by his barely parted lips which bore no trace of smile.

"Your brother is no doctor like me," Harvey said. He served these words like a tennis player, who then rushes the net, prepared to volley.

Seeing this, Ching Huo slowly brought the fingertips of his right hand together with those of his left, just in front of his chin, and fixed his gaze on Harvey's eyes. Harvey stared back, unimpressed.

"This is bullshit, Ching Huo. I don't need it. I'd rather deal with the Mafia, anyway," the doctor said, turning toward the door and the two large men, to whom he yielded nothing in height. "Gentlemen, show me out."

"The Mafia cannot deliver what you need, and you know this," Ching Huo said to Harvey's back.

"There is a deal I could make with you, but understand this," Harvey said, still facing the two bodyguards. "You need me more than I need you. And your phony Oriental posturing is costing me time and money."

"Take a seat, Dr. Harvey," Ching Huo said, his voice no longer pure disdain.

The deal Harvey outlined briefly was this. First, Ching Huo would provide certain espionage services useful to Osler. Later, there would be the potential for a joint venture, should his first assignment bear fruit. Harvey explained that in the realm of medical supplies, there was money to be made. Ching Huo would be the supplier. A new corporation, in which Osler's directors would be silent shareholders, would distribute the goods. The potential business was in the tens of millions.

"I know exactly where you stand in your organization,

Ching Huo. Bringing home this deal will give you an edge you need. Blow it, and things will not look so good."

"My brother is no doctor like you, James Harvey," Ching Huo said, his smile shifting perceptibly from that of a master towards that of an equal. "Understand this, however. We conduct business under methods developed over centuries and proven to succeed. On other things we can negotiate, but on this we do not yield."

Four . . .

Cal Kalinowsky had suggested a fishing trip about a month after the funeral.

"It'd get your mind off things," he said, buttoning his shirt. Loring had just completed a thorough physical examination. Cal was sixty-eight, a bantam-weight without an ounce of fat on his body but with some serious plaque in his arteries. His diet for sixty-four years had been red meat, potatoes, and gravy. Loring had placed a stainless steel tube—a stent—in Cal's left anterior descending artery, where there had been a blockage, thus allowing his patient to avoid bypass surgery. Now Cal hoped to return the favor.

"Everybody wants to write the prescription," Loring said. They were facing each other, sitting in front of Loring's desk. He kicked up at the sole of Cal's work boot and scowled.

"Bonefishing in the Keys," Cal offered, "a universal remedy."

"Thanks, Cal, but right now I don't want any distractions," Loring said. Cal had been inviting him for years, but he never had the time. Still, he fantasized about the flight in Cal's seaplane to some remote water and imagined the moment when the wary fish would rise to his artificial fly and how he would set the hook against a weight heavy as a boulder. Yet now, he was not eager. He explained: "I've got twenty-three years of memories I'm working through."

Instead of fishing, he went to the office every morning after making rounds at Port Hancock General and Valleyview. He had seen Carmella Parente for her three-week checkup. She was struggling to get herself on an exercise program.

"I'm willing, Loring, but the body is naughty." She winked, touched his forearm.

The months passed. He recruited Michael Bernstein to join his practice. A bright young man, Mike had good ears, too. "You listen well," he told him.

After some time, Bernstein suggested Loring take a week off. "I'm settled in. If I have any questions, Nancy can answer them."

"No doubt. After twenty years, she knows this office better than I do. But I need the routine for now. It's helping me put Janet to rest."

At night, he would return to the house, where his footsteps on the hardwood floors echoed in the dark rooms. He would turn on all the lights and, after dinner, without fail, would call Gabriella at college. "I just reheated some spaghetti. With sun-dried tomatoes," he might say, remembering that was Janet's favorite but keeping the detail to himself as you might keep a smooth stone in your trousers pocket, for you alone to touch. Then, because it was by now quite late, he would climb the stairs, turning off lights as he went, until only his bedside lamp was lit and he was settled between the sheets, under a heavy comforter. He would turn off the lamp, and in the darkness he would listen for the sounds Janet made as she drifted into sleep, little murmurs and sighs. He would turn and bury his nose in the pillow beside him, and he would think that he smelled her hair, remembering how, as she slept, she would move against him, small yet solid.

"You were not supposed to go!"

He heard himself speak the words, heard them disappear into the bedclothes and the rugs and the drapes on the tall windows, absorbed by the room without a response.

"I always thought we'd go together," he told her one June

night. She turned over in bed toward him and, with her mouth set in mock sternness, dimples forming at the corners, she replied: "Silly boy! Romantic, silly boy!"

A flash-flood of grief rose in his bosom and he cried aloud, "Oh, God, Janet! I love"—he stopped, unsure of his tense. Loved? He could not finish, for in that instant, even as tears poured from his eyes, came the first real understanding of loss. Speaking that one word, correctly, finally and emphatically informed him that she was gone while he still had life. His eyes dried almost instantly, though his cheek was cooled by the damp pillow.

In the morning, when his rounds were completed, he drove west along River Road to the rusted sign for High Life Seaplane Base, where he turned left, toward the river. Cal was standing on the silver float of a yellow seaplane, working on its engine. A worn set of coveralls, clean as the glistening cowl on the seaplane, covered his predictable uniform of khaki shirt and trousers. His view of the world in recent years had been through gold-framed glasses. His hair was trimmed close as it had been since he joined the Army Air Corps during World War II. The haircut made his ears appear to stick out like a mouse's, explaining the nickname by which he was addressed at the Port Hancock Princess Diner where, every morning he was in town, he ate breakfast at quarter past six. He reached for a screwdriver in the hip pocket of the coveralls and adjusted a drop-light glowing inside the engine compartment.

"Can you believe I lost my voltage regulator at 22:37 last night ten miles out and had to land this heap without instruments or lights?"

"Nothing about your flying would surprise me."

"It was a clear night but, hell, there ain't any lights upstream except an occasional car along River Road. And there was no moon to help out. Course, could have been fog. One time I was flying from Denver to Kansas City when the same thing happened, except there was low clouds." He launched into a story: He had read his instruments by flashlight; cut his speed to 105 knots—two miles a minute—so he could easily calculate the distance he covered; knew he was ninety miles from K.C., which, forty-five minutes later, appeared out of the fog.

"Sounds pretty frightening." Cal put the drop light in Loring's hand, positioning it.

"Trying to find the surface of the river was the tough part. Hey, help me roll this baby out and we'll take her for a test flight."

"Love to, Mouse. But I've got to get to the office. I just stopped by to see if fishing season's still on."

Kalinowsky grinned, took off his glasses and rubbed his eyes with his knuckles.

"It's always fishing season some place on the planet. When do we go?"

By 7:00 on a warm Monday morning two weeks later, they had rolled the Cessna into the water and tied it to the floating dock that jutted out beside the launching ramp. They stashed their gear—a small tent, sleeping bags, stove, frying pan and coffee pot, food, two changes of clothes with extra socks, fly fishing rods, and hip boots—behind the two side-by-side seats.

"Well? Get in!" Cal commanded. "We've got seven hours of flying ahead of us!" He walked out on the starboard float, reached up and spun the propeller twice, reached through the cockpit door and turned on the ignition and spun again. The engine caught. Cal untied the dock line and climbed up into his seat, squeezing in against Loring's right arm. As the plane headed out on the river, Loring looked down at the arcing fan of water, glowing yellow-gold in the low morning sun, that sprayed off the float. He felt the engine rev and, after a few seconds, felt the plane rise, breaking free of the water. The glassy river withdrew below the plane, and as they rose the air was cooler and the trees along the river's edge soon looked like pixie moss. They banked north, toward Maine. Loring drew a deep breath slowly through his nostrils, filling himself with air composed, it seemed, of entirely tranquil atoms. The plane rode smoothly, and the drone of the engine was somehow comforting. Cal adjusted the controls in small increments, like a cook adding the last pinches of salt, flying with no more thought than a bird.

"Did you ever have a job other than flying?"

"Sure. Four years in the electric company after the war. Saved up my money to buy a plane and some land by the river. That's when I met Marge, too. She was working in the office there and I was out on a line crew."

"My first job was tending Doc Alexander's gardens," Loring said. "I was ten. In high school, I volunteered at Port Hancock General and then got a summer orderly job. I've never been away from medicine."

"Nobody's complaining," Cal said.

"I ain't either, Cal." Loring heard himself slip comfortably into Cal's slang and felt some muscles at his shoulders ease. Indeed, Loring never thought to complain, only to please. He had no idea where his own will would have led him. His destiny was sealed, he often thought, when Sophie Willits took a liking to the foreman her father, Hiram, hired at the lumber mill. She married that logger, Nathaniel English. Between Sophie and Nate, Loring was born into certain worldly expectations and ethical ideals. The expectations were Sophie's. She had a sense of how things should be, and she imparted to her infant son an understanding that through his veins ran aristocratic blood. Never mind the immediate lack of resources. He had pedigree, she believed, and he had genius. He would rise to his natural station in the community. In Nate, on the other hand, dwelled ideals. These came from the books in his travel chest, a peculiar library in a logging camp: Plato, Thoreau, Shakespeare. Nate, when he talked to Loring, delivered a literary lecture and drew from his texts solemn rules of conduct. First among these were humility and the search for truth. A life lived on these two principals was one built on bedrock, his father often said. Never settle for less from yourself, never accept less from others.

Both Sophie and Nate understood their son to be perfection, and Loring spent his childhood attempting to earn that admiration. It wasn't easy. When he brought home a report card with four A's and one B, Sophie's praise was seasoned with hints of possible improvements. The good son listened. To do less would be to cheat his mother. His intellect, exercised by the constant search for correct solutions, grew. Folks in Port Hancock came to know young English as a competitive boy. In truth, he only competed against himself, but that was enough. His drive earned success in the classroom and on the playing field. District champion in wrestling his senior year, winner of seven meets in the pole vault. And when Loring graduated with top honors from high school, the city knew who its next doctor would be.

Loring never once questioned his future, either, although he often questioned those who did not share his vision.

"Damn!" he said in the quiet of the cockpit. "I know a thing or two about medicine, Cal."

"I was particularly hoping so when you stuck that piece of metal in me."

"Just thinking about Janet, Cal. It's so obvious she never should have died."

"She was the best, Loring. It's a shame."

"It's closer to a crime, Cal. Jim Harvey's a butcher! On that very morning, I'd been praising him to Jan. I had no idea he was so incompetent!"

"He's a big man at the hospitals, ain't he?"

Loring thought about this, lifting his rump and leaning against the plane's door to reach for the small folding knife, a gift from his father, the woodsman, which, in his office or on a trout stream, he always carried in his hip pocket.

"I've been thinking he shouldn't be," Loring said, opening the knife and testing its sharpness against his thumb.

"You going after him?"

"What do you think I should do, Cal? Janet died of a ruptured aorta. She hit the steering wheel hard, and any competent trauma surgeon, that's the first thing he'd suspect. But Jim Harvey waited two hours before he thought to check. He was betting on a heart contusion."

50

"Bad call, Lor. But it sounds like a judgment thing," Cal said as he banked the plane right and the sun bore in through the windshield. He banked left again and the sun moved away.

"That's the Chesapeake ahead," he said. "We'll be stopping in Jersey for fuel and again in Rhode Island."

It was almost dinnertime when they reached Greenville and touched down on Moosehead Lake. They refueled, bought milk, margarine, and fishing licenses. A half hour later, they glided low over a balsam forest, banked sharply to the left over a small pond and, as the pontoons touched the rippled water, scared up a flock of mergansers swimming in the reflected forest shadows. Cal steered between island-sized boulders, rubble from the last ice age, crusty with lichens. Before cutting the engine, he nudged the plane against the eastern shore, where the limbless trunk of a tree, fallen years before into the pond, formed a natural, reliable dock.

"Welcome to Heaven, Doc," Cal said, taking some parcels that Loring handed out the open door. "Smell those firs? Hear those birds, white throated sparrows? There's moose shit there on the edge of the water and, in an hour, at sunset, there'll be trout splashing everywhere. Let's pitch the tent and get fishing!"

The question of Harvey's competence had been threading through Loring's thoughts throughout the flight; and now, carrying his fly rod and pushing through thickets of alder bushes along the pond's shore, he returned again to Cal's question. Wasn't Harvey's error one of judgment, not competence?

It was, for Loring, all about standards. Competent doctors, like the best mechanics, come with all the tools. Harvey had shown, treating Janet, that he lacked basic information. There was only one way Loring could go with this.

He stopped at an archipelago of boulders reaching well out into the pond. From the third boulder out, Loring could see the plane a few hundred feet up the shore, and beyond that he could see Cal's line arcing like a whip back over the alders, then snapping forward to its full length and drifting down in the fading sunlight to the pond's surface. He stripped off a length of line from his own reel and began casting, a vision hovering inside his brow: A black hole opening in the water under his fly, and the long dark curve of a huge trout's back rising briefly, just as he jerked his rod and set the hook; and the enormous weight of the beast as he fought it up to the boulder, keeping an exquisite tension in his line—enough to hold the fish; not enough to break the delicate leader.

The sun's lower rim touched the treetops across the pond and Loring was still casting and working his tiny lure across the water, casting and retrieving, when, just to his left, a large fish jumped clear of the water, its motion grabbing Loring's attention so swiftly that he turned and saw the fish fall back into the pond. He stripped off more line and, after a few whips, sent it out across the spreading ripples.

There is no means by which a fisherman can prepare himself for the moment when fantasy comes to life, for the automatic response is a surge in the pulse so powerful it feels that the heart will escape the chest cavity. And that hammering pulse is so startling that even the most practiced fisherman may forget to set the hook in the gaping mouth at the end of his line. Loring forgot. It was a long instant between the point when his lure touched the pond's surface, rousing the hungry fish just below it, and the moment when Loring's right hand yanked desperately. He was stunned when the rod bowed sharply. The hook hidden in the fly now pierced the trout's bony lip, and Loring's hand was stopped midway in its yank as if the line were tied to a tree. But now instinct, bred through decades of experience, was engaged and Loring established that equilibrium between tension and release that could keep a five-pound fish hooked to four-pound line. After perhaps twenty minutes, the fish had grown too weary to continue its fight and Loring guided it up to his boulder. Then, dipping the tip of his rod, he let the line go slack and waited for the tired fish to spit the fly free. It was only then that Loring noticed how quickly his heart was racing and how dark the forest behind him had grown.

Cal had caught three modest-sized trout, which Loring breaded and fried over a propane stove while water boiled on another burner for the instant potatoes. The evening cold had come promptly behind the darkness. They both wore their quilted jackets as they sat on a log and ate in silence. Cal finished first and was heating water for tea.

"You going after him?" he asked, not looking at Loring.

"Getting rid of bad docs is tough, Mouse."

"But, if you're right, he could be a danger to anyone he sees."

"First, we doctors stick together. You think the Mafia's got a code of silence? Just try to get one M.D. to talk about another." He finished the last of his meal and took his metal plate a few steps to the pond to rinse it. "There are legal risks. There are ethical risks. Most guys just bury their heads."

"Yeah, and what's second?" Cal said, passing a steaming cup to Loring.

"If I'm the one complaining, I've got a couple of problems. They can dismiss me as the grieving husband."

"I'd think revenge."

Loring sipped on his tea and looked at Cal, whose face was lit by a propane lantern hung from a hemlock branch beyond him. Cal was perceptive and honest, as a good friend should be.

"You'd be right," Loring finally said. "I want his head for what he did to Janet. I want to see his license burned. But I'd be after him if his victim were a total stranger."

"You said you face a couple of problems. Credibility and what else?"

"There are a few dozen doctors and administrators in Port Hancock who have already heard enough from me, Mouse. If I wasn't sure I was right, I'd worry that I was a crackpot. I've fought with the businessmen for more equipment, more staff. I was chief of staff for eight years at Port Hancock, and I rode herd on all the departments. It was my complaining that finally got one very popular spine surgeon kicked out of the city for total incompetence. The rest of my colleagues weren't happy. He just happened to have killed a few patients. Now, they see me take after Jim Harvey, it'll be: There goes English again."

"You still haven't answered my question," Cal said, his face all in shadows as he turned to look at Loring. "Are you gonna get him?"

"I'll hook him," Loring said, looking straight into the lantern's beam. "It'll take finesse, leading him through his protectors on the staff and in the hospitals. But eventually I'll land him and I'll watch as Jim Harvey takes his last professional breath."

Five . . .

Robert Chen's reading of Dr. Thomas Grimes was off by a hair. He was wrong about his age. Chen thought Grimes had reached his late fifties. He was perhaps six feet tall and had the going-no-place build of a chest of drawers. He wore, as regularly as he breathed, a white lab coat over a starched white shirt and maroon tie. His shoes were scuffed cordovans and his hair was in perpetual need of a trim. His eyebrows were long, gray bristles, jabbing in every direction. His nose was as square as his body, and a pair of half-glasses always rested near its tip. Thomas Grimes was almost forty-seven.

Chen was mistaken about Grimes' personality, as well. His frosty behavior was responsible. Grimes studiously avoided socializing with the other Osler doctors. He answered questions with terse statements, limited to necessities. He deflected personal inquiries. He never smiled. The lamp on his desk in his cubicle in the administrative center was on late most nights, and he seldom missed an appointment. But in monthly staff meetings, Osler's business manager, Ophelia Sadler, upbraided him for slack performance.

So Chen figured he had Grimes accurately diagnosed as self-absorbed and insecure.

It was true that Thomas Grimes's attention was preoccupied. And, in a sense, he was concerned for his own security. His wife was manic depressive and had spent all their money on shopping binges. During one, she had flown by credit card to every city with a Nieman Marcus and had bought a complete outfit at each. Grimes sold his cardiology practice to Osler to raise funds to avoid bankruptcy. He then joined the group as an employee physician, work he was happy to get. His joy was short-lived. In Osler he found a machinery for making money, one that demanded of its physicians practices that Grimes felt pushed the limits of ethics. There was an emphasis on conducting tests, even when they were, at best, of marginal usefulness. Grimes was skeptical of Sadler's justification that the tests were a form of liability insurance. He also doubted that there was as much innocence as the Osler board claimed in some of the referral practices. Patients always moved from one of the primary care guys to an Osler specialist, never to an outsider. Steve Nightingale's orthopedic patients frequently became the clients of Jerry Wiegenstein, who filed slip-and-fall or motor vehicle claims. When Sadler cut several of Grimes's patients from the books because they could not pay and told Grimes he was not to provide them with care, Grimes finally balked. He told Sadler that he had some grave concerns, and he detailed his suspicions. Sadler told him he would do well to limit his diagnoses to medical ailments. Speculations like these, Sadler told him, could have severe legal and financial consequences. And so Thomas Grimes put his head down, kept his mouth shut and went about his work with his patients. On his own time, he made house calls to patients Sadler had ditched. Since Grimes was an employee physician, he technically had no patients of his own, and was assigned cases as they came in. So Sadler did not feel compelled to inform Grimes when patients were dropped from the books. Grimes found, in his late-night romps through Osler's computer files, that there was a list of patients who owed Osler money. By checking that list regularly, Grimes found, he could predict which patients he would suddenly stop seeing. From this, he created his own list: House calls. It was a list that Grimes kept secret.

Robert Chen knew none of this. But he needed some help, and Thomas Grimes appeared to be the person to ask. He found Grimes in the staff lounge, pouring a mug of coffee.

"Dr. Grimes, good morning. I wondered, could I have a moment with you?"

"I was heading back to my desk," he said, peering over the tops of his glasses as if asking: What do I need this for?

"I'll follow along, if I may."

"Sure."

Without inviting Chen to follow, Grimes moved quickly from the lounge to the administrative bay, a large circular room at the center of Osler's circular building where all tenant and employee physicians had desks, computer terminals and chairs. The lamp was glowing on Grimes's desk. Grimes sat and began tapping on his computer keyboard, ignoring Chen. Chen waited for a long moment, expecting Grimes to acknowledge him. This did not happen. So Chen forged ahead.

"I apologize for my intrusion, Doctor. But I have a request, and while perhaps there is no one at Osler Medical Group who can assist me, I thought I would ask a fellow cardiologist first."

Grimes continued to clatter at his keyboard, his back to Chen, who persisted.

"I must return to California for a week to oversee a bypass on an elderly patient. In the meantime, I have been caring here for several indigents whom Osler no longer carries." He paused, expecting a response, either positive or negative. There was none from Grimes.

"While I am gone, I need someone to cover for me with this handful of people." He hesitated again. "I visit them at home after work."

Grimes turned his chair slowly toward Chen, a scowl on his brow.

"Of course, I will reimburse whomever would see my patients," Chen said quickly.

"Aren't you violating some sacred Osler policy?" Grimes demanded.

"Am I?" Chen asked, shrinking back slightly.

"I'll say! At Osler, we only care for those who care enough to pay us, Doctor!"

"But I am seeing these patients as an individual, not as an Osler employee," Chen protested.

"Sadler doesn't care how you explain it. She'll cut off your balls if she thinks you're giving it away," Grimes said, and his scowl relaxed a bit. "I think we should discuss this elsewhere, Doctor. Perhaps we could have lunch."

They met at a pizza shop on Richmond Street, a block from City Hall in a neighborhood with a few tough, simple, family-run businesses of the kind that can survive in the corpses of dead downtowns.

"Two cardiologists ingesting thick mozzarella. A great advertisement for cholesterol and plaque!" Grimes said as they waited for their pizza slices to be reheated. "Why did you approach me?" he asked Chen when they were seated. "There are three other cardiologists at Osler, and Loring English, though he's an independent, is known for his charity work."

"I have heard of Dr. English, although I have not had the fortune to meet him. Frankly, I chose you because you, like I, are an employee physician and thus, I suspect, might be persuaded by financial consideration, given the level of income our employer offers. I confess, I know little of you other than what I have seen around the center."

"Ah, what you have seen. Of course, you've seen my encounters with Miss Sadler. I'm certain those monthly maulings have impressed you mightily."

"She does appear to focus her displeasure unevenly on you."

"For the very reason that I am going to grant your request, Doctor. I find it beyond unethical to refuse care to a patient after their money has been consumed. Osler is happy to stick it's cash hose into anyone's tank and keep pumping until it's

57

dry. Then we shove them into the hopper to make room for the next one with a full tank. It's criminal," Grimes said, edging forward in his seat and laying his unfinished pizza slice on the paper plate. "When I had my own practice, I would never have thought to cut you off because you couldn't pay. Hell, we doctors make enough in our other work. The invasion of medicine by the Sadlers and the rest of the MBAs is ripping the heart out of an honorable profession, Dr. Chen!"

"Please, call me Bob. I must say that I have too little experience with this type of practice to fully comprehend your feelings. I was of the opinion that Osler was a model institution for the efficient delivery of medical care. J.H.–Dr. Harvey–I know from our undergraduate days at UNC. He comes from a family that has given much to the medical profession."

"I guess your friend J.H. thinks it's payback time," Grimes said.

"Oh?"

"Forget it. I'm just a grouser, Bob. I'd be happy to look in on your patients while you're gone. Just drop a list off at my desk if you will. But put it in a sealed envelope, please?"

In the weeks after Chen's return from California, he and Grimes developed a shadow practice within Osler. Chen began imitating Grimes's habits. While patient records were maintained on the computer's hard drives and could be read from any terminal on the network, Grimes kept a separate computer disk for his indigent cases. Now, Chen and Grimes made copies of their disks for each other and when it was helpful dropped in on one another's patients.

Occasionally, they left the medical center separately and met at the pizza shop or another downtown joint unaccustomed to doctor visits. There, in small doses, Grimes began to unravel for Chen his view of Osler and of the direction medicine in general was taking.

"It's not that I view everything happening in medicine as awful," he said one afternoon when they had taken their seats at a chipped Formica table in the Armenian Deli. "I recall listening twenty years ago to a presentation by a doctor from mainland China who explained that your country's emphasis had been directed toward the training of more technicians as a means of helping more people at a lower level of need, rather than a few doctors handling a small slice of the critical cases. That made great sense to me. The system has to find a way to meet the most needs if it is to be a fair system of medicine."

"That is what managed care is all about, of course," Chen said.

"That's window dressing, Bob. The critical question to ask is 'Why are we doing what we're doing?' And you get the answer by looking at who is in charge."

"Government, you mean?"

"Hell, no, Bob. Look at the name of the beast. Managed care. What comes first? That word has been guiding our society since World War II. Managers have taken over everything, and they know only one way to operate. It's whatever way their generation has been taught in the business schools, and no matter what they are managing, they approach it the same way."

"Looking at the bottom line, the dollars, right?"

"I think it's more convoluted than that. If they were really looking at the bottom line dollars, there would be a lot fewer consultants and committees fucking up the works."

Chen, who was sitting facing the door in the glass storefront, saw an elderly man outside, cupping his hand over his brow to peer into the delicatessen. The man backed up a few steps, walked along the plate glass window and out of sight. Then he returned, looking down, and pulled the door open. The man had gray hair that fell to the shoulders of his tattered army jacket. His hands were hidden inside the jacket's sleeves. He wore a dark blue knit cap and ripped white sneakers. He stood for a moment inside the door, as if letting his eyes adjust to the light. Then he approached the couple at the table nearest the door.

"Sadler does love her committees," Chen said, taking a forkful of salad.

"Ah, the Oracle at Osler! But in our case, I think management is a Trojan horse."

"Tom, you've lost me."

"The shots at Osler are called from up in the flying saucer."

"Good afternoon, Gentlemen," the old man said, coming to stand beside their table, holding his cap in his dirty, scarred hands.

Grimes, startled, scowled at the man, who stepped back uneasily.

"Please, I'm sorry to bother. I don't drink anymore, and I am hungry. Could you spare some change?"

"I'll buy you lunch, friend," Grimes said. "What would you like?"

"No, that's all right, sir. I'm sorry to have bothered you," he said, and he moved on to the next table.

"He hasn't had a drink since at least noon," Grimes said. "Could you smell him?"

"He couldn't stomach the thought of food, poor soul. Now, Tom, you were saying?"

Grimes was lifting his ham on wheat sandwich to his mouth but paused, thinking. "Perhaps I've said enough for now, Bob. I've seen a lot in my two years at Osler, and I've got some strong opinions. Once I get talking, I tend to go too far. Let's save it for another day. Besides, there's some entertainment about to begin behind you."

Chen turned to see the old drunk panhandling two young women, probably City Hall secretaries, their hair lacquered perfectly, their suits tailored to at once suggest traditional values and to reveal, to greatest advantage, their marketable contours. A small man was circling the end of the deli counter, the intensity in his dark eyes leaving no doubt whom, between the women and the drunk, he preferred to have in his establishment. His arms rose, like a man preparing to scatter a flock of hens. He was a step behind the drunk when he shrieked, loud as a cockatoo, and the drunk twirled, towering over the deli man and, losing his balance, staggered back into the women's table. Like two jays, the women screamed, and the drunk spun

60

again, then began a sidelong lunge toward the front of the deli. Chen saw that the man was gasping as he stumbled past, and he saw the drunk's knees give, letting his body fall heavily to the linoleum.

Chen and Grimes leaped out of their seats and onto the drunk, whose arms were splayed to the sides. Grimes, who got there first, rolled the man onto his back and checked his eyes and the pulse on his neck. "Nothing!" he said to Chen, and then he grabbed the drunk's face in his two hands and, forcing open his jaw, planted his mouth on the drunk's mouth, forcing his breath into the man while Chen, straddling the man, placed the heels of his hands on the drunk's chest, awaiting Grimes's order.

"Now!"

Chen shoved down on the drunk's chest, paused, shoved again, paused, shoved.

"Hold!" Grimes said, and he again placed his lips around the drunk's, blew in, backed off, and was placing his mouth over the drunk's once again when the contents of the drunk's stomach erupted, a volcano of bile and booze that shot directly into Grimes's throat.

Grimes puked involuntarily and Chen felt his gorge rising.

"Oh, Christ! Get that stinking bum out of here! Jeezus! Look at all my customers leaving!" the deli man screamed, grabbing Chen's shoulder and pulling him back so violently that Chen fell and hit his head on the floor. Lifting himself, Chen seized the deli owner's arm and quietly asked:

"Did you call 911?"

"For that bum? Hell, no!"

"Then do it. Your failure will cost you in court."

"You think he's gonna sue? Hell, he's dead, anyway."

"My friend, Dr. Grimes, doesn't think so," Chen said, motioning to Grimes, who was again attempting to resuscitate the drunk. "And if he doesn't take you to court, we will. Now get on the phone!" Chen shouted, equally as loud as the deli man had been. The deli man ran behind the counter and Chen returned to help Grimes.

When the ambulance arrived, a weak pulse could be felt in the drunk's wrist, and he was breathing, although it sounded like a can of bolts was being shaken in his chest.

"Good work, Tom," Chen said as they scraped the remains of their lunch into a trash bin. "Did you ingest any of the vomitus?"

"I tried not to, but I think I'll prescribe a good dose of antibiotics for myself. Say, we're a pretty good team! Think Osler will be proud of us for adding to our patient base?"

"You're the expert in these matters, Tom. And I want to hear more of your thoughts."

"Maybe next time, we'll take a midnight stroll into a neighborhood known only to people like your friend J.H. That should open some eyes."

"I suspect you're not talking about Raleigh Gardens," Chen said.

Six . . .

Walter Scott did not aspire to a top position at Port Hancock General. Rather, he was sucked in that direction. Each time he rose, it was to fill a vacuum created immediately above him. His good works were meager. His skills in any of the aspects of business were unimpressive. But he was uncontroversial. Where do you find fault with those who are simply bland? And so when, by coincidence, he was time and again the only available candidate for promotion, he ascended unopposed. In the later years, as his trajectory arced toward the seat of the chief executive, his single discernible attribute finally won him friends among the members of the board of trustees. Walter Scott could drink. At fund-raising parties and at staff events, he could be counted on to drink doctors and benefactors alike into oblivion without himself slurring a syllable. It was to Scott's advantage that the process be accomplished quickly, for the sooner the guests were drunk, the sooner Scott's limited conversational skills acquired the appearance of erudition. At this point, when he made his pitch, clumsy as he was, he often succeeded in attracting substantial gifts. Over time he was recognized for this work, and the reward was his final promotion to chief executive.

Settling into the seat that had been his destiny, Scott discovered a problem. He was surrounded by women and men looking to him for direction, and with rare exception, they were stone sober. He could never seem to convey to them what he wanted. A greater problem, one which he would acknowledge to no one but that was clear to the more discerning among his employees, was that he often had little notion what he wanted or what was needed by the hospital. He quickly seized on the creation of committees as a means of addressing issues brought to his attention. He would allow the committee chairman to present findings to the trustees. If the trustees approved, Scott would accept credit for his wisdom. If the trustees balked, they had the committee chairman to blame.

Scott's system had worked well as long as Port Hancock General was prospering. Then two nasty words appeared in the trustees' vocabulary—"cost effective." These were followed by problems that Scott's committees seemed incapable of addressing. Now Walter Scott found himself isolated in his lofty perch, the man to whom all, including the trustees, looked to lead them through the dangerous new world of medicine.

He gazed down the length of the polished mahogany board room table, where bare spots between the packets of reports reflected the stern faces of a dozen trustees. He felt naked and exposed. He had balanced his blood alcohol level before entering the board room, but the terror within his chest was unrelieved. His vest and his suit jacket were buttoned across his broad belly, like armor fastened for a joust, and his jowls, flushed red, quivered in what could have been rage were it not fear. He was a cornered dog, and he did what any dog would do.

"Dr. Harvey, I think the problems facing PHG can best be

identified by looking at your group, Osler Medical." He paused, and the tip of his tongue darted out between his puffy lips like a lizard peeking at the world from between rocks. "I refer specifically to your creation of a surgicenter for orthopedics and other minor procedures. You have taken advantage of PHG to establish a patient base, and now you are robbing us of our lifeblood by abandoning our operating room. I believe it is highly unethical–"

"Excuse me, Walter! Excuse me," Harvey said, lowering his voice once he had halted Scott's attack. "One of our physicians has developed his own surgicenter, that's true. Dr. Nightingale made an independent decision that he felt, apparently, was in his best interest. But that was, I emphasize, an independent choice that had nothing to do with Osler Medical Group. We certainly have no control over how individual physicians practice."

"Steve Nightingale is on the board of Osler, Jim, and I'd like the board here to recognize just who our friends are." Scott's snarl was so exaggerated as to suggest parody. "First Nightingale sets up a surgicenter and gets to charge the insurance companies facility fees for every procedure, meaning we lose those fees. Then someone else is going to do the same thing with a birthing center for obstetrics and an endoscopy suite for gastroenterology."

"But Mr. Chairman, if I may?" The voice, musical as a flute, was that of Lydia Fulton, a trustee whose family of merchants had helped found Port Hancock General. Walter Scott could normally count on Lydia's loyalty, which is not to say that her contributions to board discussions were mindless. Rather, she had inherited an affinity for existing authority, a natural inclination that had served the Fulton family well in building its wealth.

"Mrs. Fulton?" Scott's puffed cheeks creased in a smile, inviting her comment.

"I only wanted to remark that I read in *Time* magazine about the spread in California of these satellite facilities, how they have replaced the same services at hospitals. Isn't this something that we simply must face?"

64

"Port Hancock is an isolated market, Mrs. Fulton," Scott began quietly, in deference to her femininity almost as much as her financial clout. "For the good of the community—to keep the hospital open—our doctors could agree not to compete."

Scott turned back toward Jim Harvey who, sitting across from Loring English, was one of three physicians on the board of trustees. The tip of Scott's tongue, moist and glistening, darted and retreated. Scott opened a manila folder and passed packets of stapled paper around the table.

"Here are the statistics. We have experienced a sharp decline in orthopedic and minor surgeries since Nightingale opened his surgicenter." Now Scott's voice regained its edge.

"My point is this. Surgicenters and their ilk are a symptom of individual greed, and they can destroy what is good for the community."

"I agree," Harvey said, shifting his voice into low range, a magnificent rumble that could crack rocks. "I perform one hundred percent of my procedures either in Port Hancock General or at Valleyview, where I have privileges. So despite what you may think, Walter, PHG is my hospital, too. And I will work damned hard to see that this hospital survives."

"Why don't you close down Nightingale?" Scott said. He glanced at Loring. "Dr. English, I'd value your opinion here."

This was not a position Loring welcomed. For starters, he and Scott were notorious enemies in this boardroom. And now, so were he and Harvey. A month earlier, as soon as he returned from the fishing trip, Loring had filed a professional complaint against Harvey with Conrad Schmidt, PHG's chief of surgery, who sat two seats from Harvey. Harvey had been notified of the complaint. He had not acknowledged Loring's presence this morning, and as Scott attempted to draw Loring into the debate, Harvey dismissively waved a hand in Loring's direction and looked out a window. There was no point in complicating his efforts against Harvey by joining this debate, and he had no idea where Scott was headed.

"Why Walter," Loring said, "I didn't know we'd made up from our last fight."

"We're tired of you playing the iconoclast," Scott snapped. "Why not actually make a contribution here?"

"Please, please! Gentlemen, we are all feeling embattled, but we are all working for the same thing." The Rev. Milton Farnham, pastor of Bethany Zion and chairman of the Port Hancock chapter of the NAACP, rose from his seat near the far end of the table and leaned forward on his fingertips. "The issue, we must all agree, is whether our patients are being well served."

"To serve them, Pastor, Port Hancock General has to be financially healthy," Scott said, unbuttoning his jacket.

Podge Durant, a born minion, unbuttoned his own jacket and edged closer to the table. Beside him, Conrad Schmidt sat at military attention in his starched white smock, stethoscope folded in its breast pocket, his pulse drumming through his carotid artery as his thoughts assembled themselves, seeking an unassailable, undeniable correctness, which they found.

"Walter, I've been critical in this room many times of your leadership of PHG—"

"Conrad, I will not tolerate—"

"And although it pains me, I to have to agree with you," Schmidt said, and Scott deflated, shrinking back from the table as he awaited Schmidt's next. "But I believe you are correct. There is no reason in the city of Port Hancock that there should be competition for the types of services that our hospital already performs. Competition clearly could kill PHG, and without PHG, there would be no charity care. Without PHG, there would be no trauma center." Schmidt, a man as tall as Harvey, but with an obviously large jaw and a bristly moustache, looked toward Harvey. He clasped his hands on the edge of the table, his posture still military.

"The only reason for competition is individual greed," Schmidt said evenly. "Doctors who operate in their own self-interest are violating the oath to which they swore. Our profession is one built on caring for others, and this rush to capitalize on every opportunity stains those principles we have embraced. I have to agree with Walter, Jim. I see Osler as a malignancy, taking that which is financially appealing and ignoring the rest. You are leading us toward ruin, sir!"

Loring, studying the other members of the board, saw them shifting uneasily in their seats, saw the unity that had always marked the Port Hancock General board dissolving. Willie Smicks, president of Neil Dunmore's bank, First Hancock, played with a pen, staring blankly. Podge Durant had slumped back in his seat, as had Rick Swaboda, executive director of the Greater Port Hancock Chamber of Commerce. Carlton Porferrio, heir to the Porferrio real estate and insurance conglomerate, gazed out a window. Bruce Groff, a tax lawyer, was unmoved and apparently uninterested, as he rooted through a briefcase stuffed with papers Loring suspected were not hospital-related. Neil Dunmore wore a bemused smile. Only Peter Warren, executive vice president of Hancock Systems, seemed to be engaged in the debate.

"Laissez-faire was okay in Adam Smith's day, Dr. Harvey," Warren said. "But we're in a different world now, where the advantage goes to those who look for short-term profits. My own company has been guilty of this, and I've told them so. Maybe your Osler Group should reconsider. Reengineering is devouring our society. And competition unchecked will hurt Port Hancock General and the community. Mr. Scott is correct, Doctor."

Three against one, Loring thought. Scott, Schmidt, and Warren all landing on Jim Harvey with both feet. Was I wrong? Is it going to be this easy?

When the meeting broke for lunch, Loring took the elevator to the ground floor and walked back past the cafeteria and the physicians' lounge toward the emergency room. He had not been here since Janet died, and entering the place required that his steps be deliberate. Reaching the ER, he took off his gray herringbone suit coat, folded it over his arm, and loosened the collar of his starched white shirt. He stopped at the emergency room command center. A clerk sat at a computer terminal and

Karen Larsen, the nurse supervisor, was talking on the phone. She gazed down at the counter, her blue eyes cheerful and unfocused, her voice hushed. Loring leaned his elbows on the counter and waited. When Larsen noticed Loring, she frowned and waved her fingertips, then accelerated the pace of her conversation, kissing the mouthpiece after she said goodbye.

"Dr. English, its great to see you." She reached for his hand. "I've been wanting to say I'm so sorry about Janet. All of us here really miss her."

"She was irreplaceable," Loring said, and he glanced around the ER, wondering in which examining room Janet's spirit began its flight from her body.

"How have you been doing? I understand you've taken Dr. Bernstein into your practice."

Loring knew that Karen Larsen did not miss a heartbeat in her hospital. "He's going to be another Dave Carn," he said.

Carn was Loring's best friend on the staff. Head of the emergency room, Carn was a walking medical encyclopedia. He more often than not led the specialists to their diagnoses when their patients were brought into the ER.

"The world could use as many of those as possible," Karen said. Loring noticed a short, blond nurse enter the command center behind Karen and sit at a computer terminal. He lowered his voice.

"There's going to be room for one more good doc in the near future," he said.

"Oh?" Karen folded her arms across her chest and cocked her head. She was more than pretty. Her red ponytail was offset by a white turtleneck, the sleeves pushed up on her tanned forearms. Even from the other side of the counter, Loring could smell her perfume, which only hinted of a sweetness Loring had first experienced when Karen was his student at Riverton. Although she was not a naturally gifted student, she was dogged, and graduated in good standing. When she was hired by Carn she flourished.

"Call it Janet's revenge. I've filed a complaint against Jim Harvey."

68

"Then you've been told," she said, her voice hushed but agitated. "It was incredible how stubborn he was." She looked over her shoulder at the nurse, then back. "I'm glad you're doing something!"

"Well, here comes the other end of the medical spectrum," Loring said. On the far side of the command center, the door of Room 3 flung open and Dave Carn burst into the room. Carn was scrawny, about five-eight, and brushed his steely white hair roughly to one side. He wore a red striped shirt and his prominent Adam's apple bounced above the tight knot of a dark blue tie. He was constantly on the move, and slammed a patient's chart into the wall-mounted chart holder without even breaking stride.

"Who's next, Juan?" he shouted to the clerk beside Karen.

"You're clear," Juan replied.

"How can that be? It's only noon!" Carn bellowed, a ballplayer arguing with an umpire. Then he saw Loring.

"Holy Mother of Cardiology! Hey, someone get security!" He circled the command center and threw his arm up around Loring's shoulder. "Get a lab coat, boy! I'm gonna put you to work for once. Hey, Florence, I got time to take the young doctor here to the lounge?" He winked at Karen.

"Be careful, Dr. English. You're in the hands of a seditionist," she said, smiling at Carn and then waving them on.

"How you holding up, Lor?" Carn asked, his arm still over Loring's shoulder as they walked along the corridor.

"I'm back on track, thanks. Got some help, too."

"Good move, Lor. This business is getting crazier by the day. 'Business.' Christ, I'm starting to talk like the stuffed shirts! You see the staff I've got in there today? Karen, who does the work of three, and one nurse from geriatrics. Christ, Lor, geriatrics! All she knows about is letting old folks die quietly, and she's thrown into the ER? It's not her fault, but she just doesn't have it. And then, when I've got four warm bodies groaning at eight-thirty this morning, who shows up but QA. And what is their idea of quality assurance? I'm saving a couple of lives, and they want me to take time out—hell, insist!—that I stop

69

what I'm doing and show them my completed charts from last week. You know where I told them to shove their charts!"

"Why don't you bring these things up at the Medical Executive Committee, Dave?"

"Bunch of politicos who are buried in their specialties, Lor. Oh, hell, I'm just an old fart who doesn't know how to adapt. I'm getting the hell out of this profession before the smell gets me. And it ain't just the suits, m'boy. It's your fellow practitioners. You wouldn't believe the stuff I run into. Guy comes in with severe abdominal pains. I ask who his doctor is, he tells me Norm Grosswirth. So I call up our esteemed former president of the medical staff. Know what he tells me?"

"Do I want to know?"

"'Give him to someone else,' he tells me. 'The guy's only worth eight bucks a month capitation fee. Cost me more than that to drive in.' And he hangs up! You and I got into medicine when people still had a philosophy of healing, Lor. Now, it's all dealing. I swear, Karen's sweet smile is the only reason I can manage to come in here. I tell Dot, if it wasn't for Karen, I'd be gone," he said as he opened the door to the doctors' lounge and let Loring inside.

"Looks like Karen's got a beau, Dave," Loring said, draping his jacket over the arm of a stuffed chair.

"Oh, her latest. Yeah, don't spread it, but it's Tom Grimes."

"I heard about his troubles with Betty. So they've broken up?"

"Not officially, and that's why Karen's keeping low. But hell, she's always kept her personal business to herself. Any man gets in the way of her nursing, she drops him like lead and moves on. Oh, she's run through a string of them. But I think Tom's a different story. He's a good doc, too, except now he's tied in with Osler."

After the lunch break, the Port Hancock board meeting moved on from the topic of competing physicians. A routine chart review by state regulators found the hospital's administration appropriate and on that positive note, Walter Scott asked for a motion to adjourn, which Podge Durant was quick to offer. As the trustees moved toward the door, Jim Harvey headed the other direction.

"Walter," he said, taking Scott by the elbow and drawing him away from the group, "I appreciate your concerns about the power that Osler wields in the community. I'd like to talk with you about ways in which we can cooperate. Could you make lunch some time next week? Say at O'Malley's?"

O'Malley's served martinis that could pass for nitroglycerin. Scott agreed.

Seven . . .

Walter Scott had not been a difficult sell. Harvey understood alcoholics. He knew Scott would find attractive any promise to ease his discomfort, and he knew Scott's job was a source of enormous pain for the chief executive. Scott liked the income, but was ambivalent about the prestige. What Harvey offered Scott was the opportunity to trade his prestige for a substantial pay increase. The job was vice chairman of the hospital that would survive a merger between Port Hancock General and the city's newer but less well equipped Valleyview Medical Center. No one had ever hinted at such a merger, but Harvey went straight at Scott with his proposal. He did not worry that the chief executive, who days before was battling him over the future of Port Hancock General, would be tied by emotion or principle to defending his turf. Harvey knew where Scott's bottom line rested—and it was not in loyalty or dominion, philosophy or morality. What Scott cared most about was his own survival, and he was smart enough to see that that was what Harvey was giving him. Or, more precisely, that was the opportunity Harvey offered. It required some work—some skillful work orchestrated by Osler's board—for that opportunity to materialize. Scott told Harvey he could count on his labor.

Jim Harvey could sense that Scott's piece was now locked in place, and he wanted to celebrate. He pointed the Range Rover across the river, toward the small ranch house where Sue Czernicki lived. Sue worked the graveyard shift this week and was home days. Her husband Chris, an ironworker, was on the job at Hancock Systems which, even as it downsized its workforce, was in the middle of an expansion project. Chris's black-and-red Ford pickup would not be in the driveway until after six. Harvey glanced at his Rolex. It was only three. Sue had begged off earlier when Harvey phoned her, but she never let him down when he pushed.

Harvey picked up his cell phone and punched four buttons.

"Tiffany, I've got an errand to run. I'll be back around five. Any messages?"

"A Mr. Chen Ching Huo called, J.H. His flight will land at Riverton International at 5:17. He asked if you would have a car there to meet him."

Harvey had never told Tiffany about the Dragon. She was his confidante in most matters, but he saw no reason to involve her in this venture. He had told her that his sudden flight to Newark back in the winter was to attend a closed meeting of physicians gathering to discuss their options in dealing with health maintenance organizations. Tiffany had no record of his travels, Harvey knew. And so there was now a need to explain Mr. Chen's arrival.

"I'll go to the airport myself, Tiffany," he said, and he felt himself go limp at the thought of bypassing the afternoon in the rancher. "Mr. Chen—and this is just for us, Tiff—is an administrator I met last winter. He's brilliant. As a consultant, he can help us cut through the managed care mess. But I don't want the board apprised. There are some tender egos we don't need to trample."

"Jim, darling, that is utter bullshit," Tiffany said without emotion. "Saddam Hussein worries more about trampled egos than you do. But don't fret. I'll handle it, whatever it is. And, oh," she paused for effect. "Sorry about your foregone errands."

"Thanks for your concern, sweetie," Harvey said, pushing a final button on the phone. He reached across the dash and flipped down the screen of his global positioning system. He punched in his code for Riverton International and, with a few more keystrokes, requested a recommended route from his location on the south side of the river. In slightly less than an hour, he was parking at the airport garage.

"I thought a man of your position would meet me with a limousine," the Dragon said when Harvey led him back to the garage. Harvey felt the sting of blood rushing to the back of his neck, responding to the hostility in the Dragon's challenge. He said nothing. To speak would be to defend, an indication of weakness.

"For the time being, I will offer you the guest suite at my place," Harvey said. "With your brother at Osler, it will be safer to hold our discussions away from the group. I will assign a maid to attend to your needs. For any personal requests, of course, I am at your call, Mr. Chen."

They left the interstate at Port Hancock and climbed into the hills north of the city, following a narrow, humped road that wound up the south face of the highest of the hills. At an inconspicuous opening in a fieldstone wall, they turned left and the pavement widened and a small green sign with gold lettering introduced Stonefield, the exclusive development that Neil Dunmore had built for Harvey and the other doctors of Osler's core. The first house on the right belonged to Brad Barnett and his wife, Natalie, who apparently loved gables. The facade of the Barnett home, sided in beige stucco, was layered in gables. One over the arched front door, one over the two-story bay window beside the door, a main gable above these two, and a big gable over the side of the garage, which had three gabled dormers that served no particular purpose since there was no room above the garage. There was even a gabled dormer over the laundry room at the rear of the house. It was in that room, on top of the clothes dryer, that Harvey had nailed Natalie Barnett. She was in the foyer in a bathrobe when he walked in that morning about two years before. Without speaking, he

73

reached for the terrycloth belt and pulled it. Natalie, standing there exposed, closed her eyes and shuddered. His right hand slipped between her legs, all the way to her buttocks, and, with his other hand on her back, he lifted her and carried her to the laundry room where, as she told her sister, he banged her brains out, the most incredible fucking she'd ever had. Natalie had hated Jim Harvey ever since.

On the other hand, Betsy Nightingale, the plump woman in the brick-faced colonial next door, adored Harvey. She and Harvey's wife Sonia had coffee together regularly, and she and her husband Dr. Steve Nightingale had two children that often played with the Harvey kids.

On a shoulder of the hill, just above Brad and Natalie Barnett's house, was the plantation-style white box of Dennis Ross. It had a two-story front porch with six towering columns. Across the street from Ross's place was Ari Urizar's house. It was three years old and of undefined style. Ari and Helen kept to themselves, seldom venturing even onto their lawn. The green paint on the cedar siding was already fading and peeling. A gardener kept the landscaping in shape, as was required of all the Stonefield property owners by deed restriction.

At the top of the hill, Harvey steered the Range Rover between two square brick columns, topped with glowing brass lanterns, into his own driveway. The driveway was a hundred yards long and was split by two circular rock gardens before reaching the house, a sprawling brick mansion. This was the house of a man trying to make a statement. The main entry was through an antique oak double door transplanted from a manor house in Louisiana. A two-story greenhouse stood next to the main house, filled with palms, vines, and fountains. Next to it was a four-car garage. Attached to the garage, in the back, were the servants' quarters, and on the right, Harvey pointed out to Mr. Chen as they approached, was the guest house.

As the Range Rover came to a stop inside the garage bay, Harvey picked up his phone and pushed a single button. "Mrs. Pelletier, could you show my guest, Mr. Chen Ching Huo, to the cottage? Thanks."

74

Immediately a door opened in front of them at the rear of the garage, and a solidly built woman with cotton white curls and stern creases in her brow entered. She opened the Dragon's door, and as Ching Huo stepped out, Mrs. Pelletier's cheeks bunched in a smile and she reached for his hand.

"Good afternoon, sir. I do hope you will be comfortable with us. Let me show you your room. Mr. Pelletier will be right behind us with your bags."

"I'll see you in the library for drinks before dinner," Harvey said across the hood of the Range Rover. "Take some time to get settled. Mrs. Pelletier will tell you when drinks and dinner are ready."

Later, Harvey offered the Dragon cognac from a liquor case in the book shelves of his panelled library. The Dragon asked instead for jasmine tea, which was served within a minute by a small black woman in a maid's uniform.

"Americans, I have found, display their wealth in predictable, and conspicuous fashion. Of course yours is the largest home on this hill, and of course you occupy the pinnacle. I believe Thorstein Veblen first pointed this out."

Harvey, suppressing his surprise that the Dragon even knew of Veblen's theory of the leisure class, retorted with a smile, "Do not the Chinese, as well as others, share the propensity for high living and elaborate ritual that seems to serve no function?"

"And what function does my visit to Port Hancock serve?" the Dragon asked, lifting a delicate tea cup to his unopened lips, the steam from its surface curling below his nose, his dark eyes gazing steadily across the cup at Harvey.

"Whatever function you want it to," Harvey said. "This is your meeting, Dragon. Tell me what you want."

"I want to know about Sue Czernicki," the Dragon said, and his lips finally opened to take in tea.

Harvey felt his heart pound two, three times hard, responding to the shot of adrenaline that the sound of Sue's name injected. The question was unexpected, and left him feeling vulnerable, something Harvey did not normally allow. He did not care that anyone might know about his visits to the rancher.

Indeed, he took no precautions precisely because he liked the challenge his openness threw out to the world. But he couldn't see why the Dragon might find this interesting or useful.

"She's a fine emergency room nurse."

"You are sloppy with your personal life," the Dragon said. "Such sloppiness could wound my business, and I will not tolerate it. Perhaps this, alone, is reason enough to cancel our liaison."

"I suppose your confusion with the use of English is forgivable," Harvey said, smiling. "The word 'sloppy' suggests carelessness. I can assure you that everything I do is done with utmost care. It is irrelevant to me whether you, or anyone else knows about my relationship with Sue Czernicki, or with any other woman, for that matter." Harvey stood and went to the closed library door and opened it.

"Miss Sloan, would you please tell Mrs. Harvey I would like to speak with her." Harvey returned to the leather armchair where he had been sitting, beside the Dragon's chair, facing a lit fire in the tile fireplace.

"Yes, sweetheart?" Sonia Harvey was standing behind them in the library door, the former Miss Kent County, still slender despite the birth of their three children, still blonde as a bottle can make you. Neither man turned to greet her.

"Would you explain for my guest, Mr. Chen, my friendship with Sue Czernicki?"

"Oh, my darling Mr. Chen, why certainly. James is very fond of nurse Czernicki. He thinks she is one of the best young emergency room nurses he has encountered, and he fucks her every chance he gets. I imagine she is very good at that, as well."

The Dragon could be seen to lurch slightly within the large arms of his chair. He turned and smiled at Sonia, then restored his gaze at the fire.

"Can I do anything else for you, sweetheart?"

"No, thanks," Harvey said, and Sonia left, closing the door silently.

"Your wealth has purchased you some things that are not

displayed, as well," the Dragon said, smiling but not looking at Harvey.

"Wealth is relative, Dragon. Were it not, you and I would not be sitting here. May we begin our discussions? If there are unnecessary restrictions that we can assist each other in removing, we will both benefit, and I see no reason to limit our scope. Do you?"

"None whatever, Dr. Harvey."

The business was to be in medical supplies. The Dragon's Triad society would become the supplier. Its source would be hijacked shipments, stolen, if practical, directly from loading docks. Sutures would be a major product, as would all disposable items. One major urban hospital on the east coast, for example, had a $21 million annual budget for sutures alone. The Triad would manufacture counterfeit medical instruments and diagnostic tools in China and smuggle them into the United States.

Dennis Ross, whom Harvey had kept ignorant of the Triad's involvement, had prepared the way for this venture. Following Harvey's instructions, Ross had a distribution company created in Wichita, with no visible ties to Osler. That company's name, Four Seasons Medical Supply Inc., would be on all invoices, and checks to Four Seasons would be written for deposit only in a bank in Colorado, from which funds would be wired automatically to a Grand Cayman bank. There was, in many hospital supply offices, one employee already tapped into the hospital supply industry, usually a purchasing officer who could direct business to the supplier who offered the best graft. Ross had cultivated friends in the industry and knew who would buy. Ari Urizar had handled the financial side, as well as the laundering of the money through outlets up and down the East Coast. Urizar, too, was given no details on the supply side of the new business. He and Ross would be introduced to the Dragon only when it was necessary, Harvey had decided.

"On another matter, Dragon," Harvey said when they had finished discussing the intricacies of the Four Seasons deal, "Osler has an imminent need for your skills with intrigue."

The Dragon rested a finger on his cheek and frowned, as if asking for more details.

"We anticipate proposing to the chairman of a major insurance company that he direct business to our group. We could offer him only a limited financial incentive to do this, a figure restrained by the volume of business his company does. He might attempt to improve on our incentive elsewhere. We could avoid the possibility of his shopping his services around, or of whispering to the regulators about our deal, if we had some knowledge of his personal life."

"You suspect there is information that he would want to protect?"

"We do not know details."

"Details can make all the difference," the Dragon smiled, and for the first time, his smile parted his lips, revealing perfectly capped teeth. "What is this gentleman's name?"

"William Scarborough. He's chief executive of Coastal Insurance."

The Dragon closed his eyes and recorded the information in the same way a good numbers runner collects bets. Again he smiled, this time with his teeth hidden. "And are there any other services we can offer?"

"Not for now, Dragon," Harvey said, standing and circling behind his chair. "I have one problem with a doctor. Loring English. But I'm handling that."

"The nature of this problem?"

"He would like to see my medical license revoked, Dragon. But I have a surprise for him." Harvey grinned. "Thanks to some loyal friends and dear, sweet Sue Czernicki."

"Another of her talents?"

"Quite. Well, dinner should be ready. Shall we—" he stopped in mid stride. "One other concern we have might benefit from your skills. A doctor in our group, Thomas Grimes, has been poking into our computer, apparently gathering information about some of our ventures that are not completely public. We could be more than embarrassed should he be up to something. Could you . . . is there some way you could inquire, have someone pose as an outsider perhaps, a regulator, and find out what he knows?"

"We would be more than happy to engage Dr. Grimes," the Dragon said.

Eight . . .

The Osler Group building was a circular structure, with waiting areas radiating out like spokes from the central administration offices. The examination rooms where the budget-minded patients were seen were tiny cubicles off the spokes. It was here, in these cramped rooms, that Thomas Grimes spent most of his time at Osler, listening to the stories of scared men and women. They didn't get to see a cardiologist if Osler's gate keepers could help it, at least not if they were enrolled in a health maintenance organization, so by the time they did they knew their hearts were in trouble.

The gatekeepers at Osler were the general practitioners and the internists, and their job, as at most practices, was to keep referrals to specialists like Grimes down. In fact, the HMO's paid a premium to gatekeepers whose efforts exceeded the organization's targets. When a gatekeeper had no choice but to refer, he or she always tried to steer business toward Osler's own specialists. Since they often succeeded, Thomas Grimes seldom lacked for patients.

There were patients who were not seen in the cubicles. These were the people who flew first class, and whose health insurance plan was not dictated by some union or employer. Their doctors were paid for individual office visits, and for as many tests as the physician wanted to order. At Osler, these patients were seen in the premium suite, where the examination rooms were as welcoming as a living room, with soft lighting, comfortable chairs, refined background music and floral wallpaper instead of the impersonal, gray green paint that was everywhere else.

Lydia Fulton flew first class, and she had one of Osler's best cardiologists. She had discovered Thomas Grimes before he sold his practice and she admired his forthrightness. She insisted that he continue as her physician, and Ophelia Sadler, Osler's administrator, was happy to oblige. Lydia's heart was laced with restricted arteries, but the damage was such that Grimes had been able to treat her successfully with drugs, avoiding the need for surgery or angioplasty. Lydia, who had the inheritance of merchant moguls, had the soul of a book-keeper, and she was punctual in keeping her appointments, whether with a doctor or an auto mechanic. She and Grimes were both on time this afternoon, and Lydia promptly raised her concern.

"Dr. Grimes, do you think, given our success with medication, that perhaps I could eliminate some of my pills?" she asked. "You've done marvelously, and the sleepiness is almost gone. But I do think that I might gain some pep if I could quit for a while. That is, if my heart will take it."

Grimes looked at Lydia, at the sweep of silver hair over her ears, and her crisply applied lipstick, not smeared like that of some women in their late seventies. He marveled at the glimmer in her blue eyes and the fine web of lines at her temples, like creases in a creamy cashmere.

"Mrs. Fulton, I respect your wishes, but I cannot give you my blessings. You are feeling as healthy as you do precisely because we've balanced your medicine. This is as good as it gets with arteries that have served you well for a few years and that now cannot deliver all the blood they once supplied. I'm sorry."

"Oh, my. Well, I just thought I'd ask. But I trust your judgment implicitly, Dr. Grimes. Now let me ask another question, and this requires doctor-patient confidentiality."

"Certainly, Mrs. Fulton."

"As you may know, I am a trustee at Port Hancock General, and Dr. Harvey is on the board, also."

80

Grimes's teeth clenched and he exhaled sharply through his nose and tensed his abdomen, bracing for something he suspected he would not like.

"Do you know any reason Walter Scott would want to discredit Dr. Harvey?" Lydia asked, her brow rising to punctuate her question. She waited while Grimes thought. He was not considering the possibilities between Scott and Harvey. Rather, he was gauging whether he should trust this woman with the information he had accumulated. Why not? She is in a position to act, he thought. But, no. Harvey is too polished. There would be too great a chance of wasting everything he had gathered.

"It's an intriguing question," he finally replied. "What stirs you to ask?"

"Oh, they had a confrontation at the last board meeting. Dear Mr. Scott seemed to believe that Osler Medical Group was not playing fair with the hospital. I really believe Dr. Harvey is tops, and poor Walter is struggling with issues that are above us all."

"I work for Dr. Harvey. I'm an employee, not a partner. I have no dealings with Mr. Scott. I'm afraid I have no insights that would help, Mrs. Fulton," Grimes said, and even as he spoke, he was thinking about all the insights he did possess concerning Osler Medical Group and wondering if Walter Scott could be the powerful ally he needed to chasten OMG.

His next few appointments were not in the premium suite. But back in the cubicles, he continued to mull over the question posed by Mrs. Fulton, and the more he thought about it, the more convinced he became that he should approach Walter Scott.

Willie Goodman, a maintenance man at Hancock Systems, was Grimes's last appointment of the day in the office. He had some house calls to make later, but he always liked to take time with Goodman after the examination was finished, so he scheduled him last.

"Your stress test looks good, Willie," he said, patting Goodman's shoulder as he returned to the cubicle with a printout. He sat in the little swivel chair by the table that served as a desk and began writing on a chart. He stopped before he was finished and, stretching his long legs, he crossed his arms, wrinkling the starch of his lab coat, and smiled at his patient. Goodman was a small man with a graying moustache that curled down at the corners of his mouth. A small tuft of graying whiskers sprouted below the center of his lower lip. His large brown eyes were made smaller by the thick lenses of his glasses. His pressed blue work uniform gave him a dignity that his narrow frame by itself might not have conveyed. His name, Goodman, was embroidered in red over the left shirt pocket. A plastic badge with his photograph was clipped to the same pocket.

"I'm amazed at your progress," Grimes said. "You've brought your cholesterol down seventy-six points in six months. How do you explain this?"

"You asked me to do some things, and I did them, Dr. Grimes. Simple as that." Goodman's slightly nasal voice, more oboe than clarinet, had a sound Grimes enjoyed.

"What did you do exactly?"

"Joined a health club. I'm on that treadmill an hour, hour and twenty minutes every day. No more hamhocks and ribs. Just chicken and peas for me. Mona, she's one angry lady. 'How come you aren't eating my good stuff? Don't you love me no more?' I tell her, 'Mona, your stuff's too good to eat!'" He winked at Grimes.

"Well, tell her she's going to have you pestering her a few more years if you keep up the good work. I guess pretty soon she's going to have you around the house a lot more, too. How close are you to retirement, Willie?"

"With this downsizing and all, fella never knows, does he? Could be next week, could be three years, when I hit sixty-five. If I had my way, I'd never leave. I've been there forty-five years, Doc. I don't know nothing else. We bought our house with my paycheck from Hancock, and sent Alisha to Howard University. You know, she's about to get her Ph.D."

"Congratulations! That's great news, Willie."

82

"We're mighty proud of her. Say, Dr. Grimes, none of my business really, but how're you doing here? They still treatin' you okay?"

"It's a paycheck, Willie."

"The reason I ask is that you're getting known in the city as 'House Call Grimes,'" Goodman said, and he didn't smile.

"They talk about it at the plant all the time. They say, 'Oh My God drops you, don't worry. House Call Grimes'll see you through.'"

"Oh My God?"

"O-M-G. Osler Medical Group. No one at Hancock Systems needs to worry. We've got the HMO—Hancock takes care of us good. But if a fella's got a cousin out of work, even though this cousin's been coming to OMG long as it's been around, if he doesn't have the fee, he isn't coming here. They turn him away at the door. It happened to ol' Miss Phyllis. You're seeing her nights now, aren't you?"

"That's confidential, Willie, who I see. But doctors have always seen people whether they could pay or couldn't. There's nothing special about it."

"You know, that's what I thought. But can you tell me: Why is Oh My God so different? Don't you all take an oath? Isn't there some rule about caring about people being healthy?"

"That's the rule I learned in medical school. Maybe they don't teach it any more, Willie," he said, standing and shaking Goodman's hand.

That night, before Grimes left the office, he followed his routine. Disks into his briefcase, locked, after making a copy for Chen. Printout of house call patients due for visits. This night, he had three. Then the phone call.

"Busy night?" he asked after waiting on hold for seven minutes.

"You wouldn't believe it," Karen said. "And we've got two temps with no ER experience. Nothing new there. Usually we're cross-training nurses from pediatrics, or worse. How's your day going?"

"It ended on a high note. I know I crab about Osler too

much, but one of my patients just let me know I'm not alone."

"Whatever made you think you're alone?" she asked, her voice quiet and deep, deeper than some men's, a voice that could hush an unruly dog.

"Guess what some of the city people call Osler?" She could not guess, and he told her. They laughed together, a laugh of shared displeasure. Grimes had not told Karen everything he knew about Osler Medical Group. He trusted her, but he wanted their relationship unaffected by his work. But in general terms he was clear about his feelings toward both Osler and his boss, Harvey. And he left it at that.

"Are you stopping by later?" Karen asked.

"Eleven-fifteen?"

"Dinner at my place?" she whispered.

"I thought I'd take you out," he said, and he reached for his wallet. There were many cash machine receipts, and three dollar bills and some change. He jotted a note on a pad on his desk. "Stop at cash machine."

"Okay, but don't get talking with one of your girlfriends and show up here at midnight!"

"Have I ever?" he asked, and they both laughed.

Grimes was putting on his jacket when he decided to try to make one more call. He was surprised that Walter Scott's home number was published. He was pleasantly surprised that Scott seemed eager to hear what he had to tell him about Osler Medical Group.

"I'd rather we meet in person, Mr. Scott," Grimes said. "What I have to tell you isn't for a phone conversation. If it reaches the authorities—and I need your assistance to make that happen—there will be indictments and jail time."

Walter Scott was silent for a long moment, and Grimes thought many things in that span, cursing his poor judgment. When Scott finally spoke, Grimes was relieved.

"I think we'd better meet soon. Call my secretary tomorrow

morning and see when I'm available. And don't mention this to anyone else, Doctor."

At nine-thirty-seven, Thomas Grimes arrived at his last appointment, the home, on an unlit country road eleven miles north of the city, of Rawson and Muriel Gore. The August sun had set and there were no outside lights on the two-room shanty that sat down from the road in a thicket of pines. There were stacks of cordwood piled between the trunks of trees, and the smell of creosote hung in the air. There was no driveway, although the dark shadow of an old dump truck lurked behind the house. Grimes parked on the roadside and, with his medical bag, a bulging paper bag, and a flashlight, searched in the darkness for the path. As he approached the solitary door, he could see through its screen window the blue flicker of a television. He knocked and then let himself in.

Muriel, an obese woman in her early fifties, was lying on a mattress on the floor on the far side of the small room. Perspiration soaked her housecoat and trickled along her brow. A row of prescription bottles stood like chess pieces on the floor beside the mattress, and there was a plastic tumbler, half filled with water. Rawson, a dozen years older than his wife, sat in a slate-blue recliner whose velour was ripped in several places. He had been a mountain-size man who had made a living harvesting trees from these woods. Now, his flesh was a thin papering over his big bones, and the cushions of his chair seemed not so much to embrace him as to engulf him.

"Mind if I turn on a light?" Grimes asked, his flashlight still glowing.

"Could you open that window beyond the stove, too?"

Rawson's voice, once a rousing bass drum, was a whisper.

Grimes pulled the chain to turn on the bulb mounted on the low ceiling. Then, setting his two bags on the floor, he walked around the stove, made from a steel tank and sitting on chipped linoleum. He pushed up the window and propped it in place with a slat lying on the sill. The place, which in the cold months was perfumed with the aroma of burning hickory, now smelled of flatulence and old kitchen trash.

Kneeling beside Muriel, Grimes checked her pulse and then, opening his bag and removing his equipment, her blood pressure.

"How have you been eating, dear?" he asked, holding her hand and watching her eyes.

"About the same, Doc," she wheezed.

"Are you getting up at all?"

"I make it out to the W.C. in the morning. I go again at night. But most of the day I stay here to keep cool, she said.

Grimes patted her hand and then went to Rawson's recliner, where he kneeled again and performed the same examination.

"You like this show?" Rawson asked. He had not looked away from the small screen since Grimes arrived. He allowed his arm to be lifted and the blood pressure cuff to be wrapped and inflated without a sideways glance.

"I don't get much chance to watch TV, Rawson. What's it about?"

Rawson launched into an explanation, and he lifted his jagged frame in his seat and turned to face Grimes, a smile replacing the stoic mask that he had worn until now.

"You'd love it, Doc. Pull up that chair and relax."

"Okay, but first, I brought some of groceries. Where can I put them?"

"Milk goes in the tin box outside by the door. Pile the rest of it over here behind my chair."

Grimes unloaded the grocery bag and then brought a wooden folding chair from the rear room, once the bedroom but now a landfill heaped with the stuff two declining lives no longer used. Grimes placed the chair between Muriel's mattress and Rawson's recliner, with his back to the stove. He promptly fell asleep. When he awoke, he looked at his watch and leaped out of the chair. "Oh, my God!" he gasped. "I've got to run."

"Get a little beauty rest, did you?" Rawson asked.

"We didn't want to disturb you, Doc," Muriel said. "Looked like you needed a nap."

"I'm supposed to be somewhere in a half hour, and I've got

to make a stop on the way. Sorry to rush," he said.

"I don't know, Muriel. Almost sound's like the doc's got a lady waiting."

Grimes was pushing an arm through his coat sleeve and gathering his flashlight and his bag and heading for the door.

"Keep taking your medicine, Rawson. And Muriel, try to walk around the room a bit. It really will help your heart."

He dashed up the hill, stumbling on sticks and rocks, fumbling with his flashlight, unable to get the switch to slide. He turned the car around and drove as quickly as the twisting road and his own tempered soul would allow. He knew there was a cash machine at the bank across the street from City Hall, five blocks from Port Hancock General.

Traffic on Port Hancock's downtown streets was limited, at this time of night, to an occasional patrol car or ambulance. The drug dealers stood on corners in Raleigh Gardens, but the downtown was decidedly clear of that business, and despite the lack of bustle that would have been there during the day, Grimes felt safe as he parked beside the bank. He left the car running and, after using his bank card to enter the vestibule, inserted the card in the cash machine. He decided to check his balance first, and as he did that he sensed that someone was approaching on the sidewalk. Assured of his bank balance, he withdrew one hundred dollars. He glanced sideways. There were three figures waiting outside the vestibule. Perhaps he should redeposit the money, he thought. If this were a mugging, he wouldn't lose the cash. Don't be so suspicious, he thought. No one gets mugged in Port Hancock. He took his wallet from his inside coat pocket and folded the five twenties inside. Removing his card from the machine, he turned and saw the three men, hands jammed in their trouser pockets, one smoking a cigarette. They all faced him, outside the glass. None was as tall as he, and they all were slightly built. He hesitated, then pushed on the door handle. Thomas Grimes was seldom intimidated.

"Good evening," he said, scanning their faces in the darkness. They were all Asian, well-groomed, and young. One wore glasses. They smiled pleasantly at him and bowed, parting to let him pass.

Grimes chuckled to himself at the trepidation he had felt. He reached in his coat pocket for the keys and remembered his car was running.

They could have stolen it if they were criminals, he told himself. He circled the front of the car, checking his watch in the streetlight. It was eleven-twenty. Karen was waiting.

He reached the car door and turned to grab the handle. The three men were coming over the curb, their legs passing through the beams of his headlights. They were not smiling.

Grimes yanked on the door handle, but the car was locked. He yanked again, this time frantically.

The first man reached him and Grimes felt himself being punched in the side, under the ribs. Then he felt an incredible pain that was not a punch but was deep inside his belly.

A second man was now behind Grimes. He could feel him somehow on his shoulders, and then he felt something sharp around his neck and he was hauled backward, away from the car and he landed hard on his back on the pavement, with the streetlight above his attackers, like the light in an operating room over the table, and the three thugs were over him, their faces in shadows like the doctors standing around an operating table.

Grimes saw a glint of silver and he tried to raise his arm, but a boot heel held his wrist firm to the pavement, and the silver came arcing toward him from the side and Grimes turned his face away, but that only exposed further the side of his neck, which the blade slashed deeply just before Grimes's thoughts ceased.

One of the men reached calmly into the inside jacket pocket of the corpse sprawled in a pool of thick blood on the pavement. The man, wearing latex gloves, withdrew a wallet. His fingers fished inside and removed the cash and some of the cash machine receipts. The three men stood then and walked around the rear of the car and down the sidewalk.

Two blocks away, an ambulance raced toward Port Hancock General, followed by a patrol car.

Nine ...

The mayor of Port Hancock, Henry Costanza, called the murder of Dr. Thomas Grimes a blight on the whole community. Costanza divided his time unequally between governing and campaigning. One cannot serve, he said, if one is not elected. Thus were his priorities ordered. In coming out forcefully against Grimes's murderer, Costanza was, in his view, both campaigning and living up to a campaign pledge to be tough on crime. He backed up his words by ordering Chief Robert C. Graves to step up patrols in Raleigh Gardens. Graves's investigation into Grimes's death included a roundup of most males above the age of thirteen who lived in or visited Raleigh Gardens. They were all brought, locked in the back seats of patrol cars, to the police station in the basement of City Hall, where they were questioned. Anger, with which the Gardens was well stocked on any day, spilled out onto the hot streets, and more patrol cars converged. The Rev. Milton Farnham preferred balance, give and take, even when you were giving more than you received. To him, confrontation could always be avoided. And yet, he sensed that in the wake of Dr. Grimes's death, he needed to shift his stance slightly. There was an assumption, he said before the members of city council, that the culprit who slaughtered Dr. Grimes was some black drug addict, when there was no other evidence than that the physician had met his end eight blocks east of the Gardens, in front of City Hall.

"One might equally assume," Rev. Farnham said, his voice building in intensity, his back to a packed gallery, "that the killer was white, since, except for the janitors, the employees at City Hall are all as white as bed sheets!"

The crowd roared its approval. Rev. Farnham turned around, a frown on his face, but grinning inside. The Sunday collection at Bethany Zion would be huge.

After three weeks, Chief Graves arrested a known distributor of crack cocaine from Riverton and called a press conference. While no murder charges had yet been filed, he said, his department was investigating a potential link between the distributor and the Grimes murder. A judge, convinced the distributor presented a risk of flight, refused bail. Graves and Costanza had a sitting duck perpetrator to keep the press off their backs. A threatened layoff at Hancock Systems became a distraction, and by Labor Day, the death of Dr. Thomas Grimes had all but disappeared from the public consciousness.

Through it all, Karen Larsen reported for work at Port Hancock General's emergency room. Dave Carn never saw a tear. Nor did he see Karen smile. Instead of her normal effort, doing the work of two, she now did the work of three, and when any nurse failed to report, Karen took the shift, some days working twenty-four hours without a break. She would not talk about her grief with Carn.

"Dammit, Karen," he said. "I'm ordering you to come with me to the physician's lounge and start opening up. It's a matter of patient safety!"

"You have no right to order me to talk, Dr. Carn," she said through clenched teeth. The rims of her eyes moistened. "And if you don't back off, I'll talk to the nurse-physician committee," she said in a low, quavering voice. She turned and joined another doctor in an examination room, knowing Carn wouldn't pursue her there.

"Talk to her," Carn told Loring English when, on the morning of the September meeting of the Medical Executive Committee, he stopped by the emergency room doctors' lounge.

"I can tell you from my recent experience, Dave, that Karen has to do this on her own."

"She's not doing it, Loring. And it's eating her up. Some people would be a bomb waiting to explode. I know Karen well enough that in her case I know the only one getting hurt is our girl. Talk to her, please?"

Loring left the doctors' lounge and headed to the emergency room. He saw the back of Karen's head first, her red hair knotted above her collar. As he approached, he could tell she was on the phone with a reluctant physician.

"It's nice that you can afford a weekend at Notre Dame for the game, Doctor," she was saying. "But one of the patients paying for your tickets is in here now, and I'm telling you: Postpone your flight and come see Mrs. Engeler. If you're not here promptly, I'll ask Dr. Carn to cite you. Goodbye, Doctor!"

She set down the receiver as if handling a Fabergé egg.

"Unruly lot, those docs," Loring said, leaning his elbows on the countertop.

"Oh, hi, Dr. English. I didn't hear you come up. We don't have one of yours in today, do we?"

"No, no. I just stopped by to say hello." He glanced around the emergency room. "And to say I'm sorry. If there's anything I can do—"

"Dr. Carn put you up to this, didn't he?"

"He tried to get me to talk to you, Karen. But I told him only you can handle your grief. It was months after I lost Janet that my feet settled squarely on the floor each morning."

"Dr. Carn doesn't seem to understand that," she said. She smiled, and abruptly her smile collapsed at the corners and tears flooded her eyes. She clutched at a box of tissues on the desktop below the counter, shoved a wad of them against her face, and, rising, ran around a corner toward the restrooms.

"That's a first," Carn said, coming up behind Loring. "Real tears."

Loring followed Karen and waited in the corridor. When she emerged, he asked if he could buy her coffee. A hesitant smile appeared on her face, then vanished.

"Sure," she said.

They took a seat at the far end of the cafeteria. Karen cupped the heavy white mug in her hands. Loring noticed her fingers. Tapered and not overly long, but extended by perfectly oval nails painted with many coats of deep, clear lacquer. He noticed her wrists, as well. Sturdy, not the wrists of a blacksmith, but with some muscle, leading into muscular forearms that disappeared under the pushed-up sleeves of her white blouse. Loring noticed too, how the blouse clung to the curve of Karen's broad shoulders and how, at the sides, under the fabric, her breasts swelled out over the sleeves, and he found himself looking to see whether her nipples showed. He suddenly became aware that his mind had wandered from Karen's grief. It was not the first time he had noticed Karen Larsen this way. She sat in the second row for his lectures sixteen years before at Riverton. She was pursued by many of the teaching doctors, but was not the kind of student who traded on her sexuality to influence her grade. At least, it occurred now to Loring, she had made no attempt to seduce him, as some other nursing students had. Perhaps he was not her type. Indeed, her type was Tom Grimes, and that was why they were now in the cafeteria.

"I didn't go to the funeral," she was saying, hunched over her coffee, drawing its warmth through her hands. "It didn't seem appropriate. But it's funny. At a time like that, I thought many times, what is appropriate? His wife is a terror who had driven Tom to near ruin. He had some good times with me. He was on his way to see me when it happened, you know."

He reached and squeezed her hand. "That must be very difficult, Karen."

"As long as I don't use certain words . . ." she paused and bit her lip, and he knew she was thinking of one of those words, a small vocabulary of loss and grief that could bring a spasm to her throat and pump her eyes full of tears. She fought them back now. "I'm working a double shift today. That seems to help. I just don't appreciate Dr. Carn trying to get me started. I just need to hold on, to ride this through."

"Do whatever it takes, Karen. And if you need someone to talk to, I've been there, too. I'd be happy to listen."

"You're sweet, Dr. English," she said. And then she took a sip of coffee, her first, and as her lips parted and touched the mug, with her face tilted down, she did something with those big eyelids, looked up from under them in some way that seemed to stop time and caused in Loring's heart a small jump, the sort he had not experienced in twenty years. He didn't notice that, just as their eyes met over her coffee, he drew a small draught of air through his nose and then held his breath, savoring the instant.

92

"MEC starts in ten minutes!" said a voice approaching from behind Loring.

"I'll be there, Conrad," Loring said, thinking: Saved from my own folly by an ill-mannered autocrat!

"Karen, I've got to go," he said, rising and touching her hand again. "But be sure to call me if you need to talk."

The Medical Executive Committee—the body that ruled on medical issues in the hospital—was the place where the largest physician egos did battle. It was the MEC, run by doctors, that held the hospital's businessmen accountable. It was the MEC that introduced new technologies and convinced the hospital to purchase the necessary supplies and equipment. It was the MEC that dealt with incompetent doctors, that voted on giving privileges to new physicians and that fought for enough medical professionals at all levels. The MEC was the neighborhood cop that kept the hospital's delivery of medical care honest.

About two-thirds of the members of the MEC had egos of a more modest size, and these doctors—all but three the heads of medical specialties—had little time for the committee, or the politics that run a hospital. Often a bare quorum was difficult to obtain at an MEC meeting. So Conrad Schmidt, as chairman of the department of surgery, had assigned himself the chore of corralling enough members to hold meetings.

There were no surprises when Loring, an at-large member, arrived with Dave Carn, who represented emergency medicine and for whom Loring once had analyzed the cast of MEC characters.

"Dave, my boy," Loring had said, "I'm going to instruct you on why you're not of more consequence in this world. Follow me as we travel down the path of importance, the roster of the Medical Executive Committee. First we have Dr. Stephen Nightingale, renowned carpenter who will replace your hip quick as Midas will check your shocks and find them wanting. A real genius—as is his fellow merchant, the good Dr. Ari Urizar, renowned slob and just the sort you want poking a

93

scope up your wazoo, a genius at finding fees where others find none. Next we come to Dr. Donald Zulauf, a real pisser who happens to be the only urologist working the pipes at Port Hancock General who has enough time to serve on the MEC which, I would suggest, may tell you something about him, except it would tell you something about you and me, too. Circling the table, we find Dr. Charlie November, chief of radiology and a former cokehead who is now a twelve-step junkie. Never saw a meeting he didn't want to attend. But at least he's a great doc. Next we have the esteemed Dr. Edward Meunch, a gregarious sort who, when he doesn't know what to do, quizzes the other cardiologists, tells a few jokes and then fakes it. The undertakers must love him. I understand they were behind his election as chairman of cardiology. At the other end of the spectrum, able to pitch forceps the length of the O.R. when he's really ticked, is that big hitter, Dr. Conrad Schmidt, almost, but not quite, certifiable. Then there's Little Napoleon, who is certifiable, Dr. Ralph Winters. Did I ever tell you about the time he comes into the O.R. on a neurosurgery consult, everyone's crammed around the table and they don't see little Ralph approaching? 'Stand back,' he yells, and all these green gowns step back and Ralphy, whose chin comes about to the top of the operating table unless he's got his footstool, steps up to the table. Except he had the wrong O.R., and the guy has a GI problem and when Ralphy reaches the table, he's got this big asshole staring at him and, Jesus, it must have been terrific to see, the thing goes off like a cannon. Gets Ralphy full in the face. But, I digress. Who else we got? Oh, sure, Helen. But she's another story," Loring had said.

That conversation was some time ago. This afternoon, most of the MEC that was coming had gathered and Helen Ramsey only needed one more for a quorum. Ramsey was chairperson of ob-gyn and president of the MEC, a job some male doctors believed she sought in order to gain control over men. Helen's skin was gray as dust, her hair dark and dull and pulled into an unattractive twist, her bones spindly as dry sticks. She was apparently unhappily married and certainly an unhappy per-

94

son. She scowled even in her official hospital photo, and complained often of the way the world treated her, even nursing old grudges from her previous career as a manager in a biotech corporation. "I was always underpaid," she would confide. "But of course, I was a woman!" She was, without question, the top ob-gyn at Port Hancock General, though, and her medical reputation, despite her personality quirks, earned her respect when she opened an MEC meeting.

"We have a packed agenda today, gentlemen," she said, her eyes cast down at papers she shuffled. "I would appreciate a one-day cessation of the petty interdepartmental disputes that so often stall our meetings."

"I suppose the dear president considers the concerns of some neurologists petty!" Ralph Winters snapped.

"If those concerns continue to be whether neuro-spines get the work that is going to ortho-spines, yes, you would be correct Dr. Winters," Helen Ramsey said, drilling a glance the length of the table. "Oh, nice that you could make it, Doctors O'Malley and Iannone," she said, without sarcasm.

Jack O'Malley's freckled face broke into a broad smile. "Glad to be here, Helen," he said, running stubby fingers through his rust-colored curls. O'Malley, chief of pediatrics and grandson of the tavern owner, took a seat beside Charlie November. Sam Iannone, head of internal medicine and the father of four adopted daughters, settled next to O'Malley.

Helen Ramsey now had one more than a quorum. It was time to turn the meeting over to Walter Scott.

"As some of you know," she said, "rumors are flying about the future of the hospital. The administration has been forcing each department to make do with less help on the floor. Insurance companies are pressuring PHG to trim costs well beyond the fat. Competition is driving down the fees the hospital can expect, and the length of patient stays is far below the levels this facility was built to provide." Ramsey turned in her seat to face Walter Scott, who sat at the end of the table to her right. "Our chief executive would like to address these problems and suggest some options. Walter?"

Scott lowered his face toward the table in preparation for pushing himself up out of his chair. His moist tongue flicked out of its lizard den and retreated as he rose, clutching his own sheaf of paper held by a rubber band. He made small theater out of removing the band and rolling it onto his wrist. Before speaking, he squared the sheets by tamping them on the table. He walked behind Ramsey to the seat opposite his, where Claire Watson, VP of human resources, sat beside Gail Osborne, nursing VP. He rested a hand on the back of Watson's chair.

"Helen has mentioned a few of the challenges Port Hancock General is facing. Here's the bottom line. This city is too small to have two hospitals, and I'm going to recommend to the trustees that we attempt to merge with Valleyview."

"No question they're duplicating some of our stuff," November said. "In radiology, we both do ultrasound and scans. If we took them over, there'd be less redundancy."

"I don't know about the other neurology guys," Winters said, his whine as irritating as a mosquito's. "But I can't see importing more competition right now. Things are tight enough."

"We're not talking about absorbing Valleyview," Scott said. "Quite the opposite." He twirled the rubber band around the fingers of both hands. "It's Port Hancock General that's the endangered species here. If we don't find a partner, the whole hospital could disappear."

"Fold Port Hancock into Valleyview?" Schmidt nearly screamed. His neck glowed red as an autumn sunset and he jumped up from his seat, flinging his chair violently, toppling it on its back. "The-hell-you-will, turncoat!"

"Conrad! Please!" Ramsey said. "Give our colleague an opportunity to explain."

"Colleague, hell! He's a drunk and a sycophant! He's got no business suggesting a merger!"

"Keep talking, Conrad. You're going to make my lawyer and me very wealthy," Scott said. His face was as flushed as Schmidt's neck, and when his words ceased, the tip of his tongue traced around the inside of his puffy lips.

"Gentlemen, will you both compose yourselves? We have important business to consider," Ramsey said, glaring at Schmidt. Ramsey watched until Schmidt settled back into his seat. "Please proceed, Mr. Scott," she said.

Port Hancock General had too much physical capital, Scott said, too expensive a plant to operate. Everything was patched together, whereas Valleyview, a newer institution, was constructed with current technology in mind. Moreover, the upstart hospital had managed to attract a high proportion of board-certified physicians, a reality that had already cost Port Hancock participation with one insurer.

"Others can be expected to drop us," Scott warned. "If we lost Coastal, for example, we would be bankrupt within a month. A merger is a defensive maneuver, the only one open to us."

"I don't understand how we suddenly became vulnerable, Walter," Loring said, rising from his seat in deference to Ramsey.

"It's classic entrenched management paralysis," said Urizar, who had tilted back his chair. "Nothing against you, Walter. But while PHG has been content to do a good job, the world has changed. Hancock Systems isn't downsizing because it can't produce integrated circuit boards any more but because shareholders demand downsizing. Fortunately for Hancock Systems, they recognize how the winds of the market are blowing. If they didn't, they'd find their stock dropping and their ability to play in the game vanishing."

"Something escapes me here," said Loring. "Aren't we charging the same amount for services as Valleyview? And aren't their expenses roughly the same as ours? Doesn't that add up to—"

"It adds up to our funeral, Dr. English," Scott interrupted. "I don't expect you to understand it with the few facts I have presented here. Hell, I don't know if you'll ever understand it. That's why doctors hire businessmen to run hospitals."

"And they run them aground!" Schmidt said.

"Cheap shot, Dr. Schmidt," Loring said with a wink at Dave

Carn. "Sure, at times we doubt Walter's competence, but does that give us a right to suggest he is acting alone in running PHG down?"

"What we need," Ramsey said, "is a steering committee to make contact with Valleyview's doctors and discuss merger prospects. Could I have a couple of volunteers?"

Loring, still on his feet, raised his hand.

"Sorry, Dr. English. I can't accept your participation. Any others?"

Helen Ramsey was not one of Loring's enemies. Her rejection startled him, and he sank to his seat confused, as she appointed Urizar and Nightingale to the committee.

Scott left then with Watson and Osborne. Ramsey cleared her throat.

"The next item on our agenda concerns you, Dr. English," she said. "We have received several complaints, and an ad hoc committee has met."

"Complaints?" Loring's hands went cold and his throat dry. "For God's sake, what are you talking about?"

"You have been charged as a disruptive physician, Dr. English. The ad hoc committee has heard testimony."

"Who complained?" Loring demanded, scanning the faces around the table. "Disruptive how?"

"The committee has a report to present to this body and a recommendation to make. I will have to ask you to leave the room, Doctor."

"This is an outrage! I insist that I be allowed to hear this report."

"It's confidential, Loring," Ramsey said. "I'm sorry. But you will have your opportunity to present a defense. Please leave now."

Ten . . .

For the first time since he and Neil Dunmore struck the deal that spawned Osler Medical Group, James Perkins Harvey III felt he had lost the helm of his enterprise. The Dragon was the problem. When the Dragon agreed to "engage" Grimes, Harvey expected subterfuge. There was no real proof that Grimes had found any damning evidence, and there was nothing hidden in Osler Medical Group's files that could lead to any penalty more problematic than a stiff fine. Doctors are seldom jailed for their stealing. Harvey had returned home late that night and found a message on his phone. He crossed back through the garage and knocked on the door of the guest suite. The Dragon greeted him with a smile.

"Dr. Grimes has agreed to be of no more concern," he told Harvey.

"What?"

"Apparently, he has met an untimely death," the Dragon said, offering Harvey a seat on his couch. "Would you like a drink from your well-stocked cabinet?"

Harvey took straight Scotch, which he downed in one gulp.

"I only asked you to question him," Harvey said, his voice suddenly hoarse.

"Our methods," the Dragon said, lighting a cigarette and blowing a cloud of smoke, "have been developed over centuries. When a man would dig into your soul, let him dig his own grave."

"An old Chinese proverb?"

"A rule of Triad society."

"I shall remember that rule," Harvey said.

As he thought about it later, Harvey understood the wisdom of the rule. An enemy left alive can be expected to return with more devilment, whereas a dead enemy is as harmless as a friend. Still, it would be many months before the mention of Thomas Grimes did not hit Harvey like a punch to the chest. He accepted this as a lesson. Not once did he consider divorc-

ing himself from the Dragon. Indeed, through his Triad con-
nections, the Dragon had assembled a thick dossier on William
Scarborough. Harvey visited Scarborough in the executive
suite at Coastal Insurance, where, on a November morning
when the hills surrounding Riverton were a leafless gray, he
presented the chief executive with a small portion of the documentation and, without bothering him with the details of his
agenda, invited him on a short cruise in the British Virgin
Islands aboard *Carassius Auratus*. "Really, Bill, don't worry
about this," Harvey said, patting the manila envelope he had
delivered. "Sorry to have even mentioned it. You ever been to
Tortola? Oh, we'll have to swing in there." Scarborough, too
stunned by the contents of the envelope to feel anger, smiled
the smile of the conquered.

"We'll do this right, too," Harvey grinned, an angler with his
fish alongside the boat. His only concern in approaching
Scarborough had been that the man could, like Harvey, have
feared nothing so much as giving quarter to another. Then
there would have been no dealing with him. But Harvey
guessed correctly that a man who yielded to his vices so readily did not have the spine to resist blackmail.

In the noon sun, Harvey, his deep tan contrasting with faded,
cut-off jeans and a white dress shirt unbuttoned and untucked,
met Scarborough at the pier and led him down the gangway to
a floating dock. A man in dark glasses, a cap with braided visor,
white slacks, and a royal blue polo shirt stood on the dock,
watching them approach.

"Captain, meet our guest, Mr. Scarborough," Harvey said,
grabbing the side of a ladder and stepping down into the
launch ahead of Scarborough. The captain offered his hand to
Scarborough, whose tentative steps revealed his unfamiliarity
with these elements. Scarborough was over six feet, thick
through the torso, like ziti to Harvey's capellini. His curly graying hair was carefully trimmed and, although he shaved twice
a day, his dark beard always cast a shadow on his jaw. On land,

he appeared to be a boulder. On the dock, he was a bag of loose marbles. But he rejected the captain's hand and climbed down to the launch unassisted.

The harbor water was barely riffled by a light breeze, and the launch, piloted by a harbor crewman, sped smoothly through the moored yachts until they pulled alongside a striking white schooner with a main mast towering behind its little companion, the foremast. The honey-brown teak glowed under thick coats of varnish. Stretched on beach towels on the foredeck were two women, both young, both wearing thongs and dark glasses, one covered modestly with a man's white dress shirt. The one in the shirt, the shorter of the two, a blond with close-cropped hair, turned her head away when the launch arrived. The other, a lanky brunette with pale blue eyes and a fetching overbite, stood and called out to the launch.

"Did you bring one for me, J.H.?"

Harvey looked back to Scarborough, whose face was almost grim. Then, as the launch nudged against the rubber fenders hanging over the side of the yacht, he turned and looked up at the brunette. "He's yours if you want him, Lucy," he said. "Lucy, meet Bill. Bill, say hello to Lucy. Our other guest is Sue, who appears to have drifted off."

Sue Czernicki looked back toward the launch party and a polite smile slipped briefly across her lips. She propped herself on her right elbow and lowered her dark glasses to look over the tops. She still wore her broad wedding band. She had told her husband Chris that she was attending a seminar in Florida paid for by the hospital. The lie was provided by Harvey when Sue had protested that she couldn't risk this trip. When she balked again, he warned her: Make your explanations and be at the airport or we're through. It should have been the invitation she had been seeking, a chance to break off this dangerous game. In her soul, she did not want Harvey, but particularly when he got tough with her, her heart weakened and she could not deny him. So she told the lie, at the same time loathing herself.

Sue rose as the launch party boarded *Carassius Auratus* and stepped to the ladder amidships, her arms folded to close the unbuttoned shirt over her bathing suit. Harvey climbed aboard first, ignoring her when he passed.

"Your stateroom is forward, down through this companionway," he said, motioning Scarborough to follow him. The wood of the ladder they descended glowed with many layers of varnish, clear as plate glass. Below deck, the walls of the broad compartments were panelled with polished rosewood and holly. There were bulkheads between the rooms of the vessel with doors that, when shut, created airtight chambers like those of a submarine, capable of keeping the boat afloat even if another part of its hull had ruptured. Fine crystal globes cast a sparkling light from the ceiling fixtures in each compartment. The two men passed first through the saloon and then, going forward, the galley and into a corridor. Off this passageway were the crew's quarters and a small lavatory, or head, complete with tile shower. The forward state room was lined with built-in bureaus crafted of the same glowing lumber as the first ladder and had its own tile lavatory and shower. Atop one bureau was a beveled mirror in a hand-carved frame, also of that wood.

"Settle in, Bill," Harvey said. "We'll be casting off momentarily. As soon as you're ready, come topside and we'll put you to work on the lines."

The schooner's sails were set and the boat heeled sharply to starboard when Scarborough emerged through the companionway. Harvey, standing behind the wheel with a foot braced against the lower starboard cockpit bench, looked at his guest with the eye of a collector who, with his latest acquisition, has nearly monopolized his field of interest. The information in the dossier had made Scarborough listen. This jaunt across the Caribbean would make him an eager collaborator. The captain, Bengt Norstrand, was in the navigation station, charting a course for a distant island. The always smiling cook, Billy Highsmith, was in the galley preparing an afternoon meal. He wore his red hair in an overgrown bush, and his small paunch was evidence that he liked his work. Harvey had already arranged for a smorgasbord in the cockpit suitable for

Scarborough's appetites. A small teak beverage cart was locked in place before the wheel, with crystal glasses and bottles of the finest branded spirits, each in its own slot. In a drawer below the bottles was a packet of rolling papers and a tin of marijuana, along with a tightly capped silver vial of cocaine. Decorating the benches in the cockpit were Lucy and Sue. At Harvey's insistence, Sue had removed the white shirt, revealing her ample, and wholly natural, proportions. Just as Scarborough raised his foot to step out of the companionway, Harvey nudged the wheel sharply to port. The huge sails, already stretched tight in the breeze, caught the wind more directly and the schooner leaned even further onto its side. Scarborough grabbed the handrails of the companionway, trying to keep himself upright. His facial muscles strained in alarm. Harvey chuckled to himself.

"You'll get your sea legs quickly," he assured the insurance man. "Choose your poison." Harvey waved to the liquor chest. "That will speed the process." He was pleased to see Scarborough take a tumbler and scoop some ice. The alcohol in his drink would work slowly, and he would be neither too juiced to concentrate nor too mellow to care about what came next. Later, the entertainment Harvey had planned would go well with either pot or coke. For now, rum seemed ideal, and that is what Scarborough poured.

They had cleared the harbor and were in deep, blue water, with the wind coming hard from the west and the water hissing just below the schooner's gunwale. Harvey lifted a radio microphone, flipped a switch and asked Norstrand for a compass bearing. He flipped another switch.

"All hands on deck!" Harvey's voice crackled from speakers above and below decks, and an instant later, Norstrand, Highsmith, and two Latino men, short and muscular, appeared. All four wore white duck trousers and blue polo shirts, and began pulling on sheets and cranking winches. *Carassius Auratus* turned her bow through the oncoming wind and, overhead, the main and foremast booms swung across the decks. Now the breeze hit Harvey squarely on the right shoulder as he stood behind the wheel. With the sails swung far out to his left, he was able to keep the boat more upright, yet she was moving even more swiftly across the sea.

"Harden the main," he called out, and the two Latino deckhands tightened up the sheet, Hector cranking the winch and Joseph taking up the slack line. The mainsail nudged closer to the boat and every square inch of its fabric drew tight as a T-shirt on a beer belly. Harvey motioned to Joseph, who took over the helm. Norstrand and Hector slipped below deck through a forward companionway. Harvey then suggested that Sue and Lucy return to their sunbathing on the foredeck while he and Scarborough talked. The three men watched from the cockpit as the women, barefoot, made their way cautiously along the high side of the deck, the wind tossing their hair. Then, for privacy, Harvey took Scarborough forward in the cockpit, away from Joseph.

"Pull out of Port Hancock General," Harvey said quietly, without a word of introduction. Foreplay is for sex, he believed. In business, deliver the point quickly and keep up the offensive. Keep your adversary on his heels and he can't outthink you. He looked at Scarborough's eyes as he delivered this punch, and he saw the appropriate confusion, bleeding into panic. A calm settled over Harvey.

"Jim, that's ridiculous. The board will never go for it. PHG is our biggest provider in the city."

"We control the board at Valleyview, and we are going to merge the two hospitals. The PHG board may need a nudge, and losing Coastal's business is going to be it. Convincing your board is your problem to solve." He still watched the eyes, the face. Scarborough's nostrils flared and his chest heaved slightly. The insurance man sucked at his drink, thinking. Good, Harvey thought. He's remembering his incentive!

"But with PHG gone, Coastal loses much of its leverage with Valleyview," Scarborough said.

"That's not a problem for us, Bill, and this is not a matter for debate. You have to decide where your loyalty lies. We will bring PHG down. I'd suggest you're safer on our side."

104

Scarborough's jaw tensed. He was a man accustomed to directing his own destiny. In a decade at Coastal, where he had been recruited as executive vice president and was groomed to be CEO, he had ridden the wave that carried the power in the medical industry into the hands of insurance executives. At age fifty-six, he was finally in a position to dictate terms. Hospital executives, once his arrogant adversaries, now cowered before him. He smoked in their no-smoking facilities and they said nothing. He made suggestions about the necessity of certain medical procedures, and they ordered their physicians to curtail those procedures. Even those who wouldn't lick his boots at least complied with his business wishes. Now, a surgeon was sitting across the cockpit of this yacht giving him orders. He considered telling Harvey to shove his dossier. Instead, he swallowed the remains of his rum and, standing unsteadily against the heel of the boat, went to the liquor cabinet and scooped some more ice, which he washed with more rum.

"That concludes our business, Bill," Harvey said. Scarborough bunched his cheeks as if swallowing a bitter pill, then raised his glass in a toast toward Harvey, who continued: "The rest of this trip is an introduction to the pleasures our partnership will provide us both."

After the buffet, served by Joseph and Hector on the cockpit table, they turned in at a small, uninhabited island and dropped anchor. Hector got a folding chair for Scarborough and set it up on the deck in the shade of the furled sails. Sue and Lucy jumped in the water with masks and snorkels, and Harvey, an all-star receiver at UNC whose off-season sport was diving, climbed the mast to the first spreaders, wing-like metal struts that pushed the supporting cables away from the mast. Standing on the spreader and holding the stainless steel cable, he looked down thirty feet to Scarborough on the deck and the women in the green water, calling to him to join them. It would be inaccurate to say he was content. Those driven by anger cannot find contentment. But he was precisely where he wanted to be. His arcing swan dive was perfectly executed, entirely under his control.

The setting sun melted in an orange pool on the horizon and the high clouds wore darkening shades of pink. Harvey and his guests dressed for dinner in *Carassius Auratus*'s crew uniform—the men in blue polo shirts and white Bermudas, the women in white tank tops and blue short skirts—and dined in the saloon on Salmon Highsmith. Harvey asked Scarborough to select the wine. Joseph took the guest into the galley, where a closet stocked top to bottom served as a wine cellar. Hector lit two candles on the table. Harvey chose the music, all Debussy.

Lucy, when she had quit swimming, had pulled a chair beside Scarborough's. She was twenty-seven, an aspiring sales-person at a medical supply company. She could talk business with Scarborough, and had. Every chance she got to agree with him, she had touched his hand, a meaningless pat. By dinner, Scarborough was squeezing Lucy's hand every other sentence. He had kicked off his sneakers, and his toes found hers under the table. Her toes traced along his instep and wrapped them-selves somehow around his little toe and squeezed back. Powerfully.

They took after-dinner drinks in the cockpit, where a mild breeze perfumed the air with the smells of the sea. Lucy brought out a cotton blanket and spread it across the starboard bench and she and Scarborough wrapped themselves in it. Across the cockpit, Sue curled for warmth beside Harvey's shoulder. They had no blanket, and her arms were puckered in goose flesh. Harvey ignored her. In the quiet darkness, Harvey watched Lucy working her long leg over Scarborough's knee as they muttered to each other. Lucy rolled a joint and she and Scarborough had smoked the whole thing by the time Harvey reached around Sue and cupped his hand against the side of her head, drawing her toward him. He stuck his nose against her hair and whispered.

"Go below and get a beach towel and the remote. And put on the *Bolero*."

Sue smiled, pecked his cheek, and with her shoulders hunched against the chill, scampered down into the glow of the companionway. When she returned, she closed the hatch and, kneeling on the cushion beside Harvey, handed him the remote and prepared to wrap a big, white terry cloth towel around his shoulders. Again he pulled her to him and whispered. She jerked back.

"No!" she whispered sharply.

He grabbed her hand and yanked her down on top of himself, holding the back of her head firmly. She struggled, but he would not let her go. Again he whispered in her ear.

"Do it!" he said, his rumbling voice no longer a whisper, and then he released her. She pushed herself off his chest and, circling his legs, climbed up on the seat and then onto the top of the cabin, just forward of the cockpit. She sat there, chest against her knees, wrapping herself in the towel, big as a blanket. Harvey glanced across the cockpit. Lucy's and Scarborough's heads poked out of the opening in their blanket, and they both looked toward Sue in anticipation. Harvey rose and stepped to the control board in front of the wheel, where he flipped a toggle. A light partway up the mast lit, throwing a beam down on Sue.

"Now," Harvey said, resuming his place on the cockpit seat, turning slightly to face Sue and pushing a button on the remote. Under the glow of the spotlight, as Ravel's *Bolero* began, she pulled the towel close, shutting her eyes. Beneath the towel, it was clear, she was pulling her tank top over her head. Then she reclined, spreading the towel over herself like a blanket, under which she now appeared to be removing her skirt. A sliver of blue fabric slid out under the edge of the white towel. With the music's rhythmic pulse still in low gear, she settled onto the cabin roof, her body fully extended. Now her hands emerged from the towel and her fingers combed slowly through her own blond hair, caressing her scalp. The towel fell off her elbows, exposing her naked shoulders. She trailed her fingers down her neck, lightly across her shoulders and then back up over her cheeks and, as the music momentarily rose, a deep breath flowed into her and her chest heaved and her breasts, now naked against the terrycloth, rose, pulling at the towel so that her small feet were exposed. Harvey glanced across the cockpit. Scarborough was sitting more upright, the blanket having slipped down behind him and Lucy, and his attention was welded to Sue's form, moving under the towel. Harvey smirked and looked back at Sue, whose fingers, fully extended, combed back up through her hair and then down along her neck and under the towel, moving smoothly over the curves of her breasts, circling each one gently and then pushing back up, vigorously, as she felt her own nipples growing erect against her fingertips. She opened her eyes a slit, enough that Harvey could see the dark glistening between her lids. He gestured to her. She closed her eyes tight, her hands still moving against her skin. She looked again, and again Harvey motioned. Damn-you creases formed on her brow, but her curled fingers did as he had insisted, appearing at the top edge of the towel and slowly, as if pulling back the sheet from a sleeping child, shoving the towel's edge all the way to her navel, exposing her breasts, creamy white globes under the mast light, and her nipples, red and rigid. Scarborough moved to the front of his seat, gripping its edge, ignoring Lucy, which was of little consequence because Lucy's hands were now up under her own tank top, caressing her own breasts as her tongue licked the inside of her lips. The music's intensity grew and one of Sue's hands slid below the edge of the towel, traced back up to her navel and then ventured deeper below the towel. She gasped and her whole body stiffened, her other hand still circling both breasts.

"Oh, Chris!" Sue moaned, "Oh! Oh Jesus!" Her knees rose and spread and *Bolero* pounded and now the towel was snarled around one of Sue's legs but otherwise she was totally naked, her body twisting side to side, as if in search of something, the fingers of one hand pressing hard against her breast, those of the other hand plunging again and again, deep between her legs.

Scarborough leaped to his feet and Harvey could see him starting forward, toward Sue, when Lucy sprang up from the cockpit seat, wrapping her arms around Scarborough's waist and tearing at his Bermuda shorts. Scarborough's forward momentum was halted at the knees by the woman tackling him, and he spun and fell along the seat, where Lucy jumped on him, grabbing his hand and holding it against her crotch, even as, up on the cabin roof, Sue screamed out the final music of her orgasm.

Harvey, unaroused by voyeurism, now, in the midst of this mass climax, felt an erection growing, triggered by the sense of power he had just experienced. Dominance, for him, felt even better than sex.

Eleven . . .

Loring was halfway down the household cleanser aisle, bent over to read a price, when Carmella Parente, pushing a cart, rounded the corner at the far end. He started to rise to greet her—his hand was in mid-wave—when she stopped abruptly and, looking over her shoulder, backed her cart out of the aisle. He put an economy box of detergent on the lower rack of his cart and headed in Carmella's direction. She was not on the next aisle—paper products. He didn't need anything there, anyway. Nor was she on either side of the isle of bread racks, where he stopped for a loaf of twelve grain, the last item on his list. He was pleased to see her just entering one of the check-out lines, however, and he pushed his cart up behind her.

"Last-minute Thanksgiving shopping?" His face cranked in a grin, prepared for her sass.

"Oh, dear," she said softly, and her head seemed to sink turtle-like down into the collar of her coat.

"Carmella?" he called to the back of her head.

She turned slowly. A worried scowl creased her brow.

"Hello, Dr. English," her voice timid as a child's.

"Dr. English? What happened to Loring Hon?"

"Oh, my, I'm so embarrassed," she said.

"Embarrassed? But why, Carmella?" He could see she was

"Really, I didn't have a choice," she said, looking away and opening her pocketbook. "I wanted to stay with you." She rummaged through the purse contents.

"Carmella, I'm not following you."

She looked up at him. "You don't . . . I thought . . . they'd already told you. They said I couldn't see you any more! That was a month ago." The shopper in front of her moved forward, and Carmella began busily loading her purchases on the conveyor belt.

"Who said that," Loring asked, nudging his cart ahead. He did not need to ask. He had been informed already by some medical plans.

Coastal Insurance, she answered.

"Please tell me you've found another cardiologist, then," he said.

No. An internist, she said. At Osler. "The insurance lady sent me there. Oh, dear! I feel like a traitor!" He saw her eyes moisten.

"Now, now, Carmella. You had no choice." He reached ahead and patted her shoulder. "The most important thing is that you get decent care. You could be seeing Mike Bernstein. He's in my office, but Coastal hasn't blackballed him."

Indeed, it was only Bernstein's presence that kept Loring's office open, so swiftly had his practice fallen apart after the Port Hancock Board of Trustees—his own board—voted to suspend his privileges indefinitely. First was the report of the ad hoc committee to the Medical Executive Committee. There had been confidential interviews with anonymous doctors and nurses. There were charges of temper tantrums, of comments hostile toward the hospital and its administration in front of patients. There were allegations that Loring had caused delays in the cath lab by arriving late for his procedures. It was all handed forward to the trustees.

But there wasn't a solitary detail. No times and dates of the alleged disruptions. No patient or staff names.

Aldie Spencer, Loring's lawyer, accompanied him when he was allowed to appear before the trustees. But Aldie was not permitted to speak or to counsel Loring. The trustees then caucused. When they returned they announced that, by a seven to four vote, Loring English's privileges to practice at Port Hancock General Hospital would, in order to preserve patient safety and avoid disruption in the hospital, be suspended indefinitely.

Aldie quickly filed for a stay in court. There was no due process, he argued in his brief. The lack of witnesses whom Loring could confront, the denial of Loring's right to counsel, the utter lack of details in the charges made this the worst kind of kangaroo court, Aldie told Judge Vincent Pushinski. The judge agreed that, in his courtroom, the charges would be thrown out. "But hospitals in this state have, historically, been given a certain leeway to conduct their affairs under slightly less stringent rules," he explained, gesturing like the apologetic hangman. "Hospitals know better than this court what their needs are, and this system has, for the most part, worked well."

Judge Pushinski's order denying a stay accompanied PHG's notice to the national medical data bank, which informs insurance companies of the status of doctors. Quickly, in order to avoid liability of their own, those companies removed Loring from their rolls of approved physicians.

Aldie immediately filed an appeal, but the appeals court delayed consideration of the case, scheduling a hearing for after the new year. So Loring, whose medical license was unaffected, continued to see men and women without insurance. And Bernstein took on those of Loring's old patients who had not been steered elsewhere.

Loring at first was stunned by the judge's ruling. He was accustomed to having all the answers, being in charge. The suddenness with which he lost all this baffled him. One possible explanation, however, comforted him. He assumed his problems arose because he had struck some nerve, perhaps with his complaint against Jim Harvey. (Even though that had fallen on deaf ears.) Perhaps with Scott. The list of antagonists was long. Just as long, Loring thought with an inner sneer, as the list of incompetents. A part of him grieved for the patients snatched from him. Although Valleyview's board had summoned its own ad hoc committee and was prepared to suspend Loring, he still had privileges at Riverton, and that blunted the pain. He was mulling these events, sitting in his office. Everyone had left for the night. A lamp with a lacquered red metal shade lit the papers on his desk. A framed photo of Janet was off in the desktop shadows. She had warned him about the cost of his battles. He smiled at her. Until now, he had been spared the price. Having finally to pay for his ideals, though, he felt not anguish but pride. He wore his suspension as a badge. Privately, inside, where his sneer lived. There was only one person whom he knew who could appreciate this sense of humble righteousness. Dave Carn applauded Loring's many stands, just as Loring cheered Carn's efforts against mindless medicine. He now picked up the phone to dial the Port Hancock General emergency room, knowing a talk with Carn would bolster his spirits.

Carn was busy with a patient. Loring asked to leave a message, which the clerk, Juan, read back.

"Just a minute, Dr. English," Juan said. "Someone wants to speak with you."

"Dr. English?" He recognized Karen Larsen's deep, musical voice, somewhere between a viola and a cello.

"Karen, I can't say I'm surprised it's you. If I'd called at midnight, I wouldn't be surprised."

"Oh, I'm not working quite so many double shifts, Dr. English. Things have settled down a bit."

"Good. I knew you would handle the situation."

"Well, I guess you're right. But the reason I picked up the phone was, remember when you offered to, you know, lend an ear?"

"Sure, Karen, any time. Is it urgent?" Loring had been tilted back in his high-backed leather chair, but now, without noticing, he had tipped forward, resting his forearms on his desk, curling around the receiver.

"No, not really. But that day in the cafeteria, that really helped. And I guess there are times when I could, well, benefit from having the same kind of talk. But I know you're busy . . ."

"I'm a whole lot less busy these days. Could you make a later dinner? My treat?"

"Only Dutch, Dr. English."

"Dutch it is. Tonight?"

The bed was a tangle of sheets and blankets when he got home, unaltered from when he left in the morning. He found Menace, a seventeen pound calico cat, settled between the folds where the sheets were mounded, on Janet's side. He loosened his tie and unbuttoned his collar and sat on the bed beside the cat. Menace rolled onto his back and stretched, offering Loring his belly. Loring looked at the night stand, where a framed picture of them standing by a wooden rowboat was propped below a lamp. He turned the lamp on to better look at the photograph. Gazing at Janet's eyes, he thought of Gabriella. He hadn't been able to reach her at college all week. She missed him at the office. Phone tag. I promised to spend more time with your child. He spoke in his thoughts to Janet's picture. And now she's too busy. Menace rolled onto his stomach and Loring began stroking his back, his mind drifting further toward his midnight dinner with Karen Larsen. He looked again at Janet. It's not a date, he told her in his mind. She just wants someone to talk with. Lifting Menace off the bed, he straightened the covers and, for the first time since Janet's death, put on a bed-spread. Then he showered and, again for the first time in a year, shaved for dinner. In the mirror, he saw a trickle of shaving cream descending his neck and dirty drops of the stuff hanging in the thicket of gray hair on his sagging chest. He groaned.

"Good thing it isn't a date," he sighed.

Oil paintings of Italian ports hung on all the walls at DiRenzo's. The paintings were not fine art but were of a quality suggesting the painter—perhaps Mrs. DiRenzo, who owned the restaurant with her husband, Guido—knew the scene well enough not to need a photograph. DiRenzo's was just a corner bar before Guido discovered people from Port Hancock General liked his cooking. It was two blocks downtown from the hospital, and now, even after midnight, when shifts changed, the dinner crowd outnumbered the regulars, who sat at the bar sipping beers while sports teams moved balls across the overhead television screens.

Loring helped Karen with her coat and, for the first time, saw her in something other than a white blouse. She must have rushed home, he thought. Her red hair fell down over the shoulders of a trim black jacket that covered a black dress, snug without being tight. She wore a simple string of pearls, sheer stockings and black pumps. Taking her coat from her shoulders, he was close enough to inhale her perfume and to see the shine of her hair and how it fell smoothly across the cloth of her jacket and, when she sat in the booth, how the jacket moved over the fabric of her dress and how the dress moved along her thigh. When he caught himself accumulating this data, he thought: Rotten old boy! It meant nothing. Never during his long, faithful marriage with Janet had he stopped noticing women. But while Karen was, rather exquisitely, a woman, she was also a grieving friend and that kept things simple for Loring.

The waiter arrived with a basket of bread and burned his fingers with one match before lighting, with the second, a candle in a glass bowl wrapped with white plastic netting.

"This is the first time I've been to dinner in months," Loring said when the waiter left. "Thanks for getting me out, Karen."

"I know what you mean, Dr. English. I've been a regular at the cafeteria for a while now."

"I'd like it if you dropped the 'doctor,' Karen. Makes me feel like I'm still the lecturer at Riverton and you're the student in the second row."

"What a memory," she said, arching one eyebrow. "Was I that conspicuous?"

114

"You were memorable, Karen. For your drive alone."

"Drive is what's gotten me everywhere, Doctor—"

"Uh, uh!—"

"Loring. Geez, that sounds funny. Not your name, just me saying it."

"You were saying? About where drive has gotten you?"

"Well, sure. I made nursing supervisor pretty quickly and not because I came in with the highest college grades. And since Tom died, I set myself a goal to get through the grief, and I'm there, or almost. There are some bad days, but mostly it's okay."

The waiter returned and took drink orders. Loring's was decaffeinated coffee. Karen ordered white wine.

"How long had you and Dr. Grimes been together, if I'm not intruding," he asked, switching into diagnostician mode, a safe way to keep this man-woman thing honest.

"It was more than a year, and you know Loring, it was the best year I'd ever had. I could drop everything for him. He had a heart big as a mountain. He was ten years older than me, and he was still motivated by ideals. I guess I'm not telling you any thing new, being a cardiologist in the same city."

"I never worked with Dr. Grimes, to be honest. We docs in private practice can get pretty isolated."

Karen started to speak, but the waiter arrived with their drinks and took their orders. When he left, she sipped her wine, thinking. Loring waited.

"Tom seemed quiet until you got to know him. I think he was just too busy all those years trying to keep his life together and to practice medicine. Things were pretty out of control with his wife."

"I'd heard hints."

Karen offered a few examples of Kathy Grimes's behavior, unpleasant and hurtful, fueled by her bitter refusal to let go of a marriage that had long ago gone sour.

"I always knew I'd been blessed with Janet," Loring said when Karen finished. "Somehow I lucked out and chose right, through no virtue of my own. Hell, I was only twenty-four when we met. But it was like we were two pieces of a puzzle, both of us adding to the strength of our marriage, and each of us fulfilling the needs of the other."

"That's so romantic, Loring. You must really miss her."

"I do, and yet, it's peculiar, I don't. It's like she's still with me in important ways. Her loss was extraordinarily painful, and it took a lot of work to get to the point where I could accept it. As you say, there are some tough days still. But on the whole, no," he said, stirring his coffee and staring down into its swirl. Maybe that's because my memories are all happy ones. Once you reconcile yourself to the loss, you can only rejoice in your luck in having good memories."

Karen clasped her hands and set her chin on them, leaning toward Loring on her elbows and smiling. "I've never heard anything so beautiful," she said, her voice a husky whisper that stirred Loring. "You had the perfect marriage."

"Perfect for me, yes. But that's the irony." He leaned back in his seat, hands on the table, eyes to the ceiling as, without warning, tears rose, sudden as an ocean sunrise. He felt Karen's hand on his, and the distraction instantly halted the flow of grief, a change of which Karen was unaware.

"The irony?" she asked, and as she leaned closer, against the edge of the table, her jacket parted, revealing the smooth flow of her skin down to the squared neck of her dress. Loring politely retrieved his hand, confused thoughts and images flickering before him.

"On the day I lost her," he said, working toward the point cautiously as a man venturing onto an icy walkway, "throughout that whole day, something had been bothering me. I finally figured it out late in the afternoon. I realized that in our twenty-one years together, everything went smoothly because she so often yielded to me. As soon as I saw this," he said, clenching his jaw against another wave of tears. He pushed through the sadness. "As soon as I knew this, I realized I could change myself, and I vowed to be there more for Janet. And that is when she left me."

Karen reached across the table, taking Loring's hand and pulling it toward her, then clasping it in both hands.

"If you cared that much to recognize one problem, you cared more than most men ever do," she said, tears filming her own eyes, chased there by her own memories. "I don't believe for a moment that Janet, or any woman, wouldn't have already recognized that truth."

His dinner with Karen had affected him in a way he had not anticipated. He felt great comfort talking with her, comfort and openness. It was an experience he would like to repeat. And this, in one sense, concerned him. He wondered if it was simply his masculinity reacting to her femininity. He wasn't ready for that, and that seemed not to be the case. He felt no lust. But he did feel warmth.

He searched his memory for his feelings toward Janet the first time they connected. They were both medical students, both a long way from home, but they did not meet at Presbyterian. It was on the train between New York and Washington, on the way home for Christmas break. He had seen her around, of course, and so when, boarding the rail car, he recognized the waves of dark hair curling just above the seat back, he stopped to say hello before he looked for a seat of his own. She had a textbook open and resting on her knee, and her smile was friendly if not too interested. The book was first-year anatomy, and Loring remarked on it. Janet invited him to take the seat by the window, which he did, but he never looked out the window until they reached Union Station. He would discover much later the pains Janet had taken to be on his train and to arrive before him. The book, he learned later, was a prop, a conversation piece. When the trip ended, Janet worried that she might have talked too much, that she bored Loring and would never again speak with him. He had made no move when they parted ways at the station to get her telephone number in New York. She spent the entire Christmas break too miserable to do anything but study. Loring? He spent the whole vacation kicking himself for failing to suggest anything resembling a date. He had gone through all the potential scenarios. Hey, why don't we grab something to eat at the station before we leave? Or: I've enjoyed this ride. Why don't we try to take the train back together? At the time, he had thought of nothing, and so he, too, told his parents he had to cram and disappeared into his room for days on end.

This thing with Karen shared some of that intensity, yet it was different. One big difference was that then, his heart was unclaimed. Now it still belonged to Janet. But he did want to hear the murmur of Karen's voice, which to him was as comforting as the soft thudding of the surf from behind the dunes. And he did think of scenes from the restaurant—the black dress and white pearls, the sharing of memories of Janet and Tom Grimes. For both of them, it was a chance to unburden themselves with someone safe, understanding. Once they got started, she had unloaded what seemed like a life's history. She talked about the men, unnamed, she had dated before Grimes. Their flaws, she said she now understood, were the very reason she had chosen them—so she would have a reason to discard them before they disappeared. She talked about her alcoholic father, and her emotionally absent mother. A cipher, she called her. And she talked about how, after one particularly draining and demoralizing relationship with a doctor who had a cocaine habit, she joined a twelve-step program for families of addicts and learned something about her own problem. It was there she met Grimes. And in him, she said, she found the opposite of all the men she had known previously.

They had talked of other things, as well. She asked about his suspension. Loring made light of it and, as a diversion, mentioned the merger rumors that were making the rounds. "In my gut, I'm suspicious," he said. "But if you're very clinical about it, if you add up the costs and the benefits, it may be necessary."

She said everyone at Port Hancock General was feeling edgy. He told her that with her qualifications, her future would be secure, with or without a merger. She was flattered, and she asked if they could do this again in few weeks. "It's given me a bigger boost than you could know," she said.

Loring's secretary, Nancy, buzzed him the next morning.

"It's the ER," she said over the intercom.

He picked up the phone.

"Good morning, Dr. English." The music of the voice untied a knot, and Loring felt himself relax back into his seat.

"Good morning, Nurse Larsen."

She laughed. "Oh, Loring. I had such a wonderful time last night. I would have sent a thank you note, but I wanted you to know right away how much I appreciated it."

"I hope I didn't keep you too late. It must have been difficult getting in to the ER this morning at seven."

"I didn't go. I'm still home in bed. I just told your secretary it was the ER so she wouldn't get suspicious."

"Suspicious?"

"Look, Loring. I mean I really enjoyed last night. You make it so easy to talk, and there was so much more I wanted to hear from you and I was wondering. Can we do it again?"

He was unaware that his finger was clicking the mouse of his desktop computer, scrolling through patient files. Something in her tone, in her melodic words, tripped a switch inside him and now he was regarding her not solely as a pleasant companion. Certainly, her choice of words was a suggestion. People become suspicious of a man and woman for only one reason, he thought. And if she were thinking in that vein, then there was an opportunity for him with Karen. He was flattered. He recognized the perils of a response. He knew there was too much of Janet yet in him to contemplate bringing another woman into his life. And yet he had always been one who allowed himself, within the limits of good sense and moral decency, to react to instinct, and that voice–that Karen voice–stirred many instincts. He decided to play it down the middle for now. He certainly had enjoyed himself at the restaurant. And her presence in his life seemed to have stimulated some of his better qualities.

"I suppose tonight would be too soon," he said, his eyes carelessly scanning his computer screen, his cheeks bunched in a grin, elongating his nostrils, creating an image that, when he had seen it in the shaving mirror many times, he thought looked moronic. He did not think about that now. When you feel cared for, you accept your flaws as virtues.

"Couldn't you play hooky?" she teased.

"Well . . . that would mean letting down my patients."

There was a long silence then, and finally Loring asked: "Karen, are you there."

"You still miss her, don't you?"

"Of course. Why?"

"Loring, look. I just remembered, I've got a prior engagement tonight," Karen said, her voice now tight in her throat, the music gone. "In fact, I'd better get going now. I'll talk to you later."

"Wait, Karen. Let's meet for coffee at lunch. No need to rush things."

"That's it, Loring," she said, barely whispering. "I was rushing, and now I'm not. Goodbye."

Twelve . . .

Merger rumors and managed care—added to Walter Scott's recent cost control measures, which included downsizing the Port Hancock Hospital staff—not only increased employee anxiety, but increased their stress levels as well. Nowhere was this more apparent than in the emergency department, where stress normally runs high anyway. Karen Larsen and ER director Dave Carn found more and more of their time devoted to filling in for their nurses and doctors.

Bill Callahan, relegated to single coverage for the first four hours of his shift, was trying not to seem irritated or impatient as he attempted to expedite a medical history from Joe Burns, a truck driver he was attending. Another trucker was passing Burns's rig on the Interstate where it begins its long descent from the mountains just west of Port Hancock. Burns was pulling an empty forty-foot box; the other rig was hauling a load of sewer pipe, and had momentum. Before his tailgate even reached Burns's door, the other trucker began to pull into Burns's lane. Burns explained all of this to Callahan in sentences interrupted by his need to inhale through his mouth. His nose and eyes were swollen shut.

"That son of a bitch," Burns said, inhaling a gulp of air, "*had* to have seen me in his right mirror." He stopped and filled his lungs several times through his mouth. Burns was a tall, stout column of a man and, even seated as he was on the gurney in examination room Three, he seemed to nearly reach the ceiling. His long, oily hair was combed straight back, the strands twisting into tendrils that fell behind his ears and brushed the yoke of his plaid shirt. The meat of his brow was traversed by one deep crease. There were red spheres the size of tennis balls where his eyes should be, and his nose had been bandaged and had bled into the bandaging.

"So, did you hit the brakes and smash your face on the steering wheel?" Callahan wondered.

"No, damn it," Burns said. "I veered to the right, into the breakdown lane." He paused for a breath. "Allowing that bastard to enter my lane." Another pause. "You want to avoid traveling in the breakdown lane." Pause and several deep breaths. "All manner of garbage collects there—its a hazard for tires."

"I need to know the details of your injury, Mr. Burns. Please go on," Callahan said, snipping the bandaging on the man's nose with scissors and lifting an edge of gauze.

Karen Larsen stepped into the room. "I've beeped Dr. Barnett for Mrs. Johnson in Two," she said. "She's continuing to hemorrhage."

"Are the floaters that nursing administration sent helping you any, Karen?"

"Not much, Dr. Callahan. They're pediatric nurses. They don't have a clue when it comes to evaluating adults. I have Sue Czernicki handling Mrs. Johnson."

"I'll be out to help you in a minute, Karen," he said, turning back to Burns. "We're a little short-handed, so I need to move along with you. Now tell me how you hurt your face."

After the other trucker passed him, Burns got back in the lane behind him. No sooner had he done this, however, than a chain came loose from on top the other truck. This freed a spare wheel rim, which fell to the road and bounced up into Burns's windshield, shattering it.

"There must be more. These sure don't look like glass injuries," Callahan said. "And I doubt we'd be talking now if that wheel hit you."

"I flashed my lights and sounded my air horn about a hundred times," Burns said. He drew another mouthful of air. "He finally pulled over. I stopped behind him."

Burns had climbed down from his idling tractor and started to walk toward the cab of the other truck. He saw the other driver climb down, a tall, lean fellow wearing a cowboy hat, a fleece-lined denim jacket, and a broad smile.

The state police had found Burns unconscious on the pavement, his nose flattened by a punch he never saw coming.

"Seems the roadways are littered with human garbage as well," Burns told Callahan.

"We have similar problems here," said Karen, who had returned to the room. "Brad Barnett's too busy for Mrs. Johnson, Dr. Callahan. He said we'll have to call in his backup, a young ob-gyn from Osler. I've called and he's on his way. Dr. Hoondal."

Dr. Kumar Hoondal made the drive from Osler to the emergency room in ten minutes. He examined Mrs. Johnson and ordered her admitted for observation. He was standing at the control center counter, filling out forms on a clipboard with a pen taped to a long piece of string that was tied to a phone cord beside Karen's computer terminal.

"Dr. Barnett will be angry with me, but I believe it is best for Mrs. Johnson that she remain here for D and C," he told Karen.

"He shouldn't second-guess you. He handed off to you."

"Handed off? Please, I do not understand."

"Dr. Barnett turned his patient over to you," Karen said, speaking slowly in the belief that would help Hoondal understand.

"Ah, this is true. But at Osler, we have rules. First among these rules is that patients should be referred to Osler physicians and facilities. Dr. Barnett will be unhappy that we are not admitting her to our own Surgicenter."

"I'm sure Dr. Barnett will understand Mrs. Johnson's needs."

"Yes, of course," Hoondal said in the way one raised in a bureaucracy agrees with something he knows to be untrue.

"You disagree?" Karen tried to look into the brown eyes of Hoondal, a man six feet tall, with broad shoulders, narrow hips and coarse black hair. She could read no insolence.

"I agree emphatically. One can appreciate the financial concerns of an entity such as Osler Medical Group. Why, those concerns were addressed immediately when each of us was interviewed for our positions."

"How was it put to you?" asked Callahan, who had come to the counter beside Hoondal.

"Put to me?"

"Explained, Dr. Hoondal," Karen offered.

"The position available was described as a revenue-generating office, RGO."

"Is that what Harvey called it?" Karen asked, shaking her head. "He's come a long way."

"Oh, no. The interview was conducted by Miss Sadler, our administrator. Do you know her?"

"Is she a doctor?" Callahan asked, absently flipping sheets on his own clipboard.

Kumar Hoondal explained that Miss Sadler, in her own words, was the business brains of Osler. He also explained how a doctor's duties at Osler included maintaining a specified high EC, or examination count. Financially, these examinations are most important for generating referrals to Osler Group's free-standing facilities. Since individual doctor fees are in many cases capped by the managed care company, it is these facilities fees that cover Osler's administrative costs and salaries.

"My visit to see Mrs. Johnson today earns Osler no more income than had she not been ill," Hoondal said. "One can perhaps appreciate, then, the consternation with which I anticipate Dr. Barnett will greet the news that Mrs. Johnson remains here rather than our Surgicenter."

"Doesn't Brad drive a Lexus?" Callahan asked.

"And Jim Harvey drives a sixty-thousand dollar Jeep," Karen said. "You've really got to feel sorry for them!"

Kumar Hoondal smiled as do those who have been raised in a bureaucracy and who recognize the unmentioned hypocrisy of their superiors.

Brad Barnett's Lexus was in the garage next to Natalie's Mercedes wagon. Natalie was in bed, naked, straddling Brad. She had insisted he stay with her until it was time for his meeting with Scarborough. She was impressing on Brad why it was important that he succeed in his negotiations with Coastal Insurance. Rising slightly, she took his hand and guided it between her legs, pressing his finger gently against her clitoris. Then she began rocking slowly against the pressure of his hand, combing her own fingers up through her loosed hair, her eyes closed, her breasts rising and nipples becoming firm. Brad knew from the wetness and the way his finger slipped into her that she was not faking. She never had to. His erection pressed against the cool skin of her cheek, and he arched himself up toward her and felt his own fingernail scratch along the top of his penis as she moved back onto him and he entered her. The orgasm they shared at ten o'clock was her fourth since six o'clock, when she had roused him, but the first since the call from the emergency room.

"It's just that I can't stand to see you taken advantage of, Bradley," she told him moments later, holding his deflated phallus in one hand and, with the other, toying with his depleted tes-

124

ticles. Brad lay still on his back, exhausted, clammy with sweat. "This is an opportunity for you. What you make of it is beyond Jim Harvey's control, and I know you can take this a long way." She bent and ran her tongue around the tip of his penis. Then she kissed it with the faintest amount of suction, enough to make Brad's balls, which were still not disinterested, jump.

"I've gotten an edge with all the other HMOs. You're saying someone will have gotten over on me if I didn't get Coastal?"

"Jim Harvey will have," she said softly. She was a woman who could kill with a feather, and she seldom needed harsh words to slip her knife under Brad's skin. "He has you out there negotiating a deal that puts money in his pocket. He might just as well be fucking me again, Brad." Natalie had reveled in telling Brad of her infidelity on top of the washer with Harvey. She had known that information would tie Brad to her more than his wedding vows. He lived in constant fear that she would abandon him, for Harvey or for some other man with whom Brad Barnett believed he could not compete. She always reminded him of her unfaithfulness, and of his own fears, when she wanted to focus his attention, and now was such a time. "If you fail to make a similar deal with Coastal, you might just as well consider yourself Dr. Harvey's procurer."

"What does that mean?" Brad snapped, rising on one elbow but leaving his pelvis and his privates within Natalie's reach.

"Oh, please. Don't worry, dear," she said, her soft voice cooing without mocking. "I loathe the man and would never again let him touch me."

"Well I guarantee you I'm going for Scarborough's throat. He'll get something from us, and I'll get something from him. It's just a matter of negotiating."

"You are an excellent negotiator, and I believe in you, Bradley," Natalie said, and then she slipped off the edge of the bed and modestly wrapped herself in a silk robe too short to cover the full curve of her rump.

Brad Barnett, who by this point had won concessions from every managed care company operating in Port Hancock except Coastal, staggered to the bathroom, an image of his pending encounter with Bill Scarborough playing in his head.

The negotiations involved Osler's capitation rate, the monthly amount the managed care company paid a doctor for each of the patients he sees. There was no standard capitation rate, or for how insurance companies reimbursed doctors. And so you could dicker.

Osler, whose doctors by now saw the majority of Port Hancock's patients, had bargaining power that no other local physicians had. And Osler's dominance of the Valleyview Medical Center board, which was made obvious during its takeover of Port Hancock General, made the group even stronger.

And so, when Brad Barnett entered the executive suite of an insurer with a proposal that the doctors in his group receive a capitation rate substantially higher than other physicians, he was listened to politely before he was offered the door.

At that point, Barnett would flex Osler's muscle. "It's a shame your company will be leaving the Port Hancock market," he would say, standing, buttoning his jacket and reaching to shake the executives hand. "Your contracts are with whom, now? Ah, yes," and he would repeat from memory the unions and employers and the number of workers covered by those contracts and the value to the insurance company of each contract. He would, again from memory, recite the precise financial loss the insurance company would suffer by failing to cover Osler's patients who, Barnett assured the executive, would certainly demand coverage elsewhere so that they could receive medical care in Port Hancock.

Now the insurance executive would be clearing his throat nervously, not wishing to be the one other corporate climbers could point to as being responsible for lost business. When the executive's distress reached a certain level—and Brad Barnett's genius as a negotiator was his ability to recognize that level, a skill learned by observing his father dealing with grocery suppliers—the physician would prescribe a cure that would leave both the executive and the doctor healthy. Barnett's remedy involved a capitation rate marginally less onerous to the insurance company than the one he had initially demanded, but still substantially higher than any other physician was paid.

"Your records will reflect that you are paying this rate," he would say, unbuttoning his jacket and settling back into the chair facing the executives desk. He never wavered from this choreography. "In fact, your checks to Osler will be for considerably less, leaving a buffer of sorts." He would pause and wait for the question, and in all of his negotiations, the question had always come. Then he would answer: "You would receive a finder's fee, of course, for your sacrifice." That fee, in most cases, would be several thousand dollars a month, an amount that Barnett would recite from memory. This might represent as much as a fifty percent pay raise—tax free—for the executive.

In a couple of instances, the executives on their own recognized that their kickback did not account for the full "buffer" and brought this to Barnett's attention. Even if they did not, he would finish his explanation by noting that his personal fee, to be paid directly to him by check from a third party, would consume the balance of the buffer.

All of the insurance executives, faced with a choice between personal enrichment or sole responsibility for lost business, had agreed to Brad Barnett's proposal. Even without the Coastal contract in his pocket, he stood to gain tens of thousands of dollars that, as Natalie had reminded him, would have otherwise flowed into Jim Harvey's account.

The Coastal deal, however, was worth almost as much as the rest combined. It required a separate approach, because Coastal's size meant that it could more easily afford to write off Osler's business. Moreover, unlike the little insurers, who had delegated the negotiations of capitation fees to middle level executives, Coastal's negotiations were handled by its chief executive. To craft a proposal that would entice William Scarborough would demand a delicate touch. Barnett could not count on his opponent's fear. Scarborough feared no one.

Driving toward Riverton in the Lexus, Brad was unable to shake an uncharacteristic tension that resided between his shoulder blades. Although its source was undetectable, something was telling him that Scarborough would be not only a tough sell, but a dangerous one. His instincts urged him to forget about Coastal. He already had enough money coming in. Then he flashed to an image of Natalie. Brad knew that she would not be satisfied with money alone. Natalie wanted to open a deep wound in Jim Harvey. Harvey showed her something she could never have, and for this she would never forgive him. And, wretched as this made him feel, Brad had no alternative but to do what she wished. He pressed the accelerator harder and the Lexus sped toward Riverton.

Thirteen . . .

In a time now lost, the word businessman meant one thing, professional meant another, and both were considered, if not always laudable, at least respectable. In the world of James Perkins Harvey III, the terms melted together and lost their meaning. Often, in place of either, one found in businesses someone called a manager. These managers, like babies, are raised on formulae. They are taught to embrace a management system, not think for themselves. They are thus very dull people, Harvey had found, more dull even than accountants and dentists are supposed to be (an unfortunate generalization). Harvey was not a manager. He was more than professional, more than a businessman. He was, he reminded himself, a medical entrepreneur, a creative force. He gathered elements, arranged them and, poof, something new and unexpected was born. Among the elements he assembled were other professionals and businessmen. And on the morning of January 9, it was one of these businessmen who phoned Harvey at his office.

"Good morning, William," he said, punching the speaker

button and setting the receiver back in its cradle, placing William Scarborough's voice at the far side of his desk, which made the contact less intimate and therefore more acceptable than an ear piece pressed against the side of his head.

Harvey listened. His features tensed.

"Son of a bitch," he said, quietly. He continued to listen, and Scarborough talked at length.

"This isn't a smokescreen to make me forget Coastal hasn't pulled out of Port Hancock General, is it?"

Scarborough answered that it was not. In fact, he said, Coastal has pulled the plug, he said.

"Now you're telling me something I want to hear. That's better, Bill. This is the sort of news that earns rewards." He chuckled to himself. The medical entrepreneur was making things happen. Minutes later, off the phone, he decided some recreation should be his reward, and he thought about Sue Czernicki's house, across the river.

"What's my afternoon like?" he asked Tiffany.

"You're scheduled for three patient visits at Valleyview this afternoon, J.H."

Enough time, he thought. But then he glanced out the window. A cold drizzle left enough water on the Osler parking lot that he could see the reflected trunks of winter-naked trees and he abandoned the idea. Ironworkers would be home.

At almost two o'clock, Harvey took his trench coat and an umbrella out of his office closet and raced from Osler's front entrance to the Range Rover, only twenty feet away in the first parking space. Before the first raindrops hit Harvey's umbrella, the Range Rover's doors were unlocked and the onboard computer was checking the adjustments of the driver's seat and the mirrors, assuring they were in their programmed locations. He opened the unlocked door confident everything was in its place.

Harvey drove past Port Hancock General's emergency room driveway, thinking of Scarborough's call. A pickup pulled out of the driveway, and it turned right, following the Range Rover. At a stop sign at the end of the block, Harvey checked both ways and prepared to turn left, up the hill toward

Valleyview. In his mirror, Harvey saw the hood of the black and red pickup close to his rear window. Impatience, he thought. Mark of a fool. He stepped on the accelerator and spun the wheel.

There was a chirping of spinning tires as Harvey completed the turn. He looked toward his mirror to confirm his judgment. The truck was nowhere in the mirror. But in the same long instant, more quickly than he could become conscious of what was there, his eyes saw the right headlight of the pickup the instant before it smashed into his door.

The Range Rover slid violently sideways. The pickup's engine raced, its tires squealed. Harvey, his head thrown sideways against the door window, looked up to the truck's mud-splattered windshield and could not make out its driver. In the same moment, the Range Rover's right wheels were caught by the high curb, and the two vehicles stopped abruptly. Harvey was thrown sideways out of his shoulder harness, his lower ribs stopping against the leather-covered arm rest, his shoulders and head whipping on toward the passenger's seat, his hands ripped from the wheel by the suddenness of the stop.

It took several moments for Harvey to realize that his foot was pressed hard on the accelerator and that the Range Rover's engine was racing, apparently knocked out of gear. He lifted his foot.

More time passed. Harvey had no concept of its duration, nor of what had happened to him. Then the pieces of the collision returned to him, the images of the impatient trucker, the headlight beside his door, the muddy windshield. He pushed himself upright and grabbed his door handle, yanking fiercely. The door was crushed, inoperable. He pushed the power window button futilely.

"You son of a bitch!" he yelled. His words could not escape the Range Rover. Frustrated, he undid his seat belt and pushed the sun roof button. The sun roof slid back and Harvey shoved on the arm rest, hoisting himself so he could stand on his seat, then pulling his torso up through the sun roof. He was ready to punch something. Hard!

"Get the fuck out here, you piece of shit!" he yelled at the pickup.

The driver's door opened slowly and the man who emerged, when his feet reached the pavement, was taller than the cab of his truck. Harvey had seen his face before, in a photo framed in silver that sat on Sue Czernicki's dresser. Chris Czernicki's chest was broad as a bull's and thick as well. His arms looked as big around as most men's legs. His blue shirt sleeves were rolled up over his biceps, which he now flexed as he pounded a fist into his palm. Harvey was drawn to the size of that fist, as big as a child's head. He thought now was perhaps a time better suited for dialogue.

"I'm phoning 911," he screamed. It embarrassed him that his voice squeaked with panic. But there was virtue, he felt, in slipping back down through the sun roof. "You'd better back off!" Harvey pushed the sun roof button, and the roof slid shut.

Chris Czernicki placed his hands on the Range Rover's hood, fingers splayed. He vaulted onto the hood, standing tall so that Harvey, who frantically punched buttons on his phone, could no longer see his face through the windshield. He looked up and saw that Czernicki was bent over the sun roof, looking down like a chimney sweep about to commence brushing.

Czernicki, for his size, moved swiftly. His elbow cranked up, and his fist came down, smashing into the sun roof glass. Chunks of glass showered over Harvey's upturned face, stinging like blown sand.

The fist now punched repeatedly against the remaining glass, clearing the whole sun roof opening.

"Police? Help! I'm being attacked in my car! Help!" Harvey cried.

Czernicki's bloody fingers, the size of hundred dollar Cuban cigars, grabbed Harvey's neck just below his jaw and yanked up. Harvey pried feebly at the hand that pulled him through the sun roof, then saw the other hand coming at the right side of his face. It hit his cheek like a slammed oak door, and inside his head Harvey's thoughts slipped like wet fish in a spinning bucket. Czernicki was standing on the Range Rover's roof now, and he pulled Harvey all the way out, propping him in front of him. He pulled Harvey's ear close to his lips.

"You filthy little scumbag," he whispered.

Harvey's eyes slowly focused on Czernicki's face. He saw the dark individual hairs of the man's eyebrows. He saw the pores of his forehead, like craters in the desert, and the creases at the corners of his eyes. As if he were touring a museum, he noticed the luminescence in the brown iris of Czernicki's eye and how the clear lens floated over it, and he saw the tears spilling from his lower lid like water pouring over the edge of a pot left under the faucet.

"Why?" the man was asking, still hushed, his fingers still around Harvey's throat, his nose almost touching Harvey's. "Explain!"

"She was available," Harvey answered, still unclear about time and place and so, probably, as honest in his answer as had he been able to think.

"The hell she was!" Czernicki spoke the words individually, hoarsely. "You piece of shit! Why her?"

Harvey could not answer, because Czernicki was already making his next statement with his free hand, which had grabbed Harvey's crotch in a crushing grip. With his other hand still on Harvey's throat, Czernicki lifted the physician over his head as if to throw him from the Range Rover's roof to the pavement. Instead, sobbing, he lowered Harvey so that he was sitting on the roof, his legs hanging over the windshield, blood streaming down the right side of his face. Harvey curled on his side like some crustacean, drawn inward by the pain of his bruised testicles.

Czernicki then stepped softly down to the hood and vaulted quietly back to the pavement on the passenger's side.

"God damn you!" he yelled, spinning and throwing one more punch that shattered the right side of the windshield, spraying glass chunks throughout the Range Rover. Then, hugging himself and hunching his shoulders, he climbed into the pickup, backed it off the Range Rover and drove slowly away.

The female nurses had gathered in the emergency room once the word spread, and they were waiting for Harvey's arrival the way workers in an office assemble for a surprise birthday party. The laughter was nervous, excited. Everyone assumed the obvious—jealous husband. None felt sympathy for Harvey, or at least none expressed anything but crude humor. When the emergency medical technicians arrived on the scene, they radioed Harvey's condition to the ER. Fractured right cheek bone; severe, jagged laceration to the cheek; scattered small lacerations to the face and hand; hematoma of the right testis.

"Bad shot, just the right one," said Virginia Hulme, a permanent day nurse whose librarian appearance, with short, frosted hair, large glasses, and a pink Angora sweater, belied a wicked streak. Her comment raced across the hospital, and the crowd gathered, each nurse attempting to act like she had business in the emergency room. The ER was, as usual, shorthanded.

"Hey, if you're going to hang around, get to work," Karen Larsen said from her seat inside the command center. "Marylou, there's a large woman in Three who needs her catheter checked. Dr. Callahan needs help in One, Betsy."

Eager to secure their place in the ER, Marylou and Betsy stepped into the respective rooms. Karen stood and, folding her arms and arching her brows, asked the illogical question: "What are the rest of you waiting for?"

She almost laughed.

Karen had arrived at Port Hancock General a couple of years before Harvey. When he joined the staff, the stories began to accumulate. A few years later, she found herself working on a night when he was called in after a severe car crash. They wrapped up the case at eleven and Harvey invited her to join him for drinks. She accepted, knowing both that he was married and that, with a longstanding reputation for philandering, he certainly had the tacit approval of his wife. She found his charm intoxicating, and for a few weeks she rode the crest of a thundering wave of passion. Once the wave flattened, she laid down the rules of their engagement. No public acknowledgments, no interfering with her life at the hospital or away. She would hold no expectations of him, but if they had time to share, great. Harvey's interest waned when he realized that Karen could take him or leave him. Feeling a bit used, he looked for more needy women, but he persisted in an effort to create in Karen an addiction that only he could serve. He wanted her to want him, and that kept him on the line as long as Karen had wanted. At the end of eleven months, his efforts had failed. She cut him loose, thanking him for his time.

Now Jim Harvey was being wheeled into the ER. She stood from her seat and looked across the counter at the gurney on which Harvey lay, an IV dripping into his arm, gauze wrapped over his right cheek and brow, covering the eye. The medics wheeled the gurney through the parting crowd of nurses and stopped at a door where Dave Carn stood.

"Karen," Carn called. "Are you free?"

She made her way through the throng and followed the medics as they rolled Harvey into Room Two. Carn was already lifting the edge of the bandage before the gurney had stopped.

"Get his vitals, Karen. Jimmy, boy! Talk to me!"

Harvey moaned.

"We do English here, Doc. You'll have to try harder. What happened? Walk into a phone pole?" Carn was grinning.

"Pulse eighty-three. Blood pressure one-forty-five over eighty," Karen reported.

"Thanks, guys," Carn said, dismissing the medics. "You sound a mite agitated for a young guy, Jimbo. Once again, what happened?"

Harvey's one eye looked glassy, perhaps from the morphine the medics had dripped in his IV. "Jussa assiden," he murmured.

"Yeah, that's what the medics reported. They also said they couldn't understand how the window got smashed on the passenger's side of your truck and how the sun roof was shattered when you didn't roll." Karen handed Carn some scissors and he cut away the dressing on Harvey's cheek, peeling back the

134

gauze to expose the wound. Harvey's right eye was swollen shut. His cheek looked like chopped meat.

"I've seen prizefighters like this," Carn told Karen. "In medical school, I worked some Saturday nights as a fight doc. It would be a very light glove, or a bare hand, that would do this much damage, though. I'd guess bare knuckles. Am I right, Jimmy?" He leaned over his patient and smiled. "There's a pool up on the second floor, I hear, Jim. Top prize is fifty bucks for the correct answer, what hit Doc Harvey. You gotta tell me the truth so the pool can pay out."

"Fuh you," Harvey muttered, and he closed his eye.

"Watch your mouth," said Carn, who was washing Harvey's wound with saline. "I won't order reconstructive surgery for any crud who cusses before my Karen here." He smiled at Karen, whose mouth twisted to the side in an evil grin.

"Fuh huh, too," Harvey said.

"I hate to ask you to do this, Karen. But could you stay with this specimen? He's not critical, but I don't trust him with any of the other nurses."

"From what the medics said, I'd guess he's harmless right now, but sure, Dr. Carn. Go on back to the cardiac room."

Carn left and Karen swung the door half shut. "You're a mess, Jim. Was this Sue's man? She says he's a giant."

"Fuh off."

"Your vocabulary's remarkably limited this afternoon, Jim. There was a time when I thought your words were programmed at birth by Miriam Webster. But then, I also thought you were the Einstein of medicine. You couldn't measure up to a real doctor in any category except ostentation."

He opened his good eye. "Who you fuhin now?" he asked. "Cahn be aythin gooh."

She thought of Loring, of their personal detente. In the last month, after Karen got her feet back under her, she had agreed to occasional lunches. These meetings were deliciously platonic. Each could inhale the aroma of romance without tasting from the menu. And so, in four weeks, as December's winds swept into January, she had allowed herself to move from across the dinner table to take the seat by Loring's side, where she felt comforted. His patience was the thing. Anyone that thoughtful, she guessed, would have to be an attentive lover.

"No, Jim, a real doctor could teach you a few tricks," she said. "In fact, the last time I worked with you, you were missing an easy diagnosis. Janet Mitchell would be here now if you'd bothered to look at the obvious."

"Wathn obyuth," he said.

"Not when you're distracted by a cute young nurse, Jim. I knew what was going on, and I talked to her about it. That's why I replaced her in the examination room. But even I saw that there was something going wrong with Dr. Mitchell, and it was clear it wasn't cardiac contusion. I just can't see how someone as sharp as you were has managed to deteriorate in his practice. It's like you've turned into a used car dealer. Just a minute, Jim. I'll be right back. I think I see Dr. Wells. Dr. Carn wants him to consult on your cheek." She leaned close to Harvey's face and, smiling and speaking softly, she said: "We'll worry about your balls later."

Later, when she thought about Harvey's visit to the emergency room, Karen again replayed the scene from the afternoon of Janet Mitchell's death, and she remembered details of the dialogue that had escaped her before. It was incredible that Harvey had ignored not just his chief nurse but his radiologist as well, bullying Dr. Raphire to dismiss his concerns, demanding that everyone accept his diagnosis. It all added up to a disaster that could have been avoided, she saw. She had always felt Harvey was too good for that. For an instant, a thought fluttered through her mind and disappeared, like a moth briefly glowing as it flies across the edge of a movie screen. It was almost, the thought said, as if Harvey had sought a bad outcome. But the chart review cleared him. Sue Czernicki's husband, on the other hand, had cleared Harvey in another sense. At this thought Karen laughed aloud.

136

Fourteen . . .

Jim Harvey was thinking like a gambler who has suffered a string of big losses and wants to win back his stake with one bet. He had a way to do it. And the more he replayed the image of that afternoon a month earlier, the more insistent became a voice demanding that he even the score.

He had not just lost a fight with Chris Czernicki. In retreating from the attack, he had yielded to a deep vein of cowardice that, since the days of his earliest recollections, he had understood ran through his marrow. The beating hurt less than the humiliation. Chris Czernicki was the only live witness to the failure of his character inside the Range Rover. But there were dead ones. In particular, there was his grandfather. James Perkins Harvey Sr. had observed the weakness in the trembling six-year-old, afraid to stand near a window of the old plantation house during a fierce lightning storm. "You'll stand there till you can take it, boy!" he had bellowed at little Jimmy. Grandfather never cursed. "No grandson of mine is going to be yellow!" Jimmy, wearing pressed seersucker shorts and a white shirt, kept his face away from Grandfather, clenching his jaw in a futile effort to staunch the flood of tears, through which came, with alarming frequency, the fragmented blue flashes of lightning until, at once with a deafening thunderclap, a jagged tongue of electricity slashed into the trunk of an ancient sycamore just off the verandah and Jimmy, involuntarily, had urinated. The thunder still deafening him, he had finally heard Grandfather's angry voice demanding that Jimmy face him. As he turned, he realized that his shorts were wet, and a deepening shame swept through him. Grandfather had put down his cup of tea, the strongest fluid to ever pass his lips, and had risen from his place on the brocade-covered love seat and walked across the parlor. All now seemed quiet, as if the lightning and thunder had expelled all other sounds from the air. He had watched Grandfather's approach, hoping for a comforting hand on the shoulder, a calm word. He saw Grandfather's hand rise, and he snuffed back the fluids that were clogging his nose, preparing for the hug he ached to feel. His face remained forward, but his eyes followed Grandfather's hand and arm, which swung back to his side. Then the hand, driven by a gust of anger whose justification Jimmy would never question, swung forward in a descending arc, slapping its open palm against his right cheek and propelling his skinny body head-long to the floor, which his left cheek hit with a force that scraped away the skin. "Coward!" Grandfather had roared.

In the weeks after Chris Czernicki beat him, Harvey searched within for the bricks of logic with which to build a wall against this resurfaced shame. But all the arguments he piled up crumbled when the memory of that afternoon slashed into his mind and heart. Then, he would visualize how he might have responded. He would picture himself climbing eagerly out of the Range Rover to confront the cuckold. He would almost feel the impact of his own knuckles against the man's jaw. He would find himself uttering aloud—more and more intelligibly as his face healed—the words he might have thrown at Czernicki, the cutting, humbling phrases that could have stopped the man in his tracks. And, just before the truth of his gutlessness reasserted itself, Harvey would imagine him-self valiantly battling his attacker, knowing the other was his superior only by virtue of physique. Then the truth would sur-face in Harvey's mind, demanding tribute. Enraged, Harvey would think of payback.

Sitting alone in his library late on a night in mid-week, Harvey poured himself a glass of cognac, passing it under his nose and inhaling its sweet fumes. He had traversed all the phases of his reverie and once again was faced with his own incapacity for bravery. He did not want to be alone with this thought, and so he telephoned Jerry Wiegenstein.

"I need to bounce some ideas off you," he said. The lawyer arrived in a half hour. Although Neil Dunmore was building a new eighteen-room house for Jerry and Debbie on a promon-tory behind the Nightingale and Urizar properties, the lawyer still lived in the restored Edwardian mansion in Port Hancock's millionaires' mile where Jerry's law firm occupied the ground floor.

Mrs. Sloan met Wiegenstein in the foyer and took his coat and scarf. "Dr. Harvey is in the library," she said, turning and gesturing for the lawyer to follow. She twisted the brass lever on the library door and shoved the door open, standing back to let Wiegenstein enter. He stepped into a darkened room with deep mahogany panelling and a fire glowing in a tile fireplace. Harvey was in the second of the two leather-upholstered chairs before the fire, dressed in sweats, his glass of cognac in his right hand, resting on the rolled arm of the chair. He looked at the lawyer and smiled.

"Jerry," he said, rising, "thanks for coming." He stepped to the bookshelf bar and took down a second glass, which he filled with cognac before refilling his own. "Smoke?" he asked, handing the glass to Wiegenstein, who was still dressed in a dark blue suit. Wiegenstein took the glass and nodded, and Harvey returned to the bar, opening a humidor and selecting two long, thick cigars. With scissors he took from the lid of the humidor, he snipped the ends off the cigars and handed one to the lawyer. Then he went to the fireplace and, with a long match stick, took a flame from the burning logs and lit his and his lawyer's cigars. They both settled into their seats and puffed in silence, until Harvey spoke.

"Okay, counselor, start your clock," he said.

"This one's on the house, J.H."

"Good. There are several items I need to discuss. First is the med supply shop. Thanks for helping Dennis get that off the ground."

"All I did was draft some sample corporations, J.H. You've paid the bill already."

"I'd like to think of us as creating this thing together, Jerry. Bills aside, the group is going to rocket in this business."

"That is my desire, J.H. Our products certainly are essential, if I understand the inventory you provided."

"And we're making two hundred percent," Harvey said.

Wiegenstein did not need to know the figure was five hundred percent. He had told Ross to keep the numbers to himself. The implication was clear, and they never mentioned it again.

"What does Ari say this will do for Osler's overall performance?"

"Triple the first year. Physician services drop to eighteen percent, with the lab and facility fees accounting for the rest."

"That's amazing," Wiegenstein said, swirling the cognac. "Seventy doctors, and they're almost superfluous in this medical group! J.H., you've got vision! That reminds me, your face seems to be healing nicely. How's your eye doing?"

Harvey's thoughts, since Wiegenstein arrived, had been fully diverted, as was his plan, but the mention of his injury brought back all the shame he had felt earlier in the evening, and with the shame came the rage.

"That son of a bitch!" Harvey screamed, pitching the cigar into the open fireplace and jumping to his feet. The lawyer stood quickly, unsure where this was going. "I'll kill him!" Harvey's voice was a growl and his face was too close for Wiegenstein to get his features in focus. "I can do it, too! You know that? I can make him dead quick as those guys got Grimes! Just like that!" he snarled, slamming the end of a bookshelf with his open palm.

"Stop, J.H!" The lawyer grabbed Harvey's shoulders. "Christ, I didn't mean to upset you. What's the problem? You're the one who got the best of it, I'd say. Your wounds will heal, but his wife still remains fucked by you, no matter what he does. Jeez, man. What are the tears for?"

"He's dead, Jerry! I'm not telling you this as my lawyer, either. If I can't do it with my own hands, I can have it done. I won't be humbled by that thick neck!"

"You're not talking sanely, J.H.! Come on, sit down! Get a grip!" He led Harvey back to his seat and took the cognac glass from the floor, handing it to the doctor. "Let's talk about the merger. I've got some questions about strategy."

Seeing that Harvey had settled, Wiegenstein eased himself into his chair. "For example, we've had some strong opposition on the Port Hancock board, particularly from Dr. Schmidt and Peter Warren."

"Schmidt's a nuisance, but he's manageable," Harvey said, gazing again through his glass at the flames.

"I've seen how you've corralled Loring English, J.H. So let's say you take Schmidt out somehow. You still have Warren to worry about. We need the vote to pass, and Warren's not only independent and stubborn; he's well respected in the community. And he's developed some backing on the board."

"Not much, I'd guess."

"By my count, the vote taken today would be close to even. Warren can count on Lydia Fulton, Farnham, and Schmidt. He needs two more, and those could include Bruce Groff, a damned Democrat to the core, and Podge Durant, although that's a swing vote."

"I thought we had the board pretty well packed," Harvey said, glancing sideways at his lawyer.

"You've got Scott and yourself, Neil and Willie Simicks, of course. But Warren may find an audience with Rick Swaboda and Carlton Porferrio, a rock-solid Republican who can listen to reason. It's just too close, J.H."

"So what do you suggest?"

"Warren's a religious man. He alone within the Hancock Systems hierarchy has stood against downsizing. He believes it's immoral, and he has spoken eloquently on the subject in the press. As you know, he's taking the position that the hospitals' merger would diminish options for patients, many of whom are his employees. That's what's got him riled. We need to neutralize that factor in some way. Convince him he's wrong, that the merger helps workers. Any ideas?"

Harvey sipped his drink, stood and took another cigar from the humidor. He took his seat again without lighting the cigar, twirling it over his tongue for a long time, gazing at the fire. He only took the cigar from his mouth when he was certain he could frame his answer succinctly.

"You're no evangelist, Jerry," Harvey said. "You'll never convert Peter Warren." He raised his glass to his mouth, tipped a small wave onto his lips, and then, without removing the glass, continued. "You must understand that I speak from experience, Jerry."

Wiegenstein nodded.

"Let me take you back a bit, to something earlier. I spoke in anger, but I spoke the truth when I talked of young Mr. Czernicki. I can kill him."

Wiegenstein did not respond when Harvey paused, so the doctor proceeded.

"I will not kill young Mr. Czernicki. No pragmatic justification exists for it, only emotion. And I will not be ruled by emotion. Emotion ignores mistakes. Which is not to say I will not act on impulses that, by coincidence, also lead to the emotion of pleasure."

"Are we still talking of Peter Warren?"

"The Port Hancock General board member, yes."

"You may have lost me."

"You are confused but not lost. I'll guide you through this."

"Thanks." Wiegenstein watched as Harvey stood, lowered another long match stick into the fire and lit his new cigar.

"When I'm skiing, there are times that are transcendent," Harvey said, standing with his back to the fire, his features lost to Wiegenstein in the shadows, and his voice, coming from that darkness, rumbling into the room like the words of a deity. "Those times are when I am descending a particularly steep slope, perhaps through a forest of lodgepole pine, and I am traveling as fast as gravity can pull me, aiming for a tree surrounded by a chasm in the snow into which I could fall and from which I could never escape." He drew on the cigar deeply and exhaled a long jet of smoke. "And knowing the risk, I somehow unhook the little lid under which we maintain what we call rational instincts, those rules that, when they guide us, defend us from committing certain errors but that simultaneously prevent us from ever experiencing true freedom." His voice had settled into a near whisper. "The lid flips up. Rationality escapes off into the sky, and I am now guided by the overwhelming power of a faith that rises inside me. If I

142

were thinking rationally, I would recognize that one instant of distraction, one miscalculation, if only by a scant fraction, would mean disaster, and knowing this, I would shrink away. The shrinking, at that speed, might well propel me into a tree. But I am no longer rational. I am existing beyond the edge of the rational, in a space where, without even a pretense at calculation, at judgment, I throw myself toward those same trees and will myself around them."

He turned toward the fire, stepped backward and fell into his seat.

"It's incredible, Jerry. You get a taste for it and you want the feeling all the time. It's like life before and after jalapeños, Jerry. Nothing tastes quite the same, quite as wonderful, without the peppers."

"J.H., I can appreciate your thrill from skiing fast. But there's a piece missing. I don't see how it applies to Peter Warren."

"One's approach to a problem such as that posed by Mr. Warren is shaped by the degree of one's enslavement to rationality, Jerry. I have tasted the supremely non-rational, more than once now, and found it liberating. I have broken, or helped break, the biggest of rules, first . . ." he paused, staring at the ash on his cigar. A thin smile alighted on his lips. " . . . with Janet Mitchell." He hesitated. "Then, through the Dragon, with Tom Grimes."

Harvey's whisper now was the only sound in the dark room. Even the fire had stopped crackling, and Jerry Wiegenstein was holding his breath.

"As a means of doing business, I find it both effective and as pleasurable as jalapeños. You don't have to worry about it, Jerry. This one's on me. Mr. Warren will be dealt in Triad style."

Fifteen . . .

In dealing with Edmund Lodge Jr., Loring English had two options. He could play hanging judge or the good uncle. Lodge sat before him now on an examination table in Loring's office, naked from the waist up, his belt undone. He already had one heart attack. His body, not plump, was soft as bread dough and about as colorless. The skin was stretched tight across his facial bones, and his brow pinched angrily toward his thin, straight nose. His jaw muscles were bunched, his shoulders hunched. His long fingers, one circled by a wedding band, gripped each other tightly on his lap. He was braced, Loring could see, for a battle. The examination had not been good. But the hanging judge would not be summoned. Lodge would meet stern lectures about the evils of long hours at the pharmacy with his conviction that he must keep up the struggle. The chain drug store next to Lodge's place was sapping his profits, Loring knew. Lodge had a decent offer from the chain to buy him out. He could be an associate pharmacist in the new store. But Lodge's pride got in the way. Eighteen years! I'm supposed to throw that away?

No, it would have to be the good uncle.

"Go ahead and put your shirt on, Ed," Loring said, turning to arrange some items on a counter. With his back to Lodge, he asked: "How's my little girl Beatrice?"

"She's made honor roll her first two marking periods as a freshman," Lodge replied. Loring could hear the pride in his voice and, as he suspected, when he turned back to Lodge, he saw his face beaming.

"High school! Good Lord, how quickly they grow. You should be very proud of her, Ed."

"Oh, I am, Dr. English. She means more to me than anything."

Loring had his man where he wanted him. He sat in a chair beside the examining table and looked up, unthreatening.

"I know she does, and that's what worries me, Ed. Because

144

I've seen you with her and I know she adores you, too."

The joy left Lodge's eyes, replaced by concern.

"I see a picture, Ed. I see Bea's father, digging in his heels and sacrificing himself to save his store." Loring watched Lodge's eyes and listened to his breathing. He spoke very softly. "And I see Bea alone, in agony, because now she does-n't have her daddy." Loring saw the tears rise in Lodge's eyes. "It makes me very sad," Loring concluded, the sting of with-held tears in his own eyes.

Minutes later, Loring ushered Edmund Lodge from the examination room, a hand on his shoulder. Lodge promised to reconsider the chain's offer, and he thanked Loring.

Mrs. Bacon was next in Loring's second-floor office in the professional building next to Port Hancock General. She had been taken to the emergency room two weeks before with chest pains. Loring had conducted a full battery of tests and found beating inside her a heart as durable as the pump on a fire engine. The pain could still be of the heart, Loring knew. And so he talked with her and listened to her answers.

"Everything okay at your job?" he asked. Helen Bacon had sold real estate in Port Hancock for half of her forty-seven years. She was attractive, with a frosting of white in her other-wise chestnut hair, trimmed short. She took care with her appearance but wore less makeup than most women in sales.

"I'm on track for a million-dollar year. Yes, it's going quite well, thank you." Her mouth smiled. Her eyes did not. She seemed to be holding her breath. Something wanted to escape her lips, Loring thought, and she was containing it. Go for the big one, he told himself.

"How are things between you and Bill?"

"Oh, he's a darling, Doctor. I was so lucky when I found him."

"Um hmmm," replied Loring, who, sitting behind his desk, looked down toward Mrs. Bacon's chart and scribbled on it with a pen, giving her time.

"I just don't know what I'd do without him," she said, look-ing sideways at the Persian rug.

"Are you worried you might have to?" He watched her mouth, her chin, which trembled. She did not answer, and he waited a moment before speaking.

"Something's come between you?"

She nodded, and her chin tucked tightly up toward her lips as she glanced up at Loring.

"Something you wish hadn't happened?" He was fishing, but an experience angler knows which pools are most promising. She rose to his question, the words spilling into the room. It had been a client, a very engaging businessman transferred from another city, shopping for a home for his family while he began his job at Hancock Systems. He triggered something in her, helped her feel a way she had forgotten. The wine during lunch on their third day of house shopping, the afternoon in the car visiting houses, the gentle touch of his hand on hers, first a pat, then a squeeze, the closeness when they moved through one hallway. Her heart had raced, beating just under her skin. It was she who decided, as the winter sun faded into dusk, that their last stop would be a home where, she knew, the family had already moved but the furniture remained.

Helen Bacon wept the tears of the condemned. Loring stepped from the room while his secretary, Nancy Fowler, a very faithful mother of four, comforted her. Lingering outside his office door, Loring returned when Helen found her composure, and Nancy left.

"You will find that your chest pains are gone," he said. "But they could return. You need to deal with this problem, and you need professional help. If your husband is the man you think he is, all is not lost, Helen." He gave her the name of a therapist and, at her request, called to make an appointment. As she left, she, as Edmund Lodge before her, thanked Loring.

"I want you to know that I signed the petition," she said, smiling easily for the first time. "I think it's terrible what they've done to you."

Moments later, Loring stood beside Nancy's desk, his hands on his hips, a grin parting his lips.

"Good work, Doc," Nancy said. "You broke that log jam."

146

"And did you hear what she said? There's a petition making the rounds! Maybe things are going to turn around in this town."

"Oh, you got a personal call," Nancy said then, handing Loring a pink memo slip. His knees went weak. Karen needed to talk with him.

She had sat at her vanity that morning in her waterfront condominium in South Hancock, looking at an image in the mirror that troubled her. It was an image framed by the bottles and jars of cosmetics that every morning were applied to the fundamental Karen Larsen to create the public super nurse. And every morning, the woman who emerged from the condo had within her the same little Karen Larsen who had always been there. It was this timid child who had, two months earlier, recoiled from Loring English at precisely the moment when most women would have pounced.

"I saw trouble," she told her reflection aloud. Here was a man whose wife of nearly three decades had died a year before, and I think he's falling for me? And say he was. How long would that last? I'm not Janet Mitchell and he'd discover that as soon as the polish dulled on the romance. Then he'd go looking for her in someone else, and I'd be left alone and in love. Girl, that's one trap into which you're never going to lead yourself, she thought.

Oh, it had been fun, flirting with Loring. But something went wrong. Some handle slipped from her fingers and she no longer controlled the situation. There was only one way it could have gone if she'd trusted him, which for a few hours she had; if she had trusted him and stuck with him. The only outcome she knew was that he would do the leaving. So she left. The only man who left me, or ever will, she thought gazing into the mirror, was Daddy.

Oh, Daddy! What a great guy, what a comedian. How many lucky little girls, dressed for school, their lunch box packed, had a new foreigner appear each morning in the kitchen to help them head off for the day. Daddy speaking his crummy

German accent. "Helloo mine dear yunk lady! Ich been ein traveling Bavarian shoe salesman. Do you haff feet? Yah?" And Daddy would kneel by her feet and wiggle her toes and promise he was coming home for dinner. At night, Mother, a humorless woman, would place the meal on the table at six o'clock and the steam would be gone from Daddy's plate by the time Karen's supper was finished. Father would be in some bar and would stumble through the back door into the darkened house while his daughter lay awake upstairs, listening.

It took her thirty-five years to learn that she really was worth more than the fifty-cent beers for which Daddy abandoned her. Finally, she had discovered that not all men were drunks. But having seen the good in Tom Grimes and having risked letting down her defenses, she was once again alone. And as good as Loring seemed to be, there was no guarantee something similar wouldn't happen with him. Or something she could never have imagined. But while this uncertainty repelled Karen, something in Loring's optimism, his eagerness to find truth, his patience—his at times clumsy mannerisms and his always gentle manner—something still drew at her heart and she ached for him to be something more than than a dear friend. She crossed her bedroom to the phone on the night stand and called.

When Loring called back that morning, she invited him to her place for a late dinner. Then she searched her drawers for candles.

"I've set things up over by the balcony," she told Loring when she greeted him at the door at midnight. "You must be starving. It'll be ready pretty soon." He followed her from the darkened vestibule, moving in the swirling wake of her perfume until, in the bright kitchen, her fragrance was nearly overpowered by the aroma of a rack of lamb with rosemary seeping from the oven. There were two covered bowls atop the range, string beans and almonds in one, small red-skinned potatoes fried in olive oil in the other. On the counter were three candles, a bottle of Bordeaux, and two plain glasses, each filled halfway to the rim. She handed him one and took the other, leaning back against the counter, cupping the bowl of her glass in both hands, allowing the base of the glass to touch gently against her skin where it was exposed by the low neckline of her silk, off-white pantsuit.

"To the best, and the most beautiful, OR nurse I've ever known," he said, raising his glass toward her. She smiled, and he saw how, when she reached to clink her glass against his, the silk moved lightly up from under her breasts and slid perceptibly along the skin of one shoulder. She was wearing her hair up, with gold teardrop earrings and a single gold chain necklace that drew his eyes to the curve of her long neck. The candlelight cast a deep shadow between her full lips and another where the silk caressed her thigh. Loring found himself staring at her, absorbing Karen's features, her sweet smell. Then he remembered the harsh wind that had blown into his life the last time he let his defenses down around Karen.

"May your life be filled with pleasant surprises," he concluded.

"Indeed," she said, her voice husky, as if she had tried to speak while swallowing. In fact, what caught in Karen's throat was a small sob of pleasure. She had prepared herself for this evening in the hopes of an exquisitely pleasant time. She had assembled most of the meal in advance, arranging with a neighbor to place the lamb in the oven so that the cooking would be completed when she returned at eleven from Port Hancock General. For most of the morning after Loring called, she culled through the clothing in her closets, discarding this outfit and that until she found the silk pantsuit. She had disrobed then and slipped into the suit naked, feeling the softness of the fabric moving across her skin. She had thought of Loring standing before her, and she had brushed the silk lightly with her fingertips, imagining the first touch of their embrace. She had shuddered and let the silk fall from her shoulders and flutter to the carpet around her feet. That would do, she thought. And no need for cumbersome pantyhose. She selected the lowest, softest bra with the simplest hook, and panties of less con sequence than tissue. If Loring took her in his arms, the rest would take care of itself.

"You were correct in your assumption," he said when he had sipped his wine and set it on the counter.

"I was?" she said, waiting for him to come to her.

"Yes. I haven't eaten all evening, anticipating this." He swept a hand toward the oven. "I'm famished!"

The way to a man's heart, she thought as the moment evaporated, and she grinned, reaching to squeeze his wrist before bending to open the oven.

"Could you hand me those pot holders, Loring?"

He did.

"Now, will you take this to the table?"

He did. Beyond the two place settings at the round table were sliding doors, and beyond these, across the darkened Hancock River, the few bright lights of downtown Port Hancock sparkled: Port Hancock General, straight ahead, and Valleyview Medical Center, to the right and up the hill. He set the platter of lamb on a trivet shaped like a fish. Karen arrived with the other dishes. She lit a candle at the table's center and Loring held her chair.

"There it glows before us, the health of our city," he said. "Not much left in the old town but the hospitals."

"And only one of them's going to survive," Karen said, spooning potatoes onto Loring's plate. "The way people are talking, this merger's going to put a lot of doctors out on the street. It is going to happen, isn't it, Loring?"

"I would guess it is."

"I hate to see Port Hancock General going. I know you may feel differently, the way they've been treating you."

"She's a grand old hospital, Karen. Some of the people running it bother me."

"I just wanted you to know, everyone thinks its outrageous. Everyone who counts. You're tops, in my book. It has to be jealousy behind it."

"It's the same thing that's behind the merger," he said, hoping to shift the subject.

"Well, greed's got to be at the bottom of that," she said. You know as well as I that Valleyview is more like a motel than a hospital."

"When I heard Coastal was withdrawing from Port Hancock, I called Reggie Wilson, Natasha's husband. He works there. Some kind of data processing VP. You know what he said? Coastal's CEO, Bill Scarborough, said Valleyview was cheaper. He claimed that by saving money, Coastal can serve more patients."

"I'll bet he said 'customers,'" Karen said, stabbing some beans with her fork and then stabbing a cubed potato. Loring laughed. "It's not just the administrators, either," she said. "I had to call one so-called doctor tonight five times before he would agree to break away from a golf video he was watching, even though his patient was in agony. Can you believe it? Some of these guys I think took a different oath than the one you did. More like a Mafia oath."

"Don't let that turn you against the profession, though," he said.

"If that doesn't, some of the patients might." She sipped some wine and ate another piece of lamb. Before she was finished chewing, she broke into a story of a woman who came in with abdominal pains.

"Dave was taking her history, and he asked if she was married. No, she said. Separated. And are you sexually active? No. When was the last time you had sex, he asks. Three nights ago, she said. But I cheated. You cheated? He thought he was going to hear something juicy. Yeah, with my husband, she said. But I wasn't sexually active, she said. I just lay there."

They laughed together at the story, and they exchanged several more, and it was one-thirty in the morning when Loring first glanced at his watch. The candle had burned to within an inch of the bronze, fish-shaped holder, but its flame still lit Karen's face, and when the light hit her eyes, it shattered in glistening spokes like headlights on a frosted windshield. Loring stopped talking and gazed into her eyes. He could see that she knew she was being appreciated, because she, too, refrained from speaking, her lips pressed shut in a nervous smile that moved from one side of her face to the other and formed little crescents beyond the corner of her mouth as it approached. Her hands rested on the edge of the table. His were in his lap, and he was leaning back in his chair, his breath coming slowly, the calm of darkness settling over him. He chose his words carefully this time.

"I really enjoy your company," he said, and he added nothing, as if he had placed his calling card in the butler's hands and was waiting in the foyer for a response from the lady of the house.

Her words floated back across the table.

"I like that," she said softly.

He extended his hand, palm up, and she placed hers in his grasp. Their fingers intertwined. For several minutes, they heard nothing but their own, and each other's, breathing.

Slowly, he unclasped their hands. Then, gently, he drew her hand to his lips, placing a whisper of a kiss on her fingers as he looked up at her eyes.

"I have missed a certain song in your voice," he said, putting his other hand over hers, as if he were holding a small bird in his palms. He had written these words on paper, then rewritten them, weighing each for its value, its truthfulness.

He had practiced saying them, listening to how they sounded, committing them to memory thinking perhaps he would never speak them to Karen. Now, the words flowed from his heart as he continued. "And there were times I thought there was nothing else I wanted than to be wrapped in the caressing embrace of your words."

Karen turned toward him and placed her free hand over Loring's. She felt the tears rising.

"But I was wrong, Karen," he said, "and that is the problem. For beautiful as your voice is, it only stirs in me the desire to be closer, to inhale your whole fragrance."

Karen bowed her head and squeezed his hands firmly.

"And now is not the time, Karen," he whispered. "Not yet. But when the time comes, I hope you will be there."

"I will," she said. "I will. But for now, one kiss."

"One, for now," Loring said and rising, he drew her to him, lifted her hands to his lips, and at that moment, without the will of either, they were touching, and her hands were leaving his and her fingers were resting on his shoulders and his arms were around her but only faintly touching.

"Kiss me!" she whispered, and her fingers rose to cradle the back of his head and his arms fully encircled her. In one hand he felt, through the shifting silk, the arching muscles in her back. In the other he held a fistful of red hair that tumbled from its restraints. Her eyes, so close, were blurry and slightly crossed and her lips, parted, glistened in the candlelight. She pressed against him, and the silk slipped off her shoulders.

"Oh, Loring," she whispered again. "Kiss me!"

The long kiss ended when Loring's pager sounded. Mike Bernstein was calling from Port Hancock General. He was in the ER, called there for one of his patients, when Carmella Parente had arrived by ambulance.

"I didn't know if the rules stop you from being here," he told Loring. "But I thought you might want to know. She was asking for you."

"Screw the rules!" Loring said. "I'll be there in ten minutes!"

Loring arrived at the emergency room, half regretting leaving Karen so abruptly and fantasizing where that kiss might have led. Mike Bernstein pointed to the room where Carmella lay hooked up to a cardiac monitor with an IV in her arm.

"The paramedics brought her in with chest pain and tachy-cardia. After her Osler doc left she called me in and asked me to call you. She's not happy with her care at Osler, referring to it as the 'factory.' My guess is her primary kept increasing her diuretics and didn't check her potassium. The low potassium obviously would have triggered tachyarrhythmia."

Carmella greeted Loring with "Lor, sorry, but I had to call you." She said she had been feeling guilty about their meeting weeks ago in the supermarket, and said she really missed hav ing him as her doctor. "I wouldn't be here if I was under your care," was how she put it.

"Carmella," Loring said, "you haven't changed a bit. I'm glad you're okay, and you know if it weren't for the damn insurance companies dictating terms, I'd still be your doctor."

"Well," she said, "I guess the old days are gone."

"Maybe so, but I've arranged for Dr. Bernstein to see you and you don't have to worry about payment. Because of the insurance, if you need to be hospitalized or need a special procedure, he'll have to arrange for an Osler physician to handle it. He knows a cardiologist there, Dr. Chen, and feels he can work it out."

"Thanks Lor. Any arrangement is better than being rushed around by the doctor they assigned me to. I don't think he knows much about hearts."

Loring wished her well and told her he would check on her every now and then himself. He left the hospital wondering where managed care was taking medicine.

Sixteen . . .

With a certainty that is mathematical, over time, the forces a son exerts in rebelling against everything his father represents create in the son a man who, far from being the father's exact opposite, is a nearly exact duplicate. The process is not completed in adolescence, either, but is constantly refined until the son's death, for the son does not need a living father, but only his image, for the rebellion to continue. A further astonishing reality is that the more effort a son expends in his rebellion, the less able he is to see himself in his father.

James Perkins Harvey Jr. might as well have been dead. A series of severe strokes had rearranged his physique, his facial structure, and his thought processes. Now he spent his days

154

propped in a wheelchair, a belt around his pelvis to keep him from slipping to the floor, his bones showing under his pajamas like poles in a slack tent, his white hair sweeping forward from his crown, extending over his brow and curling up, a jet of snow caught in a strong gust and blown over a cliff's edge. A tray was attached to the arms of his wheelchair, and a pad of lined paper rested on the tray. Dr. Harvey clutched a ballpoint pen in his right hand, all day, every day, and when he roused from sleep, his chin would rise from his chest, spittle seeping from between his sunken lips, and his hand would begin moving across the paper, leaving a continuous, bumpy line of ink, like the graph etched by a device for recording barometric pressure.

"More prescriptions, Doctor?" Jim Harvey asked, stepping into the living room of his father's suite at Green Knoll Convalescent Center. The old man's hand scribbled on for a moment before stopping, not because he was acknowledging his son's arrival but because he had drifted back into sleep. Harvey went to one of the three windows in the corner room and cranked it partially open, allowing an early February breeze to dilute the faint odor of urine. Then he wheeled his father closer to the window, beside a straight-back chair and a table with a telephone and a box of tissues. He took his father's free left hand and felt the pulse. The old man's heart was strong, stubborn against death. His hand was cold, though. Harvey cupped his other palm over the top of his father's hand, and the old man roused, his head jerking up enough for his eyes to gaze at the pad of paper. His other hand resumed its unintelligible scrawl. Harvey bent close, hoping to decipher some message, but as usual the ink dried without imparting a thought.

"If you have a moment, Father, let me bring you up to date on Osler," Harvey said quietly, standing beside the wheelchair and watching the doctor's pen move slowly across the pad. "We are doing quite well with our medical supply venture. I doubt that you ever knew where your supplies came from, let alone cared. But it's a fascinating business, Father. Great healer

155

that you were, you would have been nothing without the instruments, the sutures, the bandages. Someone has to think about providing those needs, Father, and in doing so, Osler will, in the end, profit dramatically." Harvey could hear the formality in his tone, the voice of a young manager reporting to a senior executive. Silly, he thought. He doesn't even hear me, and I'm still a supplicant.

The old man's hand had stopped and his head tipped forward. Harvey reached for a tissue and wiped saliva from the corner of his father's mouth. Then he went to the suite's kitchen and returned with a tumbler of water and a comb and, standing behind the doctor, he began taming the wave of white hair, drawing it to one side. His voice was gentle, soothing, devoid of the power his acquaintances would expect to hear. In the presence of his father, he shed his normal defenses. Unlike any time in his youth, the son could now rely on his father's presence. If the father understood nothing of what the son said, it was at least an opportunity, one never presented during the son's childhood, to talk about the things that were closest to his heart and to perhaps, in some metaphysical way, gather some praise. It was certain that his father would, at least, not scold him.

"You wouldn't believe the money there is in the simplest items," Harvey whispered, cupping his father's chin in his free hand to steady the sagging head, stroking the comb across his crown. He continued: "Stuff the hospitals buy in bulk. Sutures, for example. Riverton's annual budget for sutures is eighteen million. They do a lot of open heart, and they're a six-hundred-and-sixty-bed facility. We're going to get some of their business, deliver them a legitimate product and make a clear profit. I'd guess we're looking at seven to ten million a year at that one hospital alone. Aren't you impressed?"

"You shouldn't have to ask your daddy that, Dr. Harvey. Shame on you!"

Esther Marken, retired colonel in the U.S. Army whom Harvey had hired to administer Green Knoll when Osler consumed it, had crossed the suite's carpet silently, and Harvey, startled, spun to face her. He could not know how much she had overheard. Her next words doused his fears.

"Dr. Harvey, I only wish your daddy could understand all you've done for this community," she said, placing one hand on Harvey's shoulder, the other on the back of his father's wheelchair.

"We all wish he was clearheaded, Col. Marken. But I believe that we should treat him as if he were, in any case. That's why we have these little conversations."

"I'll leave you all alone. It's so good to see a son care about his daddy, Dr. Harvey." She gave his shoulder a squeeze and left.

"Oh, I care," he said when she was gone. "Don't I, Daddy! Daddy! Imagine how you would react if you could understand me? I could never call you anything but Sir! You demanded my respect, but I've got a secret. You never got it. How could I respect a man who spent his entire life trying to impress his papa?"

Harvey resumed combing his father's hair, and his voice, which had risen, settled like the sand once the water·has stopped swirling in a jar.

"But I loved you, Daddy. Love has nothing to do with respect. I wanted you to tuck me in at night or to play catch in the afternoon. I remember once you carried me on your shoulders. I must have been quite small, but I still can smell your scalp where I pressed my nose into your hair." He lowered his face and sniffed the white strands that crossed his father's head. A tear rose in one eye. "I waited a long time for you, Father," he said. "I waited, and I decided that I would never be like you, a slave to your father's expectations, a man without a life of his own. I saw how you were shackled by a belief that you had to match the Great Man's standard. Hell, that bastard's standard demanded nothing of himself and everything of everyone else. You were doomed, Father. The noose was tight around your neck from the start. No wonder you married a woman who didn't challenge you, who asked nothing of you. You didn't need the distraction. It was a matter of no consequence for you to abandoned her morning and night to pursue your father's ghost. She got lost in her booze. She didn't even have me around to distract her. I had to be groomed by better people than her, just as you were, Father. And now we see where your pathetic race with no finish line has led. You can't let yourself die, even though there's nothing left to live for. You poor, lost fool." He let his father's chin settle to his chest, and he wheeled him to the center of a shifting trapezoid of sunlight on the carpet.

"No, I don't respect your life, Father. I have charted my own course, and since it is of my own making, I control my future. I wish you could appreciate where I'm headed. Right now, my medical group is on the brink of controlling the sole hospital corporation in Port Hancock. We have orchestrated an accommodation by the most powerful insurer that allows us freedoms seldom experienced these days. And," Harvey said, pulling a chair to face his father, knee to knee, "we have created this medical supply system that will raise our wealth to a level you could not imagine. So rich, Father, that we, not some bank, will hold all the mortgages. So rich that, were he still alive, that son of a bitch James Perkins Harvey Sr. would have to come to us, hat in hand, if he wanted so much as a pot to piss in!"

As Harvey continued, his father's head jerked up a notch, and his hand resumed its travels across the pad of paper, moved by some neural commands whose source was not apparent.

Harvey told his father about the supplier in Atlanta who shipped truckloads of items to Valleyview Medical Center. He explained how the purchasing director at Valleyview, Ronny Spingenotti, whom the Dragon had confirmed was on the take from every supplier he could shake down, would sign the truck driver's bill of lading to indicate Valleyview had received the shipment. Then Spingenotti would direct the trucker to deliver the goods to a satellite warehouse. People had been paid off on up the line, so that audits never revealed any problems in the office of the purchasing director, never would either. Consequently, the board of directors—or those on the board who were still not under Osler's control—never would suspect what was happening. The goods were reshipped from the satellite warehouse to several hospitals, whose purchasing directors, for a percentage, had agreed to buy everything Osler's operation could produce.

There was a paper empire, created by Jerry Wiegenstein, Harvey told his father. Should anyone become suspicious, Spingenotti would fall alone. Or he would fall with the individuals similarly situated at other hospitals, medical executives who, the Dragon had determined, far from being a bulwark inside the hospital protecting patients from inefficient medical practices, were like sponges sewed inside a patient after an operation, sucking up vital cash for their own use, money that would never benefit the sick and injured. Through these individuals, Harvey told his father, Osler would extend its influence, in effect franchising the resale of already purchased medical supplies along with stolen goods. All of the dealings would be conducted through the Dragon's people, and the money would flow back through any number of shell companies, eventually enriching Osler's directors.

The father nodded down, but his hand continued to move and Harvey continued to talk.

"By any financial measure, this is a huge success, Father," he said.

In the heel of his right hand, Harvey felt his father's right shoulder become tense, and he saw that the large tendon extending along the top of the old doctor's forearm had drawn tight. The old man's hand, which in making its looping pen strokes moved with the regularity of a pendulum, now vibrated, and the pen slowed and the ink registered the shaking of the father's hand as it formed the first letter and then the next two.

"You," was clearly scrawled on the lined pad.

Harvey bent his face over his father's shoulder, his ear brushing his father's ear. Dr. Harvey lifted the tip of the ballpoint barely off the paper and then set it back, commencing the next shaky string of letters.

"Are," he wrote.

Harvey, anticipating perhaps the first thoughtful communication from his father in decades, felt his throat tighten, and moisture began rising in his eyes and his nose, and he wrapped his left arm around his father and pressed his face close to the old doctor's cold cheek. He had never felt so connected with him, and he anticipated the praise he so desperately wanted, coming miraculously, as if from the grave.

The withered, shaking hand lifted and lowered the pen again, and now the ink lines became more rounded and purposeful, and with one bold effort, the father completed his message, which would remain forever in Jim Harvey's consciousness.

"You are the poor, lost fool."

Seventeen . . .

Walter Scott injected the hospital's community with the notion of a merger in September, and in the five months following, word of the proposal spread from Port Hancock General's board room, creeping into all the wards and supply rooms, the nursing stations, the doctors, lounge, the cafeteria, and even settling down into the boiler room. Everywhere it went, the word seemed to breed and, like bacteria in compost, generate much heat if not light. Squalls of speculation swirled wherever two or more orderlies gathered. A storm of panic gripped the nursing stations, where talk sizzled like a downed electrical line, arcing from horror stories of cases botched by the already depleted staff to rumors of layoffs. And heated arguments would arise between physicians passing in the hallways, defending or attacking what was universally predicted to be the death of Port Hancock General.

During this same period, Loring had been struggling to rescue his life's work. There had been long evening hours with Aldie Spencer, working to construct an assault in the appeals court. He had plenty of time for this work, with so many of his patients turning to doctors acceptable to their medical plans. Loring had no time to worry about the hospital merger.

That changed whenever he would meet for breakfast with Peter Warren, his old colleague on the PHG board. Warren, along with Conrad Schmidt, Lydia Fulton, and Rev. Farnham, voted against Loring's suspension, and Peter called Loring once a week to schedule a breakfast at the Port Hancock Princess. After coffee and small talk, Warren would demand to know how Loring was doing. Assured that his friend was surviving, he would usually want to share with Loring the latest on the merger.

"Something stinks here," he said often. "I can't put my finger on it, but it sure resembles the back side of a barn. We're the spinal column of medicine in the city and suddenly we're told we can't go it alone. Then, for its own undisclosed reasons, the biggest insurer cuts us adrift. That, my fellow outcast, is what should be investigated! Collusion between Valleyview and Coastal Insurance!"

"When you think Valleyview, think Osler," Loring suggested once, then wished he had not. He didn't need his comments coming back to him in court, no matter how right he believed he was. Not that he worried about Peter Warren. Indeed, Warren had the respect of every honest member of Port Hancock General's board. Where Conrad Schmidt's acid words turned good women and men against him, Peter Warren spoke with compassion and fairness. Walter Scott, who could slap Schmidt down without a sideways glance, would defer when Warren spoke, even when the words shot bullets directly into the heart of Scott's plans. If you won over Peter Warren, you did it with facts. And Warren had not lost yet. He still had a core of four nay votes, with three more possible.

But even his own chief executive at Hancock Systems, Serge Luftmeier, had asked Warren to back off. It was the same herd instinct he had witnessed throughout industry. Conventional wisdom ruled, and no one questioned where the conventional wisdom originated. Those who did question became enemies of the people, obstacles to progress.

The "mixer," as Scott dubbed the social event scheduled for the Valentine's Day weekend, was designed to allow the professionals from PHG to learn more about Valleyview. Peter Warren almost ignored the mixer, whose guests included the physicians and board members from both hospitals. But to maintain any hope of influencing good works in Port Hancock, he had to swallow his pride, attend the event, and smile at those whom he knew to be the real enemy.

They would be everywhere in the Grande Ballroom of Riverton's Park Place Hotel.

"Honey," Warren's wife Marion had said when she found him in his office at home that evening, "maybe you should hold off." He had splashed some Scotch on ice.

"A rare occasion these days, dear," he had replied. "But then, these are rare times."

"It's just that we don't know how alcohol will react with your heart medicine, Pete," Marion had continued. "You don't want another attack of arrhythmia during the party."

"That would be one way to escape, now, wouldn't it," he had said, and he put down his glass and gave her a hug.

Now they were entering the Grande Ballroom hand-in-hand. Before them were two towering ice sculptures, one in the shape of Port Hancock General's initials, the other carved into Valleyview's corporate logo. Somewhere behind the sculptures, a swing band played, cornets and trombones muted, clarinets bubbling. From the direction of the music, perhaps from behind the PHG ice sculpture, Walter Scott descended on the Warrens.

"Marion, you remember Mr. Scott," Warren said. "He's the reason we're here."

Scott took Marion's hand but looked at Warren. His face was almost grim.

"You'll want to meet Derrick Keating," he told Warren. "I'll introduce you in a minute. He's talking with Dr. Harvey right now."

"We'll circulate, then, Walter. I see my dear friend Lydia Fulton. Marion, let's see how Lydia is doing. Excuse us, Walter."

Lydia Fulton and Marion Warren served together on various committees that, with greater or lesser pretentiousness, worked to make Port Hancock a better place to live. A few years older, Lydia had taken Marion under her wing when Peter joined Hancock Systems as a senior vice president. They had combined their energies to restore parks, institute hot meals for the elderly at an old schoolhouse, and raise money for a youth orchestra, among other projects.

"My darling Marion, how perfectly wonderful to see you here. Isn't this just the most splendid affair?" Lydia asked, embracing first Marion then Peter. "I do believe that, whether we like the merger, this is a marvelous way to bury the hatchet, don't you, Peter?"

Warren winced. So even Lydia was caving! He could not find it in himself to disabuse Lydia Fulton of her glowing view of the world, even if it ignored the very evils which he believed were leading to ruin.

"Great to see you, Lydia. If you'll excuse me, I think I'll sample the buffet while you ladies talk shop."

He moved to a long table draped in pressed linen, with a shower of yellow, blue and pink flowers spilling over the edges at its center and, for several yards on either side, one silver platter after another of exquisitely crafted hors d'oeuvres.

"Ah, here you are, Pete."

Walter Scott had approached from behind. When Warren turned, he saw a tall, broad-shouldered man at Scott's side. Derrick Keating wore a navy blue double-breasted suit that fit perfectly. His dark hair, if it did not look so natural, could have been glued in place, so precisely was it combed and trimmed. His tanned cheeks were shaved beyond a hint of whiskers. The features you noticed on his face, beyond his brilliant blue eyes, were the deep dimples that formed on either cheek and the perfectly aligned, sparkling white teeth that emerged when he smiled. Derrick Keating's smile made a simple statement: I'm the boss.

"Mr. Warren," he said, extending his hand. "We're only temporary opponents. After the vote, I'd like to talk with you about the future of our two great institutions."

"You get right to the point," Warren said, his hand not yet released by Keating.

"Of course. I see no benefit to our customers wasting time on party talk . . . may I call you Pete?"

"As you wish."

"In my view, Pete, we have a product that is in great demand, and it is our mission to deliver that product as efficiently as possible. Responding to the forces of the marketplace, we will fine-tune our business so that the consumer will be the beneficiary."

"Port Hancock General is a non-profit, not a corporation that has to respond to shareholders, Mr. Keating."

"That kind of thinking has left PHG where it is: vulnerable. I'd think that, as a businessman, you'd have some appreciation of this."

Keating's smile had transformed. It now said: I doubt your value as a human being. Warren's face said: I doubt your honesty.

"Tell me, Mr. Keating, have Valleyview's efficiencies created a financial surplus?"

"Twenty-eight percent in the last fiscal year, Pete," he said, and his smile said: Top that!

"And where are those twenty-eight percent today?"

"Plowed back into the hospital and its ancillaries," Keating said. "We expect to fund a new wing in the next year. We've already invested in several satellite facilities. An MRI lab, along with radiology. A birthing center. A surgicenter." "Hmm, all in competition with Port Hancock General. But of course, when PHG is consumed, you won't have to worry about competition."

"Another way to look at it is that our customers won't be paying for duplication," Keating said.

"Of course, it's only a small part of the twenty-eight percent," Warren said, raising his hand slowly and taking the lapel of Keating's silk jacket between his thumb and index finger, rubbing the fabric. "But it should be noted that four hundred and eighty thousand dollars last year was paid to Valleyview's chief executive. A healthy reward for serving the community, wouldn't you say?"

Warren turned and walked away from Keating and Scott. I could use a drink, he thought.

Peter Warren understood that Walter Scott was a weasel. He had seen him operate at the Port Hancock General board meetings for the last several years. Scott's techniques were seldom forthright. Warren also knew of Scott's drinking problems. Warren saw in the scowl that constantly creased Scott's face the sort of unhappy mask worn by the tormented.

Now Scott was in league with Keating, a prince who saw a larger crown in his future, a medical executive who saw patients as customers, who saw healing as a product. It made Warren ill. He looked around the room at the fixed smiles, the phony embraces. He wanted to stand on a chair and shout at them, rattle them awake! Instead, he saw the bar against a side wall and made his way toward it, shaking hands as he went, each handshake draining a portion of his self respect, so that when he reached the bar, his tank was nearly empty.

"Scotch. Make it a double," he told the bartender, a young Asian man.

"Sure, Doc," the man said with a smile that displayed most of his front teeth. The bartender scooped some ice into a glass and filled it to the rim with twelve-year-old liquor.

Warren put a dollar bill on the bar but did not leave. "Nice music," he said. "Free booze, too. You getting a lot of customers?"

"Not so many," the bartender answered. "They're talking too much. Maybe listening to music."

A young woman in white and black approached with a silver tray of peppers stuffed with mushrooms, and Warren took one, setting it before him on the bar. He had not realized how hungry he was, and, washing the food down with his drink, he soon had exhausted his supply of both food and beverage,

There were more young women with food, and the bartender was quick to fill his glass. Warren lost count of—as well as concern over—the number of drinks he had consumed. He took two more stuffed peppers, and the third one tasted a bit odd. He sprinkled it with salt and asked for a glass of water.

"Lime, Doc?" the bartender offered, and he twisted a slice into the glass of ice and water.

"Peter, old boy. Never thought we'd see you here!" It was Larry Bunch, vice president for finance of Port Hancock General, whose heavy hand landed on Warren's shoulder.

"You sound happy for a guy who's about to be made superfluous," Warren said, trying to steady his gaze and get Bunch in focus.

"Superfluous? Got the wrong guy, Guy! I'm the comptroller of the new outfit. I just got done talking with Mr. Keating. Deal's done. I'm in. Congratulate me!"

"For siding with a den of asps?"

"Oh, come on Pete. For God's sake! It's just business! It's not like we're selling out our country. Geez, man, I'm thrilled. It's a whole new challenge."

"A damn site easier work than the challenge of keeping Port Hancock General afloat, no doubt."

"Well, you're sure a wet blanket, Pete. Least you could do is wish me luck."

"You're going to need it. Here's hoping you avoid indictment," Warren said, raising his glass. Just as the drink touched his lips, a wave of nausea gripped him and his head spun. He set down his Scotch.

"Excuse me, Larry," he said, grasping the edge of the bar for steadiness, then lurching toward the Grande Ballroom's entrance. It was not that time stood still but that the murmurs and shouts in the crowded room blended into a dull hum, and his own feelings were numbed as he pushed his way, frantically, between people, shoving them aside like vines along a jungle path leading to a pool of cool water. He did not see Marion pushing toward him through the crowd. He did not notice that sweat now poured from his every pore, although he realized that as he stepped through the ballroom door into the lobby, his heart raced erratically. The arrhythmia! he thought, straining now to get his breath. He leaned against the wall beside a reproduction Queen Anne wing chair and felt the side of his head touch the wall as his lungs pleaded for air. It was as if he had inhaled a plastic bag, for as hard as he pulled, nothing moved into his chest. He clutched at his breast and managed one muffled grunt. Then he fell forward, landing across both arms of the chair and rolling sideways, tumbling one complete turn to land face down on the deep carpet.

"Help! Help! My husband! Help!" Marion Warren screamed to the ballroom filled with doctors. Peter Warren's heart raced out of control, vibrating so fast that no blood moved in his vessels and, soon after his nose pushed into the carpet, the cells in his brain, denied fresh oxygen, ceased to function.

The Port Hancock General Hospital Board of Trustees voted eleven days after the mixer and approved a merger with Valleyview Medical Center, effective April 1. Port Hancock General became City Campus. Its maternity and pediatric floors were immediately closed, and its radiology department transferred all MRI and ultrasound work to facilities owned by what had been Valleyview's not-for-profit foundation, now renamed Hancock Medical Services, or HMS for short. More improvements would come in the months ahead, Derrick Keating wrote in a newsletter called "Caregivers" that was distributed at both campuses of HMS. Beyond the initial layoff of forty-six nurses and fifty-eight other employees, whose departure he chalked up to progressive management's keen understanding of the marketplace, Keating promised further "refine ments in the overall operation of HMS to position us for the Twenty-first Century."

"The tough decisions we make today provide the sound basis for growth, for cost containment and, most importantly, for customer satisfaction," Keating wrote. "After all," he concluded, "caring is our calling."

Eighteen...

Entering Dutch's Outdoorsman Barber Shop was like discovering some kind of weird museum. The usual mirrors ran the length of the side walls, all the way to the back of the long, narrow room. But over the mirrors were Dutch's trophies. There was a stuffed moose head, a caribou, and an elk. There were several stuffed deer heads, one entire bobcat, a skunk and a gray fox, along with the head of a wild boar with one tusk broken. No one knew whether the tusk was broken before or after the boar was mounted. But then, no one knew anything but the price Dutch had paid for those trophies and for the three dozen mounted fish that were also displayed above the mirrors. Charlie Dewees—"Dutch Junior"—was adjusting some yellow iris in a vase in the front window, and his chair was empty, but Loring, after he had stomped the slush off his boots and hung his coat on a wall hook, sat in one of the chrome and brown vinyl seats along the wall and picked up an outdoors magazine.

"Next?" Dutch Junior asked, as if it were five o'clock and the shop was filled. He was lighting a cigarette, squinting against the expected sting of the smoke, as Loring let himself down on the barber chair.

"Not to be prying, Doc English. But ain't it about time y'got a new style?"

Loring looked at himself and little Dutch in the mirror. Dutch was about five-five, wore beltless slacks and shirts made of some kind of plastic weave, unbuttoned to his breast bone. He had kept his black hair in a pompadour since high school.

"I'll change when you do," Loring said.

Dutch Junior, whose father, Dutch Senior, owned the shop and the trophies but no longer cut hair, fastened Loring's bib in place and took the electric clippers from their hook under the shelf below the mirror. He spun Loring around and began trimming his neck.

"Ye hear what's happening up at Hancock Systems, Doc?" Dutch asked, tugging the bib tight around Loring's neck.

Loring loved gossip, and visiting the Outdoorsman's was like going to the well.

"That's what I come in here to find out, Junior."

"They told the unions they won't negotiate a new contract when the old one expires. Going to farm the work out. Makes me mad as spit, all this town's done for that company. Though I don't believe one speck of it. They know they've got the guys by the short hairs, and they figure they can save some money for the shareholders. Probably take away more of their medical coverage, though what's left now ain't worth the poke, let alone the pig."

The door opened, drawing Dutch's attention and obviating Loring's reply. A very short and very round woman, with a kerchief over her head and the bare hand of a boy of perhaps seven in her grasp, stomped her boots and then bent to brush the muddy slush off the child's feet.

"There's a broom beside the door, ma'am," Dutch said. He set down his clippers and picked up his smoke. "No need ye should be using your bare hands."

"Thanks, Mr. Dewees," the woman said. "Haven't seen snow this early since we left Pennsylvania the year after Billy was born."

"You been in Port Hancock that long?" Dutch asked. "I don't recall seeing you around back then."

"No, we come here from New Mexico. Billy's daddy left us there. Went back to Indiana. Indiana, Pennsylvania, that is. Confusing, ain't it?"

"Didn't like New Mexico, huh?" Dutch asked. The woman had finished helping Billy take off his coat, and she was settling onto one of the brown vinyl seats along the wall.

"No, I guess he didn't," she said. "But Billy had to be there, the doctors said. Allergies."

"I s'pose that's a good place for people with allergies," Dutch said.

"If you can find work, it is. But I couldn't. Too many nurses want to live there. And I gotta have work to support Billy. So we came here, and I sort of lucked out, I guess."

"You got a job?"

"In a doctor's office. Not just a doctor, but an allergist."

"You *guess* you lucked out? Sounds perfect as a locomotive and a caboose," Dutch said, crushing out his cigarette and bringing the clippers back to Loring's neck.

"You're right. Don't know why I said that," the woman replied, and Loring, who had closed his eyes while Dutch buzzed the clippers up his temples, looked at the woman and saw on her the face of one who believes she has spoken out of turn. He wondered about this.

"This here's Doc English." Dutch pointed with his clippers. "Port Hancock's finest, although some folks up at the hospital don't seem to understand. You know, Doc, I heard something that made sense about that."

Loring peered sideways at Dutch, trying not to move his head.

"Yeah, couple fellows talking. They said that big group, Osler, is behind your troubles at the hospital. Said you tried to get one of their docs disciplined and then suddenly the hospital's suspending you."

"That's one way to read it," Loring said, not wishing to expose himself to more anonymous charges.

"Why'd ye go after one of them docs? They're pretty powerful. Seems a bit risky, if y'ask me." Dutch picked up some shears and began trimming above Loring's ears. Loring thought a moment before answering.

"An incompetent doctor is a risk to everyone," he said.

"There's a woman on the phone for you," Nancy announced one morning about two weeks later.

Karen, Loring thought. He had taken her call every morning since the night he first visited her place overlooking the river, and each new day seemed to draw Karen closer to Loring, although not geographically. Their schedules were opposites, and due to cutbacks at the hospital, Karen seldom had a day off. When she did, she needed to recover from physical exhaustion, so he never suggested more than dinner. And he let her do the calling during working hours. This served as a sort of welcome governor of their relationship, an external brake, applied by forces in the universe to help keep them from going too fast and burning all their emotional fuel. Still, when the phone rang and he knew it was going to be Karen, Loring felt a glow spread throughout, as he did now.

"Karen?"

There was silence, then a stammering voice. "Dr. English?" He did not recognize the caller.

"Yes, this is Loring English," he said, and the glow dissolved and he heard his own voice go flat.

"I'm sorry to bother you, Dr. English, but I thought maybe you could help me." It was not the voice of a local woman, he realized.

"Can I have your name?"

"Oh, certainly. I'm Mrs. Wheeler. Dotty. Dotty Wheeler. And my son's Billy Wheeler. I met you at the barber shop."

"Oh, right! Mrs. Wheeler! Thanks for calling. What can I do for you?"

"Mr. Dewees told me about you and Dr. Harvey," she said, and waited.

"I can't discuss that, Mrs. Wheeler. I'm sorry."

"No, no. I just thought maybe you could help with something that's bothering me." Dotty Wheeler explained that she worked at Osler, where she was sent by an agency. She filled in for other nurses when they were out, but usually was assigned to the office of Dr. Ross.

"I found something," she said, her statement ending as a

question. "Could you meet me? I think it could be important."

"In what way, Mrs. Wheeler?"

"You said an incompetent doctor is dangerous, right?"

"Absolutely, you—"

"I can show you one, Dr. English," the woman interrupted. "But I can't stay on the phone any longer. My break is over. Can we meet?"

Loring found Cal Kalinowsky at the counter when he got to the diner at seven the next morning. Cal was melting what appeared to be butter on a wheat English muffin, and the aroma of the fresh muffin, mixing with that of Cal's hot, black coffee, made Loring's saliva flow.

"Another layer of paste for your heart arteries, Mouse?"

"I bring my own non-fat margarine and leave it with Millie," Kalinowski said before he took another bite of the muffin. "Millie, show the doc here my margarine."

"While you're at it, could I have the same as my friend?" Loring asked the waitress. "Maybe he'll lend me some of his non-fat."

"What brings you in here today, Doc?" asked Millie, a bony woman of about forty with hair the color of ashes and skin that seemed to be glued directly onto bone.

"I'm meeting a lady," Loring said, sliding a knife through the white plastic margarine tub.

"I'd heard you were seeing someone," Kalinowski said. "That's good, Doc."

"Yes, it is good. But that's not the lady I'm meeting."

"Oh, one of those, are you. Damn, this is a different type of dog than I thought I knew." Kalinowsky winked at Loring through his gold rimmed glasses, but wore an expression that suggested to Loring that his fishing buddy expected better of him. Loring decided not to disabuse Mouse.

"Here she comes now," Loring said when he saw Dotty Wheeler in the parking lot. "This is hush-hush stuff, Mouse, so I'll have to leave you now," and Loring winked back at his pal.

172

Loring brought his coffee and muffin and led Mrs. Wheeler to a secluded booth near the windows. She sat away from the window, piling her heavy coat on the seat beside her and glancing over her shoulder at the other patrons of the diner.

"I don't suspect anyone from Osler would be here," she said. "But I can't afford to be seen. You understand, don't you?"

"I can only guess," Loring said. "What are we here for?"

"Do you know Dr. Dennis Ross?"

"I've seen the name," Loring said. "What about him?"

"My Billy has allergies, and that's why I took the job at Osler, because they had an allergist. He's been seeing Dr. Ross ever since we came to Port Hancock."

"Has the treatment been adequate?" Loring asked, catching himself only when it was too late, realizing he was pushing for an answer rather than letting Mrs. Wheeler tell her story.

"Billy's doing fine. But that's not why I wanted to talk to you." She paused, expecting Loring to speak. He saw she waited and urged her on.

"I am a floater at Osler. When I come in in the morning, they assign me wherever they need me. Usually, it's Dr. Ross's. He's very busy. So one morning three weeks ago—before that big snow storm—I was in Dr. Ross's office. There are some doctors at Oh My God who have their own offices—I think they're the owners—and the rest share a big central office. Anyway, I reported to Dr. Ross's office and was told to file some charts. I was filing in the W's and I saw Billy's chart, so I took it out, just out of curiosity."

The waitress came and Mrs. Wheeler waved her off, but Loring ordered coffee for her and a refill for himself. When the waitress had left, Mrs. Wheeler opened her large shoulder bag and took out a folded piece of paper, unfolding it and handing it across the table. Loring scanned what appeared to be a photocopy of a standard medical chart.

"I don't see the problem," he said.

"Under procedures. What do you read?"

"Two separate tests and one injection on December 12.

Before that, the same injection November 15. Also October 14, also with the tests."

"Billy has been given no injections by Dr. Ross, Dr. English."

"None?"

"And he didn't visit the office in October, either."

"You don't think this is some kind of clerical error?"

"I was assigned back to Dr. Ross's office week before last. He used me in the room with an elderly woman and with a child, and I took notes on how he treated them. I went back to his office last week during a break, just to hang out with the secretary—"

"And?" Loring asked, edging up to his side of the table, one of his long knees bumping Mrs. Wheeler's. "Oh, I'm sorry," he said, embarrassed. She didn't seem to notice.

"And I got talking with her, asking her questions about how to file stuff, like I wasn't certain. Now I'd studied my notes before I went in, and so I pulled out the old lady's file to use as an example, and sure enough, there was an injection and a test listed that he had never performed. So I pulled out another folder, for the little girl Dr. Ross had seen, and guess what?"

Now Mrs. Wheeler was up close to the table, her elbows pushed forward.

"More false entries?

"Identical. What do you think?"

"Could you get copies of these other files to me, Mrs. Wheeler?" he said. "I agree something looks wrong here."

Mrs. Wheeler phoned Loring at his office the next Monday. She had the photocopies. On Tuesday morning, he met her at the diner, where she handed him a business-size envelope somewhat thicker than a letter might be. Within an hour, Loring had called Reggie Wilson at Coastal Insurance and then faxed him copies of Ross's charts. Reggie promised to cross-check his data base for Ross's account and these patients. After lunch, Reggie called back.

"The good news is two of the patients are covered by Coastal," Reggie said. "I checked with our medical review people. It looks like a scam."

"And?" Loring waited for the rest.

"Medical review sent it on up to the executive suite, and it snapped back like it was tied to a rubber band. Not interested!"

By three o'clock, Loring had another call.

"Dr. English, I am putting you on notice that you have violated Dr. Dennis Ross's privacy, and right to protection from illegal search and seizure," Jerry Wiegenstein said without pleasantries. "A written notice will follow this phone call. I want you to return the original documents and any copies you may have made to me directly and immediately! Do you understand?"

In his entire life, Loring English had never been spoken to in this manner. There was something almost threatening in Wiegenstein's tone. Loring clenched his jaws.

"What are you talking about?" he said evenly.

"You faxed copies of Dr. Ross's records to Coastal Insurance. Your fax address was on the copies. No doubt your previously demonstrated personal bias against Osler Medical Group is once again behind this irresponsible act." Wiegenstein spoke without pause, as if he had no need to breathe. "I am further investigating whether your possession of these documents constitutes burglary, Dr. English," the lawyer said, pressing on into the silence that he correctly read not as timidity but as speechlessness. "Tell me now where you acquired the documents, Doctor!"

"I see," was the only response Loring could summon, so startled was he.

"The source, Dr. English?"

"Oh, I'm sorry, Mr. Wiegenstein," Loring said, collecting his thoughts. "I don't believe it is my privilege to provide you with that information. Doctor-patient confidentiality, you know."

"Fine. I made you an offer. As for the documents, you may

either hand deliver them—and I mean all of them—this after-noon or send them by registered mail, although if I were in your shoes, I would not let them out of my sight until I handed them over in this office. And by the way . . ." The lawyer paused for the first time. "I believe the powers at Riverton University have some concerns about disruptive physicians."

When the lawyer hung up, Loring settled the phone back onto its console and pondered Wiegenstein's attack and Osler's score. First there was Jim Harvey's incompetence. Then there was Osler's disregard for Carmella Parente's health by having her managed by a primary care doctor whose cardiology knowledge was suspect. Now this defense of what even Coastal's medical review experts saw as fraud. What is going on there, he wondered. Our lives as doctors are dedicated to the pursuit of physical truth. Just how far have these people strayed?

Nineteen . . .

Steven Nightingale, seated as usual between Ross and Dunmore, tugged his nose. Harvey ignored him. Regardless of the subject, there was no situation in which Nightingale doubted the significance of his own contribution. His contributions to Osler board meetings, in truth, frequently amounted to clutter. Harvey allowed no clutter. Not that Nightingale's contributions to Osler Medical Group were insignificant. Harvey valued the medical work he brought to the group almost as much as he val-ued the way the orthopedic surgeon served as a glue holding pieces of Osler's core together. Steve's deals with Wiegenstein kept the lawyer happy. Their personal injury cases fattened both their wallets and made them co-conspirators, binding them to each other and thus to Osler in a way mere loyalty could not. Loyalty, among idealists, although often cherished, is yet subordinate to ideals. Neither Nightingale nor Wiegenstein embraced overriding ideals. For this, Harvey valued them both. Indeed, among all the Osler board members, Harvey believed, he alone, with the possible exception of Neil Dunmore, was motivated by an ideal.

While Nightingale was valuable, he was not an innovator. He was instead methodical. He went about his task of developing a practice in orthopedics the same way a carpenter goes about constructing homes; that is, following a plan with no view toward the possibilities in the real estate next door. Wiegenstein, who thought not as a carpenter but as a developer, had approached Nightingale with the idea of combining their talents on personal injury cases. Once Nightingale had been shown the details–Wiegenstein would recruit phony injury victims for whom Nightingale would craft bogus examination reports that the lawyer would use as the basis for a suit. The doctor worked intelligently, concocting plausible diagnoses that could not be refuted by an insurance company's expert. At heart, though, Nightingale was a simple, if not sandaled, carpenter. Harvey, knowing this, kept Nightingale focused where he could best serve. Harvey had another view of Brad Barnett.

"I'd like to take this opportunity, before the entire board, to thank Dr. Barnett for his work as our capitation negotiator," Harvey said, circling the table to stand behind the gynecologist. Clamping Barnett's shoulders with both hands and massaging his neck with his thumbs, Harvey continued: "Alone, dealing with executives of a dozen insurance firms, Brad has won for Osler a capitation rate that averages fifty-five percent above the standard rate paid physicians in Port Hancock." Harvey injected his voice now with its deepest resonance as he said: "A round of applause for Dr. Bradley Barnett!"

The rest of the board rose from its seats, and the clapping was hearty and lasted more than a minute, with whoops from Dunmore and Ross punctuating the outpouring. Even Ari Urizar, whose crumb-coated fingers had been delivering without interruption chips from a bowl to his lips, rose and clapped. Urizar reached down to pat Brad's forearm.

"Good work, Buddy," Urizar said, leaving a dandruff of crumbs on Brad's coat sleeve. "Damn good work."

Barnett had seldom, in his life of struggles, felt warmly embraced. Even upon graduation from high school, when he was called to the podium to receive seven different academic awards and scholarships and his entire class, which, due to his confinement after school in the grocery store or in his studies, knew little of him, rose to its feet to cheer his crowning as top scholar—even then he had not felt as accepted by others as he did now. A warmth spread up from his neck, into his ears and under his hair and through the skin under his eyebrows, and a deeper breath filled his chest and his eyes moistened.

"In appreciation of Brad's efforts, which will return millions to Osler in the next fiscal year, I move that the board authorize a one-time bonus of fifty thousand dollars, to be paid upon the close of the fiscal year," Harvey said, returning to his desk at the squared end of the conference table.

"Here, here," Dunmore said, "there's none more deserving. I second the motion."

The deep voices of the doctors and the entrepreneur rose together to approve the bonus. As the board members filed from the room at the end of the meeting, Harvey quietly asked Brad Barnett to remain.

"That's okay, Tiffany. Dr. Barnett and I will only be a minute," he said, and when Tiffany had closed the door behind her, Harvey shook Barnett's hand warmly. "Really, Brad, I've gained respect anew for you. Here, have a seat. Let's talk a moment. I've got a proposition."

A swirl of thoughts were occupying Barnett as he settled tentatively into Wiegenstein's chair, facing Harvey. Only he knew of the cut he had taken from all twelve insurers, including Coastal. The fifty thousand bonus amounted to mere quarter of his own take from the skimming. Now, at a certain level, he felt like a cheat, given the warmth with which his work had been received by these close friends. A desire to confess to Harvey built inside him. But there was an image foremost in his thoughts: Natalie. She stood before him like a towering gate keeper, and he could not dislodge from his throat the cry that strained within.

Harvey's offer didn't change this.

"I'm leaving for five days of skiing in British Columbia on Wednesday, Brad, and I'd be honored to have you as my guest. Just the two of us, like back at Johns Hopkins."

"Those were some great days, weren't they?" Brad warmed to the thought. "Crashing the trails all day, closing the bars at night and falling into the sack back at Mom and Dad's in Montpelier?"

"You showed me a great time, Brad. I'd never tried skiing before that first time."

"You took to it like no one I've ever seen. Must have been your experience as a running back."

"That and gymnastics. So, what do you say? We'll be taken to the Caribou Monashees, heli-skiing. Just a week, you and me and the mountains, my treat. Is it a deal?"

The four-wheel-drive van that picked them up at the airport took them directly to their log chalet at the heli-skiing resort at Dominion River. The driver, when he had carried their bags into the chalet, told them dinner would be at eight and in the fading light pointed to the main lodge, another log building, long and low with smoke curling up from its central stone chimney. "If I were you, I'd call up the massage room before dinner and work out the kinks from your flight," he suggested.

"A massage sounds good, Brad," Harvey said when the driver had left. "I know the head masseuse. Let me call up and schedule us for, what, a half hour from now?"

Brad Barnett grinned. This was all too much, he thought. He had put away his guilt and, for this trip, his concerns over Natalie, as well. He was prepared to enjoy Dominion River's every offering, from its pampering to its powder snow. He showered and put on a pair of jeans and a maroon turtleneck jersey and met Harvey in the chalet's kitchen, where Harvey was pouring them each a bourbon. Harvey raised his glass and, looking toward the fire through the currents in the gold liquid, offered a toast.

"To Osler, to you, and to me, Brad. And to the future and its potential."

Barnett raised his glass to clink Harvey's.

"And now," Harvey said, swallowing his bourbon, "to Brenda's!"

Brenda, the head masseuse, was behind the counter in the health center in the basement of the main lodge. She wore black Spandex under pink shorts and an extra large white T-shirt with aqua graphics. The shorts flared away from the curve of her thighs and the T-shirt fell like a stage curtain from the outermost points of her full, high chest. Her dark hair was pulled into a thick pony tail. Her fingernails were polished the same shade as the shorts and, to Brad Barnett, seemed too long for one whose job involved touching human skin.

"Dr. Barnett, meet my dear friend, Brenda. We've known each other for several years now, haven't we?"

An embarrassed smile crossed Brenda's lips and she glanced sidelong at Brad, then back to Harvey.

"Who do you have for Dr. Barnett tonight, Brenda?"

"Trinka is available, Dr. Harvey," Brenda said formally.

"Great. Let's get started."

Trinka, wearing the same outfit as Brenda, came through a door behind the counter. In Brad Barnett's eyes, she was everything Natalie was not. She was blonde, her hair cut short, above the ears, and clipped close on the nape of the neck. Her eyes were round and as blue as Wedgwood china, and her lips were full as pillows, but parted just to the left of center by the tip of a perfectly white tooth that bit gently on the lower lip. She smiled at Barnett and dimples formed on her smooth cheeks.

"This way, Dr. Barnett," she chirped, coming around the counter in bouncing steps and reaching for his hand. She led him back along a thickly carpeted hallway lighted by lamps set on low tables every few feet, and she opened a door on the left, standing aside to let Brad in.

180

"You may disrobe in that booth, Dr. Barnett. There's a towel in there. I'll be ready when you are."

Barnett emerged in less than a minute with the towel wrapped around his middle. Trinka positioned him on the table, face down. She went to the wall of the small room and turned one knob, dimming the lights, and another, producing soft music. Then she circled to the head of the table and began working her fingers over Brad's shoulder and neck muscles. He closed his eyes and noticed the fragrance of her perfume. He felt her hands working gently along the individual muscles, following them down his back, and at first this had an unwinding effect and he drifted just above sleep. But Trinka pressed on, following the muscles across the small of his back and then, tentatively, her fingers splayed, she pushed the towel down and, leaning over him from the head of the table so that parts of her were actually touching the back of his head, she drove her firm fingers down across his buttocks and then slowly dragged them back, the heels of her hands plowing up the muscles and the tips of her fingernails raking the skin. Brad drifted no longer. With one pass of Trinka's hands across his rump, the doctor found himself lying atop an erection rigid as an oak log.

"Is this good?" Trinka whispered, drawing her hands back up to his shoulders. He groaned. "Then it's time to turn you over," she said, and she nudged his shoulders. "Ooh, my," she whispered, "I guess it is good."

Brenda and Trinka left the chalet some time during the night. Harvey saw them out. Brad Barnett was deep in blissful sleep. Even before they had brought the women to the chalet, the doctors had had a busy night. There was the welcoming banquet in the main lodge around the massive central fireplace, a masonry marvel of river-polished boulders that were as big around as the pine logs that constituted the walls of the lodge. Close to the fireplace flames, the aroma was of burning pitch pine, but by the tables, with their green and white checked linen, the scent of veal cordon bleu kicked the salivary glands into action. The diners—there were twenty-seven of them who had paid five thousand dollars each for a week at Dominion River—were serenaded by an Austrian musician in lederhosen playing mountain waltzes on a concertina. Following the dinner, there was the introductory presentation, complete with a film on techniques for surviving an avalanche, using a personal emergency transceiver, and approaching or leaving a helicopter without losing one's scalp. When the introduction was finished, there was the cordial visit at the bar with Gunter Klass, who owned the lodge and who even flew one of the helicopters on occasion.

Harvey roused Brad at quarter to six with some difficulty. "Time for Wally," he called through the door to the tumble of sheets and calico bedspread. "Warmups are mandatory!"

Brad stumbled to the bathroom, dressed in the same jeans and turtleneck, and joined Harvey in the kitchen, where he accepted a cup of steaming black coffee. Their bags were already packed with their powder suits. Their boots and skis were waiting in the rental office. The warmups brought some life to Brad's eyes, and the breakfast restored his vigor.

"Jesus, I can't believe we're here, J.H.," he said, strapping on his transceiver outside his powder suit, a waterproof, insulated jump suit.

"Weather's not perfect. Overcast, but flyable," Harvey said, zipping the front of his suit over his transceiver. "But March is pretty warm here. We'll be working up a sweat."

Wally met them at the helipad. Walter Schiller, from Innsbruck, had been a guide at Dominion River for four years and had never lost a client. He was a strong powder skier, and he led the expert groups, the screamers and hot dogs who liked to pull out all the stops. Harvey had skied with Wally for the past three years, and he had assured Wally that Brad, even if he was from Vermont, was up to the challenge.

"I will not expect from you disobedience," Wally told Brad, glancing over his equipment as the helicopter rotors slowly began turning and the jet engine whine of the Huey gained pitch. "The rule is this: Do only as I say. Heli-skiing is dangerous, please. We tell you about avalanche, about tree holes into which you fall *und* get killed. I will allow this not at all. Ski close with your buddy, no problems. *Verstehen sie?*"

Speak English, Brad thought, his excitement somewhat diminished by Wally's controlling attitude. He sensed Wally's disrespect. "Asshole," he muttered to Harvey as they stooped to pick up the ends of their skis. Hunched, they dragged their skis toward the chopper, in line with the eight other skiers in Wally's group. They dropped their skis in the snow beside the Huey's door and climbed in while Wally strapped the equipment into baskets on the helicopter skids. Inside, Harvey and Brad buckled their seat belts along one wall with three other skiers. On the far wall, the other five were buckling. Wally climbed into the co-pilot's seat and gave Bill Gartz, who more than twenty years before had flown chopper evacuations out of Saigon, a thumbs up. Gartz, who even on the coldest days wore no cap over his shiny bald dome, tipped the stick forward and the Huey tilted and then lifted quickly, banking immediately to the left so that Harvey and Brad, looking across the chopper out the side window, were seeing nothing but snow. Gartz accelerated and the Huey swung back past level and they saw gray sky. A light snow was falling, but Gartz could fly as long as there was visibility. He maneuvered over the Dominion River, which churned now under thick domes of translucent ice, and followed it up the valley, toward where the old logging fields formed a patchwork on the mountainsides. Now Brad could see large groves of snow-caked pines climbing up a steep slope. The helicopter was rising. They flew over broad clearcut areas and then skimmed over a ridge and maintained altitude as the valley fell away once again. On the far side of this valley, perhaps ten minutes into the flight, the helicopter turned toward the mountain and climbed sharply. There was forest and then there was snowfield, above the timber line, and the Huey banked and circled, then leveled and, with the racket of its rotors bouncing back from the snow, settled onto a narrow ridge where large orange flags marked the corners of the landing site. With hand signals, Wally directed his ten charges out the door and away from the chopper. He unloaded the gear and scampered to meet the skiers as Gartz lifted off, banking and diving immediately back down one side of the ridge toward a broad stand of lodgepole pines.

"Listen up," Wally said, standing apart now like a drill instructor. "We ski through the trees, and out the bottom we ski into big, open area. The chopper will be there. Be sure, stick together. Now, check your transceivers. Put them on transmit. Then pass by me so I can tell are you working."

The skiers formed a line and passed Wally, whose transceiver was on receive, as it would be were he looking for a skier buried under an avalanche. Convinced the signals were strong, Wally led the group across the shin-deep snow to the pile of equipment, where he gave them instructions once again on sticking with their buddies when they hit the tree line. Then he stepped into his ski bindings, grabbed his poles and shoved off the lip of the ridge, dropping almost vertically for twenty feet before sinking into waist-deep powder, and beginning a series of turns which the two skiers he had chosen as buddies attempted to match.

The pairs of buddies each now shoved off the top together, each pair looking for their own path of unbroken snow.

"See you at the tree line," Harvey yelled over his shoulder, lowering his goggles and pushing himself into the air on his poles. He dropped airborne far down the slope before landing in a geyser of fluffy snow. Brad's launching was a split second later, and the two, shrieking like kindergartners, carved trails that left a fresh path of figure eights down the slope.

At the tree line, Harvey picked a route to the far left, well away from the snow broken by the others, and Brad followed, hollering replies to Harvey's shouts. The snow billowed around his chest in a way Brad seldom experienced in Vermont, coating and melting on his cheeks and his teeth, which were exposed by an uncontrolled grin. In one sense, it was almost like floating, the snow was so soft and the turning was so easy. In another, it was like driving the wrong way on the interstate, dodging traffic, as the trees came flying at him,

184

the gray bark of their tall trunks a blur, the holes around their trunks, of which Wally had repeatedly warned the group, gaping like the mouths of killer sharks. It was fun and fear combined, and Brad's adrenaline was pumping hard as, out of the corner of his eye, he kept sight of Harvey, plunging along his own path perhaps forty feet to the left and a hundred feet ahead.

Brad kept his distance from the trees, and that kept him behind Harvey. As much as he disliked Wally's attitude, Brad believed the warnings about the trees. The pines had branches only at the very top, but this thick canopy was laden with snow and kept snow from falling directly around the tree trunk. This left a well around the tree, twelve or more feet deep, into which a careless skier could fall. Injury, Wally said, was certain. Death was possible, and there had been three deaths at Dominion River. Lost bodies were a reality at some other tree skiing fields in the province, Wally had said, but all three corpses were found at Dominion River.

The fear was there, but so was the thrill, and Brad was gaining a rhythm that he had misplaced since he last skied. And with the rhythm, Brad began gaining on Harvey, whose shouts were at times muffled by the trees and who disappeared for long moments and then reappeared. Harvey had disappeared once again when, as he swerved above one dark-trunked tree, Brad saw him stopped farther down the mountain. In seconds, Brad was beginning a turn that would pass in front of Harvey and bring him to a halt below him, a few feet above the next tree. But Harvey began sliding across the slope, and just as Brad passed in front, the tips of Harvey's skis clipped the tail of Brad's, sending him spinning backward toward the tree and its hole, deep as an elevator shaft. Brad attempted to fling himself to the side, and the motion caused his ski bindings to release. Sliding on his belly, feet first, he plunged over the rim and into the tree hole. His back bounced off the rough bark of the tree trunk and he was pitched, face first, into the snow wall just as his feet hit the ground, snapping something in his right leg. A hot pain shot through his knee, thigh, and hip and he crumpled to the ground. A pile of snow fell on his back and then all was quiet and dark. He wasn't certain which way was up until he heard Harvey's voice.

"You're in pretty deep, Brad!"

He pushed with his arms against the snow and broke free. Snow was packed inside his goggles. He slid them back on his head and looked up. Perhaps fifteen feet above Brad, the tips of Jim Harvey's skis poked over the lower edge of the hole.

"No shit, J.H. Help me out! I've hurt my leg!"

"Oh, I wasn't talking about your current predicament, Brad," Harvey said, leaning forward on his poles to look down into the hole. He lifted his goggles so that Barnett could see there was no mirth in his eyes.

"What . . . what do you mean, J.H.?" Barnett asked, twisting to get a better look at Harvey.

"I think you know, Brad. You dug yourself in deep with Bill Scarborough. What did you think your take would be, Brad? One-fifty? Two hundred?"

"What the hell are you talking about, J.H.? What about Scarborough?" Brad saw a look in Harvey's eyes he remembered well; the look of the ship's captain derailing a mutiny and willing to use the sword if necessary. He sensed that denial would not work, but he needed time to respond.

Harvey wasn't going to give him the time, however.

"It's too bad you couldn't be satisfied with your cut from Osler," Harvey said calmly. "Hell, Brad, I know you could have been satisfied. It's that bitch Natalie who drove you. And I forgive you for that."

Brad saw Harvey's shoulders settle and believed his forgiveness was genuine. Harvey's face disappeared, and the tips of his skis began sidestepping along the rim of the hole, toward the uphill side.

"Look, J.H., you're right. You're right in everything. About me. About Natalie. I let it get out of control, and I'm sorry." He turned to look up at Harvey's new position, and he was starting to rise on his good leg to accept Harvey's help out of the hole when the rim of the hole above him collapsed and fell on

186

him, burying him to his shoulders under hundreds of pounds of snow. When the flurry of powdery snow that followed this small avalanche had settled, Brad saw Harvey once more, standing immediately above where the avalanche started.

"That one was for cheating me, Brad," Harvey said quietly. "The next one's going to be for lying. And the one after that, the one that could be the lid on your coffin, that may be just for the hell of it, Brad. Because somehow I just don't believe you're sorry and I suspect that I might be better off if you just disappeared today." He reached his hand out over the edge of the hole so Brad could see what dangled from it. Brad patted at his chest, as if searching for a pack of cigarettes.

"That's right, Brad. Your transceiver came off when you fell. No one will ever find you in that hole. But I'm certain you'll feel little pain. The cold numbs you, they say, and then you simply go to sleep."

"Don't do this, J.H. Please!" Brad cried, and tears flooded his eyes. "We're doctors, for God's sake! You can't take a life!"

"It happens every day, Brad. How many lives have you lost and wondered: Could I have saved her? I know I've had my share. We all have, Brad. So what's one more? What harm is it, compared with the harm you could do to Osler if I let you live?"

Harvey kicked another avalanche into the shaft, and Brad was buried to his neck.

"Oh, God, J.H., this is twisted! Please, please! Let me live!"

"Begging becomes you, Brad," Harvey said flatly. "Of course I'll spare you. Why shouldn't I? Your life on earth will be a living hell when Natalie finds out. But wait! Perhaps she won't learn of your capitulation. You can be useful to Osler in many ways. If you're willing to deal."

Twenty . . .

Grieving relatives, when they came to Podge Durant's funeral home, almost always accepted his suggestions and his prices as readily as they accepted his condolences. But Podge, whose inheritance of the business spared him a life as a supermarket shelf stocker—the other career for which he had an aptitude—was aware that at all other times, in the minds of every member of the community, including those whose dearest loved ones he had disemboweled and embalmed, the name Podge Durant commanded scant respect. And so, of course, respect was what Podge wanted most.

That is why, after the merger, Podge accepted the invitation to remain on the board of the combined hospitals. Even better to Podge's liking, he no longer was a trustee—a musty old noun, like an irrelevant text untouched for decades on a back shelf at the library. Now, he was a member of the board of directors. The matters of the hospital were no longer just left in his trustworthy lap. He now was in a position to direct the future of the institution, and from everything he saw, Valleyview, now christened Hancock Medical Services, had a brimming future.

Joining Podge on the new board were Lydia Fulton, a woman drawn by civic duty, and the Rev. Milton Farnham, similarly motivated; Mayor Henry Costanza, to whom civic duty translated into votes; bank president Willie Smicks, Rick Swaboda of the chamber of commerce, real estate agent Carlton Porferrio, and Neil Dunmore, each of whose altruism was tempered by an eye for personal profit; and doctors Jim Harvey, Steve Nightingale, and Ari Urizar. Konrad Schmidt, although he remained chief of surgery of the City Campus, was so distressed by what he saw as the high-handedness of the merger that he refused the invitation to join the new board, as did tax lawyer Bruce Groff, who gave no reason. Peter Warren's health had not returned following his very public collapse from the accidental poisoning by a combination of alcohol and *Coprinus* mushrooms at the mixer before the merger vote, so he was unable to accept the offer. If he had, the small board room at HMS would have been all the more cramped. Loring English, discredited in the community, had received no invitation.

Not until April 1. Derrick Keating called, asking him to be a guest at the monthly HMS board meeting. It was no April Fool's joke. And so Loring arrived in the little conference room early and took a chair against the wall. He recognized his colleagues from the PHG board, seated around the plain, rectangular table, and some of the others whom he knew to have been Valleyview board members. There were several strangers, as well. To Loring's right was Mandy Levine, an original Valleyview member representing Hancock Systems, and to his left sat Walter Scott, who now held little authority within HMS but carried the title of chief operating officer.

The high-backed leather chair of chief executive Derrick Keating was at the end of the table with the room's only windows behind it. At precisely ten o'clock, as Loring twisted in his seat to keep his knees from hitting the back of Wallace Reid's chair, the boardroom door opened and Keating, led by a young woman with an armload of folders topped by a jar filled with M&M's, entered and went directly to his seat.

"First order of business, chart reviews," Keating said, shuffling papers busily without looking at his board members. The young woman had set the candy jar by his right hand, and Keating now uncapped the jar and scooped a handful.

"If we might first have a moment of prayer," Rev. Farnham asked, "of thanksgiving for the deliverance of Dr. Barnett from death's door by his good friend, Dr. Harvey."

"Your comment is well taken, but out of order," Keating told the preacher. He flipped some candy into his mouth. "Please bring that up under other new business." The board dispensed with the medical chart reviews before moving into a discussion of a proposal from Hancock Systems to contract with HMS for nursing services at the factory.

Mandy Levine rose beside Loring, a thin body grown stout, with slender legs and arms protruding from a short-sleeved suit. Baby fat robbed her face of distinguishing features; a flat voice suggested adenoids. Her inner beauty, Peter Warren had once told Loring, was that she was a hell of a comptroller.

"As you know, Hancock Systems has been repositioning for the new, competitive marketplace," she began. "In furtherance of this effort, the company has taken a look at its medical department and come to a conclusion." Six nurses on three shifts was uneconomical. Nearly a quarter million in salaries.

"You folks have always had a reputation for taking care of your workers," Henry Costanza said.

"Amen!" said the Rev. Farnham.

"Repositioning demands, however, that we accomplish the same goal with less expense," Levine said. Her tone allowed no room for debate. "Under our proposal, HMS would establish a Scheduled Healthcare Office Time, or SHOT, system," Levine said, bending to pick up a folder from between her chair and Loring's. A SHOT nurse would make scheduled stops at the factory. Employees needing routine care would be advised to report during scheduled hours.

"HMS would earn an administrative fee," Levine said, "and you wouldn't need to increase your staff. Nurses could be scheduled in off-peak hours to prevent conflicts. We will work with the hospital to accommodate your needs."

"It's a win-win," said Keating, rising to draw attention from his board and to put his approval stamp on the proposal. "And it's good customer relations between HMS and the city's major employer."

The unasked question begged to escape Loring's lips, but he stifled it. His restraint was rewarded.

"Well it certainly sounds economical," Lydia Fulton said, "but is it medically sound? What happens in an emergency?"

Employees would be trained as medics, Levine promised, turning away from Lydia toward a more receptive end of the table. The original reason for a factory nurse—to keep noncritical cases on the job—would be accomplished, she told Keating, at a savings of about one hundred and fifty thousand dollars. Lydia attempted to pose a followup question, but Keating pointed to Ari Urizar who, holding one hand over his mouth to keep half chewed pretzels inside, waved the other.

"If it's in order, I move we authorize the chief executive to negotiate with Hancock Systems to provide nursing services."

Nightingale seconded the motion and Keating immediately called for a vote, which passed with only Lydia Fulton and Milton Farnham opposed.

Without hesitation, Keating moved on.

"Next order of business, Emergency Room Coordinator. The position is responsible for assuring productivity and enhanced career development, including cross-training."

Loring's mind began to wander, his eyes drifting out the window behind Keating into a brilliant April morning whose hot sun sucked the sap up into the landscape. He felt like a kid in a classroom where hormones are competing with first-year algebra. What the hell am I doing here, listening to talk of productivity and enhanced career development and repositioning? His thoughts had not drifted so far that Keating's next words couldn't snap him back into the moment.

"For your information, I have selected for this new position, which will oversee nursing at both the Valleyview and City campuses, an outstanding young nurse, Karen Larsen."

Loring, caught by surprise, let out a small, gleeful whoop at the news. He tried to recover composure by faking a cough, and in that moment, he saw Jim Harvey, sitting on the far side of the table two chairs from Keating, rising to his feet.

"Derrick, I believe this is a level of staffing that requires board approval," Harvey said. "Not to second guess your judgment, but particularly at this juncture when the staffs of the two institutions are still adjusting, such an appointment should enjoy particularly broad support, as board approval would suggest."

"The appointment is within the bylaws," Keating said, reaching into the candy jar. "Particularly in the realm of medical staffing, where I have already received recommendations from department heads, there is no issue." He flipped two of the candies into his mouth, ending discussion. "Our next item will, however, require board approval. We have as our guest today Dr. Loring English, a medical giant poorly treated by our predecessor, Port Hancock General."

That caught Loring's attention. Beside him, Walter Scott tugged at the sides of his suit coat, drawing them together and buttoning them, arming for the defense. Loring's focus was locked on the chief executive.

Keating explained that a reporter from the Port Hancock Journal had called, sniffing out a story. His questions all centered on Loring's suspension. Keating decided to review the case himself. He found what he called the "sorry history of this medical community," a history in which, he regretted, the old Valleyview had shared. He hoped, he told his new board, that HMS would treat Dr. English with the dignity his contributions to medicine in the Hancock River Valley deserved.

"At our next meeting, I will entertain a motion to revoke Dr. English's suspension and to make a public apology for his hardship," Keating said, and with that he stood, facing Loring, and began clapping, slowly, rhythmically.

Lydia Fulton, Milton Farnham, and Podge Durant all stood and applauded, and gradually some of the others joined in, even Neil Dunmore, who smiled warmly at Loring and nodded his head in approval. At the end, only the Osler doctors were seated, and they, too, stood before Keating's applause ceased.

Loring had experienced this sensation before when he'd missed a diagnosis and the patient nevertheless responded to his therapy. Everything he had tried to salvage his career seemed inadequate. Aldie Spencer promised only the long haul in court. Loring's own quest against Harvey had been effectively stalled, despite the help that Reggie Wilson had offered. At every turn, when he had tried on his own to battle the forces degrading medicine, he had been ineffective. It was, without question, not the longest but rather the first losing streak in Loring English's life. Now, through none of his efforts and from a man for whom he had no respect, his salvation appeared to be arriving. He later would describe the scene to Karen as surreal. He had half expected Walter Scott to throw off his suit and reveal himself as the Dalai Lama. He would make this observation after he had reported to Karen the other extraordinary event of the board meeting, her own promotion.

The meeting ended with Keating inviting the board members to visit the newly installed microwave medical waste processor at City Campus. "Environmentally, it's an improved technology over the old gas-fired incinerator, meaning good public relations. And we'll save hundreds of thousands. But most important, it signals our continued support of City Campus," Keating was saying as Harvey began shoving papers theatrically into a briefcase.

Neil Dunmore saw that Jim Harvey was furious, but he did not pursue the matter until they had reached the parking lot and were standing between Dunmore's Jaguar and the Range Rover, parked near a blossoming cherry tree.

"I had the bastard buried alive and suddenly the guy I've put in charge of the vault is rolling the stone away!" Harvey fumed, throwing his suit jacket across the front seat of the Rover. "Can you believe the brass?"

"You must admit, he had you outmaneuvered," Dunmore chuckled. "Whatever he was after."

"Whatever indeed. You know how much we jacked up his pay to get him—"

"Jim," Dunmore interrupted softly, "why don't we get in my car and talk. Our voices are carrying."

Once inside the Jaguar, Harvey complained bitterly about Keating's disloyalty. His income had risen after the merger to three quarters of a million. He had been put at the controls of a sprawling empire much more grand than his credentials warranted, simply because Harvey and Osler needed a puppet. Now the puppet had cut his own strings and was attempting to actually work the controls. Harvey could see Osler's grand plans succumbing. Dunmore doubted Keating posed such a great problem.

"What you have to ask yourself, Neil, is why Keating wants to promote English."

"You have an idea?"

"Simply because he knows we were behind the suspension. He's throwing down a challenge, and if we don't flatten him, he will rip HMS out of our hands."

And why, Dunmore asked, had Harvey objected to what appeared to be a natural promotion in the nursing staff?

Harvey did not respond with complete honesty, for he did not mention the element of pique, his memory of how Karen had dismissed him at the end of their affair. What he did tell Dunmore was the truth.

"Are you familiar with Karen Larsen?" Harvey asked.

"I don't recall having met her."

"You would remember, Neil. I can assure you."

"A knockout?"

"Very attractive."

"What has this to do with your objection."

"Not a thing. But do you know who she's dating? Of course not, if you don't know her. Well, it's Loring English. They're keeping it quiet if not secret. But here's the problem, or the potential. With Karen and English as a team, working with Keating, they may well pursue Loring's holy war against my license and that other matter that Jerry handled last month."

"The Dennis Ross thing? You ought to be careful with your boys, J.H.," Dunmore winked.

"You know the range of practices our fellow Osler board members engage in as well as I, and you know that we are in no position to limit them, given their involvement with our own ventures."

"Jerry snuffed out that problem. Had the help of that Coastal CEO."

"So you weren't sleeping at the switch. Good, Neil. Well, Scarborough is, indeed, our bosom friend. He caught wind that English was poking around and tipped us. Then he placed a couple of moles on the good doctor's source inside Coastal."

"So that avenue is sealed off to English. And so far, Jim, Keating hasn't succeeded in rehabilitating the doctor. Why don't we worry when the time comes to worry?"

"Keating is dangerous, Neil. He's on the move, and he's shown who he's going to court. It's not Osler."

"He does create a dynamic image, Jim. But he's all style, no substance. Tell you what. I'll go have a talk with him, let him know he should tone it down. How about that, Jim."

"I don't know, Neil," Harvey said, pulling on the door handle to leave. "I doubt there are strong enough words for Derrick Keating."

Twenty-one . . .

An explanation is needed for why Muriel Gore lived her life of captivity inside the little forest cabin she shared with Rawson, her husband, and it is this. Beyond her physical incapacity, which was severe but not totally crippling, there was a further shackle. Muriel was terribly afraid of the unknown. She had not ventured outside the cabin in four years, and there had been times that Thomas Grimes had wondered if her obesity had increased to the point where, if she needed to leave, it would require taking a chain saw to the cabin's door. Grimes died before he learned the answer. Robert Chen, who had inherited Grimes's list of house calls, was a witness to the solution early on a hot morning in May. Rawson had phoned Chen to ask for help because Muriel's breathing had become even more labored than normal. Chen called the police and then sped to the cabin, where he found Muriel lying on a litter on the cabin floor and medics smearing petroleum jelly on the door frame. The cabin's windows were nailed shut, the air was stagnant and the temperature in the room at six-thirty had to be above ninety degrees. The doctor bent to examine his patient, over whose mouth was strapped an oxygen mask, and was met by the most perfectly relaxed eyes, for while Muriel feared the unknown, she did not fear death. What happened to a person upon death was, for Muriel, an absolute known. Her Bible had long ago explained it all.

"I'll ride with you to the hospital," Chen said, taking Muriel's hand but staying clear of the medics, who now were lifting the litter. The ambulance was air-conditioned and Muriel, with sweat still beading on her brow, shivered. Chen pulled the white blanket up to her chin and rested his palm on her forehead. Through the clear oxygen mask, he could see her mouth curl in a smile. "You will be fine, Mrs. Gore," he said with more certainty than he felt.

Another ambulance was backed up to the Valleyview Campus emergency room door and had to be moved before Muriel was unloaded. Chen raced by her side as the litter was wheeled through the automatic doors and around the corner to the cardiac room, the first examining station on the right. The hospital staff now took over, applying wires to many parts of Muriel's body and engaging several large pieces of electronic equipment, which beeped and blinked and produced a paper chart that Chen grabbed and read intently.

"Is the catheterization suite available?" he asked, still scanning the chart.

"They're on standby," the redhead in the jeans and white blouse answered.

Chen, whose back had been to Muriel, lowered the chart and turned to her. "Now I described catheterization to you on the ride, Mrs. Gore. We're giving you some clot-busting drugs, but I suspect you're going to need angioplasty in at least one place. I'll need you to sign a consent. Do you think you can do that?"

Muriel nodded and winked.

"Nurse, could I have a consent form?"

Karen Larsen already had one in her hand on a clipboard and passed it to Chen with a pen. The doctor held the clipboard and showed Muriel where to sign, which she did with a firm hand. Then, under Karen's direction, Muriel was moved from the examining table to a gurney. With an IV hanging from a stand at her side and dripping medication into her arm,

Muriel was wheeled out of the cardiac room to the elevators, again with Chen at her side.

There were, as Chen had suspected, two pinched arteries in Muriel's heart, and the procedure to open them and insert stainless steel stents—the expandable tubes that would keep the vessels open once the balloon was deflated—took three hours. Chen stood beside Muriel's gurney for another hour, holding gauze against the place where he had punctured her groin to insert the catheters in the femoral artery. She talked as though from a dream but clearly understood all that was happening.

"You'll do fine, Mrs. Gore," Chen said when he finally removed the gauze and there was no more bleeding.

"God's will be done," she said, smiling.

Chen made it a point to return to the emergency room and locate the redhead.

"I wish to applaud the efficiency with which your staff handled Mrs. Gore," he told Karen, whom he found emerging from one of the examination rooms. "Our emergency room never functioned so smoothly."

"Thanks, Dr. Chen. I guess this is the first time we've worked together," she said as he followed her across the emergency room. "You've never worked at Port Hancock . . . uh, City Campus, have you?"

"The services of Osler employees have been withheld from your old hospital since I arrived."

"It figures. Too bad. From what I saw in there, Doctor, you're a skillful cardiologist." They stopped outside the closed door of an examination room.

"You have many fine cardiologists at City Division. Dr. Michael Bernstein is one of my acquaintances. I have found his abilities top notch."

"Mike's doing great," Karen said, reaching for the door handle. "And we may be getting Loring English back. He's the best."

"Ah, perhaps I should feel threatened by competition. But there should be room for the best. We lost one of them not long ago."

"Oh, who was that?" Karen asked, pushing the door open

slightly. Laughter came through the crack in the door, the giggles of an adult male.

"Dr. Thomas Grimes," Chen replied, and Karen yanked the door shut, a reflex at hearing Grimes's name unexpectedly.

"I've really got to go, Dr. Chen," she said hurriedly. "Many patients waiting."

"I must be on my way as well. I have an afternoon flight to California, and I must attend to Mrs. Gore's husband before I leave. Very pleasant speaking with you and working with you, Nurse Larsen."

Karen nodded, waved and pushed open the examination room door, eager to immerse herself in work and push aside the disturbing reminder of Grimes's death. Inside the room, she found a gaunt young man with a face gray as a death mask, his mouth twisted in a jack-o-lantern smile, his brow furrowed and questioning. Matt Willow's contorted expression jerked Karen away from the memory of Tom Grimes.

"Welcome back, Matthew. I thought the rehab must have worked. But from your smell, I'd say you've been on a ride for a week at least. God, you junkies stink. It's been a long time since I've seen you like this."

"Yeah, man. Times have been good," the boy said slowly. "No time like the present, man, oh yeah, like a Christmas present. Hooo! This stuff is good, man, know what I mean?" Matt Willow broke into the hollow laughter of a dead soul, and while he felt that he could easily fly to the ceiling of the examination room, it was obvious to Karen from his soiled, ripped clothes and the bruises on his arms and from the way his cheeks sunk into his mouth that this seventeen-year-old was spiraling toward Hell.

Matthew Willow had been found at daybreak, unconscious, on a roadside to the west of Port Hancock, and the medics who responded rushed him to Valleyview Campus by the most direct route. Among the few vehicles on the road at that early hour was a Range Rover, headed west, toward the mountains.

Dr. James Perkins Harvey III turned off the highway about twenty-five miles from the city and followed first a country road and then an old logging road until he reached a small, brown shingled hunting cabin. Green shutters were padlocked over the cabin's windows and a large padlock was on the front door hasp.

Harvey parked the Range Rover and rolled up his sleeves before stepping out of the air conditioning. He stood for a moment outside the vehicle, observing the woods and listening. A few birds chattered high in the foliage, where the leaves moved in a light breeze that could not reach down to the forest floor. Harvey filled his lungs with the fresh air and smelled the sweetness of the forest, then reached in his pocket for the key to the cabin.

The sound of his steps on the porch planks reminded him of his last visit to the cabin, when his footsteps were accompanied by the hammering of spiked heels. She was a visiting executive from a national agency that certifies hospitals. He believed, from their conversations, that she might respond to the feel of rough floorboards on her naked backside, and he was proved correct when, once inside the cabin, they had not touched the two cots. Now, as he entered the cabin alone, Harvey left the door open for the light it provided. He went to the old, white range in the rear corner, took a match from a cardboard box and lit one burner. Then from the chipped porcelain sink he drew some water into a tea kettle, which he set on the flame. Steam was beginning to waft from the kettle's spout when he heard the sound of twigs cracking under the weight of tires and then heard the whump of a car door being shut. He was pouring water into two mugs, one with instant coffee and the other with a tea bag, when the light in the cabin dimmed as a figure entered the doorway.

"You obviously had no problems with the directions," Harvey said.

"None."

"The tea is jasmine."

"Excellent."

"It's rather stuffy in here. Please, take off your jacket."

"I like the heat, Doctor."

"As you wish, Dragon. I asked you to come so that we might discuss face to face the progress of our businesses and work out any issues that may have arisen."

"Do you have issues, Doctor?" the Dragon asked, joining the fingertips of both hands in a bridge before his chest.

"My issues are only with regard to the health of our efforts. From our end, the electronic transfers have been prompt and the operations appear to be flowing smoothly. Have a seat, Dragon."

They each pulled a wooden, armless chair up to a rectangular table covered with a yellow oilcloth, facing each other in the half light of the cabin.

"I have some questions about the medical supply contract," Harvey said.

Dragon sipped his tea deliberately, gazing through the vapor at Harvey without responding.

"We have no mechanism to feel assured that we remain your sole client. We would not be pleased should you choose to engage additional distributors," Harvey said.

"Feel assured that that is not our intention. We believe you have the capability of adequately protecting your interests, and we respect that ability."

"Good. As long as we remain clear on this."

"We do, Doctor. Now, there must be some other business that brought us here. Perhaps we could discuss that as well so that I might be on my way to the airport."

Harvey rose and went to the door, then returned. "Good, You came alone. I want to mention some names to you and a situation. Consider this my compliment to you, that I would raise this subject and seek your advice."

The Dragon smiled. "Of course."

"There are a couple of individuals, Dragon. One man's name is Derrick Keating," Harvey said, and he detailed the administrator's grab for power. "I just want you to be aware, in case we should have to take steps."

"We agree that now is not the time," the Dragon said without seeking a response. "You mentioned another individual?"

"Loring English. Dr. Loring English, but that, too, can wait. I simply wanted you to be familiar with the situation. For now, he is under observation with no reports of imminent problems."

"Fine. Then I must take my leave."

Harvey escorted the Dragon to his car, an inconspicuous white Toyota four-door which was parked beside the Range Rover. The Dragon got in and turned the key, but the car would not start.

"A minor matter were it not for my flight, Doctor. This is a rental car and I must return it to the airport before I leave."

"Take the Range Rover, Dragon. I'll call for a tow before you leave and wait with the car. Just leave the Rover in the long-term parking lot with the key in the glove box. Call my secretary and tell her what letter you parked next to so I can find it."

"You are a gentleman," the Dragon said.

Port Hancock Taxi Company, way past its prime, used fifteen-year-old Dodge Diplomats painted white with green doors. Bob Gray, who, upon early retirement as a supervisor from Hancock Systems was just hitting his prime, was the company's sole driver. His noon run into the woods to the north of the city ended on a roadside where a cabin without a driveway was visible down the hillside through the trees.

"No charge, Doc," Gray told Robert Chen, who was passing him a twenty dollar bill from the back seat. "I've heard from the guys at the plant what you've been doin' for folks. Least I can do is give you a lift."

"I must insist," Chen said. "You've used your gas and your time."

"Bet you did the same for these folks, else your car wouldn't be parked here, not that I'm askin', mind you."

"I appreciate your effort, Mr. Gray. And I liked your joke about the parsley."

"Now, don't you go passin' that one around or I'll get me a reputation."

"Thank you again, Mr. Gray," Chen said, closing the cab door. When Gray had left, Chen passed his car which he had left parked on the shoulder and descended the bank. He found Rawson Gore sitting before his television, wearing a dark green sweater. The door of the cabin was open, but the air inside was still and hot. Chen checked Rawson's pulse and temperature and found them normal. He noticed that the man was not sweating.

"You appear to be fine. Mrs. Gore will be staying in the hospital for two days. I will check her when I return from California. Is there anything you need?"

"Nope," the man said, his eyes unaverted from the television.

"Then I'll be leaving," Chen said. Rawson did not respond.

By the time Chen had picked up his luggage at home, it was two in the afternoon. His flight left Riverton International at five, and the drive to the airport was ninety minutes, so there was no time for lunch. He took two apples from the refrigerator. He was finishing the second apple when he turned into the long-term parking lot at the airport and, searching for a parking spot, pulled in beside a Range Rover with a vanity license plate—OSLER. Chen knew the vehicle. He wondered whether Dr. Harvey or his wife were taking a trip. The answer was of little concern to him, and by the time he reached the airline concourse he had forgotten about the Rover.

"Put your bags on the conveyor and step through the arch," the attendant in the uniform said, looking away from Chen with the sort of professional distraction practiced by toll booth attendants. When he had retrieved his bags on the other side of the arch, he found Gate D-2 and got a boarding pass. It was when he turned to find a seat that he saw the back of a familiar head. It had been at least five years since he had seen his brother, and another five could pass happily if Chen could avoid encountering the Dragon. He found a seat behind a pillar. A woman with fleshy arms, gray hair and a print dress was in the next seat, reading *People* magazine. On the cover was a story about crime and so, of course, the question surfaced. Why is my brother in Riverton? But Chen employed a mental exercise he used whenever complete concentration was necessary. By focusing his attention then on the case in California that had beckoned him, he was able to remove the question about the Dragon from his consciousness.

And then the memory of the Range Rover in the parking lot presented itself, asking another question.

"There could be no connection," he said aloud, startling himself and the woman, who looked up from her magazine and turned away from Robert Chen.

Twenty-two . . .

A steaming mug of coffee sat beside the architectural plans over which Derrick Keating was huddled when his secretary, Dana Resnick, led Lydia Fulton into the conference room. Keating, the sleeves of his silk shirt folded up below the elbows, his tie loosened and the collar button undone, could have met Lydia in his office, but he preferred this setting, this image—the chief executive immersed in his work, able to see the big picture and the details. He did not look up from the plans, which showed Valleyview's ground floor, when Mrs. Resnick reached his side, as if he were preoccupied with some concept on which the future of the hospital hinged. In fact, he had no idea what the plan showed, other than some corridors and some rooms. Mrs. Resnick spoke quietly.

"Mr. Keating? Mrs. Fulton is here."

Keating hesitated before he looked to the side. Then, his glance engaging Lydia's, he broke into a warm smile that creased the tanned skin at the corners of his blue eyes, and his perfect teeth were revealed by the parting of his lips.

"Lydia, Lydia! So glad you were able to come over!"

"Hancock Medical Services has become my priority, Mr. Keating," Lydia said, allowing him to take her hand between his. Keating made a minor study of which individuals disliked being touched and those who responded to his hands. Drawing her by her left hand to stand in front of him and face the table on which the plans rested, he settled his free hand on Lydia's shoulder.

"Look at this, dear," he said, bending over her other shoulder, adjusting his voice to communicate intimacy, trust. "Nothing has changed, despite our growth. I was just pondering—you know, blue-skying, as they say—whether we're missing something by not analyzing our facilities, now that we have Port Hancock's incredible team with us."

"Dear, old Port Hancock General. I do miss her," Lydia said. She turned her face toward Keating, who moved aside to allow her to look up at him. "But what we have now is probably a whole lot better."

"We can improve," Keating said. He allowed the smile to fade, the brow to furrow. "That's why I asked you to stop by. I would be grateful if you would consider some thoughts—not plans, yet, but ideas I've had. Board meetings are filled with egos, but there are a handful of members whose judgment I respect and you are chief among them. I wanted your reaction to some suggestions. No commitment, mind you. Just your thoughts. Here, let's step back into my office, if you don't mind."

When they both had settled into comfortable chairs around a coffee table—Keating with his mug of coffee and Lydia with tea that Mrs. Resnick had brought—Keating explained how HMS acquired medical supplies.

"I think we could do better with competitive bids, even though Larry Bunch says we're getting lower prices than other hospitals he's surveyed," Keating said, sitting back and crossing his legs, affecting a casual pose to help Lydia become relaxed and open.

"I'm surprised we don't already have competitive bids. My

family always used them," she said. "What is your idea, Mr. Keating?"

"Really only that. But as you know, we have some hide-bound traditionalists on the board, some don't-fix-it-if-it-ain't-broke folks. I don't expect easy sailing if I propose we go out for bids."

"Would it help if I made the proposal, Derrick?" Lydia asked.

"It could make all the difference, Lydia," he said. "You have such a nice, unthreatening way. Would you, dear?" Keating said, sliding forward in his chair and reaching to lightly touch Lydia's hand. "I would be grateful, and I know the hospital would benefit."

"You can count on me," she said, smiling.

"Then there is one other item," Keating said, "if it's not an imposition. You may recall that last month, I suggested we return Dr. English to our fold."

"It's about time someone saw the injustice," Lydia said.

"Again, I need someone to make a motion at this month's meeting. Would you do me the honor?"

"Ah, well, there is a problem that just occurred to me," she said, setting her tea cup in its saucer and folding her hands. "I must be out of town the last two weeks of the month. Otherwise I would love to bring both issues to the floor."

Keating slumped back in his chair. Lydia was the ideal vessel to float his ideas before a board peopled by Osler's principals. Although Osler's members did not by themselves constitute a majority, they had influence with the rest. Lydia's old-money stature was the most promising counterbalance. He settled on his best option.

"Then we'll do it at the June meeting, if you'll be there."

"I will," Lydia said, patting her clasped hands on her knees lightly, soft smile wrinkles tucking back her cheeks.

Although Derrick Keating did not know of Osler Medical Group's connection with Four Seasons, the firm supplying HMS, he did know that Larry Bunch had been suggested as comptroller of the combined hospitals by Walter Scott. And he knew that Walter Scott had brought the board of Port Hancock General in line for the merger at the request of people associated with Osler. He assumed, therefore, that when Bunch renewed the deal with Four Seasons, the Osler people were informed.

Now, since the visit by Neil Dunmore, Keating was looking for any way to weaken Osler's grip on him and on HMS. If it meant denying their friendly vendors an income from the hospital, he would make that happen. He was, he reminded himself, the chief executive of this institution. It was absurd that Dunmore, a simple developer, should think he could come into the hospital and tell Keating how to function. "I remind you that you serve at the will of the board," Dunmore had said when Keating had rejected the suggestion that his style in running the board meetings was offensive to some members. "Osler controls a clear majority on the board, and that majority answers to one man," Dunmore had told Keating. "That one man isn't you."

Although Dunmore mentioned no name, it was clear to Keating that Dr. James Harvey was the power Dunmore had in mind. Stuff it, Keating thought. I set out to separate myself from my keepers and I won't stop. Bringing Loring back when Harvey was behind the suspension had been his device. It was a stone thrown into a hornet's nest. Now, in the wake of Dunmore's visit, he needed to further assert his independence.

Keating had searched, then, for a gesture with impact. If his suspicions were correct, Four Seasons was the appropriate target. He knew he had hit pay dirt when he got the call several days after Lydia Fulton's visit from Tiffany Blaise, who said Dr. Harvey wished to meet with him to discuss HMS's medical supply contracts.

"I simply won't have time until next month," Keating told Tiffany. "I'll ask Mrs. Resnick to pencil something in, perhaps in the second week of August."

"That's okay, Mr. Keating," Tiffany said, her voice as melodic as a coloratura's. "Dr. Harvey will make a point to stop you when he sees you in the hospital. He said it won't take all that long."

Indeed, it was that same afternoon when Harvey appeared before Dana Resnick.

"How's your husband doing, Mrs. Resnick," he asked. "I haven't seen him in months."

"Oh, he's doing great, Dr. Harvey," she said, standing and folding her arms across her thick chest. Dana Resnick was a natural blond, a mother of three with the extra pounds to prove it. Her hair was done in tight curls, short above the ears and up the neck. She wore eyeglasses with pale pink frames and lenses of a thickness that exaggerated both her eyes and the bags under them. "He always says what a miracle worker you are, Dr. Harvey. You caught the problem so quick! He always tells people they should use you."

"I appreciate that, Mrs. Resnick. It's good to know when you've helped someone."

"Oh, Lord, Dr. Harvey. I guess you've helped hundreds of folks here in Port Hancock."

"Well, I could use some help of my own, Mrs. Resnick. I need just a minute with Mr. Keating." Harvey, still standing before the secretary's desk, leaned forward, placing his hands on her desktop. He whispered. "I know Derrick's busy, but I'm certain he will welcome this interruption, if you'd just buzz me in. No introduction necessary." He winked at the woman.

"Anything for you, Dr. Harvey," she said, lowering her own voice to a whisper, and as Harvey stepped around her desk, the door to Keating's office buzzed open.

By the time he left Derrick Keating's office, Jim Harvey had painted, with short, bold brush strokes, a rather stark picture of the administrator's future.

"Let's just assume that your hearing is better now than it was when Neil Dunmore visited," Harvey said once inside the door, which he shut quietly before advancing on Keating like a boxer coming out of his corner, chin lowered, eyes fixed, his words flashing like left jabs as he circled the desk. Keating, who had been tilted back in his chair before Harvey entered, was too stunned to change his position. "Your salary is seven hundred and thirty seven thousand, Derrick. Your mortgage is one-point-two, and you serve at the will of the HMS board. Your contract has a buyout provision that could keep you whole, unless malfeasance is discovered. Sit down, Derrick," Harvey said, now beside Keating, who was trying to get to his feet. Keating sat down. "There are any number of ways malfeasance can be proven, Derrick. And your board of directors, whom you believe you can buffalo into changing suppliers, is stacked against you. Your dismissal from HMS would be publicly humiliating, Derrick. Do not question that. And you would enjoy a future in the health care industry equal to that of an M&M in a furnace." Harvey scooped a handful of candies from the giant brandy snifter on Keating's desktop and popped several onto his tongue. He stepped back to gauge, as the candies dissolved, Keating's response. The usual confident smile was erased. The muscles over Keating's jaw flexed as he ground his teeth, but he did not speak. Harvey was pleased. "Questions or comments?" he asked.

Keating looked down at his desktop. Harvey waited. He would have waited all afternoon for Keating's response. That was unnecessary. The administrator, whose hands had been folded in his lap, unclasped them and, with a palms-up gesture, asked: "Is there anything else?"

There was no way Harvey could know, as he left Keating's office, that the administrator had already seized on a plan to corner him. What Harvey read as meekness in Keating's face was in fact a skillfully crafted mask covering a certain glee. Even as Harvey was giving him his marching orders, Keating was envisioning the outline of the doctor's defeat. Seldom had Harvey so misjudged another man, but in his ignorance, he felt a surge of strength, a weightlifter's rush. He strode out of Keating's office, waved his thanks to Dana Resnick and believed that he had but one more account with Keating to bring into balance, the matter of Karen Larsen's promotion. It was a fait accompli, to be sure. Keating, unwittingly, had Harvey boxed in. Unwittingly because no one, including Karen, was aware that when she had broken off their affair seven years earlier, Harvey had vowed to himself either to restore the relationship so that he could be the one to end it or to end her career. Keating's move left him only one out. He headed toward the elevator intent on pursuing her vigorously and successfully. On his way to the emergency room, when he glanced into the cafeteria, he saw Karen standing third in line at the cash register. Taking an apple from the glass shelf of a countertop display, he worked his way past two nurses waiting to have an order from the grill filled and moved quietly into line behind Karen.

"Seldom have I seen Nurse Larsen absent from her duty post," he said in a stage whisper. The two nurses turned to look, and Karen, startled, jumped slightly. "Is this what the new medicine has come to mean?" He took a bite of the apple.

Regaining her composure, Karen twisted her mouth to the side, a snarling gesture that caused her cheek to crease in a fine crescent line just beyond the mouth's corner.

"Well, Adam and the forbidden fruit!" she said, turning back toward the cash register.

"Hardly forbidden," he said, turning the meaning of her words. "Simply not sampled for too many years."

"Nor will it ever be, Jim," she said, stepping forward to pay the cashier. Harvey dropped a dollar bill on the counter and followed Karen across the cafeteria to a table by a window.

"May I, please?" he said as she took her seat.

"I'd prefer that you didn't," she said, still not looking at him as she removed the cling wrap from a slice of banana nut bread.

"There are few women whom I respect enough to honor that request, Karen," he said. He shifted out of his normal vocal rumble into a softer tone that sounded chastened as a tardy altar boy. "You're quite aware of that. I plead guilty. For you, however, I have the deepest respect, and I'll take my leave. I had only wanted to say hello and see how you're doing."

"I'm doing quite rotten right now, Jim. Your timing is uncharacteristically lousy."

"I'm sorry to hear that on at least two levels. What's the problem?"

"A case in the ER that I just had to escape. Nothing momentous. Just another human louse, the kind we seem to see too often."

"The details?"

"Twenty-five, a bundle of big bills rolled up in his pocket. He and his pal had been drinking and they got in his Porsche. When they hit the iron fence that runs along the Fulton mansion, the passenger's side of the Porsche was shredded. The cop who brought him in said it was like a tin can that's been run over by a lawn mower. This guy gets a broken knee. His pal was cut in two."

"Not nice," Harvey said, and he motioned to the seat opposite Karen, a question in his eyes. She shrugged, and he sat.

"This guy's in the ER weeping over the pain in his knee, which must be numb with all the needles the EMTs shot into it, and he's asking the cop about his car. His damned car! Meanwhile his pal's body still lies in two neatly severed halves in that car, but this character doesn't once ask about him. It's disgusting!"

"Could it be that he was in severe denial from shock?"

"That would be a charitable interpretation." Karen took a small bite of her banana nut bread.

"And you aren't feeling charitable today? That's uncharacteristically harsh of the Karen Larsen I remember."

"A lot of things have changed about me that you wouldn't recognize, Jim."

"Enough hasn't that, sitting across from you, I can't take my eyes off yours, Karen," he said. His gaze was indeed fixed on her, and some of the vocal rumble returned, and Karen felt a small, familiar and not totally unpleasant tremor in her chest. She bit the inside of her mouth gently. I shouldn't have let this start, she thought. I shouldn't have made a reference to myself, either.

"Really, I was just looking for some solitude, Jim. If you don't mind."

"Of course, Karen," he said, easing back from the table. He took another bite from the apple and chewed it, looking out the window, and then bit again. When he had swallowed, he spoke without looking back. "I still feel the loss."

"I really wanted to be alone, but I can see that's not going to work," she said, pushing back from the table and scraping the legs of her seat across the floor loudly.

He followed her out into the corridor. "No, no, Karen. I'm a fool and I apologize. I told the truth, but I can see you don't want to hear it."

"Got that straight, Doctor!" she said, marching ahead of him. He stepped briskly to her side as they approached, on the left, the short hall that led to the emergency room.

"Karen, I'll always care for you. You know that in your heart."

Dave Carn was stitching together the knee of a skateboarder when Loring came to the emergency room, expecting to find Karen.

"Tell him what you were doing, son," Carn commanded the boy. "Never mind. I'll tell him. He was trying to ride his board down the handrail in front of the high school. There are seventeen steps there. I counted them once myself."

"I hung the whole thing, too," the boy said.

"Forgot about the landing, though," Loring said. "No harm done. There's plenty more skin where that knee came from."

"Lucky he didn't crack the knee cap, Dr. English. His insurance company's going to be paying for x-rays. I told him it should come out of his allowance."

"My folks will sue the school. They've got plenty of money to pay for it," the boy said.

"Family values!" Loring said. "What would this country be

without them? Say, Dave, have you seen Karen? I need to talk with her."

Carn knotted a stitch and then ushered Loring from the examination room, closing the door behind him. He looked both ways and then, whispering, asked: "What's going on between you two? Are you making any progress?"

"We're good friends, Dave. Really. I sure do enjoy her company."

"Hmmm," Carn said, tugging on his chin. "I thought I heard more in her voice than friendship."

"You're losing your touch, Dr. Carn. Now, where is she?"

"Cafeteria. She took a break to get away from a lout in Room Three. Why don't you go meet her?"

Loring was heading out of the emergency room when he thought he heard Karen's voice around the corner. He definitely identified the words he heard next as coming from Jim Harvey, and they caused a flush of hot blood to race across his scalp and the hair along that path to stand erect.

Twenty-three . . .

There was a smell inside Eddie Beiler's gym that Loring had forgotten. He rediscovered it the day after he ran into Karen and Jim Harvey in the City Campus corridor. It was sweat and wintergreen ointment, sweetness and pungency stirred together. Loring liked it, and he was working hard at making his own contribution to the mix. Perspiration flooded from his brow and soaked his fingers, intertwined and pressing against the matted hair on the back of his head, as he strained through a lengthy set of sit-ups. Eddie, a retired light middleweight whose neck now rose directly from his chest to his chin with no pause for an Adam's apple or a jaw, squatted and held down Loring's ankles.

212

"You don't want to overdo it, Doc," Eddie advised.

"Loring gasped between repetitions, "gotta . . . drop . . . this . . . paunch."

"Thirty-five, Doc," said Eddie, who had been counting for Loring. "Let's move over to the bag. You're on schedule with the abs. Your arms need some work."

Loring dropped back on the mat without removing his hands from behind his head. He closed his eyes and felt the warmth of blood returning to his strained stomach muscles.

"You've been hitting it pretty hard for a week now, Doc," Eddie said, a worried look on his face. "You have a bad physical or something?"

Loring propped himself on an elbow and grinned, shaking his head. "Or something, Eddie."

"Ho-lee shit! It's a god-damned woman, ain't it!"

"I guess you only had about two choices, right, Eddie?"

"But why're you working out so fierce? Either she's a young'un, or you got yerself some competition."

"You get two more points, Eddie," Loring said, pushing himself up from the floor.

"You got competition, I'd better be teaching you some self-defense moves, Doc. No extra charge."

"Karen, I'll always care for you. You know that in your heart."

These words had, over the last week and at the most inopportune moments, repeatedly surfaced in Loring's mind with the nasty insistence of a pimple that's ready to break. He had somehow managed to contain himself on that afternoon when Karen and Jim Harvey rounded the corner in the corridor, as if he had heard nothing. Karen had no such success. A flash of red swept up from her neck when she saw Loring and, as she marched past him toward the emergency room, she scowled and demanded: "I think you need to talk with Dr. Harvey, Loring!"

Harvey had shrugged at Loring, stopping. "Apparently I upset her," he said.

"Apparently," Loring replied. "But how?"

"You figure women out and you tell me, Dr. English," he said, turning to retreat back toward the cafeteria. Loring watched him go but his mind was preoccupied with a number of racing thoughts. He followed Karen to the emergency room and found her behind the counter, typing furiously.

"What did he mean: 'you know that in your heart,' Karen?" he asked quietly.

"Come with me," Karen said, rounding the end of the counter and taking him by the elbow. She led him to the doctor's lounge, nearly shoved him inside and locked the door behind them. Her eyes were filled with tears as she told Loring about her affair with Harvey and how she had ended it. Dating another woman's husband, she said, had not been a problem for her. That should be obvious, considering Tom Grimes. Loring listened, taking a box of tissues from a desk and handing Karen one. And, she said, there was something safe in Harvey's disrespect for women, a confidence that she could never get close to him and therefore, by her acceptance of this fact, that she was protected from disappointment. "I kept the relationship while it served my need to have someone around. When that wore out, I ended it," she said. "That's the way they all were before Tom Grimes. And you," she said, squeezing her eyes shut as if trying to wring out the tears, and shaking her lowered head from side to side, anticipating the worst from Loring.

"I . . . I understand, Karen," he said. "We both had lives before we met. I understand. I was caught off guard by Dr. Harvey, I admit. But it's okay." He reached for her and took her by the shoulders. "I trust you," he said, drawing her to him. "And I have no claim. Not yet."

"Oh, but you do," she said, looking directly at him through a film of tears.

Even with trust, though, Loring thought that getting in shape couldn't hurt. He knew how his paunch looked in a mirror, and he knew that Jim Harvey carried no such baggage. So he began

214

visiting Eddie's gym every day. He found himself, during the mental isolation imposed by his workouts, thinking about Karen's silence about her past with Harvey and her support of him as he pursued punishment for Harvey's incompetence. He shifted this matter from one mental hand to the other, testing its weight, its worthiness. Did she see, as he did, corruption in Harvey, or was she guided by the bitter flavor of a romance that had ended? Each day after he left the gym, he would stop in the emergency room to see Karen, sometimes at Valleyview Campus, others at City Campus. She saw his concern, and she freely rehashed the matter. Harvey's a jerk, she would say. The proof is the way he was pursuing me that afternoon in the cafeteria. But I dropped him knowing he was a jerk. Your dislike for him, she told Loring, is well placed.

In time, Loring's doubts about Karen ceased.

His doubts about James Perkins Harvey III were, however, buttressed by a phone call he received at home one night from Janet's former partner Natasha Wilson. Natasha had sold her practice to Osler Medical Group and had become an Osler employee. She had a lot more time to spend with patients, and she was enjoying most aspects of her work.

"Up until I had a run-in with Ophelia Sadler," she told Loring, who took the call seated in his favorite chair, a tattered, overstuffed recliner upholstered in a coarse, mud-colored fabric and reeking subtly of dust, pets, and body odor. He had been tilted back in the dark, slowly sharpening his pocket knife against a stone and listening to a Bach tape. Menace the cat had climbed into his lap just before the phone on the table beside him rang.

"Sadler's the business manager," Natasha explained, "and its among her jobs to push the doctors to meet the group's productivity goals."

"Now that's a medical term I've never heard," Loring laughed.

"As you might guess, it has nothing to do with medicine. As Ophelia once explained it to me: 'You are an employee and as such have a responsibility to attain certain productivity goals.'

215

Loosely translated, this means 'You'd better be cramming in as many patient visits in any twenty-four-hour period as you can. And don't spend too much time with any one patient.'"

"Does she actually object if you linger with a sick child?"

"Loring, let me put it this way. You are assigned an examination room each morning, and there is a punch-pad just inside the door. You punch one button when the exam begins and another when it ends, and the times are recorded by the central computer."

"I suppose you know that's outrageous, Natasha," Loring said. "or else you wouldn't be calling me."

"That's not why I called," she said. "A couple of months ago, I got some mail from an insurance company by mistake. Normally, the Osler mailroom would handle any incoming insurance mail. This slipped through."

Inside the envelope from Carecard, a medical plan, was a notice that from the period of March through April, Natasha had been found to have ordered an excessive number of spinal taps. The insurer was withholding payment until the matter was resolved.

"No way I'd ordered too many taps, Loring. And when I went to Sadler demanding an explanation, she told me that under my employment contract, I had no right to see Osler's financial records, even those concerning my own patients. Can you believe that?"

"So what have you done?"

"One of the fellows here, Dr. Chen—you may know him, he's a cardiologist—"

"I've never met him, Natasha."

"Anyway, he overheard my conversation with Sadler. It's difficult to miss when she's talking, Loring. Her voice sounds like ripping metal. He came up to me later and helped me sleuth through the computer to look at the records." Natasha and Chen had worked for an hour before they began to make sense of the insurance codes, and then it became clear that there were numerous mistakes in Natasha's files. There was no distinct pattern to suggest the workings of fraud. Rather, there

216

would be an extra injection here, an unnecessary blood test there, radiology charges in cases of rashes or bee stings. But the mistakes occurred in about ten percent of the patient files.

"Dr. Chen told me something interesting then," Natasha said. "He said Dr. Grimes had once told him of similar irregularities in his billing. He said Dr. Grimes died before he explained the whole situation. But when I told Reggie about this, he thought it was worth looking into. So he did some work on the files at Coastal Insurance."

Reginald Wilson's role as head of data processing at Coastal gave him all the access codes to the company's powerful computer. It was no trick for him to inspect files or run statistical regressions. As he cruised through the company's computer memory, he began to see patterns, cases of fraud from the past by other physicians that might indicate what to look for at Osler Medical Group.

"Reggie's right here. Given your interest in Osler, we thought you might want to hear what he found."

"If it points to Osler and Jim Harvey, you bet!" Since Derrick Keating had announced his effort to restore Loring's hospital privileges and to renounce his discipline, Loring had begun to think in terms of renewing his own campaign against Harvey. As soon as he was stricken from the national data bank as a problem physician, Harvey's license would become his target. Whatever Reggie had to say could be valuable ammunition. And as Reggie began to talk, Loring's radar started beeping.

One of the case studies he found in the files, Reggie said, concerned an Ohio orthopedic surgeon. He ran a couple of side businesses, including one, which he set up in his brother's name, that sold passive-motion beds. Most insurance companies, including Coastal, wouldn't pay for the bed because they didn't consider it therapeutic. But workers' comp would pay. So the doctor culled his practice to treat primarily workers' comp patients. He operated on them and then, after the operation, prescribed the passive-motion bed and told them of a convenient place where they could buy it. He made a couple grand on each bed, and the bed did absolutely nothing

"He's double-dipping," Loring said, settling back in his chair in the big, quiet house, stroking Menace, who stretched and began purring.

"No, he's triple-dipping. There's more!" Reggie said. "He does what's called a spinoscopy test, not a standard test. It's a computerized system that looks at the motion of the spine. It's supposed to distinguish between real and phony back claims. It doesn't work, but he orders the test and then performs it on every single patient."

"Is he still practicing?"

"As of the time of the case study, he was. But he's not alone. There are the neurosurgeons and their myelograms, where you put a needle into the nerve sack in the lower back and inject dye. It's something like an MRI. Am I telling you something you already know?"

"On the contrary. This is fascinating. Go ahead, Reggie."

"The guy ordering the test, which is of limited use, is also the guy performing the test. But these docs get paid for procedures, so guess how many they do? I've got a hammer and everything looks like a nail!"

"How does any of this relate to Osler, though," Loring wondered aloud.

"Just wait. I was talking today with Kent Erickson, the medical director for Statewide Mutual. They handle Medicare and Medicaid for all the providers in Port Hancock."

"That's got to be big business."

"I'd guess they've got nearly two million covered lives."

"Covered Lives! That ranks right up there in my medical dictionary with productivity goals!" Loring howled.

"I know, I know. Natasha's always catching me using the jargon, too," Reggie said. "But soulless as the insurance business is, wait till you hear this! Kent caught one doc who had all this chart documentation in his office to get reimbursed for his patients. If he had had a business manager who could check what he was putting on the charts, he might never have been caught. Insurance companies pay docs by levels. Say a level one is a procedure that requires the doc to spend five minutes with a patient and level five requires thirty-five minutes."

"This part I know about, unfortunately." Loring laughed like the condemned.

"Okay, so the doc gets compensated accordingly, right? So this doc had all level fours and level fives in his files. A business manager would have seen this and, at the end of the month, told him he had too many high-level patients. Cut it back."

"That's all it would have taken?"

"Sure.

"And then he could have gotten away with it, you're saying?"

"You docs are all so smart!"

"Was it hard to catch him?"

"Kent says the damned system is so bureaucratic that it is hard to get these guys. So much backlog and so many claims being sent through. They can get away with it for a long time, but normally they'll get caught, Kent said. Like this guy. Eventually, Kent said, Statewide noticed that he was falling out of profile. While he had all the documentation, and he got by with spot checks, when Kent went and looked at all his books, there weren't enough hours in the day for the doc to have spent so much time with his patients. It was physically impossible!"

"That's outrageous, Reggie. They must have bagged that one."

"Yeah, but there are plenty more. According to Kent, there are a couple of other docs he's looking at but has never been able to nab. When they seem to be pushing the code—when their charts start to draw Statewide's attention for Medicare and Medicaid—they back off and the problem seems to go away. Kent said it's like these docs have some kind of an early warning system. And guess where these docs work?"

"Could it be?"

"You are quick, Doc! I spent the afternoon, after talking with Kent, going over the Osler files, and I can see precisely the pattern he's seen! If you chart it, you see a series of mountain peaks, where one doctor or another is pushing the code and then falls off. But Osler has seventy docs, Loring! If you exam ine the spectrum, from obstetrics to geriatrics, they have several docs right up there and the tilt light should be going off for Osler as a whole, if not for any one of their docs!"

"How does Natasha fair in this measure?" Loring asked.

"She's had her ups and downs, too. There's the same pattern everywhere."

"So where do we go from here, Reggie?"

"I'm going to draft a report for Bill Scarborough, our CEO. To hell with chain of command in this case. Last time, when we looked at Dr. Ross, my concerns got derailed. But Scarborough won't ignore this when it lands on his desk."

Twenty-four . . .

Audrey Mills was a regular visitor to the Port Hancock General emergency room, and her bipolar condition was a constant challenge to the staff.

Doctors and nurses are not the only ones who know about medical problems, and you could not tell Audrey Mills otherwise. When she was in a hypomanic state she particularly distrusted nurses, who always seem to doubt your ailments. Like the red blotches that had appeared under Audrey's armpits. She saw how the nurse at triage looked at her dismissively.

"It's a heat rash," the woman had told her. "Go home and put some cold compresses on it. If you insist, apply a thin coat of cortisone ointment."

That nurse, it was clear to Audrey, wouldn't know a heat rash from poison ivy. You had to learn to deal with these people, Audrey had discovered, if you wanted to get quality medical care. You had to push your way past the numbskulls until you reached a skillful physician who could recognize the malady that afflicted you. And once past the triage nurse, Audrey had been pushing, but to no avail.

220

Now she was sitting along one of those walls, across from the emergency room command center, and she had been here for twenty minutes, as if her problems were not of the moment of those other people who had come in after her and already were being seen by doctors. They had wheeled one stretcher directly in front of her, so she could see that the man with the bloody bandage on his head was conscious and talking coherently, if not with proper diction.

Audrey Mills sighed, placed her hands on her thighs, fingers pointing in, and pushed her heavy, uncooperative body up from her chair. Due to her height, she could not see, from her seat, whether anyone was behind the command center counter. But when she reached the counter, she saw that the nice red-headed nurse she remembered from previous visits was still there, on the phone. Audrey moved along the counter until she was opposite the nurse and was going to clear her throat and make some demands when she overheard something that intrigued her. She decided to just listen for a moment.

"I understand, darling," the redhead said. "But you should think about it." Her voice was deep, yet soft as velvet, a voice that lulled Audrey

Think about what? Audrey wondered, and she tried to move closer. The redhead was listening, not speaking, and she was twirling a strand of her hair behind her ear, with the phone pressed to the other ear. She did not look up at Audrey, and that would have infuriated Audrey had it not been for her curiosity.

"In time, honey. Don't push. There's nothing I want more than to see you reinstated to practice again. But you have to be careful, especially after your encounter with that creep lawyer Weigenstein. We have some digging to do. Reggie will have access to the files, and you'll have to get those first if you are going to nail Osler."

The redhead again listened, and Audrey wondered what Osler was and who was going to nail it.

"I don't think either of us has a problem with lumping Osler as a whole in with Ross. Still, I think it's worth our effort to track Ross down, and Reggie's in a good position to do that. Get Ross, get Harvey, and then talk to Bernstein about rejoining the practice. For now, you still have your work at the university. Although," the redhead said, reducing her voice to a near whisper and curling down over the phone even more, her lips almost touching the mouthpiece, "I don't know that I trust those nursing students there. I squirmed a few times when I was in your class, you know."

Audrey Mills, who knew that, given her intelligence and powers of observation, she should have remained in college and become a doctor herself, now observed, among other tiny details, the way the redhead nurse's nipples poked out of her white turtleneck, and Audrey herself felt curiously aroused.

"Gotta go, honey," the redhead said, straightening herself and letting the strand of hair unwind from her finger. "We have a full house and Dave needs me." She set the phone back on its cradle and looked up. "Yes, Miss Mills?"

Audrey cleared her throat, since she hadn't had the chance when she first approached the counter.

"I see that Dr. Callahan is available, and I must insist that I be seen next." Audrey switched her gaze to the young doctor, who had just emerged from a room on the far side of the command center and was circling the counter rapidly.

"I'm sorry Miss Mills, but Dr. Callahan is on his way to take care of a young child with a bad leg fracture. I'll call you when a doctor is free." She smiled at Audrey, but Audrey wasn't falling for this ploy. She scowled.

"This place isn't so busy that you couldn't take time out to talk to 'honey,'" she said, tilting back her head so that she could look down the short ridge of her nose. She saw the redhead was blushing and decided to press on.

"I am not at all satisfied with the concern I've been shown for my condition," Audrey said, with increasing rapidity of speech. "This hospital may well need to be reported to the state health department."

Karen was suddenly aware that Audrey could become a full-blown manic.

"I'm truly sorry," the redhead said. "I'm the head nurse, and it's my responsibility to see that you are well taken care of. Would you step over here for a moment and we'll review your triage report?" She gestured toward the end of the counter, and Audrey glanced in that direction and then followed the redhead, who picked up a clipboard and flipped through the few sheets fastened there. "Hmmmm," she said, pouting and flipping back to the first page to reread it. "We don't have an examination room free, but would you mind if we stepped into the ladies' room and I take a peek at you?"

"Why, of course not," Audrey said, and scurried after the nurse, who shut the restroom door behind them and asked Audrey to unbutton her house dress, which she did. The nurse looked at the blotches. Finally, someone was taking Audrey seriously!"

"How long have you had these?" the redhead asked.

"I first noticed them last Thursday—"

"Last Thursday!" the redhead gasped. "And you're just showing up now? Miss Mills, I know you've been to this emergency room enough to realize that you should seek assistance promptly!" Karen left briefly and returned with a hospital gown. "Here," she said, "remove your house dress and put this on. Then come back out to the counter."

Audrey did as she was told, and when she returned to the command center, she was guided to the door of one of the examination rooms, which the nurse pushed partially open.

"Dr. Carn. I have a bipolar regular who needs evaluation and a medical check for a dermatology problem. May I place her on a gurney and park her in the holding area for a transfer to the fifth floor?"

"Okay, Karen, I trust your judgment. Go right ahead."

Audrey, annoyed as she was, didn't argue. After all, in the past she always got better treatment on the fifth floor than in the emergency room.

The redhead led Audrey to a gurney against the wall opposite the counter and helped her onto it. She placed Audrey's house dress and the clipboard on the foot of the gurney and began wheeling her towards the corridor at the far end of the emergency room.

"Here we are Audrey," the redhead said. "I'll park you here and someone will be down shortly from the fifth floor. Just be patient and remain calm and stay on the stretcher for as long as it takes. If you need anything call and I'll come back to check on you." She pulled a sheet up to Audrey's chin and patted her head gently before retreating back to the command desk.

Alone in the hallway, Audrey raised her head from the pillow to examine her surroundings. If there is one thing that Audrey Mills was it was curious. Proud and curious. She took pride in her quest for information, a quest that at the moment involved reading the signs protruding above each door within view. The first on her side was Medical Supplies, followed by Janitor and an exit sign. On the far wall of the corridor were signs for Vending Machines and, directly opposite Audrey, Doctors Lounge. Shouldn't there be an apostrophe on "Doctors"? Audrey thought. There were two chairs without arms along the corridor wall on either side of the doctors' lounge door, which was partially open. Audrey heard voices coming from inside the lounge, and she settled her head back on the pillow and closed her eyes, the better to hear them.

" . . . waste of time," she heard. It was a deep male voice. "It's an outrage," said the voice of a woman, a flat voice that sounded as if the woman's nose was pinched shut. "You have to hire extra staff off the top to deal with them. Then the other day one of the managed care companies had one of our secretaries on hold forty minutes. Forty minutes! We've got a patient in the examining room, naked, and this functionary in Atlanta, who is trained to say 'no' and doesn't know how to react if the answer might be 'yes,' is taking her sweet time finding out whether we have permission to treat this guy!"

"It's got nothing to do with getting people healthy, that's what gets me," said a second male voice, and Audrey thought it might be good if the transfer from the fifth floor was a bit slow. She wanted to hear more.

224

"Neither does Osler's advertising," said Deep Voice. "Billboards, television, radio. Osler's all over the place pushing everything from their surgicenter and MRI to every innovation in medicine."

"They even imply that you'd be taking your life in your hands to see docs outside Osler," the second male voice, almost too soft for Audrey to hear, said. "It hasn't helped my neurology practice any, but I'm managing to stay independent."

"You may not survive much longer, though, Ed." It was a third male voice. "This new physical referral service—have you seen it? I suspect Osler's behind that, too."

"Got an application in the mail the other day," the woman said. "They want everything down to your high school diploma. And they hint that you'll be squeezed entirely out of the system if you don't join. They claim to have screened all the physicians and, for a fee, will refer patients to the best in the area. I didn't see anything on the application that would suggest they are screening, as long as you're willing to hand over their fee."

"They're double-dipping?" Deep Voice said.

"They want to get us and the patients both," the third male voice said.

"Pity the poor patient wheeled in here and needing help," Soft Voice said. "They can't know which way to turn."

Audrey, of course, thought of herself, lying helpless on this gurney, in the grip of her bipolar condition, her life hanging in the balance. She wanted to hear more, but the door to the lounge was pulled open, there was the shuffle of shoe leather and the squeak of sneakers on linoleum and all the voices moved toward the end of the corridor, away from the emergency room. Audrey didn't open her eyes in time to see their faces, and that, to her, was a clear loss. These were obviously among the caring doctors and, given her medical history, Audrey might have need for every one of them. Yet she couldn't even identify them by sight.

She watched them walk four abreast to the far end of the

hall, where one of the men pushed open the fire doors to allow the rest through.

Audrey was engrossed in her thoughts when she saw the doors swing open and saw a tall, heavy man start down the corridor. At the same time, she heard footsteps coming from the direction of the emergency room. She did not bother to close her eyes this time.

The first voice, high and raspy, came from the person approaching the emergency room.

"Good morning, Whalen. I've been meaning to talk with you about the emergency spine call schedule and we might as well get into it here and now."

Audrey thought immediately, when she heard this voice, of the manager of her apartment building, an unsympathetic creature if God ever made one. She suspected that Whalen and this fellow were not best friends.

"What's on your mind, Dr. Barth," said the big man, whose voice belied his youthfulness. Audrey could see Whalen's face, a dark beard along a square jaw, horn-rimmed glasses, and short hair. He did not smile as he looked down at Dr. Barth, a man so short his elbows barely reached Audrey's eye level.

"I understand you've been talking to my friend, Conrad Schmidt, about the supposed unfairness of the spine call."

"That's correct," Whalen said, folding his arms across his chest and spreading his feet. He towered in the center of the corridor, an apparently immovable object, Audrey thought. "I'm just trying to make sure that all qualified spine surgeons are given equal time on the schedule. Right now, Doug Quillman, the other fellowship-trained orthopedic spine surgeon, and me are the only doctors not represented on the schedule."

"And it's going to remain that way," Barth said, tucking a folder he was carrying under one arm so that his fist was against his hip, his elbow pointing directly toward Audrey. "You see, young man, we neurosurgeons know the spinal cord and are trained to take care of neurological trauma. You orthopedics should stick to your bones and leave the neurology to us. Quillman and his orthopedic group knew their place and have stayed there since he arrived two years ago. Now you come along and in six months you want to change the entire system? I think you'll find you won't get much support from the chief of surgery. You'd do better to back off."

Audrey could see the muscles of Whalen's jaw flex and his nostrils flare. He paused before he spoke, then delivered his words evenly, his anger contained.

"Dr. Barth, let's stick to the facts. Fellowship spine-trained physicians, whether orthopedic or neurosurgeons, are equally qualified to manage and immobilize spine cases. There is only one reason to disqualify orthopedics, and that is fees. With all due respect, Doctor, to keep us off of the emergency room call list is restraint of trade."

"You're damn right we're trying to restrain you, with all your board certifications and fellowships. We got along fine before you arrived, son. So until you've been around as long as the rest of us, I'm telling you to back off!" Barth's voice had increased steadily in pitch and now his fist was shaking in the general direction of Whalen.

"Your partner Finkowski already has two or three cases being reviewed by the surgical quality assurance office for mis-management concerns," Whalen said. "I'm not about to back off, Dr. Barth. This is about quality of care and fairness to physicians, not about Wayne Barth's bank balance."

Audrey was amazed at the directness of the attack and, quite honestly, pretty damned disturbed at the suggestion this Dr. Whalen was making. It seemed to her he was saying that some doctors were working on peoples' spines and lacked the qual-ifications. She was not reassured by Dr. Barth's response.

"Slanderous comments like that will put your money in my bank account, kid," Barth said. "Watch your tongue and stay away from Schmidt!" He pushed past Whalen and headed down the corridor.

"Good day, Doctor," Whalen said to the neurosurgeon who had disappeared behind his back.

"Insolent little prick!" Barth screamed just before the fire doors slapped shut.

It was only then that Whalen noticed Audrey on the gurney and saw that she was staring at him. He came toward her, and a warm smile spread across his face.

"I'm sorry, ma'am. We doctors don't always agree," he said, touching her shoulder and then entering the doctors' lounge.

Audrey took stock. Thus far she had heard that managed care was bringing inefficiency to doctors' offices, and advertising was helping drive competent doctors from their practices. And she had heard that competition between physicians for the same type of work can leave a patient in the hands of an incompetent, if the incompetent is part of the old boy network. What she needed was some plain old-fashioned doctoring, and she began to long for the people from the fifth floor to appear.

Instead, she got Stanley Randall. When Stanley's medication was balanced, he was a brilliant thoracic surgeon. But Stanley was self-medicated, and his idea of balance depended on his widely swinging moods. Since he enjoyed his manic stages, he tended to seek a balance that strayed into this range, and in his mania, when his brilliance shone for all to admire, he often felt there was absolutely nothing wrong with him. Stanley was out of a brief depression and into mania when he pushed through the fire doors and came charging down the corridor. He glanced at Audrey, grinned broadly, and asked why she was on a gurney in this area. Audrey was explaining as Randall picked up her chart from the bottom of the gurney. Since she could read his name tag, pinned askew on his smock, and knew that he was an M.D., she figured he might help her. She was taken aback by his response.

"Holy camoly!" he hooted. "A genuine bipolar." He was grinning as before, and flipped rapidly through the three sheets on the clipboard, again and again.

"Doctor, do you know about bipolar?"

"Do I know about bipolar?" Randall responded, "I'm one myself." He gripped his chin between his thumb and index finger and folded his free arm across his slender abdomen. "I can act like a real wing nut at times, Miss Mills." He laughed aloud at his own remarks. "How about you?"

228

"No, no!" Audrey protested. "I may be bipolar, but I've got a real medical problem." She pulled the hospital gown from under the sheet, exposing not only her reddened armpit but also her bosom and protruding belly.

"What am I looking at? I see a heat rash, aggravated, I'd say, by constant rubbing. Maybe you should get a new bra, Miss Mills." He laughed again.

"I fail to see the humor, Dr. Randall," Audrey said, rising on both elbows. "I came here with a serious problem and I'm headed to the fifth floor for examination!" Audrey was getting just about as angry as she could, and was close to tears as well.

"The fifth floor in this hospital is the psyche unit, Miss Mills," Randall cried, staggering back and falling into a chair in a fit of laughter.

Audrey was about to get off the gurney and leave when she noticed Joann Perkins, a familiar face from the fifth floor, approaching.

"I'm glad you're here. I don't know what's the matter with me, but get me out of here!" Audrey said, thinking to herself that perhaps she should report this crazy doctor to the state medical board.

Joann smiled at Randall, excused herself, and wheeled Audrey off toward the elevator.

Twenty-five . . .

The sun rose at 5:35 that Sunday to find Derrick Keating almost dressed. He wore purple nylon running shorts and a white T-shirt with the faded logo of Port Hancock National's successor, the giant Valubank, and he was lacing on his running shoes when the digital clock flicked to 5:36. He stepped out into the first level shafts of light beaming through the forest of mature pines that surrounded his home, and he jogged the three hundred yards to the gate where the *Times* was waiting in its box, along with the *Port Hancock Journal*. He removed the first section from the *Journal* and tucked the rest, along with the bulky *Times,* under his arm. Then he headed back to the house, walking slowly as he read the lead story.

"Hospitals Chief Sees Profits in Purchasing," was the headline running across four columns.

Keating smiled. On Friday, KJAK-TV in Riverton had televised a story sympathetic to Loring English, detailing the history of his suspension and revealing Keating's proposal to restore him.

Now this newspaper article. Keating's plans were unfolding on cue. He had allowed Lydia Fulton to take the topic of competitive bidding to the *Journal*. "If we're surrounded by fence-straddlers," she had told him, "the best way to lead them is let them believe public opinion favors us. They always respond to conventional wisdom."

The journal ran a small piece based on Lydia's phone call to the editor. Then medical writer B. Morton Martin had called Keating, seeking more details. Martin had expanded the story to look at how the medical industry was dealing with supplies. But he had used Keating and the anecdote involving Hancock Medical Services and the Four Seasons contract as the lead to the story. Keating was quoted as saying that "layers of middlemen who supply hospitals are skimming resources that could better be used to strengthen the institution's finances, giving a community hospital such as HMS the opportunity, through profits, to expand its services to its customers."

B. Morton Martin used that quote high in the story, and it appeared on page one before the jump. No way could Jim Harvey miss that, Keating thought. No way his people can retaliate without giving me more ammunition. Keating spanked the side of his naked thigh with the folded front section, a congratulatory slap one jock might give another after scoring a point, and then he jogged back up to the front door, where he deposited the *Journal* and *Times*. Stretching his arms over his head, he saw the sun lighting the lower branches of the pines, part of a forest planted during the Great Depression around the Port Hancock Reservoir, which his five-acre estate bordered. He headed toward the pines, reaching the gate he had built in the rusted wire fence that surrounded the city-owned land and closing the gate behind him.

Keating liked to run at first light, a time when he could be alone on the narrow gravel trail that meandered eight miles through the trees around the Reservoir Tract. There were no intrusions by other runners at this hour to break his pace. He wore a sophisticated digital watch with which he could time his speed from one to the next of the concrete posts, painted yellow, that marked tenths of a mile along the path. He could recall precisely his previous best time between individual posts and his most recent time, and this concentration on pace was for Keating a form of meditation, holding at bay the thoughts that normally hounded him.

Before he reached the running path, he had to walk for some distance under the canopy of pines, through which a faint breeze whispered, and across the brown pine needles that carpeted the forest floor. He inhaled the fragrance of pine pitch oozing from the bark of the trees in the June warmth. At the edge of the path, he turned and urinated against the trunk of a tree, standing with his hands on his hips and allowing his plumbing to work without direction. Then he bent to touch his toes, a pose that he held for half a minute as blood rushed into his forehead and temples.

Although he heard the song of a bird high in the pines, as soon as he began running, that music and all other external input was replaced by the sound of his own breath, sucked in for four strides, then exhaled for two, a rhythm that he never altered, regardless of the pitch of the trail, which rose and fell regularly. As he passed the first yellow post, he glanced at his watch and found he was two seconds behind his normal pace. He adjusted his stride and tempo minutely. By the second post, he was one second behind and at the third, which he reached at precisely the moment he had expected, he recalibrated his stride, knowing now that he would hit all the marks along the trail on time. By the sixth yellow post, an itching sweat had broken out on Keating's scalp and shins, and by the eleventh, perspiration flowed comfortably from all his pores and his breathing had settled into an unstrained cycle, allowing him to sink into a nearly anesthetized dreaminess.

This reverie was broken when, at a sharp bend between the forty-third and forty-forth yellow posts, Keating saw another jogger approaching, moving sluggishly over the gravel. The man was thickset, with dark hair and a zippered royal blue polyester running jacket and matching trousers. His head was down, eyes cast at the path along which his just-out-of-the-box-white sneakers shuffled. Keating took in this image instantly, and in that same moment he felt the degree of irritation a tourist might experience when, just as he depresses his camera's shutter release, a stranger strays into his scenic snapshot. He muttered a barely audible "good morning" to the man as they neared each other but avoided eye contact, and when he had passed the man, who registered in his rapidly retreating thoughts as Asian, he again focused on the sound of his own breath, drawn in for four strides, flushed for two.

The next sound, which Keating heard only briefly, was that of a groan rising from his chest and stopping in his throat, unable to escape.

A steel cable, pulled tightly around his neck, cut the flow of blood through his carotid arteries and fractured and compressed his larynx, denying breath to his lungs and blood to his brain. At the same time, as strong hands yanked back on the wire, a knee hit Keating in the lumbar spine, snapping his backbone at his hyperextended neck and lower back.

He was unconscious before his back hit the ground, where he was allowed by the thickset man to gently fall onto a sheet of plastic, placed there by a second individual.

This second man now crouched at Keating's feet, removing his running shoes. The man, tall as Keating and athletic, removed his sandals and pulled on Keating's shoes. He exchanged a few words in Cantonese with the stocky man, and then, using the plastic sheet, they lifted Keating's lifeless body and stuffed it in a plastic garment bag. The taller man then ran ahead along the trail, in the direction Keating had been moving, carrying his own sandals in his hands. The stocky man sprayed inside the bag with an aerosol can and then carried the bag across the pine needles to an open pit at a far corner of the reservoir tract. He dumped the bag into the pit and shoveled in soil that had been piled on a green plastic tarp. From a plastic trash bag that had been filled earlier with dry pine needles, he littered Keating's grave site, leaving it almost undetectable.

The search dogs brought by police later that day circled the running path, following the scent of Keating's shoes, a scent that led off the path through a maintenance gate and to a paved country road, where the scent disappeared.

The hospital administrator was replaced at the end of the week by the temporary appointment of Walter Scott, in whose opinion all contracts, including those with Four Seasons, were inviolate.

Twenty-six . . .

By Wednesday morning, everyone in Port Hancock had been made aware of Derrick Keating's disappearance, first by an eleven o'clock news story Tuesday on KJAK and then by the Journal's front page. Loring English was, for his own reasons, jolted by the news when, after reaching the little office he shared with another doctor at Riverton University Medical Center, he finally opened his paper. He read through the entire article once and then a second time. Then he clicked on his computer and logged onto the Internet, searching for more details. The *Journal* said one theory held that Keating had been abducted, perhaps for ransom. The story listed Keating's salary as a half million but noted that a major health provider could generate substantial cash if ransom was demanded. The *Journal* also noted that on Sunday, the day Keating's wife reported him missing, the hospital administrator was the subject of a major news story concerning hospital contracts. The *Journal* did not mention KJAK's item linking Keating and Loring.

The Internet provided no more information than the *Journal*, however, so Loring took the elevator to the cafeteria and brought a cup of coffee back to his office. Although he had rounds to make, if Keating was in fact gone, he needed to sort through the implications. In the last few weeks, Loring had been anticipating the June HMS board meeting when, Keating had told him, Loring's privileges would be restored. He had begun contacting his former patients. And, through Aldie Spencer, he had notified the national data bank of the impending change, hoping to shorten the reaction time of insurance companies in acknowledging him as an acceptable physician. This was crucial, for while he had managed to survive the last nine months, his finances were strained to their limit. With the handful of patients he still saw in Riverton, he earned enough to pay Nancy Fowler and keep up the office rent. But his personal bills were eating into his retirement fund.

And now Keating, his savior, was missing. Loring put down his coffee and sighed, staring blankly at the *Journal* front page. His mind kicked into neutral, unwilling to focus on the possibilities. He was stirred from this funk when the phone rang. It was Natasha Wilson.

"I just talked with Karen," Natasha said. "She's coming to dinner with us tonight. How about you, Loring?"

He hadn't had dinner with Karen for a long time. Natasha's invitation shot some life into his veins, and, just for an instant, he remembered the winter night of that long, lovely kiss. Since then, it had been almost all phone romance with only a few lunches, time snatched from his work day, limited by Karen's own schedule.

"Great!" he said, and he shoved the Keating matter to the rear of his consciousness and spent the rest of the morning making rounds, lingering with patients when each examination was completed to chat about their families, their jobs.

On the way to City Campus, where he had agreed to meet Karen, he stopped at Eddie Beiler's gym for an early workout. That done, he showered and rubbed on his wintergreen and headed for the emergency room.

"I've been meaning to ask you, Loring," she said when they reached his old Buick wagon. "Have you changed your aftershave? You smell like peppermint."

"Is that all you've noticed?" he asked, laughing. "Can't you see the return of my sinewy, youthful physique?"

A pretty scowl puckered her brow, and she slowly shook her head.

"You mean all that sweat's wasted? Damn! I'm going to demand my money back from Eddie!"

"You're becoming a jock?" she asked, a sweet smile appearing below the still hovering scowl. "Just for me? Oh, Loring, that's so precious!"

"And I lost three pounds," he said, letting her into the Buick. They both laughed and agreed they needed to spend more time together.

Bella Fontana, a restaurant offering a fine northern Italian menu, was in the hills to the north of Port Hancock. Shortly after leaving the city a dog bolted in front of them nearly causing Loring swerve off the road.

"Hey, get your seat belt on, Dr. English!" Karen commanded. "Do you know how many injuries I see because people are too stupid or lazy to buckle up?"

Loring pulled the belt over his shoulder with one hand, and let go of the wheel to pass it to his other hand.

They then settled into the subject that was on everybody's minds at both HMS campuses: What happened to Derrick Keating?

"The guy is a real dazzler," Loring offered. "Maybe he's tucked away on a beach somewhere with some cutie."

"I doubt a successful CEO would risk his career that way, and so do you, Loring," Karen said.

"Maybe he embezzled hospital funds, transferred them offshore, then disappeared before he got caught."

"I don't think he embezzled anything. Someone would have found a problem by now. I suspect foul play, Loring," Karen said.

"A conspiracy theory? I like that!" He nudged her with his elbow. They had arrived at Bella Fontana, and Loring parked beside Natasha's Jeep at the far end of the lot. The air above the pavement was thick with heat, but they were quickly in the coolness of the restaurant.

"You're right," Natasha said when they were seated in a darkened booth and had ordered drinks—an ale for Loring, white wine for the women, and seltzer with a twist of lime for Reginald. "Why not a conspiracy? When you think of the fact we've lost two young, healthy men in the last two years. Tom Grimes, may his soul rest, and now Keating?"

"I'll suggest another element," Loring said. He glanced around the crowded restaurant in whose air noisy conversation surged and retreated. He saw no familiar faces. "I hope this doesn't sound egocentric. But recently Keating had gone public with some fairly controversial proposals." Loring described the medical supplies contracts. Lydia Fulton had called him, asking his advice after Keating had enlisted her. Loring had thought about the dominant position of Osler doctors on the HMS board and told Lydia she should support Keating.

"And, of course, there is the matter of Keating and yours truly," Loring said, pausing to sip his ale. The thought had badgered him all day, a child born of idleness, tugging at him while he talked with patients, pulling him back to the *Journal* article again and again, urging him to seek clues. "If Keating's gone, I remain discredited and effectively barred from bothering Jim Harvey."

As a theory, even Loring saw—having spoken the words and hearing how flat they fell—it was preposterous.

To his surprise, he was alone in that view.

"Add it all up," Reggie said, his voice hushed. "Keating, who has been a non-factor, suddenly acts like he's in charge."

"He sure chose the wrong cause to champion when he picked you, Lor," Karen said.

236

"And he should have known better, from what the Osler gossip mill says," Natasha added.

"Oh?"

"Sure, Loring. They say Keating was hand-picked by Jim Harvey to run Valleyview. And everyone at Osler is convinced Harvey is behind your suspension. I guess that wouldn't be news to *you*."

The appetizers were served then, and the conversation continued in hushed tones. By the time the entrées were finished, the four had embraced the theory that Keating's vanishing act was linked to Loring. A piece seemed to have fallen in place for Loring, the final stone completing a wall of evidence naming James Harvey as not just an incompetent but a medical evil, a physician whose science dealt not in the search for truth and fact but in the creation of wealth and power. But Harvey's was an evil to which most seemed blind, or at best were unwilling to see. Now Reggie told Loring about his report to Coastal Insurance's brass. Armed with the patterns of Osler's doctors—one after another nearing the limits on numerous procedures, apparently warned off at the last minute—he had filed his report directly with William Scarborough. The chief executive had come down from his lofty corner office to Reggie's floor, marching past Reggie's secretary, Cynthia Ansel, slamming the door behind him and informing Reggie in scalding terms that he was never to waste Coastal's time on a meaningless project like this packet of nothing. With those words, he had slapped Reggie's thick report loudly on his desk and left.

"I guess I need not ask you for more favors," Loring said, shaking his head.

"On the contrary, Loring," Reggie said, putting his arm around Natasha and drawing her tight to his side. "As long as this lady is under Jim Harvey's thumb, I'll be digging wherever I think I might find something. In fact, I was hoping you might join me one night. Together, with your knowledge of medicine and mine of computers, we've got the weapons, don't you think?"

It was mid-July before Loring got a call from Reggie, who

had been deluged with end-of-fiscal-year projects, asking if he could come one night to Coastal. Is tonight too soon? Loring asked.

Not only is there a place in the modern corporation for the Cynthia Ansels of the world, their role is critical. Lacking a human bond anywhere in their lives that they believe they can trust, the Miss Ansels choose instead to invest themselves in the corporation, an entity that, in their experience, rewards their devotion at least once every week, without fail, and that, despite the efforts of some of the others who are also employed by the corporation, never rejects them. If a superior were, for example, to suggest that Cynthia Ansel's performance did not meet his or her expectations, Miss Ansel would understand that the problem was not with the corporation but with that particular superior. Her loyalty would remain intact. She might be motivated to use her many talents to dislodge the offending superior because of his or her clearly proven lack of aptitude. Indeed, in the service of the corporation, she would maintain a file of those employees whom she believed were incompetent, and if called upon by the corporation to expose them, she would, without a trace of glee but with definite pride, do her duty.

William Scarborough, the first time he summoned Cynthia Ansel to his office on the eighth floor, served her tea and sugar cookies, praised her work and revealed that the corporation was not only aware of her many contributions but was pleased to promote her from the clerical staff to the title of executive secretary. He explained that this appointment carried with it duties involving confidential matters. She could compare her new role, he suggested, to that of a scribe in a secret order, one who knows the innermost workings of the corporation but is sworn not to reveal them.

Cynthia Ansel's bosom swelled with pride and she shifted in her seat, as if adjusting the robes of her new office. She was prepared to serve!

Scarborough then told Miss Ansel that her boss, Reginald

238

Wilson, had been found to have dealt, sub rosa, with one Dr. English on matters that were outside the scope of his authority. The corporation would benefit greatly if Miss Ansel were to take note of any future such dealings, he told her.

So on that July afternoon, as soon as Reginald Wilson finished his phone conversation with Loring English, Miss Ansel, who had, with great caution, been eavesdropping on the line, called Scarborough's secretary and, using the code words the chief executive had given her to gain direct access to him, arranged to visit the eighth floor. Scarborough met her at the entrance to his office and closed the door behind her.

"You asked me to tell you if I found Mr. Wilson was engaging in covert dealings with outside organizations, Mr. Scarborough," she said immediately after the door shut.

"Indeed, I did, Miss Ansel," he said, showing her to a seat before his desk. He then leaned against the front of the desk, folding his arms across his chest. "Please go on."

Miss Ansel repeated the conversation between Loring and Reginald Wilson without omitting a word or an inflection. Then, her lips pulled tight against her teeth, she concluded: "I thought there may well be some significance in this. Mr. Wilson seems to have a very strange idea of what we do here at Coastal Insurance."

"The corporation is indebted to you, Miss Ansel. May I call you Cynthia?"

Again her bosom rose with pride in her accomplishment. It was the first time anyone at Coastal had requested to use her first name. It was as if she had been inducted to the inner circle of power.

"Oh, please, Mr. Scarborough—"

"No, no, Cynthia. Call me Bill. You've done a great job, Cynthia. Of course, as always, this is completely confidential, and I have absolute trust in you in that regard."

"Absolutely, Mr. Scarborough," she said. He did not correct her formality.

"One more thing. I'll be calling Mr. Wilson up for a meeting this afternoon. When he leaves the office, there will be some repairmen who have some work to perform on his computer. Would you see that they get in and out quietly?"

"It would be my deepest pleasure," Miss Ansel said.

Loring spent the morning in his Port Hancock office and then drove after lunch to Riverton, where he visited a few patients. At six o'clock, he drove under looming thunderclouds to the Coastal Tower, on the west side of the city. The rain began in large drops as he was turning into Coastal's huge parking lot. He thought he could make it to the door when he quickly found a spot halfway across the lot, but even running he was too slow. The sky opened as if a thousand garden hoses were aimed down on him, full blast, and while his small umbrella helped keep his hair dry, his shoes, socks, and the bottoms of his trousers were soaked when he pushed through the revolving door into the lobby where Reggie was waiting.

"Man, and I thought you could walk on water!" Reggie said.

"I tried, Reg. I tried."

"Let's get up to my office," Reggie said. "I've got some dry stuff in my gym bag. We're about the same size."

"I'll be okay. I just need to wring out my socks and drain my loafers."

"Well, come on up. You can use my bathroom."

Loring shook off his umbrella and followed Reggie to the elevator. He changed his mind and accepted the dry clothes, and when he had them on, he joined Reggie at his desk.

"Thanks, Reg. I was one drowned rat," Loring said, padding silently across dense, lichen-colored carpet.

"I hope you'll find the rats are here in our records, Doc," Reggie said. He clicked his mouse to bring a file up onto the screen.

"What do you think we're looking for?" Loring asked, rolling his chair closer.

"I am absolutely certain that Osler is submitting phony billing, but they've got the documentation to back it up—records that show what each doctor did with or to each

240

patient—so there's nothing I can do. I have no patient complaints. If someone would come in and say their notice of payment is out of whack, that they didn't get the services, that would help. Like your Mrs. Wheeler did. But for one thing, what patient ever reads the codes on those statements or understands them?"

"Aren't you talking about 'covered lives?'" Loring asked, a smirk twisting his lips.

"Okay. I deserved that," Reggie said. "Anyway, I was thinking that if we could look through Osler's file for, say, cardiologists and then compare those figures with the stats from other cardiologists outside of Osler, we could tell if something's really up. But I need your expertise. You would know if things look kosher or not."

"What are we waiting for?" Loring asked, waving Reggie back to his computer. "If you can show a pattern of their docs always billing at the maximum, I can show you some probable crooks. Let's get to work, the night is slipping away. Where do we begin?"

"Let's start with the heart of the matter. The cardiologists."

Reggie began feeding data from the cardiologist's files into the computer. They had been working several hours and darkness had long since drawn up over Riverton when Reggie's eyes froze on the screen.

"Look at this, Doc. Here's an Osler guy who, every day of the week, has this one code. What's that?"

"Hypertension recheck. Now that's screwy. He must have been running some sort of clinic to have that many cases."

"Well, if we go back here to April and look at the same doc, we see the same thing. And look," Reginald said, moving to another screen, "here's another doc, same code, same thing."

"Yeah, Reggie, they're maxing on these procedures and, if I read your screen right, they're all getting paid. I think we're on to something. We can crack this case tonight!"

Reggie pushed back from the computer, stopping his chair beside Loring's. A don't-be-ridiculous look drove his mouth back into deep dimples on either side. "A week from now, Doc, maybe. If I work every night. You've gotta have patience. Don't be in such a rush."

"I'll be the poster boy of patience, Reggie. I have willpower you can't believe."

"Oh, I can believe it, Doc. That I certainly do believe." Reggie's grin broadened.

"Now, now . . . what precisely are you inferring?" Loring asked. He saw that Reggie had another meaning in mind, but he was without a clue.

"About the only one I know with more patience than you is Karen Larsen. That girl's been waiting for you for months, the way I heard it."

"What do you mean, Reggie? We're fine."

"What Natasha tells me is that Karen thinks of nothing but you. But you don't seem all that interested. She figures she isn't ever going to find another like you, so she's biding her time. I guess she thinks you're better as a friend than any other man is as a lover."

"Oh," Loring said, rubbing his thumb up over the stubble that had grown on his chin. He thought in silence for some time, knowing that Reginald was watching him, waiting for a response. "I think Karen's terrific," he said finally.

"But?"

"No buts. She's terrific. You know, when I first started seeing her, it was only a year after I lost Janet, and I had these terribly opposed feelings. The grief was still there, and yet I found Karen warm, exciting, really all the things I was missing in Janet. And I almost let myself yield. But I thought: Is this the way I want to go, just forgetting about Janet and taking up with the first girl who interests me? I didn't lead my life that way while Janet was alive because I valued our love. I guess I just had to put Janet to rest and, frankly, I haven't been ready to take that step yet."

"I hear you, Doc. And I guess Karen understands. You're just too good of a couple, though. I'd hate to see her give up and move on. You're good for each other. It shows, Doc."

"You know, I agree with you. It's been long enough. And

242

when I think of Janet, it's a warm feeling, not the pain it was for a long time. I would have been no good to Karen, that pain always gnawing. Now's a different story, though."

"Good, Doc. Then you work on that and I'll work on our problem. But let's knock off for now. It'll be nearly two when we get back to Port Hancock, and I for one need at least four hours sleep."

After Reggie and Loring left Coastal, another light remained on, one floor above, in the corner office. When, through the receiver on his desk, William Scarborough heard Reggie's door close, he picked up his phone and dialed. Before he heard a ring, he hung up. Then he rolled open a lower desk drawer, removing a bottle of Chivas and a glass, into which he poured from the bottle. He leaned his elbows on his desk, brought the glass to his lips and, without sipping, set it back on the green blotter. He ran the fingers of his free hand up into his scalp, letting his brow come to rest in its palm.

"I've lost control," he said aloud. "I built a reputation for honesty, and now this." He raised the glass again and sniffed the whisky. "Either I break an honest man, or I fall myself." He set the glass back on the blotter and brought his other palm to his brow, as well, pushing the heels of his hands into his eye sockets, so that within his skull he saw flashing blue and yellow lights. "Damn Harvey! Damn those photos! But I must survive. No prison. No, no, no. No prison and no poverty. Sorry, Reggie, much as I admire you. Sorry your work is wasted." Scarborough sat straight, working over his face with the fingers of one hand, taking the glass in the other, then opening his eyes and drawing off a small mouthful of Scotch. He dialed again, and after listening to the recorded message, he began to speak. By morning, James Perkins Harvey III would be aware of Loring English's new fascination with Osler Medical Group.

243

Twenty-seven . . .

The gang gathered in the doctors' lounge at Riverton University Medical Center was of one mind. Osler Medical Group harbored some of the finest, and some of the most incompetent, physicians on the planet.

"You've got guys like DeBeerie, who can make excising a pituitary tumor look easy as slicing cucumbers and Chen, who I've personally seen opening coronary arteries that were nearly invisible, they were so blocked," said Roger Caswell, a cardiologist with whom Loring had once shared teaching duties.

"Yeah, but then you've got a butcher like Urizar," Len Szramka said. "The man should be put in chains, the way he tortures patients. I know of two intestines he's perforated, because we got them here. He handles a colonoscopy as if he's mining!"

"And what about that obstetrician, what's her name?" Caswell asked.

"Oh, 'Midnight' Melchior! Ghastly woman," said Lenore Trossbach, herself a gynecologist. "She did a hysterectomy on a seventeen-year-old. Never even tested her for pregnancy! Can you believe it? The girl was beginning the second trimester. Melchior claimed after the fact that the fetus, which everyone in the operating room saw and which she disposed of against hospital regulations, had somehow infected the uterus. The girl had come in with false labor, apparently, and hadn't told her parents she was pregnant. She confessed afterward. I hear Melchior is one of Osler's top-grossing doctors, though."

"That says it all, doesn't it?" Szramka asked.

Loring asked the Riverton doctors to compile a list of botched Osler cases. They were delighted, and Loring left the hospital even more enthusiastic about his pursuit of Osler.

The three men employed by the Dragon to deal with Loring were waiting in an idling Ford F350 pickup across the street from the hospital entrance when Loring left. It was two nights after he had met with Reginald Wilson. Loring had heard a traffic report almost as soon as the Buick wagon's radio came to life. The interstate to Port Hancock was closed due to an overturned tractor-trailer. He would have to take the mountain road. That suited him. He was in no rush. A slow drive home would give him time to think. There was a lot to sort through, and even before he reached the stop sign at the hospital's exit, he was categorizing the issues with which he had to deal. There was not only the Osler matter, with the new insights his Riverton friends had supplied, but there was the Karen issue, which Reginald had brought into focus. And there was Gabriella, who never seemed to have time for a visit. Ironic, but there it was. The sin of the father visited on him by the child, he thought, turning left, toward the mountain road. He did not notice the pickup, parked across the highway. Nor did he see, in the flat light of dusk, the cloud of dirt the pickup created when, its rear wheels spinning, it lurched from the grassy shoulder onto the pavement.

As for Osler, Loring thought, turning off the highway at the fork where the mountain road headed north, Reggie has found the smoking gun. Every other group or private practice in Coastal's files operated somewhere between sixty and eighty percent of their theoretical capacity for billings. Osler was above ninety-five percent. Consistently. What more evidence do we need? Reggie said it looks like they've got access to Coastal's computer algorithms that calculate what the limits are, and they've embedded that information in their own system. That keeps them from going over profile.

Now, Loring thought, how do I use this information?

The few cars coming toward him as he rose in the foothills had their headlights on, having lost the sun earlier in the ravines that creased the mountains. When one approached with its high beams blazing, Loring thought to pull on his own lights. He noticed then that he hadn't buckled his belt, and he thought about Karen's scolding, as if she were sitting beside him now. I've never had an accident, he told her image, a smile crossing his face. You're acting like a wife.

The smile flattened and his foot involuntarily eased off the accelerator. I don't need another wife, he thought. Janet's my wife. How could I replace her? What would that mean about the honesty of my love for her?

Now there were headlights close behind in Loring's mirrors, and he was entering the first no-passing curve leading into the mountains. He stepped on the accelerator and brought the Buick back up to the speed limit. The headlights backed off.

No, I could never substitute for Janet, he thought. And yet Karen's in my thoughts more frequently. What exactly are those thoughts, though? He tried, without success, to compare his feelings for Karen to his love for Janet. It's entirely different. I saw Janet as bone of my bone. There never was another before her. She filled that spot in me completely, and her dying didn't remove her. In a sense, there's no vacancy there for Karen to fill.

So what have I been doing, Loring thought, if not preparing a place for Karen in my life? Why have I invested this time in her, and she in me, if there wasn't room? It would be a different sort of place, not quite so exclusive. And she brings her own ghost. I'll never evict Tom Grimes. From what Reggie says, Karen has accepted this. Damn, these women are smart. Why haven't I looked at this more closely?

The road, paved in concrete slabs whose joints passed under the Buick's tires with a rhythmic pa-pluck-pa-pluck, had climbed halfway to the Port Hancock Pass, where the Appalachian trail crosses, and Loring was now steering through the first of several hairpin turns. When he braked for the sharpest part of the turn, the headlights behind him got close enough to shine down onto the Buick's dashboard, suggesting to Loring the vehicle was a truck, one whose driver was apparently unfamiliar with these turns and, thus, failed to brake in time.

Setting aside for the minute the Karen issue, Loring now turned his attention to Gabriella, whom he had not seen since Christmas.

The other woman, Loring thought. Ironic that she's the one

I spend my time pursuing, she who is, indeed, flesh of my flesh. More so than I wish to admit. She's as tied to her life at school as I ever was to my medicine. She's consumed with study. Bet she doesn't think of home on her own once in a month. And I'm proud of her for it, even if it means I don't get to see her, don't even get to talk with her. I wouldn't think of telling Gabbie her focus is too narrow. Just like I wouldn't think of telling her about Karen. Whoa! Do I sense guilt here, good Doctor? Do I sense a fear of rejection, should she think there was anything going on? Not that there has been, but am I so in need of approval that I shrink from letting my daughter know I have a woman friend? That's it! She's coming home and meeting Karen, if I have to go up to the college and drag her back!

Loring was touching the brakes once again, lightly, well in advance of the approaching turn. The mountain dropped off sharply to the right, and he felt safer giving the trucker behind him sufficient warning. Even before he recognized the sound of the truck slamming the Buick's tailgate, he felt the back of his seat shoving him forward. His foot, already on the brake, jammed the pedal to the floor, and the old, nearly bald tires locked and screamed along the concrete. The Buick's headlights were, for an instant that lingered like a snapshot, flooding the steel beam guard rail that wrapped around the edge of the curve. Beyond the guard rail was blackness, toward which Loring was sliding at increasing speed.

"Dammit!" Loring yelled as the thought of his unattached seat belt flashed into his mind, quickly followed by the memory of Karen's disapproving words.

The front bumper laid the guard rail over and the front of the Buick was, suddenly, silently airborne. Loring felt the car tipping forward, sensed his weight case off the seat. Like an astronaut, he thought. Preparing himself for the jolt of the impact, he pulled on the steering wheel, attempting to draw it to his chest, to wedge himself against something solid to keep from being thrown outside the station wagon.

The pickup had slid to a stop, the light of its headlamps lost in the darkness over the Mountainside. The three men inside jumped out and ran to the twisted guardrail. The forest around them was silent, but there was the smell of gasoline in the humid evening air. They spoke in Cantonese, their words coming in bursts, two talking at once, then all three. The one with the glasses shouted above the others, silencing them.

"We are professionals, not street boys! Gather your wits! You, get the flashlight from the cab. We can see nothing in this darkness."

The taller of the three scurried to the passenger's side of the pickup and returned to the others, who were standing between the headlights. Glasses spoke again.

"Follow me," he said, moving to the left, away from the truck's lights but still near the guard rail. "Shine that down the bank. We must determine the results." The tall man did as he was told. In the middle of one sweep, its beam was reflected from perhaps one hundred feet down the rocky slope. The tall man returned the beam to that spot, illuminating the chrome trim on the Buick's rain gutter. The car had come to a halt in a round catch basin, and the only part not submerged was the roof and the very top of the side windows below it. The tall man swept the light back and forth along the water and then around the edge of the catch basin. Nothing moved.

"Xian, lead us down to the car. We must be certain," said Glasses.

"There's no need," Xian said. "Clearly the man died from the wreck or he was drowned."

Glasses drew a small gun from the hip pocket of his blue jeans. He weighed it in his hands without pointing it. "We in the Triad do not seek the simpler path, only the correct one. Do as you are told."

"Oh, the wise leader," the tall man said. "You only wish you were in the Triad. They use you and reward you with crusts and stale water and promises."

"I will find my reward beyond your corpse," Glasses said. "Lead us!"

The tall one turned and lifted his leg over the guardrail. But the third man, the shortest, tugged at Glasses' sleeve, pointing off to the north, where the headlights of a vehicle descending from Port Hancock Pass flickered through the trees.

"Wait!" Glasses called to the tall man. "We must leave! Everyone in the truck, immediately!"

The short one, the driver, wheeled the truck backward in an arc until they were headed down the mountain. Then he sped down, around the curve, barely keeping the tires on the concrete but gaining distance ahead of the lights that they knew were approaching from behind.

The Buick had bounced twice on its bottom before belly-flopping into the catch basin. The first contact slammed Loring's chest against the steering wheel. The steering column collapsed and in collapsing absorbed some of the force generated by Loring's body weight. Still, the impact of his ribs against his thumbs separated one thumb at the large knuckle and severely strained the other, and his head banged against the windshield. At the same time, the Buick lost some of its velocity. But because it landed between the rocks on its four tires, the car was catapulted again into the air by its springs. The Buick next glanced off the downward tilting face of a large boulder, the edge of which ripped off the fuel tank, rupturing it. Somehow, the tank's contents were not ignited. The Buick's forward motion was slowed again so that when it hit the catch basin, it merely settled to the bottom, where a submerged boulder caught the right side, causing the station wagon to tilt to the left. Loring was dazed, but the sensation of water rising around his left elbow brought him quickly into a disarranged present. He could see lights out the passenger windows and struggled from under the steering wheel, reaching across to grab the far side of the bench seat, which slanted up toward the light. When he had pulled himself up and could see through the top of the window, he saw what could be headlights above. The water was rising now to his waist, and he tried to sort through his options.

Would opening the door cause the car to sink further? Was he injured more seriously than he realized? Were the people who went with the headlights just bad drivers? He remembered the force with which the truck continued to push him, even after the first impact, and how he had stood on the brake without effect. Images and questions revolved in his mind like the facets of a kaleidoscope, changing shape slightly as they shifted. He strained to clear his mind, to focus on one piece, but each became a handful of smoke. Yet one thought managed to float barely above the rest, a thought that saved his life. This, he somehow sensed, may not have been an accident. He decided to wait. He edged closer to the window and saw the shadowy forms of three men. They were talking loudly. They were not speaking English. Nor was it Spanish, he thought, groping through his memory for the right tongue.

And then the voices and the lights were gone. But the water was at Loring's shoulders.

"So I pushed the door open," he told Gabriella, who had been in his room at Riverton University Medical Center when he awakened after the surgery. There was nothing the doctors could do for the broken ribs. He would have to simply live with the pain that came with each breath. They had put his right hand in a cast to immobilize the thumb, and they had stitched his scalp back together where the windshield had rolled back his forehead like a window shade. The emergency room doctor at Riverton, Winston Thayer, had called his good friend, Dave Carn, who dispatched Karen Larsen to Loring's side. It was Karen who called Gabriella and who now sat in a chair near the door while Loring talked with his daughter.

"Daddy, I can't believe you!" Gabriella said, a cross scowl on her forehead. "You couldn't have buckled your belt? You, a doctor? And just how fast were you driving, anyway? I can't believe you slid off that road."

"I stand accused, or lie accused, as it were," Loring whispered so as not to have to breathe too deeply. He had, in the moments after he gained consciousness, put it together–the truck, the headlights over his wrecked car, the voices of men, speaking some other tongue, who had left the mountain before his rescuers arrived. And he had decided not to share this with Gabriella. She didn't need to be burdened with his suspicions. He saw a change in her expression and asked: "What, you think something's funny?"

"Yes, Dad," she said, her scowl released from her brow by a smile like he'd seen on her face every Christmas when she was much younger.

"And what . . ." he said, pausing because he felt an involuntary laugh attempting to escape his chest to express his pleasure at seeing his girl. " . . . what is that?"

"Dad, you didn't tell me you had a girlfriend!" Loring looked past Gabbie to Karen, who stared down at her hands folded in her lap. She was in jeans and a white turtleneck, her hospital nameplate still pinned to her chest. She peeked sideways at Loring and gave a small, I didn't-say-anything shrug.

"I don't know . . . whether that's the way . . . Karen would . . . describe herself, Kiddo," he whispered.

"Well?" Gabbie asked, "C'mon, Dad. One of you. What's going on here?"

At that moment, the end of the dinner cart poked through the door beside Karen, and an orderly put a tray of styrofoam containers on a table which he lowered over Loring's bed. "Just soup tonight, Dr English. With a little bitty custard for when you're finished. Mean-looking bandage, Doc. You hurting bad?"

"I'm fine, Gary," Loring said, reading the orderly's nameplate. "My girlfriend and my daughter are helping me. Thanks for the meal."

Gary left, and Gabbie bent and kissed Loring on the nose. "Good, choice, Dad," she whispered. "I like her a lot."

Loring was discharged the next afternoon, a Wednesday. Gabbie had returned to college with a promise to visit on the weekend. Karen, who had taken the week off from HMS, drove Loring home.

"What did Gabbie whisper to you yesterday?" she asked as they rolled along the interstate in her hatchback.

"She likes you," Loring said softly, unwilling to test his ribcage. Karen had tilted his seat back so that he could breathe easier. "She thinks I have great taste in women."

"Do you?" The way Karen asked had a nervous quality, the tone of a student asking a teacher for her grade.

"Oh, I have . . ." he took a breath, " . . . standards like the . . . Bureau of Weights and . . . Measures."

"And is there anyone who meets those standards besides Janet Mitchell?"

Loring felt a new pain in his chest, cutting through the aching from his snapped ribs. It was the sword of guilt.

"Janet died more than eighteen months ago, Karen. It took a long time for her to rest peacefully in my heart."

"You have the right to that time. I'm sorry for being pushy, Loring," Karen said, patting his arm. She glanced away from traffic for a moment and smiled.

"You don't need to push . . . anymore," he said. "Janet is . . . gone. Now there is . . . only you and me."

Twenty-eight . . .

Arrogance, unpleasant as we find it in others, is the one human quality upon which the race can rely to bring about change. Churchill and Hitler, Napoleon and Newton, they all believed that what they thought or had to say was something the rest of the world should accept. Those who succeed in creating change wrap their arrogance in some other personal attribute that allowed the masses to swallow their message, whether it be eloquence or demagoguery.

Conrad Schmidt's arrogance was swaddled in very little. He had no personal warmth. His way with words was akin to a logger's use of the chain saw. But among his colleagues, Schmidt was recognized as a brilliant surgeon. And, despite his legendary fits of rage in the OR, his devotion to medicine was unquestioned. This helped temper people's reaction to his arrogance, as did the fact that the rest of the physicians who practiced under the Hancock Medical Services umbrella had all suffered through the same swift and disturbing decline in the hospitals' operations since Walter Scott assumed control. When Schmidt called for an evening meeting of the medical staff in the City Campus auditorium, then, no one was absent.

"Things just aren't getting done, at least here at City Campus," said Sam Ianone, one of those who came early and stood in a small crowd by an entrance at the rear of the auditorium.

"Or they're getting done the wrong way," said Kumar Hoondal. "They sent down an edict: No more overtime for nurses. You did see this, didn't you? And they hired per diems instead. The nurses' union, of course, complained because it was a clear violation of an existing contract. We were lucky, I'd say, that we had any nurses on duty."

"They named this nitwit, Pamela somebody, director of technical support," said Sheldon Bennett, a senior radiologist. "Only last week. First I heard of it, she came to the department asking me to explain to her what a gamma camera is and how it works. I asked her, 'Young lady, may I inquire why you want to know?' She said, 'Well, doctor, it is my job to decide whether the hospital should buy a new one from company X or company Y.' I said, 'Don't you think maybe you should ask someone who knows what the thing is, a radiologist, perhaps, to decide whether we need a new one at all?' She replied, 'Oh, no, Doctor. Those decisions have already been made by administration. This is too important to the bottom line to be left to anyone who possesses less than a high degree of business acumen.' I liked that. 'Acumen,'" she said."

Dave Carn, who had just arrived, nudged into the group by the entrance. "This sounds like the work of Walter Scott, all right. Remember when he was running Port Hancock? He allowed the pharmacist to dictate when certain meds would be distributed. So all of a sudden, Coumadin is being administered at night only, and all of the lab's blood evaluations are coming back screwed up."

"Yeah, and the syringes?" said Ianone. "Remember when these cheap syringes were showing up on all the floors, and when the anesthesiologists went for a needle, all they could find was crap? Boy, were they pissed."

The stories were traded this way until Schmidt arrived at precisely eight o'clock. He selected one doctor to stand watch at each of the entrances, ordering them to deny access to any but staff physicians. As he stepped up onto the stage, someone dimmed the auditorium lights so that only the footlights were illuminated. When Schmidt reached the microphone at center stage and turned toward his audience, his face—the huge jaw, the thick nose, the sunken eye sockets—was etched like a vampire's in reversed shadows. His brow was twisted in a snarling fury. His starched white lab coat, on the other hand, glowed with a holy radiance. The total image was of a demon inside an angel's robes.

"This room is secure," he said without switching on the microphone, his unamplified voice carrying through the chatter. There was instant silence. "There are no members of the administration in this room. There will be no one here to tell you that what you have been experiencing has not happened. We are here because of that administration. Specifically, we are here due to the incompetence of Walter Scott. We are here because if we, as doctors, do not heal our hospital, we will no longer be able to heal our patients!"

A murmur rose in the darkened auditorium.

"Why don't we call in the state department of health?" a voice called from the seats.

"No, no. We should go en masse to the next board meeting," another responded.

"Shouldn't we first assess our problems?" asked a third, and the sounds of a dozen conversations rose across the hall like gulls squawking around tossed crusts.

"Please!" Schmidt bellowed, and the silence returned. "I have asked Helen Ramsey to speak to you. The problems we see every day have been a matter of discussion within the Medical Executive Committee. Helen, if you please?"

Dr. Ramsey climbed the steps to the stage. Her voice, soft by nature, was adequate for communicating to the MEC members within the confines of a conference room. It was lost in the auditorium, however. Schmidt reached forward, turned on the microphone and slid its stand toward Ramsey. She removed the mike from its stand and paced to the left side of the stage, away from Schmidt.

"Conrad has raised an issue that we've been struggling with and, frankly, had hoped to deal with through the normal give and take that goes on with the administration. Perhaps I don't see things quite so starkly as Dr. Schmidt. But I do have my concerns which, again in all honesty, are not uniformly shared by all the members of the MEC."

Ramsey listed the failings of Hancock Medical Services, the same items that the doctors had already acknowledged among themselves.

"While the Medical Executive Committee does, indeed, represent you before the board of directors, and while the MEC has absolute authority in all medical decisions, I can inform you that you can expect no sudden action by my committee, given the thinking of its members. Therefore, if you believe, as Conrad does, that the situation at HMS is critical, please feel free to engage yourselves in a dialogue with the administration or to take any other action you might wish."

Ramsey stepped down from the stage and blended back into the darkness and silence of the hall. Schmidt turned off the microphone.

"I am looking for volunteers to form an ad hoc committee," he said. "Come up to the stage and leave your name and number on one of the clipboards. I'll get back to you."

Schmidt's next move was to phone the Port Hancock Journal the following morning and ask for B. Morton Martin, the medical writer. In Schmidt's view, what was happening at HMS was page one news. How could it miss? You had two hundred doctors upset enough to come to a meeting. You had an alcoholic administrator flushing the city's only hospital down the sewer. And you obviously, Keating told Martin, had the power of Osler Medical Group attempting, through the actions of their doctors on the MEC, to thwart reforms.

Martin invited Schmidt to visit his office with any documentation he had, and Schmidt said he would be over that afternoon. He arrived on the second floor of the *Journal* with a folder in his hand and was escorted to a cubicle with steel and frosted glass walls near the back of the newsroom, as far removed from windows as was possible. Martin's desk was heaped with papers. There were obvious coffee stains on the side of his computer monitor. The only personal touch was a small tole lamp that glowed from the top of a file cabinet beside Martin's right elbow. The reporter was tapping on his keyboard when Schmidt arrived, and he kept his eyes on his screen but motioned with his left hand for Schmidt to take a seat at his side. He finished typing then swung to face the doctor, his knees brushing Schmidt's.

"Whatcha got?" asked Martin, a shorter than average man with wiry brown hair, a moustache that covered his top lip, and square eyeglasses with black plastic rims. He wore chinos and a blue oxford buttondown shirt with a blue plaid necktie.

"As I told you, I have a conspiracy between Osler Medical Group and the HMS executives to defraud the City of Port Hancock and its residents. That should be enough, I would think."

"Depends. What's in the folder?"

"Names of doctors who have volunteered to fight against the ruin of hospital services."

"Yeah? But what about documents? What have you got that says there's a conspiracy? What data can you show me that details this decline you're talking about?"

"Well, I'm just here to point you in the right direction. It would be a simple matter for you to take it from there."

"Hey, you wouldn't believe how many hot scoop charmers I run into. Suspicions aren't enough. Look, Doc, I'm not trying to be difficult, but neither of us can risk any liability here. I'm willing to work with you, but you gotta do some homework for me, Doc, if you want anything in the paper."

"Doesn't it pique your curiosity that two hundred doctors would come to a meeting called to deal with a hospital's problems?"

"Sure, and I can write that up for starters. It might be worth about three inches on page fourteen, or somewhere back in the business section. To go further we have to work with something more than hearsay."

"Well, you can quote me. Osler Medical Group is at the heart of this. And Walter Scott, who is overseeing HMS's death throes, is an incompetent and a drunk."

"That may be true, but what's your proof? Get me documents and hard evidence and we can do something. Until then I agree, though, that two hundred angry doctors might make a story. Give me your list of names and I'll see what I can do."

In the *Journal* the following morning, under B. Morton Martin's byline, an uninspired article reported on the doctors' meeting and quoted several who said that there was a sense of malaise at the hospital, a sense that the leadership was in turmoil following the disappearance of Derrick Keating.

Robert Chen had been unable to get to the meeting at eight o'clock. He was still making the rounds with his charity patients. And when he arrived at the auditorium a half hour late, he found the door locked from the inside. He read Martin's report two days later at breakfast, and then he stopped Leonard DeBeerie, one of those doctors whom Martin quoted, in Osler's parking lot at lunch. DeBeerie had volunteered for Schmidt's ad hoc committee, and he suggested Chen get involved, as well. "You've got the managed care angle down better than the rest of us," he told Chen. "Your California experience could come in handy."

Chen went to the first committee meeting later that week already armed with an informed opinion about Osler Medical Group's role in Valleyview's decline. His interest in Osler's practices had been whetted by Tom Grimes and later spurred by Natasha Wilson's troubles with Carecard. He was not ready to share his complete vision with his colleagues. His research was incomplete. But the evidence had been pointing in the same direction from the moment he first logged on to Osler's database and began a study of the group's medical and financial habits. His inquiry eventually expanded past the computer, to Osler's mailroom, where he formed a friendship with Joshua Goodman, the first cousin of Tom Grimes's patient, Willie Goodman. Grimes had found Joshua the mailroom job when he was laid off at Hancock Systems. In time, Chen imposed on Joshua, a heavy gentleman with a short left leg and a pronounced limp, to keep track of certain addresses that originated or received Osler's mail. Between this information and his ongoing strolls through the computer, Chen was developing what he believed was a picture of something far more sinister than phony billing. He didn't know exactly what.

But these vague suspicions convinced Chen that if the ad hoc committee were to be effective, it could use his help. He arrived at Schmidt's home with DeBeerie, who parked along the curb because the driveway was already filled.

"Good to see we're not alone in this," DeBeerie said, pushing the doorbell. Schmidt greeted them with the warmth of a maitre d' at quitting time.

"Snacks in the kitchen, through that door beyond the couch," he said with a dismissive wave. Chen looked around the living room, where physicians he knew and some he did not engaged in earnest conversations. Doug Quillman, an orthopedic spine surgeon, sat on the couch talking with Mora Weintraub, a thoracic surgeon. Bill Callahan leaned on his elbow on the fireplace mantle, chewing on a stalk of celery that shared his lanky proportions, listening to Jack O'Malley, a fam-

258

ily practitioner who worked alone and, ever since Port Hancock General was absorbed, no longer had a seat on the MEC. In the kitchen, a dull-yellow room that suffered from the lack of a woman in Schmidt's life, Chen found Helen Ramsey, Michael Bernstein and pediatrician Bill Deveney, another sole practitioner and one of the senior physicians in Port Hancock.

"It saddens me," Deveney was saying. "Good medical care was once a given in this town, and we only had a dozen doctors."

"The machines are more sophisticated, but they seem to have robbed us of something," Ramsey replied. Deveney stroked his sweeping white moustache as he stared at the floor, shaking his head from side to side. "Robert, good to see you came," Ramsey said when she noticed Chen approaching. "I knew you were one of the idealists."

Chen was about to respond when Schmidt, having moved to the kitchen door, clapped his hands loudly.

"The meeting of the Port Hancock Doctors Ad Hoc Committee will come to order! Please take a seat."

Someone had brought some dining room chairs into the living room, and Chen sat in one, next to Bill Callahan.

"Ten of us," Schmidt said. "Well, ten's a good number. There are a couple others who said they would come, but I don't know that we'd be any better off to wait, so let's start. My idea is for each of us to take a few minutes and outline what we see as the problems facing the hospital. I've put a tape recorder over there on the mantle, and with your permission I'll record the comments and transcribe them later should we decide to issue a report or statement or the like. In deference to his longevity, I will ask Dr. Deveney to start." Schmidt remained standing in the doorway, and Deveney, who walked with a plain ebony cane and suffered from mild arthritis, remained in the wing chair where he had settled. He reminisced for a quarter hour about earlier, better times in Port Hancock before Schmidt interrupted and thanked him for his thoughts. Then, limiting each doctor to five minutes of "considered opinion," he selected Helen Ramsey next. When she finished, hands were in the air, each doctor eager to volunteer his or her thoughts.

Chen was both comforted and troubled that each speaker appeared to have become disillusioned by a different aspect of medicine and could cite specific areas in which the residents of Port Hancock had been short changed. The doctors assigned blame, as well. It was government regulations or it was insurance company paperwork or it was managed care or the pressures of an ephemeral force identified as the "bottom line." To Chen's surprise, there did not appear to be the unifying theme he had expected. None of the eight who had spoken when he and Schmidt were the only ones left had ventured a thought about the role of Osler Medical Group in the city's health care decline. And to Robert Chen, that connection was the only one worth mentioning.

"I am pleased," he said, standing slowly when Schmidt asked if he had comments, "that Dr. DeBeerie and I are the only two from the Osler Group to attend, for that frees me to suggest that the presence of this megagroup in our community may be a factor we should consider." Chen launched into a discussion stitching together each of the other doctors, complaints in a quilt that, when assembled, covered the broad range of Osler's activities, from its creation of satellite facilities that sapped the strength of the hospital to its dominance of Ramsey's Medical Executive Committee.

The doorbell rang, and Schmidt motioned for Chen to continue as he walked behind him to greet his late guest. Chen obliged, for he was now well into an explanation of the sprawling structure of the Osler Group. He saw no need at this point to even hint at the petty illegality he had discovered within his employer's walls. Indeed, he would keep that information, and his greater suspicions, well protected until he had turned over to authorities his documentation. But even without revealing these things, he felt it important to expose to the light of public awareness the way in which Osler's legitimate businesses undermined the city's sleeping, complacent doctors and the health care services on which the city's trusting citizenry relied.

When Chen had finished his five minutes, he settled onto his chair. Immediately, he felt a hand on his shoulder and heard a familiar voice.

"A fine presentation, Robert," Brad Barnett said. "J.H. will be fascinated."

Robert Chen had not visited the flying saucer, Osler's executive suite sitting atop the circular building, since that December day nearly two years earlier when his UNC classmate had interviewed and hired him. He felt no slight in this fact. Harvey traveled always at a different level of society than Chen. Nor did he experience envy. But on the morning after the meeting in Schmidt's home, when he reached the office and listened to his messages, he felt the flames of anger and the frost of anxiety passing through him and, oddly, he felt shame when he heard Ophelia Sadler's scolding voice ordering him to report to Dr. Harvey's office at eleven-fifteen.

In the one hundred and thirty-five minutes before that engagement, Chen had time to consider where he would next seek employment, how he would manage to find physicians to handle his charity cases and how meager his bank account truly was and whether he would have to reduce the monthly check he sent to his mother in Hong Kong. These concerns still swirled in Chen's brain when he approached Tiffany Blaise's desk. She smiled at him warmly.

"Take a seat, Dr. Chen. I'll announce you," she said. Perhaps, he thought, this is not about my comments last night. Certainly J.H. respects the First Amendment. Tiffany returned and asked him to follow her. She closed the door behind him once he had entered J.H.'s office.

"Robert, please, have a seat," Harvey said. He was in a starched white shirt, sleeves rolled to the elbows and a tie splashed with neon colors over a black background, knotted firmly at his neck. Chen recognized the chair in which he had sat during his only other visit here. "I'm sorry to have had to call you in, Robert," Harvey said, easing into his chair, his eyes opened widely and fixed, unwaveringly, on Chen's. "But as you are aware, your contract with us specifies certain limitations, and I have been informed that you have exceeded those limitations."

"I apologize, J.H." Chen said. "You are within your rights to take action."

"You are an honorable gentleman, Robert, and I know that you in no way intended disrespect either to me or to Osler by the analysis you gave to your friends last night. Nevertheless, you have agreed to withhold comments that might be construed as unflattering to Osler Medical Group. This is a standard contractual element in today's medicine, and it is necessary in the strenuously competitive environment in which we operate. I am certain that, with your admirable focus on the practice of medicine, you are unaware of these considerations, just as your remarks last night, as conveyed to me by Dr. Barnett, reveal your unfamiliarity with the demands placed on a medical group of this size."

"I have reread my contract, J.H.," Chen said, folding his hands. "I understand the consequences of my actions, and I am prepared to remove my belongings from Osler this morning."

"Oh, heavens, no, Robert! Bobby! Dear God, that's the last thing I want!" Harvey said, standing and extending both hands to Chen. "You are a valued member of our group. Your work brings credit to Osler. I only request that, in the future, you share your thoughts with me before you share them with others. This alienation you apparently have felt is unhealthy for all of us. I simply ask that you confide first in me."

Chen was not a man who lied easily. on this occasion, however, the truth seemed his willing victim.

"It would be my honor," he said.

Twenty-nine . . .

Jim Harvey could not afford the public relations disaster that firing Robert Chen would create. Nor could he risk allowing Chen to see the fear and rage he felt when he realized someone within his organization was questioning his integrity. The unpleasant truth was that Chen had forced Harvey to acknowledge the degree to which he had been trading on his family's reputation in medicine. His rage stemmed from having to admit this. His fear was related to that sensation caused in the knees by imagining you're standing at the edge of a high cliff and the rock you're on has started to tilt. For the first time, Jim Harvey saw the means by which his empire could be destroyed. And all he could do, at least for the moment, was to politely ask one of his employees to seek his counsel, to buy his explanations. This did not fill Harvey with a sense of power.

Nor had he been reassured by the Loring English matter. He had, upon receiving Bill Scarborough's call, contacted the Dragon and told him that English was digging too deeply.

"You recall the Triad's rules."

"Yes, yes. And I suppose that's why I mentioned the problem. Of course, I would want no one else included."

"And why would there be?"

"Well, he is close to a nurse. They may be dating. I'm not certain. I wouldn't want her involved."

"We conduct our business with the skill, if you will, of a surgeon, Dr. Harvey."

"I have no question that you do, Dragon."

Harvey's confidence had been broken, however, when Loring English survived the car wreck on the mountain.

"I inspected the scene myself," the Dragon reported. "My people had planned properly. They had staged the truck accident on the interstate. And if you will only drive along that mountain road you will see that they chose their spot wisely. I cannot fault them. There will be no such miracle the next time, I assure you."

"Your guarantees are hollow, Dragon," Harvey had told him. "My people inform me that English is healing and is appearing some nights at his Riverton office to work alone. And now he is always driven from Port Hancock in a taxi. Another 'accident' would not be advisable. But you must do something!"

So the Dragon's people wired devices to Loring's home and work phones, and they began listening to tapes of his conversations and made detailed logs of his habits, his plans. They also constructed a small surprise, really a trifle, that they would deliver to Loring at the appropriate moment. Into a gelatin capsule—which would dissolve in thirty minutes when immersed in water—they put powdered cyanide which, when introduced to water, creates cyanide gas, a substance used to execute society's worst criminals. The second time, the Dragon's men would succeed. And the evidence would vanish.

Loring's convalescence lasted until Labor Day. The pain from the ribs eased after a week or so, but his right hand remained useless in its cast and he still had severe headaches. For the first time in her career, Karen Larsen had taken vacation. She told Dave Carn to expect her back when he saw her, and she moved into a guest bedroom at Loring's house and kept him in his recliner in front of the television while she cooked for him and administered his pain medication. She was, even here, still a nurse. And she was more.

"Sit with me for a while, Karen," he said one time when she had brought him a fresh mug of coffee. He flicked the television off with the remote. "Let's talk."

"Your ribs must be feeling better," she said, moving an ottoman next to the recliner. Seated facing him, she leaned her elbows on the arm of his chair, resting her chin in her hands.

"Just don't make me laugh," he said with a scowl. "We must restrict ourselves to serious matters."

She reached to brush back his hair, which had fallen over his eyes, and her hand felt cool against the unbandaged part of his brow and her wrist had a fragrance that, when Loring inhaled it, reordered, in that instant, the nature of his thoughts. He looked at the skin of her arm, so close, and then his eyes traveled along the smooth underside to the elbow, then refocused on her lips, the only part of her face not blocked from his view by her arms. They were full lips, slightly parted, moist as dewy red berries. His glance descended along the curve of her throat, the knobs of her collarbone and the freckled skin draped below it that disappeared under her button-down blouse.

"Did you have something on your mind?" she asked.

"You've been a good nurse," he said.

"Why, thank you, Doctor. It is my pleasure to serve." She withdrew her hand from his brow, and he saw a serious, which is to say not entirely happy, expression in her eyes and noticed that her lips had closed firmly.

"You've been a good friend, too." He reached for her hand as he said this, drawing it to his chest and cupping it in one palm against the bandaged other palm. "I have grown to expect that you will be in my life, to think of my days as including you." He squeezed her hand. "I've been afraid of the word 'love.' It is such a serious word, and I didn't want to use it frivolously."

Karen now entwined the fingers of both hands with Loring's, and he raised them to his lips and kissed the back of her hand, which was warm against his lips.

"Are you still afraid?" she asked.

"I am not uncertain about my feelings toward you," he said, and he tilted the recliner forward bringing his face to the same level as Karen's, and so close that her features blurred in his eyes. "If love is an unconditional acceptance," he said, again kissing her fingers, then keeping them near his lips; "if love is the glow that races through me when you are near; if love is the desire, whenever we are apart, that we should rejoin each other; if love is wanting to hear your voice, your words, your thoughts and to inhale your aroma and to feel the touch of your fingers, Karen, then I love you."

One of Karen's hands fell from Loring's and she ran the back of an index finger under her eye, leaving a mascara smear. With some effort, Loring pushed himself out of the recliner and drew her by her other hand up to him. Her eyes searched his face through the blur of tears, and her fingers traced lightly along his cheeks, her forearms pressed against his chest. Loring's arms were circling Karen, barely touching the cloth of her blouse as he looked down into her eyes. They could feel the shallow puffs of each other's breath against their faces, and when their lips finally met, it was the kiss of a feather against a spring breeze, elegant, with all the exquisite promises that restraint always possesses. They remained cradled in this near weightlessness, their eyes closed, still but for the movement of their breathing, which was deep and luxurious. And then Loring stepped back.

"When the time comes," he said in a near whisper, "it will be perfect."

The following Monday, after having his bandages removed, Loring returned to work. He took a taxi and spent the next several days reading automotive reports. By the end of the week, he had concluded what type of vehicle he should buy, although he was not certain that even this choice would protect him as well as the old tank of a Buick had. On Saturday morning, he phoned Karen, who had returned to her condo, to tell her he would be around later in the afternoon, and he once again dialed Port Hancock Taxi Company, which dispatched Bob Gray to pick him up at his front door.

"I'll be requiring your service for a while, Bobby," he said. "We have several stops to make." By noon, the taxi had visited the countryside and returned to Port Hancock's shopping district. At Luddington's, one of the few fine apparel shops surviving in downtown Port Hancock, Loring opened the neatly folded piece of paper on which, when Karen was still staying in his guest bedroom, he had written the various sizes she wore—blouse, shoes, skirt, dress, undergarments, pantyhose.

He asked the elderly clerk with blue-white hair if she would be familiar with the styles worn by a lady in her mid-thirties. The clerk called to a younger woman, who accompanied Loring through each of Luddington's departments until he had assembled a substantial wardrobe. As he wrote out the check, he asked the woman to remove the tags, pins, and clips.

"You want help with that," Gray asked when Loring returned to the taxi and began placing the shopping bags in one of two suitcases he had brought. It was just after noon, and the September heat reflected off the sidewalk with enough intensity to cause sweat to bead on Loring's brow in the short distance from Luddington's door to the taxi.

"No, thanks, Bobby. I'll do this while you drive over to Rafferty's."

Gray pulled into the service parking lot of Rafferty's Mercedes-Volvo and waited while Loring went around a corner, into the sales office. It was fifteen minutes before Loring returned, the keys to a new Mercedes sedan in his hand. Loring reached in the back seat and took the suitcases, disappearing once again inside the dealership.

"All set," he told Gray when he climbed in the back seat. "Next stop, Riverview Condominiums." The cabbie looked at Loring through his mirror and shook his head.

"Yer grinning like a teenage fool, Doc," he said. "What exactly are you up to?"

"Can't stand the suspense, can you, Bobby?"

"I can wait," Gray laughed.

"You won't have to wait long," Loring said, folding his hands behind his head and stretching his legs luxuriously.

"Should I bring my pocketbook?" Karen asked when Loring told her they were taking a taxi ride.

"Do you keep your lipstick in it?" he asked.

"Of course," she said, arching one eyebrow and scowling with the other in a manner that demanded an explanation.

"Well, then, of course, bring your pocketbook."

"Why won't you tell me where we're going? I don't like surprises."

"I guess, then, that you don't like tomorrow."

"I have hope for tomorrow."

"That's a fine answer," he said, taking her hand and tugging her toward the taxi. "And so do I."

"I didn't know what to wear. You didn't say where we're going."

"Shorts are fine. And I like that blouse. You've got great taste."

Without waiting for instructions, Bob Gray started the Diplomat and drove back to Rafferty's, whistling "Some Enchanted Evening" loudly.

"You've been a wonderful driver, Bobby," Loring said, handing him several bills. "But I've brought along a new chauffeur. She'll be taking care of me from now on."

"Be careful, Miss," Gray said, winking. "This is one crafty fellow you're dealing with."

Karen blushed, and Loring, having stepped out of the cab, reached for her hand and led her to the front door of the showroom, outside of which was parked a dark green Mercedes with tan leather upholstery. As they neared the car, Loring pressed the button on the key ring and the doors unlocked. Still holding Karen's hand, he pulled open the driver's door.

"I'd rather be the passenger than the driver the first time out. Would you do me the great favor?"

"My lord, Loring. You went from a bashed-up Buick to this? I've never even been in one of these before, let alone driven one."

"The salesman told me that it won't drive itself. You really must use the steering wheel," Loring said. "But it has a computer that will do all the thinking. Go on. Get in!"

Loring navigated for Karen, and she piloted the car cautiously around Port Hancock, making wide turns and braking for minor bumps.

"Let's take it out on the Cramer Mountain Road," Loring said. "I want to see what this thing will do."

"Maybe you should be driving, then."

"Oh, no, girl. I'm just going to relax and let you do the

work." Loring opened the glove box and took out a compact disc, which he inserted in the dashboard.

"'The Piano.' Loring, that's my favorite," Karen said, reaching across the console and patting his arm.

"I knew it was nine months ago. A lot has happened since then."

"A lot of surprises," Karen said. She drove the Mercedes onto the mountain road to the west of Port Hancock. They listened to the music without speaking. As they approached a small, carved wooden sign on the left, Loring turned down the volume on the CD player.

"Let's drive up to Eagle's Nest Inn and take in the view," he suggested.

Karen turned onto the narrow, crowned asphalt road just beyond the sign. The sun was still high, sending beams through the green canopy of sycamores and lighting the humid air in slanting shafts that played across the car as it passed under them. The road wound left and right and back again as the car climbed the side of the mountain. They emerged from the trees near the pinnacle, where the road split into the halves of a grand circular driveway that led past the white-columned entrance to Eagle's Nest. When they were nearly to the inn, Loring directed Karen to turn right, along an even narrower driveway.

"The best view is out here," he said. The driveway led along the top of a mountain ridge, and on either side, separated from each other by broad sections of forest, were occasional small white cottages. Each cottage was surrounded by a deck that, on the far side, was cantilevered over the descending slope of the mountain. "Slow down," Loring said. "Here, turn down this driveway." He pointed to the left, and Karen guided the Mercedes down to the back door of one of the cottages. "The very best view of the valley is from here," Loring said.

"Do they mind? The people who live here?"

"Oh, no, it's part of the inn," Loring said. "They are really quite pleased. Wait a minute. I'll come around and open your door."

"What? I can drive your car but I'm incapable of opening my own door?"

"Let me be a gentleman. I need the practice." He circled the car and held Karen's hand as she stepped out. Then, lacing his fingers between hers, he led her to the cottage steps. "Let's go around front," he said, his voice barely a whisper. "The view is spectacular."

As they rounded the far corner of the house, Karen stopped short. The mountain fell away below the deck sharply, so that just beyond the deck railing were the tops of tall trees, like the lumpy domes of green cumulus. A warm breeze was rising up that slope, carrying with it the smells of the late summer forest. Cicadas buzzed. Leaves rustled. Karen stepped up to the rail and spread her arms out to each side, tilted her head back and inhaled deeply. Loring stood behind her, looking at the wisps of red hair that curled down over the crisp white collar of her blouse. The breeze, as it washed past her, brought him the scent of her perfume, and he thought of the times when he was convalescing, when she would lean over him and he could smell her body, near, warm. He stepped closer, so that his chest brushed against the bun into which her hair was drawn. He reached lightly around her then, and her outstretched arms fell over his and her hands took his and held them at the center of her bosom. She looked up at him, looking down at her over her shoulder, and she did not move, except to settle back against him, so that they were touching fully. Her hair was now brushing his cheek, and the cool curve of her ear was against his nose and his lips, and her aroma was filling him. He brought his hand up to touch her face, and he felt her breast yield under his rising forearm and saw her eyes close and he closed his own, kissing the edge of her ear and turning her toward him, his lips brushing across her cheek. Their lips met, and it was not the light, delicate kiss it had been but a swirling fury that built in an increasingly demanding rhythm, lips swirling against lips and necks, hands swirling across fabric and skin. Two years of restraint was ended. Flung to the far corners. Under the high sun, buttons were unfastening, zippers unzipping. Karen's neatly pinned bun unraveled and her hair fell down her back. She felt the warmth of his hand on her neck, a warmth that moved across her shoulder, peeling away her blouse there and then circling her back to bare the other shoulder. She felt the soft hair on the naked small of his back in her palms, felt the waist of his trousers brush up across the back of her hands as she pushed her fingers under his belt and pulled him toward her and felt his hands now against her in the same way, cupping her under her shorts, which were sliding down over her hips, cupping her and lifting her, so that when her shorts slipped past her ankles, her legs were free to wrap around him, only to find that, somehow, in all the fury, his legs were as naked as hers and the hair of his chest was moving up against her nipples and, with Loring still standing on the deck in the sunlight, her orgasm was beginning, sucking breath from her lungs and screams from her throat. Screams upon screams. His and hers. And the warmth of the wooden deck beneath her, the warmth and the roughness, and the motion that now was rhythmically subsiding, like the waves of a retreating tide.

After a few moments, Loring laughed, holding her tight, lying naked on the cottage deck.

"We'd better gather our clothes, for now," he said, standing and handing Karen her shorts and blouse.

"For now? You mean you have more planned?" Karen asked.

He collected his own clothes and dressed and took a key from his pocket. "We'll spend the night," he said, and he put the key in a sliding glass door off the deck.

"You mean this was a seduction? You planned this? You naughty boy!"

"The plan didn't include the fireworks on the deck," he said, pulling on the door handle. The door would not budge, so he removed the key and reinserted it. "We were supposed to be in on that bed."

"I'll give it a try if you will," Karen said, tucking in her blouse.

"Neither of us will if this key doesn't work any better in the front door," he said, taking her hand and leading her around the cottage. The front door opened easily, and Loring picked Karen up and carried her inside. A fresh bouquet of lavender iris and butter-yellow daffodils were in a vase on the credenza in the front room of the two-room cottage. There was a card, which Karen opened.

"Oh, Loring, I love you, too." she said, reaching her arms out to him. "If love means wanting you in my life forever, wanting to come home to you every night for the rest of my life." They embraced. "I've loved you for a very long time, Loring. I love you now," she said, her voice acquiring its deepest hum. "I want you now," she said. "Properly, between fresh sheets!"

An hour or so later—Loring had no concept of time, except that the long shadows of afternoon could be seen on the trees below the deck—there was a knock on the cottage door, and Loring, shirtless, stumbling as he pulled on his trousers, hobbled from the bedroom by the deck to the living room. When he returned, he was carrying a bouquet of a dozen deep red roses in a cut-glass vase.

"You're sweet, Loring," Karen said. "A spendthrift, but sweet."

"These aren't from me," he said. "There's a card, though." He set the roses down on a nightstand halfway between the bed and the sliding doors and opened the card. "'Best wishes' is all it says. Must be from the management."

"Now, that's very thoughtful. I wonder if they send flowers to every guest. Oooo, they smell so good!"

"In a room occupied by the beauty of Karen Larsen," Loring said, crawling on his knees across the king-sized bed, "flowers of any hue or fragrance are superfluous. From the first crocus of spring to the final mum of autumn, they should all wilt in embarrassment in the presence of this red orchid." He braced himself over Karen, who had pulled the sheet up to her shoulders, and he looked down into her eyes. She reached up and unbuckled his belt and unbuttoned and unzipped his trousers, which she shoved back to his knees.

"My, my, Doctor, you certainly do have some marvelous

272

instruments," she said, staring at him. "And it looks like you're prepared to use them again."

Loring lifted one hand and took the sheet near her chin, tugging it down slowly, sitting upright to get a better look at what he was uncovering. She smiled and let the sheet fall, and the fabric had just exposed her navel when Loring caught the scent of almonds, overpowering the perfume of the roses. He lurched back, at the same time grabbing Karen's wrist and yanking her from the bed, away from the roses, and dragging her violently into the living room, where he clamped his hand across her face and yelled: "Don't breathe!" Karen nodded vigorously. Loring took his hand from her mouth and, holding his own breath, tried to open the front door. The knob would not turn. He tugged at it again and again, but the door was frozen into the wall. Loring waved for Karen to stay by the door, then he ran back into the bedroom, snatching blankets from atop a small chest. His lungs were aching for oxygen, but he didn't breathe, running back to the front room where he wrapped Karen in one blanket and then made a shawl for himself of the other. Again he motioned her to stand still, and he ran into the bedroom. He ducked sideways just before he reached the jammed sliding door, and his shoulder hit the glass first. He stayed on his feet, and his momentum carried him through the shattering glass to the deck. Turning, he waved to Karen and called.

"Run! Run, baby!"

Thirty . . .

The manager of the Eagle's Nest, having easily opened the front door that Loring had told him was jammed, saw the wreckage in his cottage and turned slowly toward Loring, folding his arms across his chest.

"And the gas bomb?" he asked, a principal interrogating a

truant. The manager was a solidly built fellow. His appearance was dominated by eyeglasses whose magnification appeared to pull the flesh around his eyes up to the lenses. His face was composed of fat bunches at the cheeks, chin and on either side of his forehead, where sweat beaded. Almost invisible solitary strands of hair rose like wafting vapors from his otherwise bald scalp. He wore beltless gray trousers and a maroon turtleneck jersey, stretched to its limits about his waist. The man was somewhat shorter than Loring, and when he stood with his belly almost touching Loring, looking up and waiting for an answer, he acquired the appearance of an impatient tug boat.

Loring was perplexed. He had told the manager about the fragrance of the roses and the smell that supplanted it. But when he emptied the vase for the manager in the cottage sink, all that came out was water. The only evidence that something had happened in the cottage were the shattered sliding door, the shards of glass on the deck and the snarled blankets and bed sheets.

"Obviously," Loring said, standing again, "the gas has dissipated, and however it was delivered was consumed in the process."

"It's obvious that I rented you a cottage and now I have a thousand-dollar repair facing me. Look, mister, I don't care how you and your girlfriend carry on. Just tell me how you're going to pay me."

The man had once again moved his belly up to Loring, an act of aggression that stirred in Loring a reflex taught him by Eddie Beiler, one that would leave the manager on the floor, writhing in pain. Not very Hippocratic, Loring thought.

"You have my credit card imprint," he told the manager. "For now, bill me. I'll sign it blank."

"Well, okay," the manager said, taking a half step back. "That's fair." He smiled at Loring. "That's darned reasonable. Of course," he said, edging forward slightly, "that would include labor for cleaning up this mess."

"Of course," Loring said. "Now, if you'll excuse us, we need to gather our belongings."

274

"Sure, I understand," the manager said. "You can't stay here. I'll open another cottage for you."

"That won't be necessary," Loring said over his shoulder, heading out the front door. Karen was waiting in the Mercedes, still shaken. As they drove slowly down the mountain, leery of any car that approached or that overtook them, she asked where they were going.

"Police. We've got to report this. There must be some evidence. Fingerprints, maybe chemical residue from the gas."

They parked in front of City Hall in a no parking zone by the massive stone front steps. Descending to the basement under a white "police" sign with blue letters, they passed through a door into the dim fluorescence of a corridor. At the far end was a steel bar gate, floor to ceiling. A row of bus terminal green vinyl seats were against the left wall, and on the right wall was a bulletproof window with a speaker hole. There was no one on the other side of the window, so Loring pushed a button. They heard the scraping of a chair across a floor, and less than quickly an officer appeared, chewing as he walked. He was tall and not particularly fit. His gun belt, with a holster on one side and a walkie-talkie on the other, was hitched up under his arms like a child's inflatable pool toy. He came to a halt opposite the speaker hole and looked at Loring without speaking. A chunk of lettuce was stuck to his cheek beside his mouth.

"Sorry to bother you, but I want to report an assault," Loring said, recognizing instantly the imposition this officer felt that Loring and Karen represented and knowing things would go better if he could refrain from telling the sonofabitch public employee that the taxpayers' meter was running and he should get his ass moving.

The officer, without speaking, walked back out of sight and, several seconds later, appeared with a form, which he slid into the tray under the bottom of the window.

"You gotta pen?" the officer asked.

Loring felt his pockets and shrugged. The officer again disappeared, this time for a bit longer, and returned with a cheap ballpoint, which he slid under the window.

"Fill it out," the officer said, and left to resume his lunch.

Loring and Karen sat together on the seats and completed the form with the diligence either one of them would have applied to a medical chart. There were thorough descriptions of the room, the delivery man, the flowers, the time of day, the weather. They omitted an explanation of what they had been doing in the cottage, but they reported on their talk with the manager and the fact that there was nothing in the vase when it was emptied.

The officer told them to remain in the corridor after they buzzed for him and gave him the form.

"What happens now?" Loring asked.

"Detectives gotta review things," the cop said.

They waited another forty-five minutes, a time during which the corridor and the office on the other side of the bulletproof window remained quiet, before Loring again punched the buzzer.

"Oh, you still here?" the officer asked, and he smiled slightly at their foolishness.

"Yeah, we are scared out of our wits, and we want some police action," Loring said sharply. "What is the holdup?"

The officer's smile faded. "You hold on!" he told Loring.

"We've been holding on. What have you been doing? Sleeping? Has anyone read our report? What exactly is the delay, officer?"

"The detective was out on another case, and he just got back, Mister. He'll get to you when he gets to you."

"Officer, I'm certain Chief Graves expects more professional behavior of you. My name, which you undoubtedly do not know because you haven't bothered to look at the form, is Dr. English. Chief Graves's wife, Beth, is a patient of mine, and I of course have her home phone number. If I do not speak immediately with the detective, I will step outside to my car and phone Mrs. Graves, who, I'm certain, will put her husband on the line. And then you and your detective will have not only my report to consider but your futures with the department. What shall it be?"

276

"Sorry, doc, sorry!" the officer said, tugging on his gun belt. "Just a minute." He scurried out of sight, and in seconds another officer, in plain clothes with a badge pinned to his belt, was at the barred gate, unlocking it.

"I'm Detective Johnston," the man said. "Please step this way."

They followed him into a room with a basement window high on the pale yellow wall and a wooden table with three wooden chairs.

"Frankly, Dr. English, there's not much I can do for you," he said. "I've read your report, and I've talked with Mr. Phillips, the manager at Eagle's Nest. The alleged gas bomb, there is no evidence—"

"What about fingerprints? Maybe a chemical analysis of the carpet for cyanide?"

"As I was saying, Doctor, there is no other evidence that would warrant even a drive up the mountain. Quite honestly, the damage that was done in the cottage, according to both you and Mr. Phillips, isn't all that uncommon. Folks get up there for a rendezvous, things don't quite work out and something gets broken. Happens more frequently than you might guess."

"Are you saying we had a fight and broke the window?" Loring asked. His teeth were grinding and his breath was shallow in his nostrils. His clenched fists pushed against the sharp edge of the table and he was on the front of his seat. He did not feel Karen pulling back on his arm. "Someone attempts to gas us, only a month after I'm run off the road in Riverton, and you blame us? Damn!" He stood, and his calves hit the chair with enough force to topple it.

"You've got quite a temper, Doctor," the detective said calmly. "I'm beginning to wonder if I shouldn't be questioning Miss Larsen about possible domestic violence. From your display right now, I'd say there may be a link. And you had an auto wreck a few weeks ago? Maybe we need to think about your abuse of alcohol or drugs, Dr. English. There may be a nasty little pattern here." Johnston was grinning, his words snapping at Loring like whip cracks.

"A damned pattern of utter incompetence!" Loring bellowed. "Too bad you don't hate to collect your paycheck as much as you hate to follow up on a citizen's cry for help, detective Johnston. Come on, Karen. We'll have to fend for ourselves."

They stayed in Karen's condominium the rest of the weekend on the theory that it was less isolated than Loring's place in the country and, unlike his home, had a deadbolt on the door. They talked well into Sunday morning, woke late and, at Loring's request, rushed to dress and get to noon Mass at St. Anthony's. Karen had never attended a Mass and held Loring's hand throughout, kneeling and standing as he did but totally at a loss to find her place in the missal. Afterwards, they stopped at the Port Hancock Princess for breakfast. They asked for the end booth and sat beside each other, facing the door, Loring on the outside. The place was packed with regular Sunday customers. Several said hello to Loring, and Cal Kalinowski sat down opposite them in the booth to, as he said, "shoot the breeze." The waitress, a thin woman with uneven teeth and limp, dark hair held away from her face with pins, was in constant motion. When they waved for their bill, she scowled at them both, in turn.

"Y'all hardly touched your stuff. Something wrong?"

"No, no. It was great, Alma," Loring said, sliding a five dollar bill under his saucer. "We just weren't hungry."

"I can wrap it for you," she offered.

They declined, and as they walked to the car, they laughed together—for the first time since Eagle Lodge—at the thought of grits in a doggie bag.

Sleep was no more restful for them on Sunday night than it had been Saturday, but they were up early Monday because Karen was scheduled at Valleyview Campus for the seven to three shift. Loring drove her to work and walked her into the emergency room. The nurse in the triage office looked up from her book and smiled at them. Bill Callahan was on duty and greeted them both.

"Let me know if anything unusual happens, honey," Loring said when Karen had ushered him back to the entrance.

"I will, sweetheart," she said, rising on her toes and closing her eyes for a kiss. He held her, then set her back at arm's length.

"And please, don't leave the hospital until I get here."

"I'm a big girl, Lor," she said. "I can take care of myself as well today as I could on Friday, when you weren't with me."

"I know, I know. But things are different now, too."

"Are they?" she asked.

"In every way," he said, and he kissed her again, not the brushing of lips but a hollow-mouthed, wet kiss that stirred them both as they had not been stirred since the cottage. She pushed herself against him, then slid across him, feeling him against her belly.

"Good," she whispered. "I hoped you hadn't lost interest. Now get out of here before I go to a pay phone and call in sick."

The unusual happened at precisely 1:27, when James Perkins Harvey III appeared at the emergency room command center on the opposite side of the counter from Karen. A lump caught in her throat when she attempted to speak, and cold trickles of sweat raced down her sides.

"Your patient, Doctor?" she said, her usual contralto replaced by a scratchy whisper.

"Karen, we need to talk. Is there some place we can be alone."

She shuddered imperceptibly and thought, Get a grip, girl. You're tough enough for this. He can't do anything here.

"Do you have a patient here, Doctor?" she repeated, evenly, in her natural voice.

"I must talk with you, Karen," said Harvey, whose voice now was the one lowered to a whisper. "There are things that must be said, feelings that must be expressed."

"Am I dealing with a stalker," she asked, increasing her vol ume a notch, more as a warning than in an attempt to draw the attention of others. "I have made my position clear, Dr. Harvey. *Do—you—have—a—patient—here*?"

"No, I do not, but I have the patience to wait for you, Karen," he said, moving away from the counter. "Mistakes have been made. I'll admit that. Terrible mistakes. And they should not be allowed to interfere with the free flow of trust and caring that is possible between us. I will work to see that these things are restored, and I will have the patience to be ready when you are, Karen." Harvey turned, then, and left the emergency room, and Karen slumped back in her chair.

Callahan, who had been in Room Three opposite the command center, emerged with concern on his face.

"Is there a problem?"

"Taken care of, Doctor," she said.

"Are you certain?"

"Quite," she said, and a grin cranked the side of her mouth and she gave Callahan a thumbs up. Inside, however, Karen Larsen had felt the heat of her spirit drain away, leaving her soul shivering against the possibilities that a moment alone with Harvey could create.

Thirty-one . . .

That same afternoon, Gabriella called her father, as she had done every weekday since his accident. Until she had seen her father in the hospital, she had believed him invulnerable. Now she worried not only about his physical health but his spirits. She was particularly concerned about Loring's suspension. Seeing him on his back in bandages, for the first time she could contemplate the potential his burdens carried for eroding his always buoyant soul. She vowed to be there for him, not simply because she was feeling guilty and selfish but because she was her parents' daughter, nourished by their sense of nurture. She reached him in his Riverton office.

"Anything new?" she asked.

Loring had anticipated Gabbie's call, and he had his answer ready. "I've asked Karen to marry me."

It was the perfect bombshell, as conversation pieces go, guaranteed to preoccupy Gabbie not only throughout this conversation but for weeks to come. And indeed, in her excitement over the news, she cut her phone call short with her father's blessing so that she could call Karen with congratulations.

Gabriella English had been an independent spirit since an early age, but nonetheless felt bonded to the support and structure that her parents offered. Part of whom she was included her parents, ideals. Chief among these was a concern for truth. It was, then, stunning to Gabriella when she coyly questioned Karen about the big news, anticipating a heart-to-heart with her future stepmother.

"He never mentioned the cottage?" asked Karen, who went on to explain their suspicions, the possible connection with Loring's accident, with Keating's disappearance.

"I can't believe something like that happened and he didn't tell me! I'm really pissed, Karen."

"Don't be, Gabbie. I'm sure he didn't want you to get involved."

"For God's sake! I'm a grown woman!"

"I know. But just be thankful you have a dad like Loring," Karen said. "He knows there's nothing you can do. But to tell you the truth, something has to be done to bring this all to a head. I'm afraid what might happen to your father if he keeps poking around without knowing exactly what we're up against."

"Any ideas?"

"In fact, I do," Karen said. "But first, you have to promise not to let your father hear a word of this. Is it a deal?"

"That's a hard promise to make not knowing what you're going to say," Gabriella said.

"Either yes or no, Gabbie. It won't work if Loring knows. But if I don't try, we may lose him."

"You don't really give me a choice, Karen. Okay, what is it?"

Jim Harvey, Karen explained, was the key. A dominating individual, he would be in control of Osler's schemes. If the group was involved in this violence, Harvey would be the one making the decisions. Karen explained her relationship with Harvey to Gabriella and told her about Harvey's renewed interest in her.

"Sounds like he's on to you, Karen. I doubt his advances are genuine."

"Of course they're not," Karen said. "But the man has one incredible blind spot. He's had so much luck with women that he thinks he is in complete charge. There is no way that he could see it coming if a woman were to turn the tables on him."

"Such a woman as you?"

"You've got it, honey."

"But how?

"Poetically," Karen said. She would call Harvey and tell him she had rebuffed him because she was afraid of her feelings. But having reconsidered, she wanted to see him. She would suggest a rendezvous.

"You're right," Gabriella said. "Dad should never know about this."

"Oh, he'll know afterward. Don't worry. Nothing will happen," Karen said. She would seduce Harvey, reminding him of a particular form of foreplay that involved her kneeling behind him, massaging his chest, then his temples with her hands, and finally the back of his neck with her breasts. Once she had him in this position, Karen told Gabriella, she would inject him with ketamine.

"I know all about that," Gabriella said. "That's an ingredient in the date rape drug."

"Exactly. It puts the patient in a catatonic state, awake but unable to move. And it works fast, even when injected in muscle," Karen said. "Within a minute, he'll be falling sharply and in less than two minutes, the ketamine will have taken hold."

"I don't know, Karen. Once he gets jabbed, he'll know something's up. He'll turn on you."

"I've got that covered, Gabbie. I'll be wearing a broach with a lot of sharp edges. I'm good with injections, so he won't feel much. But what he does feel, I'll cover by apologizing for scratching him with my broach."

"Okay, but this is pretty chancy, Karen. Don't you think you should have a backup?"

"Like you? No, I don't think so. Believe me, I can handle Jim Harvey. Anyway, next I'll insert a heparin lock. You know what that is?"

"A needle with a tube and a stopper, right?"

"Pretty much. It's used so you won't have to keep stabbing a patient with new IVs. You put in the heparin lock, and then each time you need to change the IV, you insert the new needle into the stopper in the lock, not into the vein. I'll insert one of these in his arm, tape it in place, and then I'll load him up with Pentothal. He'll tell me anything I want to know. And I'll be taping."

"I see what you're planning. Sounds like it will work. Then you beat it out of there with your tape and go to the cops, and Dr. Harvey will be out of business for good."

"That's pretty much the plan. Except for your role."

The plan worked well, up to a point. Harvey wanted Karen to spend the weekend with him on his yacht, which was now berthed on the Chesapeake. They would sail on the bay in perfect seclusion, except for the yacht's captain, who, Harvey said, was a discreet gentleman. The weekend wouldn't do, Karen said. Couldn't we go tomorrow? Of course, Harvey said. I share your eagerness.

Karen had to work fast. She gathered her supplies from the drug room, to which she, as supervisor of the emergency room, had both keys. She took a substantial quantity of thiopental sodium. She found two epi-pins, spring loaded injection devices about the size of a pen light, and she filled them with doses of ketamine; one for Harvey and one for the captain. She took two heparin locks, a roll of tape and some alcohol and cotton balls.

Next, she phoned Dave Carn at City Campus and told him she had a last-minute opportunity to take a two-day course at Johns Hopkins. She was due for retesting. Take off, he told her.

Before she called Loring to tell him about the course and her sudden change of plans, she phoned Cal Kalinowski. She asked him if she could have his confidence. Then she told him of her need.

"Girl, count me in," he said with an enthusiasm that reassured Karen. He told her to stop by his place before she left and pick up a hand-held GPS receiver, an electronic device the size of a cell phone that would give her location on the water. "I'll show you how to work it and give you some instructions for the ship's radio, too. And don't worry. Loring'll never know."

Finally, it was time to speak with Loring. Karen hesitated. The thought of tricking him had come too easily. It was not the way she wanted their relationship to work. But these were extraordinary times, she thought. If I can bring all this to an end, we may have a chance together. But if I don't act, we may both be dead. She picked up the receiver and dialed Riverton.

On Thursday morning, the day's heat was already in the streets at nine o'clock and there was the promise of record temperatures by early afternoon. It did not feel to Karen like a day to pursue a romantic idyll on an unshaded yacht on a placid expanse of water, which she mentioned to Harvey when he met her at Riverton International. Loring had taken her to the airport for what he believed was her flight to Baltimore. She had ordered a ticket as part of her ruse and had gone to her gate with him to wait for the flight. Loring was pleased that Karen was leaving town, out of harm's way, he thought. He stayed until eight-thirty, but then left for his office. Harvey's Range Rover was parked one level above Loring's Mercedes in the airport garage, and their paths crossed in the concourse, but neither saw the other.

" *Carassius Auratus* is air-conditioned," Harvey said, slinging her overnight bag over his shoulder and taking her hand. "We'll swim, of course. You brought your bathing suit?" He laced his fingers through hers as they walked. In the Range Rover, Karen was pleased to find that the front bucket seats each had armrests and were separated by a broad console. Still, Harvey again reached for her hand as he drove, and disguising her revulsion at his touch was a test for Karen. Good practice, she thought, for his seduction, and she visualized how this charade would play out on the yacht. They drove out of the parking garage, but they did not take the airport exit. Instead, Harvey circled the runways to a low, silver hangar and pulled the Range Rover onto the concrete apron, stopping beside a jet helicopter, whose engine was whining to life.

"We'll be there in a half hour," he said, smiling at Karen in a way she once had found rather attractive but that now caused her skin to crawl.

"Yours?" she asked as he opened her door.

"The group's. A business expense," he said. "Have you flown in one before?"

She had not, so he instructed her to keep her head down as they passed under the rotors, which were slashing overhead at an accelerating pace. In less than a minute, they were buckled in their seats directly behind the pilot and lifting off the concrete. At five thousand feet, they passed over Riverton University Medical Center, and they climbed even further before they crossed the Hancock River, several miles below Port Hancock.

"Here's the bay," Harvey said after about twenty minutes in the air, pointing across Karen to the right window of the helicopter. "We'll be at the marina in no time."

The helicopter began a rapid descent over a thick forest along the western edge of the bay, then banked sharply to the right and settled in a cloud of dust on a gravel parking lot. As the rotors slowed and the dust thinned, Karen could see the tall masts of sailboats, clustered like the dead gray trunks of cedar in a swamp. *Carassius Auratus* was in a slip near the main bulkhead, a location from which it was admired by all the sailors

285

passing to their own boats farther removed from the shore. The taller of its two masts was the loftiest spar in the marina. The captain, Bengt Norstrand, was waiting on the finger pier to greet his employer and Karen.

"Ready to cast off, Captain?" Harvey asked, handing Karen's bag to Norstrand. "Captain Norstrand will put your things in the aft cabin, Karen. He's the only crew today; he's even the cook. Why don't we go below and see what he's fixed for us." He led Karen down a ladder into the coolness of the salon, where an urn of coffee sat at the center of the table surrounded by pastries and small dishes of cheese. Norstrand emerged from a doorway to the rear. "We'll be casting off presently," he told Harvey, climbing the ladder to the cockpit. Karen was taking a seat by the table when she felt the boat begin to move. A chill passed through her, one which caused a visible shiver.

"The air conditioning's too high," Harvey said. "When we've had a bite, why don't you go back and change into a bathing suit and we'll go on deck. You'll find the air on the bay is comfortable."

The yacht was passing the last point of land and emerging in the bay when Karen climbed back up the ladder into the heat. Her bathing suit was a one-piece, the most dowdy navy blue design she could find, with ruffles along the top edge and the hem and no cleavage visible. It could not camouflage Karen's figure, however, and she could feel Norstrand's leer. On the bay, there was wind that rinsed away some of the sun's heat and tossed her hair, which she had let fall over her shoulders when she changed. The boat was heeled slightly to starboard, the wind coming over the port rail and the water slipping silently along its sides. Harvey, standing on the high side and leaning against the lifelines, was now in a bathing suit, as well—a speedo that left little to the imagination concerning either his endowment or his level of anticipation. Karen sat on the opposite side of the cockpit, her knees pressed primly together, her elbows resting on her thighs so that her arms concealed her bosom.

286

"This is really rather delightful," she said. "Much nicer than I expected."

"Relax and enjoy yourself," Harvey said, looking down at her. "These are the days that create the best memories. Playing hooky on a boat! What could be better?"

They stopped at noon in a small cove to swim. By late afternoon, they were under way again, somewhere in the middle of the bay, a thick haze obliterating the shore from view. At about six o'clock, Harvey took the wheel to steer the yacht, sending Norstrand below to prepare dinner, and Karen stretched out along the cockpit seat, taking care to avoid any suggestion of seductiveness, affecting instead a prim, reserved posture of a girl who needs some coaxing. When Norstrand returned forty-five minutes later, Harvey yielded the helm to him and, reaching for Karen's hand, drew her toward the companionway. In the salon, he showed her to her seat on the settee by the table and then sat beside her. The soft blond hair of his thighs brushed against *her*, and when he leaned to fetch something across the table, she felt his shoulder, warm against hers. Clever, she thought, and so, so subtle.

As they ate, Harvey talked. He talked about the yacht, about her work at HMS, about his own struggle to create a new method of delivering health care in a difficult climate. His voice, rumbling quietly near her ear, was almost hypnotic. He talked some more about her career, about her reputation in medicine, every reference ringing with praise of the sort that Karen had spent her professional life seeking. He knows, she thought, what works. She looked into his eyes, holding her forkful of speared salad in mid-air, searching for the flash of evil she knew those solemn lenses must contain. He stopped talking then and returned her stare for a long, silent moment. He breathed in deeply and then spoke even more quietly.

"You are irreplaceable," he said, and she felt his hand on her elbow and saw that, with his other hand, he was reaching to take the fork from her. She did not resist as he turned her toward him and, having set the fork on her plate, with one hand still on her elbow, cupped the side of her face with the other, gently as if he were handling a bird. His fingertips reached to the back of her neck, and with the slightest pressure, they pulled her head toward him, her lips toward his.

The creep, she thought, while letting the kiss happen. The filthy scum, she thought as his tongue entered her mouth, searching for hers, and his hand slid down to her shoulder, his thumb stroking even further below. She pulled back slightly, enough to disengage her lips.

"Why don't you wait here a minute," she whispered. "Wait here and I'll get changed." His hand slid off her shoulder and down her arm, his thumb tracing along the side of her breast. As she moved back across the settee, she noticed that he was fully aroused. Good, she thought. "I'll call for you in a minute," she whispered, backing off the settee and stepping through the door into the rear cabin. She locked the cabin door latch and, opening her bag, began arranging her goods. The last step was to change into a negligee pinned between the breasts with a gaudy rhinestone broach. She tucked one of the epi-pins inside her bra, which she had replaced when she got out of the bathing suit. She looked at herself in the mirror on the back of the door, then called to Harvey through the door.

"Remember that thing you liked me to do with your head?" she said in her deepest voice. His words came back from just beyond the door.

"I hoped you hadn't forgotten."

She unlocked the latch and stepped aside as Harvey entered the small cabin, whose berth extended the width of the boat and all the way to the rear wall of the cabin. She took his hand and led him to the edge of the berth, turning him around and shoving him gently back, so that he was sitting on the edge, his feet on the floor. Then she climbed onto the berth and, on her knees, moved behind his naked back. She wrapped her arms around his chest, letting her fingers play with his chest hairs as she looked down at her broach to assure herself that it was in position near his neck. She brought her fingers up along the sides of his neck and, as Harvey leaned back onto her, began combing through the hair on the back of his head. Karen had just looked up to a brass-rimmed clock on the bulkhead and noticed that it was five past eight when there was a knocking at the cabin door.

"Dammit!" Harvey growled. "Yes, Captain?"

"You've got a call, Doctor. Sounds important."

"Tell them I'll call back," Harvey said, tilting his head back and looking up at Karen. She saw that his erection had lifted his suit away from his body.

"You'd really better take this now," the captain insisted.

"Stay here," Harvey whispered to Karen. "Okay, I'm coming." He adjusted the bikini and stepped into the salon, closing the door behind him. Karen jumped off the berth and pressed her ear against the door's mirror.

"They're sending the helicopter out," the captain was saying. "Some fellow named English is causing problems at the morgue. It's all coming apart."

"Who called."

"The lawyer," the captain said. "He said there's been one death already. You've got to go."

"You're right," Harvey said, stepping farther away from the cabin door and lowering his voice. All Karen heard was a murmur that ended with her name.

"They're here," the captain said in a normal voice, and Karen heard the thumping of helicopter blades. When she looked out a porthole at one end of the berth, she saw Jim Harvey jumping overboard and swimming to a rope ladder that had been lowered from the chopper. Water was spraying against the side of the yacht. The view from the porthole was blurred by droplets of mist that gathered on the glass and were illuminated by the low rays of the sun. As the sound of the helicopter faded to nothing, Karen heard the engine of the yacht start. But the sun continued to pour in from the starboard porthole, the same side of the boat it had been on all afternoon. Clearly, the captain was not turning back to the marina.

Thirty-two . . .

Loring English could not have pinpointed the time. His best guess would have been that it was early, perhaps when he first opened one of his father's books and struggled through the archaic prose. But he embraced the concept immediately, the notion that the heavy baggage carried by privilege is duty. Noblesse oblige. Raised by his mother with a sense that through his veins ran aristocratic blood, he therefore felt bound, even as a child, to always seek out a responsible path. As an adult, by reason of his superior intelligence, he rose to a vocation that, for hundreds of years, society had elevated to the level of nobility. Physicians were, by virtue of their life-and-death powers, only one rung below God, on a par with saints. Their lives were financially rewarding. Their incomes, in the minds of the masses, reflected their station at the pinnacle of the marketplace. The doctor's house was the grandest in town, his car the most luxurious and few, if any, begrudged him these rewards because the doctor earned them. He was the savior who appeared in the middle of the night. He was the deliverer of new life, as important as semen and ova to the propagation of the human race. Medicine was a complicated science, but not quite so complicated that one man, with superior mental powers, could not absorb it all and use this science for the lesser members of his community. This was medicine when Loring English entered medical school.

The profession changed. The science advanced, adding layer upon layer of understanding, hundreds of words to describe the ever expanding knowledge of man about medicine, and even by the time Loring had completed medical school, it was clear to him that he needed to focus his attention on one discipline. Cardiology, at that time, was one of the handful of specialties, and so he studied the heart for a few more years before entering practice as something not quite as unique or omniscient as a family doctor, but still revered.

Then specialized medicine became the norm, research

swamped the profession with more details than one individual could retain and doctors, increasingly, became technicians. They continued, through their ability to restrict trade in their profession, to claim the same high financial rewards. But their prestige became diluted. Since no one of them knew it all, none of them was quite as close to God. Thus was the nobility of physicians lost, and this became not just their loss but the community's. For as the technicians replaced the deities, so did avarice replace responsibility. The physician as technical wizard traded on his skills to secure personal wealth. The specter of this wealth was to businessmen like roadkill to vultures. So that as Loring English entered the later years of his career, it was not uncommon that the chairman of a medical insurance company was rewarded with millions of dollars a year, while a family physician could find himself employed on the same salary as the local high school principal. In this environment, the physician who focused on medical care for the sick slid to the bottom while the doctor whose eye was on the dollars crafted himself a new sort of pedestal.

Loring still followed the course of duty. And on a night when Karen had told him she would be in Baltimore, he saw no reason he should not remain at his Riverton office, reviewing the case studies gathered by his Riverton colleagues, pursuing the evil that now he was convinced infected Osler Medical Group.

It was shortly before seven o'clock when the phone on Loring's desk first rang. He ignored it, choosing instead to screen his calls. It could be Gabriella. She had called on Tuesday and asked Loring to go to dinner with her this night. He knew where to call her. If it was Karen, she would leave a number. Loring was glad to see Karen getting out of town and, he felt, away from danger. Her absence also gave him some uninterrupted time to focus on consolidating the evidence he had gathered. It would have been better had he been able to walk through Osler's doors and unlock Jim Harvey's files, Loring knew. But he compared this sleuthing through documents to a review of medical charts. If he could build a solid case based on Osler's record among Riverton doctors and with Reggie's discoveries inside Coastal, he would be in a position to demand a physical examination of Osler's operation, complete with depositions from individual physicians. He would prove the fraud that corrupted the entire practice. Finally, James Harvey would be made to pay for Janet's death.

The red light was now lit on Loring's phone, and he dialed to get this new message. The voice he heard was unfamiliar, but the caller was clearly frightened.

"This is Robert Chen!" the voice said. "This is Dr. Robert Chen. I am calling from Osler Medical Group. I, I, I . . ." there was a pause. "Dr. Natasha Wilson informed me that you are investigating Osler. Yes. We must talk. This is urgent! I, I, I . . ." Loring could hear breathing for several seconds before the voice returned. "Please call me back immediately if you are there!" Chen's voice said, and then he left a telephone number.

Loring dialed the number, and after five rings, he got the Osler business office message, listing office hours.

"Damn!" he said aloud. He wondered what Natasha had told Chen. He looked through his pocket calendar and found her home number, which he dialed. He got another answering machine, and he left a message for Natasha to call him at work. He attempted to resume his labor on the computer, but Chen's desperate voice haunted him. When the phone rang again, he grabbed at the receiver.

"Yes!" he shouted.

"Dr. English?" The voice was timid.

"Yes, yes. Who is this?"

"This is Robert Chen. We have not met, Dr. English."

"I got your message, Dr. Chen. You said it is urgent?"

"More than I had thought, Dr. English. I must speak quickly. My life is in danger. They are listening." Chen's voice was calm now, almost at peace, Loring thought.

"I am listening," Loring said.

"I have the information you are seeking. If I die, it will go with my body. I must say this to you alone, a not unusual statement."

"Where is the information?" Loring asked, but even as he spoke, he heard Chen hang up his receiver. "Jeezus!" he shouted aloud. Then he dialed the operator and asked for the Port Hancock police department. "Yes, I want you to connect me, quickly please."

The phone rang seven times before a woman's voice came on the line.

"There is an assault under way at Osler Medical Group on Hillcrest," Loring told the woman.

"Are you the victim?"

"No, no. Dr. Robert Chen."

"Who is the assailant, sir?"

"I don't know. I don't know, dammit! Will you get some cops up there?"

"Now you hold on, mister. Is this some kind of a crank call?"

"My name is Dr. Loring English. I just received a frantic call from Dr. Chen. He said he is at Osler, and someone is trying to kill him."

"Why didn't he just dial 9-1-1, then? Why did he call you?"

"I don't know why. Will you please send someone over?"

"A unit is on its way, Dr. English. Please explain your involvement for our records?"

"I'm a friend, and I'm on my way to Osler. Goodbye."

Robert Chen's investigation of his employer was less like angioplasty, more like open heart surgery. He had split Osler's protective shell, had stuck his hands inside places which James Perkins Harvey III believed were impenetrable, and what he found was a malignancy that appalled him, that was metastasized to every part of the organization, corrupting the work of good physicians, including his own, connecting this supposed health care provider to potential destroyers of health, purveyors of stolen, inferior, and adulterated medical goods. He had carefully made records of his findings, and he had periodically stashed those records—on computer disks and on microcassettes—in a safe deposit box in a bank in Riverton. His cache was nearly complete, and he had been prepared to take the package to the police when he discovered a more intriguing line of inquiry involving Dr. Brad Barnett. On this night, Chen had locked himself after hours in one of the administrative offices. He had logged on to the computer using Ophelia Sadler's password, which he had acquired by watching her and memorizing her keystrokes. Secure in the belief that he was alone at Osler, he had turned off the terminal and had stepped out in the corridor on his way back to his cubicle to retrieve some papers. When he logged off, two men sitting in another private office stood up from their seats before a computer screen and headed for the room Chen was just leaving. Chen saw them rounding a far corner when he stepped into the corridor, and he quickly stepped back into the office, relocking the door.

In that instant, Robert Chen realized that there was, indeed, a connection between James Harvey and the man in the corridor, the man at the airport, Ching Huo, his brother, the Dragon.

Moments later, he recognized the voice that followed the knock on the office door. He did not answer, but, with his heart racing, lifted the receiver and dialed a phone number he had never before called. When he got the recording, he left a message and then quickly disconnected. He believed he had whispered his message. He had not, but it did not matter. As Chen had wandered through Osler's computer files, he had been noticed. Sadler had alerted Harvey of the invasion. Harvey told her he would contact an electronics detective service. He called the Dragon. The Dragon's people had no difficulty eavesdropping on Chen electronically, and on this night, it had been clear that Chen had accumulated too much information and that steps must be taken. The Dragon had decided to allow his brother to complete his work and to approach him only when he left the locked room. The Dragon's timing was uncharacteristically imprecise, allowing Chen to return to the sanctuary of the office. The Dragon would not wait for his brother to come out, but neither did he believe in using force where it was unnecessary.

294

"My honorable brother," the Dragon said, leaning a shoulder gently against the office door. "We are on opposite sides of this door, and of life, kind brother. This should not be. Allow me to enter your side."

Inside the office, Chen stared at the blank screen of his computer. He considered turning the machine on, an idea he then rejected. There was nothing more to do. He had secured every bit of evidence they would need. He placed one of two cassettes he had brought in the microcassette recorder, and in a relaxed voice barely above a whisper, he began to speak. When he had finished, he turned off the recorder and removed the cassette. From a stainless steel dispenser on the wall, he took a latex glove and from his smock pocket, he took a pair of bandage scissors. He snipped off the glove's middle finger, and he slid the cassette into the thumb. Then he stood and took his wallet from his rear trouser pocket. In the opened wallet, he found a brass key, which he placed in the latex finger beside the cassette. Stretching the latex, he tied a knot in the open end of the finger so that the cassette and the key were secured inside. He unbuckled his belt then, glancing around the office. He didn't see what he wanted, so as his trousers fell to his ankles, he checked through the drawers of the desk beside the computer. Still he found nothing, and so he worked his cheeks against his tongue until his mouth was filled with saliva, and then, holding the glove finger with its contents just below his mouth, he drooled saliva along it until it was coated. With one hand, he shoved down his briefs. He then squatted and placed the package against his rectum, increasing the pressure until the sphincter yielded and the lubricated thumb rose into the anal canal. He stood then, replaced his clothing, straightened his shirt, put the remains of the latex glove in one pocket and his wallet in the other and dialed Loring's number at Riverton once more.

When the call was completed, Robert Chen stepped to the office door, which he opened. He looked at his brother and smiled.

"Ching Huo, please join me," he said. The Dragon and the

man with him entered the office, and the second man closed and locked the door.

"Please take your seat," the Dragon told his brother. "Our business should be conducted formally."

"Of course," Chen said. He noticed that his brother and the other man were wearing gloves of the type he had just used. He sat in the chair and rolled forward to the desk, looking straight ahead. He felt the muzzle of the pistol against the side of his head.

As the body of his brother fell forward, the Dragon was already placing the discharged pistol in the right hand. He noticed the tape recorder then and the cassette.

"Most convenient," the Dragon said to his accomplice. "My brother and I always sounded the same as children. Perhaps we still do?"

"Identical," the man said.

"Good," the Dragon said, unwrapping the fresh cassette and placing it in the machine. "First we will do this. Then we will leave. This is not the place for us any longer. Let the doctors heal themselves." He laughed, and then he pushed the record button on the tape recorder and brought the machine near his mouth.

"I want to leave some instructions," the Dragon said as the player began recording. "And I want to explain why I took my own life . . ."

Thirty-three . . .

Carassius Auratus continued on its southeastward course, with the late summer darkness drawn up over its bow by the last long fingers of sunlight that settled off its stern. Karen had remained in the aft cabin with the door locked until after the retreating sound of the helicopter had dissolved in the muffled clatter of the yacht's diesel. She could not stay put. Loring was at a morgue, probably at City Campus. In some way, his safety was threatened. Jim Harvey never abandoned what he thought was guaranteed sex for a suffering patient, Karen knew. His departure from the yacht signaled the seriousness Harvey placed on thwarting Loring.

Karen went through her overnight bag and selected blue jeans and a button-front blouse. When she was dressed, she tied on her sneakers and then took the second epi-pin from the bag. She placed it on the top of the cabin's dresser, and then, looking in the mirror on the back of the door, pulled her hair up into a tight twist, which she pinned securely in place. The first epi-pin was still in her bra. She now took the second and inserted it into the top of her twisted hair, checked her appearance once in the mirror and then opened the cabin door. Norstrand stood at the big wheel in the darkness, the light from his instruments shining up on his face. He glanced at Karen as she emerged from the companionway.

"Well, Captain, what was that all about?" she asked, standing before Norstrand, off to his left, looking out at the waters. A nearly full moon was rising in the east, large, yellow, just above the horizon. Its light reflected in a thousand scalloped ripples that stretched toward the eastern shore of the bay. The boat moved smoothly across the water with very little roll or pitch. The captain remained silent. Karen turned and looked at his face, expressionless yet eerie in the blue-green glow of the lights. "Where did Jim go?" she asked.

"Dr. Harvey's business is his own," Norstrand said, his fingertips resting atop the wheel, moving it by increments, left and right, port and starboard.

"And did he tell you to return me to the marina?"

Norstrand did not respond, his eyes fixed at some point off in the darkness.

"Where are we headed, Captain?"

Norstrand, without turning his head, allowed his eyes to drift toward Karen, and his lips slowly curled up at the corners.

"My instructions are to take care of you," he said, and he reached in front of the wheel to the instrument panel and moved one of the controls. He then stepped to the side of the wheel, facing Karen, his feet apart, his hips rolling with the slight movement of the yacht from side to side. Karen understood his intention, knew the message his posture was broadcasting. He was not flirting. He was a predator. And now he was moving toward her. Karen glanced toward the companionway, an image of the lock inside the aft cabin door claiming her attention, and as she began to move, so did the captain. His lunge caught Karen before she had completed a step across the cockpit. His large hands were on her shoulders, his body upon hers, trapping her back against the wall beside the companionway, his knee driving between her legs, so that she could move neither to the side nor up or down, until he released one shoulder and she began to squirm. But now she felt his fingernails against her collarbone and then heard the tearing of fabric as he ripped the blouse off her right side. Her hands were free, and she was shoving against him as he jammed his head against her ear and bit into her neck. Karen was reacting, not thinking. Her screams, weak from his weight against her and her inability to breathe, came back to her loud, reflected by the side of his head. His free hand now was jammed under the back of her jeans, and he was attempting to shove the jeans down over her hips while the thick fingers of that hand clawed around her rump and pushed into her rectum. Now he removed his other hand from her shoulder and began to lift her, still pressing against her. Karen's arms were free, and she pushed against his shoulders without effect. She felt her jeans being stripped down her legs, and it was only now that she remembered the epi-pin. It was remarkable, she would later realize, that she could at this moment have thought so clinically. The ketamine, she knew, would take a minute, perhaps two, to take effect. That was not enough time. She could be raped and dead by then. Unless she could hit an artery or vein.

In one motion, she reached to the back of her head, seized

the epi-pin and, clutching it like a dagger, shoved it into the captain's neck.

"Cunt!" the man screamed, standing so suddenly that Karen, released from his grip, fell to the cockpit floor at his feet. He bent to reach for her, a figure all in shadows above her. The blue jeans were snarled around Karen's ankles, ensnaring her feet. She attempted to roll away, the cold roughness of the fiberglass against her thigh. She was on her knees and grasping for the edge of the companionway, and the captain's hands were clutching her naked pelvis, pulling her back. And then he was on top of her, she face down on the cockpit floor, her legs splayed to the sides, his chest on her back, his legs between hers.

Karen froze.

The captain did not move.

There was near silence. The yacht's engine turned slowly somewhere below the deck. A light breeze slapped a halyard against one of the masts. Still the captain did not stir. Karen pushed to one side, and Norstrand rolled off her back. She made it to her knees, then to her feet and felt the breeze wash against her naked breasts and legs. She reached down to draw up her jeans but had to steady herself first. She removed the torn blouse and the bra, still hooked around her ribs. For the first time, she looked at Norstrand, sprawled on his back, his eyes open, staring blankly toward the stars, and it occurred to her dreamy mind, in which everything seemed to have been set in a slow gear, that she should restrain the man. She felt for her second epi-pin but realized that it had been in her bra, which was now gone. She began to search the cockpit deck, but then decided she should in some way bind the captain. Shaking, she climbed down the ladder into the salon, where one wall-mounted lamp was lit. She looked through drawers in the galley for anything, finally selecting a roll of silver duct tape. She returned to the cockpit and rolled Norstrand face down. Then she taped his wrists together firmly and then his ankles. From the emergency room, she had acquired a knowledge of restraints, and the ones she improvised were designed to resist twisting, stretching and clawing. She then ran the tape around both the wrist and ankle wrappings, pulling hard so that Norstrand's feet were jerked up toward his back, almost touching his hands. She looped the tape in this way several times. Then she wrapped the tape around his head in a manner that sealed his mouth. Finally, kneeling beside Norstrand, she bound his arms and torso in a mummy wrapping. Then she stood and, as she took a moment to inspect her work, the boat rolled to the left and she heard a clattering across the deck. She picked up the unused epi-pin and tucked it in her jeans, then descended into the salon where she found the radio. She dialed to channel seventy-two and pushed the button on the microphone.

"Yellow Bird, Yellow Bird. This is Redhead calling Yellow Bird."

"Redhead, this is Yellow Bird. Over."

"Cal, come quick. Oh, Jesus, come quick," Karen said, and she began to sob.

Patiently, Cal talked Karen through a reading of the yacht's compass and the GPS he had given her.

"Okay, Karen. I'll be reaching you in about fifteen minutes," Cal said. "Get a life jacket on and grab anything you need to bring. You're going to have to do some swimming."

Cal touched down on the Chesapeake twelve minutes later beside Carassius Auratus, which was making way under a computer programmed automatic pilot. Over the radio, Cal talked Karen through the steps to shut down the yacht's engine. Then he taxied beside the boat and stepped out onto the starboard float, where, after Karen jumped overboard and swam to the plane, he helped her out of the water. Within five minutes of Cal's arrival, Yellow Bird was airborne with Redhead, and Cal had radioed a land-based telephone operator. Before she called Loring's home to leave a message for Gabriella, she called the Port Hancock police.

"Is this in any way connected with one Dr. Loring English?" the dispatcher asked.

"Why yes," Karen said. "So you are aware of the situation?"

"We've already responded to his call, ma'am." "You've sent police to the morgue?"

"Not the morgue, ma'am. We resolved the issue before the body was transported."

"But something's going on at the morgue. You've got to send a unit there. It's urgent."

"You'll have to give me the nature of the crime we're investigating, ma'am."

"Well, I don't know exactly," Karen said. "All I know is that Dr. English is at the morgue and some very evil people are upset that he is there." She could hear how pathetic this explanation sounded and wasn't surprised at the response.

"We've already been alerted to Dr. English's theories on conspiracies, ma'am," the woman said. "We are not dispatching units unless we have a complaint of specific criminal activity. Do you have such a complaint?"

Karen's thumb nearly drove the button through the side of the microphone as she made her response, not unlike the response Loring had uttered ninety minutes earlier to one of the city's most decorated detectives.

Thirty-four . . .

Loring had experienced the scene many times before. At the wheel of a car passing through rural darkness, its tires screaming on every curve, racing toward a soul in desperate need of his help, Loring would enumerate and then place in some sequence of priority the things he must do when he arrived at the patient's side. In this case, Loring had new technology, a car phone mounted on the console. He could be giving aid even before he reached Robert Chen. Indeed, he had, by phoning the police, already given as much help as was possible. If the police arrived in time, then Chen's life could be saved. But if not . . . Loring's hands gripped the wheel more firmly and his foot pressed harder on the accelerator at the thought, and the Mercedes leaned heavily around a turn on the mountain road between Riverton and Port Hancock. The interstate was closed again, forcing Loring to take the more treacherous route, his speed curbed by the twists of the pavement around the darkened folds of the mountain. When he was about halfway to Port Hancock, he slowed and punched in the number for Osler Medical Group. A male voice answered just as Loring was glancing at the dashboard clock. It was 8:17.

"Is this Osler Medical Group?" Loring asked.

"Who is calling?" said the man.

It occurred to Loring that the same person who had been threatening Robert Chen could be on the phone, and so he chose to be obtuse.

"May I speak to Dr. Chen?"

"This is the Port Hancock Police Department. May I have your name?" the man said.

"This is Dr. Loring English. I'm headed to Port Hancock and I wanted to be certain that you had responded to my call. Is Dr. Chen okay?"

"What do you know about Dr. Chen?"

"I am the one who called the police, officer. I reported the threat to his life. Is he okay?"

"I'm sorry, but I am not at liberty to discuss the case."

"Officer, give me your name," Loring said, attempting to control his rising frustration. The Mercedes had slowed to a near crawl, Loring's attention drawn by this conversation that was going no place, as well.

"This is Detective Emile Johnston."

"Aha, that explains it," Loring said, and his foot jammed on the accelerator and the Mercedes lurched into a short straightaway.

"Excuse me, sir?"

"You're the sonofabitch who wouldn't investigate an attempted murder at Eagle's Nest. No wonder I can't get information from you!"

"Oh, yes," the detective said. "It comes back to me. You're the conspiracy theorist, right? Gas bombs in a motel room? And didn't you have a car wreck you were somehow trying to link to a broken door at the motel?"

"I am on my way to Osler, Detective." Loring calmed his voice. No sense riling an incompetent, he thought. "I would just like to know if Dr. Chen is okay."

"A guy who puts a pistol to his head and pulls the trigger probably couldn't be in any better condition than the good doctor," Johnston said.

"He's dead?" Loring's question was a reflex. He always knew the instant he had lost a patient, and now he felt that same thickness in his throat, as if he'd swallowed something too large, something that scratched on the way down and left a feeling that would not let go. He knew now that Robert Chen, whom he had never met and whose name until an hour earlier was but a scrap of awareness in Loring's memory, was gone, that his call had come too late and that the disease which Loring had, for months, been attempting to diagnose, had claimed a victim.

"Are you calling this a suicide?" he asked.

"I sure would like your advice in solving this, Dr. English. All I have to go on is a gun in the dead man's hand, a taped suicide statement in the man's own voice and no evidence of foul play. What would you say?"

"Dr. Chen phoned me a half hour ago. He said his life was in danger, and he suggested there were people who wanted to silence him."

"Yeah, he mentioned those voices in his tape. Said he heard them all the time; they were telling him to do bad things and he had to escape them. That's why he shot himself, Dr. English."

"I'll be there in twenty minutes, detective. There has to be some evidence on the body that would suggest murder."

"Don't waste your time, Doc. You'll have to find a conspiracy some place else."

"Just don't move the body until I get there."

"The body's already gone to the morgue at City Campus, Doc. So you'll just have to wait for the autopsy to prove you right."

The road straightened on the Port Hancock side of the mountain, and Loring took the Mercedes up to eighty. His fingers felt across the keypad on the phone, and he dialed Dave Carn's extension. A nurse answered at the City Campus emergency room. Carn was not on duty. Loring asked for Patty McCullough, the woman in charge of the mobile intensive care unit. Mrs. McCullough told Loring that Bill was the emergency medical technician on duty and, no, they weren't busy at the moment.

"Can you have Bill meet me in five minutes at the end of Ferry Street?" Loring asked.

"Are you okay, Dr. English?"

"Yeah, sure, Patty. But I need this favor, and I need you and Bill to keep it quiet. Can you do this for me, Patty?"

"It's pretty irregular, Dr. English."

"Hey, isn't that my reputation around the hospital, Patty? You know me! Just this once, girl. It's for a good cause."

"Oh, gee. Well, okay, Dr. English. But if Bill gets a call, he's going to have to leave or turn around, no matter what."

"Understood. Good girl, Patty. Thanks for doing an old guy a favor."

The ambulance was already parked at the foot of Ferry Street, in a lot built by the city for the urban fishermen who spent their days standing on the old ferry dock, their lines slanting out over the river. Loring pulled the Mercedes around to the river side of the ambulance, so that it was hidden from the city. When he got out, Bill rolled down his window and Loring explained what he wanted. He went to the back of the rig, where Bill opened the doors. Loring climbed inside and sat beside the stretcher, on which a sheet and blanket were already folded. He waved to Bill through the cab window and then felt the movement. Through the side windows, he saw red lights sweeping across the brick storefronts as the ambulance drove back through the downtown toward City Campus. When he felt the rig begin the climb on the last block before the hospital, Loring unfolded the blanket and sheet and shifted himself onto the stretcher, pulling the covers back over himself and settling his head on the pillow. The ambulance stopped and then began backing. Loring pulled the covers across his face and waited. He heard the rear door swing open, then heard the sound of an overhead garage door rising.

"Okay," Bill whispered. "We're here. I'm going to roll you inside. I checked and there's no one around."

The stretcher jerked sharply toward the rear, and Loring's neck slid back against the pillow. He heard the spring-loaded legs of the stretcher snap down into position, first under his knees and then under his shoulders, and he felt himself being rolled along a rough surface and then onto a smooth one.

"We're here," Bill said, no longer whispering. Loring pushed back the covers and sat up. They were in a dimly-lit corridor that, ahead of him, bent to the right. "I've got to run. A call came in just before we arrived. You're on your own, Doc."

"I'm indebted, Bill. Take off!"

"Be careful, Doc. I don't know what you're up to. I hope you do."

"I haven't got a clue, Bill. Scram!"

"Okay. You know your way around," Bill said, turning to leave.

"Wait, is the room locked?"

"Yeah. You're gonna need a key." Bill twisted a key off a crowded ring. "This fits everything down here."

"Enough said. I'll drop the key off in the emergency room when I'm done. Now go!"

"I'm gone, Doc."

With the key clutched in his hand, Loring headed toward the bend in the corridor. Along the walls were the debris of industrial change. Office chairs with wheels missing, bulky computer terminals smudged with the dirt of many hands, old beds with hand cranks, a stack of laminated signs taken from doors and hallways with no-longer-accurate directions to maternity and radiology, to cardiology and intensive care.

Here, the linoleum floor was chipped and not recently scrubbed, and a preponderance of the fluorescent tubes in the ceiling were dead. Loring made his way around a discarded mop bucket, still half filled with grimy cold water. He moved between stacked boxes holding hundreds of pounds of computer printouts. The corridor bent once again, to the left, and then, as Bill had reminded Loring, on the right, just before the sign for "medical waste disposal" was a set of locked double doors.

Loring inserted the key and pushed through. Inside, he found a short passageway and then a square room, in which the temperature was not above fifty. Straight ahead was another passageway leading to another room. To the right, six cold storage lockers occupied one wall. Three lockers were at chest level and three at knee level. He opened the three on the bottom. All were empty. He began opening the top doors and found a body draped in a white sheet in the middle locker. He left that door open and looked in the final locker to assure himself there were no other corpses. Then he pulled on the cold metal handle of the stainless steel tray on which the draped body lay. The tray and the body rolled out from the locker like the grease pan in a broiler, suspended over the floor. Loring lifted the sheet and saw the body of an Asian male, dressed in charcoal slacks and a white shirt with black socks. Blood, almost black, was caked on the right side of the head. Loring pushed at the skin on a hand and found it rigid, perhaps as much from the cold storage as from rigor mortis. He lifted the hand. The elbow bent slightly, normal, he thought, since Robert Chen still lived in this body less than two hours before. Loring went into the next room and returned with a steel gurney. He rolled Chen's body onto the gurney, face down, then wheeled it back to the second room, slightly larger than the first, an area of stainless steel counters and cabinets. A high, trough-like stainless steel table was in the center of the room. It had a sink-drain in the middle and, at one end, two deep basins with faucets. Over this autopsy table was a circular lamp, mounted on an articulated arm. A large circular scale—the kind butchers used to use to weight meat—hung above one end of the table, a basket suspended below it. Loring pushed the gurney beside the table and rolled Chen's body onto the table, face up. Then he went to the counter where he found a regular kitchen drawer full of knives, scissors, disposable scalpel blades and handles, rib-cracking shears, an electric autopsy saw, forceps. He found an apron, some latex gloves and a tape recorder, which he took. He unzipped and unbuttoned Chen's clothing, removing it from the body. He turned on the tape.

"Here begins an unofficial autopsy on the body of Robert Chen," he said, speaking slowly as he looked the length of the naked corpse. "In a telephone conversation shortly before his death, Dr. Chen told this investigator, Loring English, that he wished his body to be examined immediately and that information I am seeking, quote, will go with the body, end quote." Loring stopped, and after a long moment he sighed. "Unfortunately, that cryptic message is all Dr. Chen left. It's just like every other step in this case, folks. A lot of suspicion. No leads."

As soon as Detective Johnston left Osler, which was immediately after he had spoken with Loring English, Jerry Wiegenstein dialed the ship-to-shore operator, who patched him through to the yacht. It was another thirty minutes before James Perkins Harvey III arrived at Osler Medical Group, the helicopter settling in the designated area beside the parking lot, its strobe lights illuminating the face of Wiegenstein, who leaned against his Lexus, waiting. Harvey alighted and the lawyer, taking the doctor by the elbow, led him toward Osler's private executive entrance. They were inside before either spoke.

"Mr. Ching Huo has left," Wiegenstein said.

"He's gone after English?"

"He's simply gone, J.H." The lawyer fell into a seat opposite Harvey's desk. "You're on your own."

Harvey went to the broad window behind his desk and stared out. "What do we do?"

"I have no further advice for you," Wiegenstein said. "You have many options. Some of them are legal. Some are not. You are by now familiar with choices of this nature, and you will no doubt find a suitable solution."

"Why did the Dragon go?" Harvey asked, still facing into the darkness.

"Perhaps he is grieving for his brother."

"What exactly happened?" Harvey asked. He returned to his desk and settled slowly in his chair. His eyes pondered something on his desktop, as if he were lost in contemplation.

"The police tell me that Robert Chen was despondent, that he was schizophrenic and that he killed himself to escape voices giving him evil commands. I guess that's not so far off the mark, is it?"

"Spare me your moral view, Jerry. What really happened?"

"I checked the surveillance tapes. It was rather simple. Mr. Chen and his employees were performing under their security contract with Osler when they discovered Dr. Chen was violating computer security. They determined the nature of his eavesdropping and concluded that the data he was gathering would, in the hands of certain parties, constitute a threat to Osler. They chose to eliminate that threat, and they did a rather clever job. There was only one problem, and that, as I told you on *Carassius,* was that Chen had called Loring English."

"Were they working together?"

"They apparently didn't even know one another. But Chen told English that if he died, his secrets would accompany his body. If I had been given that message and then had been told by the police, as English was, that the body was headed for the morgue, guess where I'd be going."

"You're telling me English is at the morgue searching Chen's body?"

"I have no direct knowledge of that, Doctor. I offer only the

308

symptoms and observations. Make of it whatever diagnosis you wish. As for me, I am removing myself from representation of Osler Medical Group immediately. This will constitute my notice to you. I will turn over your files in the morning. Good luck, J.H."

"Were it that simple, Jerry, I would gladly release you. But if I fall, you do as well."

"I can assure you that my ass is covered, J.H. I'm bailing. If you want to save your own, you'd better start thinking, and fast."

"Give me your keys, Jerry. My Rover's at the airport."

"Sorry, J.H. I can't afford to implicate myself any further."

"Then I'll implicate you," Harvey said, standing abruptly, taking four strides around the desk and, with both hands, yanking the lawyer up from his seat. Clutching Wiegenstein's lapel with his left hand, Harvey punched the lawyer's jaw with his right. When he slumped to the carpet, Harvey reached into his pockets and removed his car keys.

As the white-gold sedan pulled into the emergency parking lot at City Campus, Gabriella English was eight miles to the north, in the kitchen of her father's house, desperately dialing through a list of phone numbers she had found in her father's desk. In Karen's plan, Gabbie was the decoy. Her dinner date with her father was designed to keep Loring occupied. But after many calls to each of his offices, she had not been able to reach her father. Then she heard Karen's message. Panic set in. Finally, she had reached Patty McCullough at City Campus. Mrs. McCullough was too busy to talk, but she suggested Gabbie would find her father if she found Bill, the ambulance driver. "Come down to the ER. Bill will be back in time," Mrs. McCullough offered. Gabbie thanked her but decided to try a few more phone calls.

Meanwhile, at precisely the moment when James Harvey ran through the emergency entrance at what once had been the proud institution known as Port Hancock General, a radio message was being successfully transmitted from a yellow Cessna to the Port Hancock Taxi Company dispatcher. Karen Larsen would need a ride in five minutes from the foot of Ferry Street.

Thirty-five . . .

Chen's words played across Loring's mind as his hands worked with the tissues of Chen's cadaver.

I have the information you are seeking. If I die, it will go with my body. I must say this to you alone, a not unusual statement.

I know nothing of this man, and yet I have chosen to believe him, not the police, Loring thought. Is my choice rational? The detective claims this is suicide. No question it is death by gunshot, he thought. Loring had examined the wound, created, he guessed, by a medium-caliber bullet, perhaps a thirty-two. Looking closely, he could see the chunks of shattered bone, tipped up around the edge of the wound like the rubble of an earthquake, glued in place by the congealed blood. The brain, dark as caviar, oozed from the bullet hole and collected in the scoop of the ear. Chen had died instantly, perhaps—although medical science had no way of determining—painlessly. Loring had left the wound untouched in order to preserve forensic evidence. It was bad enough that he planned to pursue this examination as far as needed, that a charge of abuse of a corpse could be lodged, certainly, in the spectrum of crimes, at least fractionally more serious than disruptive physician. He had decided to work alone to avoid the risk of exposing a helper to charges. He would disturb as little as possible, but he already had pried open the lips and then the jaw and, adjusting the overhead lamp so that its light flooded the mouth, moved the tongue from side to side, looking for . . . what? He opened and closed the eyelids and, a bit sheepishly, tapped on each eyeball with a scalpel handle to determine if it were perhaps glass, a possible canister containing "information." The eyes were, however, human. Loring tilted the head back and shone the lamp into the nostrils, then probed with a slender stainless steel pick. He discovered nothing unusual.

Why, Loring wondered, had Chen babbled so if he felt his life was endangered? Why hadn't he used their time on the phone to be more explicit, or at least to leave a clue? He tilted the head to one side and then the other, peering into Chen's ears, expecting little and finding nothing.

Maybe I misunderstood, Loring thought. Maybe it was simply the desperate cry of one who knows that his thoughts will die with him.

"But, no," Loring said aloud. "He could have called anyone, but he thought calling me would do him some good. Stop and think! What is the patient telling you? That he swallowed something? 'I have the information you are seeking.' It could be he ingested the information. 'If I die, it will go with my body.' The premise still holds up," Loring said, turning from the autopsy table and opening the drawer full of implements. He took an autopsy knife, long as a roast knife, its blade and handle made of one piece of stainless steel. "I can cut him open and examine his stomach. But first, what else did he say? 'I must say this to you alone, a not unusual statement.' Well, that means absolutely nothing, doesn't it. Come on, fellow. Call yourself a doctor?" Loring set the autopsy knife back on the counter. "What's not an unusual statement? 'I must say this to you alone?' Say what?"

Loring picked up the tape recorder and turned it off, and he hitched himself up onto the counter opposite Chen's body. The words kept circulating and Loring's mind drifted and shifted into a sort of neutral gear, where no energy was being exerted but his thoughts simply moved themselves, arranged themselves as they pleased, and the thoughts and Chen's words looped around and through each other, like night crawlers in a bait box. "I must say this to you alone" kept surfacing and diving, followed by "A not unusual statement," which rose and fell, as well, one puzzling phrase chasing another, but Loring was no longer puzzled or lost. His mind was detached, exerting no leverage, attempting neither to force nor to figure, simply waiting as he watched the lifeless form on the metal table. And now Loring saw a part of one phrase as if it stood alone: Say this to you alone. Say what? Why, of course, say: 'A not unusual statement.' And now, through the thicket of thoughts and words, these four words played, and Loring sensed that they would solve the puzzle if he allowed them time. He slipped down from the counter and turned the recorder back on, and he resumed his examination of the body, inspecting, feeling, and as he went, the vague sense of a new word began playing with the phrases in his mind, although Loring did not at first recognize the word, which was acronym.

Loring worked for several minutes, his face unmoved by expression. When the thought finally formed itself, he did not speak or smile but simply rolled the body onto its side, pulling the knees toward him so that, bent, they protruded over the side of the table. He circled the table and, extending the middle finger of his gloved right hand, probed the anus, and when he felt the hard object in the rectum, he thought: A Not Unusual Statement. He went to the drawer and took the forceps, and with these he pulled the little package from inside Robert Chen's corpse. He set the package on the counter top and, with a scalpel, sliced the latex open, revealing the tape and the key.

"I have now examined the anal canal," he said into the recorder, "and have found an audio tape that I will now attempt to play in this recorder." He turned off the machine, ejected the one tape and inserted Chen's. The voice he heard was calm, and the instructions were simple.

"Use this key to enter my safe deposit box at Riverton National Bank's main office. The box is number one-thirty-seven. If you do not have a box of your own there, you may need to purchase one before they will allow you to enter the vault. In any case, in the box you will find a complete set of storage disks, along with instructions and accompanying audio cassettes. The total package documents several criminal activities conducted by Osler Medical Group and its physicians, Dr. English. James Harvey has become a virus, using medicine to destroy, not to heal."

It was not that Chen's words were a surprise. The thing that slammed Loring English so hard in the chest was that Chen chose the same phrase Janet Mitchell had used on her last day. The virus was infecting Port Hancock even then, but it took

312

better eyes than mine to see, Loring thought, better ears than mine to hear! And now it has taken Robert Chen's life!

Loring stripped off his latex gloves and then shoved Chen's tape and key into a fresh glove, which he tied off at the wrist. He put the glove in his hip pocket, rolled Chen's body onto its back and then rolled it back onto the gurney, face down. After returning the utensils to the drawer and turning off the lamp, he pushed the gurney, feet first, back toward the cold storage room and was in the passageway when the double doors to the corridor swung slowly open and James Perkins Harvey III stood facing him. Harvey stepped through the doors and allowed them to close behind him. Loring stopped pushing the gurney.

"Loring, you're a little out of place, aren't you?" Harvey said, his voice deep but still, the threat in it like the reflected light of an approaching, but yet unseen, subway, warning of potential violence. He stepped forward, his hands coming to rest on the sides of the gurney at Chen's feet. "Really, there is little more to be done for Robert, now that he has done this to himself."

An anger ripped inside Loring, one prepared to scream out the sins of Jim Harvey. But for the moment, there was a priority, a need to deliver the key and the tape into safe hands. Loring decided to play along.

"A friend asked me to confirm the cause, Jim. Amazing how quickly word spread."

"Utterly amazing. I understood that it was you who informed the police. I guess I was mistaken."

"No. no. That's true. Chen called me distraught. I didn't know what to make of it and called the authorities. Too late, though." Loring gestured at Chen's bloodied head.

"I find that I am more comfortable wearing a suit I've bought for myself rather than one I've borrowed, Dr. English. Lying does not suit you, sir. You are too accustomed to the truth."

"Excuse me?"

"Loring, I, too, feel more comfortable in this place dealing with undeniable facts. Death is so sobering, isn't it?" Harvey paused, as if inviting Loring's comment. "The facts as I understand them are these. That both you and Robert Chen had developed a fascination with the inner workings of Osler Medical Group." Harvey gently pushed the end of the gurney to the side and began moving toward Loring's end. Loring pushed his end of the gurney toward Harvey, so that Chen's body now lay at an angle across the passageway and the gurney, touching walls at both ends, formed a barricade. Harvey stepped back. "It's okay, Loring. Osler is worthy of your interest. But it's not for the reason you suppose."

"I always supposed Osler succeeded through your practice of top-quality medicine, Jim."

"I know you are sincere, Loring. You're attempting a subterfuge, but I believe you truly felt that of Osler. At least until Janet's unfortunate accident." Harvey stepped up to the gurney again, separated from Loring only by the width of Chen's shoulders. "You see, you still fail to appreciate what Osler has accomplished."

"And that is?"

"The medical profession is as dead as this heap of bone and tissue between us, Loring."

"You believe that?"

"The beasts that survive are the medical businesses, and to continue that survival, these beasts must feed. They must consume and grow. You see it, Loring?" Harvey asked. Although his mouth turned up at the corners, his expression was no smile. Fear drew the skin tight across his face, stretched it into a transparent mask through which Loring could see the anger and sadness and terror that were gripping Harvey.

"I do see it, Jim," Loring said. "And I'm sorry."

"Sorry!" Harvey thundered. "Indeed you are sorry! The whole lot of you. You play at being omnipotent, tricking people into believing you are something you could never be!" He shoved at the edge of the gurney with such violence that Loring lost his footing and stumbled. "You pretend to heal, and you know there is no healing. There is only death, guaranteed. Just ask our friend here!" He shoved the gurney again, and now Loring was standing back in the autopsy room. One more shove and Harvey would be clear of the gurney, so Loring braced his feet and shoved back.

Harvey was unmoved.

"I'm the more honest of us two," he said, calm once again. "I admit my humanity, and knowing the limits of medicine, I have chosen to be among the survivors. In the ruins, I have built a fortress. There is little that can challenge me. But you might," he said, stretching both arms across Chen's corpse, the palms of his hands up, fingertips inches from Loring's arms. "If you leave here, you may possess the weapons to destroy me." Harvey's hands moved swiftly now, but Loring had anticipated and stepped back just in time to avoid letting his wrists fall into Harvey's grasp. In stepping back, he moved his weight off the gurney, and Harvey, having missed the target of his lunge, fell forward against the end of the gurney, spinning it around Loring, into the autopsy room, so that now Chen's feet were again pointing toward the double doors and Harvey had free movement to the inner room. Loring's only chance lay in the corridor. He dashed for the double doors and was pulling them open when he felt his arm go weak from the axe-like blow of the side of Harvey's fist as it smashed down onto the tendons between Loring's neck and shoulder. Loring's entire side collapsed, and as he spiraled toward the floor, he was caught on the nose by another punch, on the jaw by a third and Loring's conscious thoughts ceased.

Harvey opened one of the lower cold storage lockers and rolled out the empty tray. He lifted Loring and set him on the tray, which he pushed back into the locker, closing the door. He opened the double doors slightly and checked the corridor. Seeing no one, he lifted Chen's body and placed it on the tray with the sheet, which Loring had left extended over the floor. Harvey covered Chen's body with the sheet and shoved the tray back into the locker.

"Not good enough," Harvey muttered to himself. He opened the lower door and pulled Loring out of the locker. Kneeling beside the tray, he felt Loring's pulse.

"Okay, old fellow. I have a better plan, more poetic," he said. He stepped into the autopsy room, rummaged through the drawers and returned with two lengths of medical tubing. With one piece, he bound Loring's ankles and with the other tied his wrists together and to the back of his belt. He hoisted Loring onto his shoulder, shoved the tray back into the locker, closed the locker door and tugged open one of the double doors, stepping into the corridor and turning right. He stopped under the "medical waste" sign and looked back along the corridor. He tilted his head to one side. There had been a sound, perhaps footsteps. Harvey waited for several seconds, listening for another disturbance of the silence, but there was none. He pushed on the door under the sign and, with Loring still unconscious, carried him inside. To the left were a pile of cardboard boxes and several red plastic bags, bulging with contents and tied at the top. To the right was a small office cubicle. A heap of papers threatened to slide off the desktop, and a homemade ceramic ashtray under the computer console was filled with a mountain of butts surrounded by a beach of gray ashes. Straight ahead of Harvey was another room, into which he moved, and in that room was Derrick Keating's legacy for City Campus, the medical waste microwave, ten feet high, ten feet wide and twenty-four feet long, built of steel, painted off-white, and resembling, except for the control box on the side and the hydraulic truck tailgate lift on the near end, a dumpster. Harvey settled Loring on his back on the tailgate lift and straightened his legs. He opened the metal door on the control panel and examined the array of square, colored buttons. When he pressed a black button, the lift began rising and there was a repeated beeping, the sound of a truck's reverse warning signal. The lift rose to level with Harvey's waist and he pushed the button again, stopping the machinery. Harvey went to stand beside Loring.

"Come on, Dr. English," he said. "Time to wake up." He

swung his arm back and brought it forward in a vicious slap that glanced off Loring's cheek."

"That's it, come on back to me. I can see your eyes flickering!"

Loring did not feel pain. In his mind, thought competed with dream. He sensed, and thought this must be a dream, that his jaw had been moved half way across his face. When his eyes opened, he saw no objects, only light, shattered as if coming through crystals. His first thoroughly conscious sensation was the smell of his own blood, already clotting in his nose from the punch. His second realization was that his hands were under a heavy weight and against something hard and cold. It was the sound of Harvey's voice, the deep rumble of the subway emerging full speed from the dark tunnel into the station, that brought Loring into full awareness.

"Glad you have returned, Dr. English," Harvey said. "As much as you love to examine the inner workings of things, it would have been a shame had you not been aware, before you experienced its naked power, of the fascinating heart of this cutting edge technology, excuse the pun."

Loring tried to sit but fell back. He tried to speak, but his mouth would not work, and now a blinding pain shot through his forehead and he closed his eyes.

"Overhead, you will see a large convex mirror, Doctor. If you look into the mirror—please, Loring, do open your eyes. That's it. If you look into the mirror, you will see on the top of this device a large, steel lid. I am going to push a button, and the platform on which you are lying will begin to rise, and after a bit more than a minute, that lid will begin to open."

Harvey returned to the control panel and again pushed the one black button. The beeping resumed, and with it Loring heard the muffled hum of machinery.

"Now keep your eye on the mirror, Doctor, and you'll see, once the lid has opened, the spinning blades. Under the lid is a hopper, and at the bottom of that hopper is a shredder. The literature says it's capable of chopping five hundred and fifty pounds of medical waste into unrecognizable flakes every hour. Imagine!"

Loring could hear the machinery working if he could not see it, and he could feel himself being lifted toward the top of the machine, toward the gaping mouth of the hopper.

"When you reach the top, the platform will tilt and you will slide into the hopper. It shouldn't be too long before the pain stops, Loring. But, you're thinking, there will be blood everywhere! Ah, these folks have thought of everything. Steam jets will come on and wash your residue down through the shredder, and when you are, shall we say, deconstituted, that's when your fine little chunks will be fed into the microwaves. There are six microwaves in all, and they will cook your flesh to the point that even rats won't recognize it as food. Isn't our new technology marvelous, Loring?"

From the sound, Loring concluded that the lift was now almost to the top of the hopper. His eyes still glazed, his mind yet fogged, he rolled onto his left side, bending his knees, searching for the edge of this machine, trying to judge which side might be safety, which the microwave. He rolled to his right and his knees hit a hard, moving surface. The sound of the machinery was now very clear, and he sensed the platform was beginning to tilt.

"Here it comes," Harvey said, his words gleeful. "Oh, darn. The lid's open but the blades are spinning so fast you can't tell what you're looking at, can you? Let me explain."

Now or never, Loring thought, and he was about to roll sharply to the left, throwing himself off the lift and taking his chances, when the lift stopped moving.

There was, for several seconds, only the sound of the whirling shredder blades coasting to a stop. The near silence was broken not by Harvey's voice but by another.

"Give it up, Jim."

Again there was silence. Then the platform flinched under Loring, sending his pulse racing and injecting his arteries with adrenaline, causing his muscles to strain, pushing against the tubes that bound him. But the platform was now level, and, if he could believe his senses, Loring was descending. Somehow, Karen had arrived in time, Loring believed. She had saved him. Loring waited to hear the voices of the police who had accompanied Karen, but the next voice was Harvey's.

"This is perfect," Harvey said. "You'll join your lover in eternity." He laughed gently. "Really! This is prophetic! Come here, Karen. Come take a ride with the doctor!"

Loring strained to look down toward the floor. Beyond the dazzling shards of light, he could see two shadows, two forms, one near the machine directly below him and one probably Karen, since Harvey was still lowering the lift farther away. And that one was moving to the right, circling toward the machine. I could drop on him, Loring thought. I could distract him, but then what. He felt his descent halt.

"What's this?" Harvey's voice was now coming from slightly above Loring. "An epi-pin? Good girl. Hand it over."

"Untie him, Jim."

"What? Am I supposed to fear you and that little needle?"

"You know I know how to use it, Jim. Untie him!" Her voice was low, firm, without fear. She was standing near Loring's feet and as her words ended, he felt a tugging at whatever was binding his ankles, and there was a loosening.

"That's enough, Karen," Harvey said, his voice moving away from Loring, toward Karen. "Either give me the pin or I'll take it. Ha!"

"You bastard!" Karen shouted.

Loring strained to see but could not. He tried to rise, but his hands, pinned under his rump, pulled him back down.

"Do struggle, Karen. It will only make your blood pump faster. What's in this, anyway? Did you use it on my captain? I'm sure you chose wisely."

Loring could see the two forms as one. He guessed from Karen's silence what had happened, and he realized that survival now depended on him alone. Act like a doctor! He commanded himself. Use your senses, all of them! For the first time, he focused his attention on his restraints. Moving his legs slightly, he found that Karen had managed to undo those bindings. That left his wrists. Loring arched his body slightly, allowing his fingers enough room to curl under him and probe at the restraint. Pliable, he thought, pliable strands. Still arched, he strained against the tubing, hoping to give himself some room, but when he relaxed, the strands still bound him tightly.

"Relax, Dr. English," Harvey said. "Your lady friend is about to join you, and you are about to join your wife. It gives me a warm feeling, knowing the role I've played in it all from the beginning." With a grunt, Harvey hoisted Karen and dropped her on the platform beside Loring.

Parts of our lives are so familiar that they become invisible to us even when obvious to those around us. There are people who wear glasses who will search for hours for them only to find them atop their head. Similarly, there had been times when, on a fishing trip, Loring English would be in need of a sharp object and curse himself for having failed to anticipate the need. And all the while, his little pocket knife was at the bottom of his hip pocket, where it resided every day of his life. In despair, with the weight of Karen pressing beside him and the lift rising again toward the top of the microwave, he relaxed his muscles and fell from the arch he had created in his attempt to free his wrists. And in falling, his buttocks pressed down on the back of one hand and Loring felt, and recognized, the lump in his hip pocket.

"I remember that afternoon so well, Loring," Harvey said over the hum and beeping of the lift and the whirl of the shredder blades. "Janet looked ghastly, and I knew that I had to work fast if I was going to save her."

Loring jerked his elbows up, straining against the tubing, and he extended his index and middle fingers together and probed for the opening of the pocket.

"So I called for some tests. I know you aren't one for a lot of tests, and neither am I, Loring. But think what I was dealing with! The busiest pediatrician in Port Hancock! If I failed to save her, who would care for all those babies and children?"

Loring's fingers found the pocket and he jammed them to the bottom, using them like pliers to seize the little knife. Gently, he began to pull the knife toward the opening.

"Who, indeed? If you think in a broader way—if you think

like a modern medical decision maker—you see not only the practice of a pediatrician, Loring. You see the medical needs of the child's parents and grandparents. You see cardiologists like yourself and GI guys and even trauma surgeons like me. You see dermatologists and proctologists and radiologists, all of whom could get referrals from this one pediatrician. You see a whole group practice that could benefit, could secure its survival."

The knife now was in Loring's hand, and he had rolled slightly to the side and was attempting to work the blade free. But the sound of the shredder blades now was much clearer, and, he believed, he had only seconds left. His mind shifted now to what he must do once the tubes were sliced from his wrist, and he remembered the advice of Eddie Beiler.

"After all, isn't medicine all about survival, Loring? And here I was, faced with a choice, really the same choice all of us in medicine face now. Who will survive? Will it be the old lady with good insurance or the welfare child who can't afford to pay? Will it be the hospital, by cutting staff beyond the bone or will it be the guy brought in from a car wreck who needs quick, expert emergency care? You see the sort of quandary I faced, Loring?"

Loring's thumbnail finally found the notch and he had just gotten the knife opened when the lift stopped. He began slicing the tubes, the honed tip of the blade slashing at the skin above his wrist as he felt the first section of tubing pop free.

"I have to finish this story before I send you on, Loring," Harvey said. "I apologize for the delay. But, you see, I realized on that afternoon that, if I did not discover a ruptured aorta quickly, then Janet would be lost. And if that happened, her enormous practice would, given the control I could exert, shift into Osler's hands. I had analyzed the situation carefully. And so, I thought, why not perform a few more tests, just to make certain."

Within Loring English's mind, there was no room for both the fury that Harvey's confession had now created and the concentration he needed to secure his and Karen's survival. The fury burst through his lips.

"You bastard!" He screamed as he sliced through all of the remaining tubing and deeply into his own arm. His legs and wrists free, he looked over the edge of the lift and, four feet below, he saw the shape of Harvey's head. With one shove, he threw himself over Karen and down, onto that form, grabbing with both arms, feeling Harvey's shoulders under his forearms, hearing Harvey's breath and voice close to his face and feeling Harvey's arms wrapping around his ribs in a crushing grip, lifting him off the floor. Eddie Beiler's first bit of advice flashed before Loring, and he grabbed Harvey's ears, one in each hand, and, lowering his head, he yanked. He felt the smash of Harvey's face against the top of his head. Using Harvey's ears as handles, he shoved his head far back and again yanked it forward, this time driving his skull into Harvey's jaw. He felt Harvey's grasp around his ribs weaken, then disappear.

Eddie Beiler's second instruction now elbowed into Loring's thoughts, and as his feet hit the floor, he spun the dazed doctor and jumped on his back, wrapping his right arm around Harvey's neck, balling his fist against the carotid mass on his neck. At the same time, Loring flung his left arm around the other side of Harvey's neck, grabbing his own right elbow and pressing his left biceps against his balled right fist, depressing the carotid artery. Harvey staggered two steps away from the microwave as the blood stopped flowing to his brain, and, with Loring riding his back, he fell to the floor. Straddling Harvey, Loring rolled him onto his back and felt his neck for a pulse; its thrum was strong. Through the gauze of his damaged eyes, he strained to see Harvey's features, but could not. He took Harvey's jaw in his left hand and moved his head from side to side, and as he did, a shudder passed through Loring English, and a piece of him that was closer to James Perkins Harvey III than he had ever realized surfaced in his thoughts, and his fist balled again, his elbow cocked and with absolute confidence that what he was doing was noble, he swung and his knuckles connected squarely with Harvey's chin, cracking the bone beneath the flesh.

"Damn you!" Loring shouted. "Damn all of you!"

322

Officer Bruce Stottlemire of the Port Hancock Police, when he saw the blue compact speeding toward City Campus, threw on his lights and pursued. Gabriella jammed on the brakes in front of the emergency room and left her lights on and door open when she raced inside. Stottlemire's patrol car slid to a stop behind the compact and the officer sprinted behind the young woman, whom he found at the emergency room command center. A tall, young man with short dark hair was listening to the young woman, his head cocked to the side.

"This way," the young man shouted, and he led the young woman and the officer to a door under a stairwell sign. The footsteps of the three echoed off the stairwell walls and then off the walls of a long, dingy corridor, where they came to a halt by the morgue. Finding no one in the morgue, the three returned to the corridor and heard shouts coming from the door under the medical waste sign. They burst in to find two men on the floor and a woman ten feet above, lying unconscious on a steel lift.

The blades of the shredder were still spinning and that, along with the heavy panting and grieving sobs of the smaller of the two men, provided the only sounds of life in these, the entrails of the world of medicine.

Epilogue

B. Morton Martin's epic tale was published four months later in the *Sunday Journal Magazine* under the headline "Doctor Daring." The gist of Martin's story was that Loring, alone and unaided, uncovered a festering gang of criminals whom everyone else had overlooked. The more Loring read, the angrier he became. By Monday morning, he couldn't wait to get to his office at City Campus and phone Martin at the *Journal*.

"I'd like to commend you on your writing," he began when

Martin, gruff in the defensive, suspicious manner of a meter maid, answered. Martin's voice softened immediately, and Loring proceeded. "I'd like to praise your reporting as well, except there's not one damned honest fact in the whole story!"

Martin was experienced at dodging criticism.

"Well, you're wrong right off the bat, Dr. English. Shall I list the details? Dr. Harvey's lawyers are, in fact, planning an insanity defense. Dr. Urizar's wife has relocated offshore. I spoke with her by phone. Dr. Barnett has been offered a deal by the attorney general to cooperate, as has Dr. Ross. No one has reported those facts before, I should add. Dr. Nightingale is under guard at a mental facility. All five have been indicted on charges ranging from murder to extortion to grand larceny. Neil Dunmore is in Costa Rica and is not expected to return any time soon. The lawyer Wiegenstein faces possible disbarment. Ching Huo, the Chinese gangster, has slipped back into the murk like a startled eel retreats into the mud. And none of this would have happened if one Dr. Loring English hadn't risked his neck, which is the point of my story. So what's your complaint?"

"Let me read a few lines to you, Mr. Martin," Loring said, and he smoothed the creased magazine pages on his desktop. "'As darkness drew across Port Hancock, English was racing from his office in Riverton, the only man on the face of the earth who had the goods on the bad guys. Having been informed by police of Dr. Chen's murder, English knew that he alone could link the death to the details of larceny and murder on a massive scale that he had discovered in months of diligent detective work . . .' where did you come up with that nonsense?"

There was a pause at the other end of the line before Martin responded.

"You refused to be interviewed, Doctor. So I did the next best thing. I talked to more than forty of your colleagues, and then I pieced it together."

"Well, that's great, but the pieces don't fit!" Loring said, shoving his chair back from his desk.

"The best we ever do is an approximation of the truth,"

Martin said. "I'd say this is a damned good approximation, no thanks to you. But I'd still like to hear your story. I see a book in it. A bestseller, Doctor."

Loring expressed his disinterest by gently setting the receiver on its cradle. He had no more time for Martin or any other reporter. The job of restoring the hospital in the wake of the collapse of Osler Medical Group had called him—or more precisely, the new chairman of the renamed hospital had called.

In the weeks immediately after what the *Journal* had dubbed Medigate exploded into the city's consciousness, Loring's days were consumed with assisting criminal investigators piecing together the crimes spawned by James Harvey. Robert Chen's tapes gave some raw facts and disclosed the electronic paths to follow. But the prosecutors needed a consultant familiar with the medical industry who could explain how it all fit. Loring accepted the assignment with the understanding that the public would be informed at each step of the way.

"Jim Harvey succeeded because no one was watching," Loring told Winthrop Pettingil, the attorney general, a politician not unlike Mayor Henry Costanza, although from the other major party. "The money's still here. The motive still exists. We need the eyes of the community on the medical establishment if we're to have any chance of avoiding another Osler."

Meanwhile, Hancock Medical Services was being meticulously reconstructed. Lydia Fulton, at a special board meeting, called for a vote of no confidence and Walter Scott was fired, although the lucrative severance package arranged for him by Harvey was found to be binding and Scott's future comfort was assured. The board also voted to restore Loring's privileges and to rename HMS Port Hancock Medical Center. In time, the board, at Loring's urging, named Peter Warren as its chief executive. Warren immediately asked Loring to become chief of medicine.

"Take it," Karen said. "You'll need something to occupy you when I'm spending long nights with Dave Carn. I'll bet you can still see a few patients, even if you're riding a desk most of the day."

And then, a few weeks after Martin's article, came a meeting with William Scarborough, who wanted to talk about Coastal Insurance and Port Hancock Medical Center. Loring recalled Reggie Wilson's encounters with Scarborough and expected the worst.

"I couldn't believe it," Loring told Karen that night. She snuggled under his arm as he sat against a pile of pillows propped against the headboard of their bed. A picture of Gabriella was on Loring's nightstand, beside a larger photograph of him and Karen on their wedding day, Thanksgiving weekend. A large framed photograph of Janet Mitchell and another of Tom Grimes were hung between two windows in the living room, where they got the morning light.

"What couldn't you believe?" she asked.

"Here is the man who wouldn't go after Harvey. Now he tells us we're the model hospital he's always looked for, and I'd have to say his interest seemed genuine."

"It gives you a good feeling, doesn't it, honey?" Karen asked, wriggling closer and looking up at Loring. She smiled and closed her eyes.

"It sure does," he said, reaching across her to turn off the lamp. In the darkness, he slipped down from his pillows so that her cheek was against his shoulder and the smell of her hair was in his nose. He closed his eyes in the peaceful darkness, where the sound of Karen's slow breathing began to draw him into sleep.

"Just one thing," she whispered.

"Unhuh," he muttered.

"You said you can't believe it?"

"Mmmhmmm."

"Don't."

A NOTE TO THE READER

When we collaborated on *Malignant Decisions,* our purpose was to describe and address, in the context of a fictitious medical thriller, the changes and problems facing the health care profession today. Unfortunately, scattered within a noble profession are a few unscrupulous physicians, motivated by financial gain. Yet the greater number of physicians are ethical, providing the quality of care expected of them. Among their ranks are those who serve as department chairpersons, members of hospital boards, insurance company advisors, and officers of county and state societies. Their dedication is the insurance that the unscrupulous and incompetent will not prevail. We, the authors, are confident that Americans will continue to be provided with the world's highest level of medical care.

–Walt McConnell, M.D., and D.A. Campbell

ABOUT THE AUTHORS

Walt McConnell, M.D. practiced family and emergency medicine for thirty-six years. He was associated with Dover General Hospital in New Jersey, the hospital where he was born in 1931. He received his B.S. in biology from Bucknell University and his M.D. from Jefferson Medical College in Philadelphia.

Since his retirement in 1996, he has concentrated on writing, travel, photography, and part-time work as a cruise ship physician. He is the author of *The Snowbird Tram: One of the World's Great Tramways,* a history of the pioneering tram at the Snowbird, Utah ski resort. In 1989 he reached 27,000 feet on Mount Everest as the leader of the first New Jersey Everest expedition. McConnell is an accomplished distance runner and continues to compete in cross-country and track meets and world masters' events. He and his wife Isabel have traveled, biked, hiked, skied, and rafted in more than seventy countries. They live in Bolton Landing, New York where they enjoy frequent visits from their four children and their spouses, and their seven grandchildren.

D. A. Campbell is the author of *The Sea's Bitter Harvest,* the story of thirteen deadly days in the Atlantic clam dredging industry. He retired in 2000 from the *Philadelphia Inquirer* after twenty-five years as a staff writer. He received numerous awards in his thirty-three-year career as a journalist, including a first place award for newspaper writing in 2000 from the National Association of Black Journalists, and the 2001 Society of Professional Journalists, Keystone State Professional Chapter, award for feature writing. He lives with his wife, Monica, their two dogs, Thelma and Louise, and three cats in Burlington, New Jersey.